GREENHÆLAN

CHRONICLES OF ALGARTH #1

L.A. WEBSTER

Copyright © 2020 by Lyn Webster

First paperback edition February 2020

Book design by Katya Dibb
katdibb.wixsite.com/design-cat
Images from Jude Infantini and
Corey Agopian on Unsplash, and iStock.

ISBN 978-0-6487175-1-5 (paperback)
ISBN 978-0-6487175-0-8 (ebook)

Published by Gateshaper Books
www.lynwebster.com

This book is dedicated to Ken, Ethan and Megan:
my first readers, and still the most important.

ONE

Sara

Sara dragged her slippered feet into the kitchen, giving her hair a desultory rub with the towel. Three days in Sydney, culminating with a nightmarish drive on rain-slick dirt roads peppered with suicidal kangaroos, had left her drained and almost as jumpy as the animals. What she needed was wine, followed by bed.

The phone buzzed, snatching her breath in mid-yawn and setting her heart thudding. The stone counter amplified the normally muted tone, transforming it into a bullying demand for attention. If only she'd switched it off earlier. If only she could ignore it now. But the hard truth was she couldn't afford to miss even one potential client. Not while she was still building her business. Clamping the towel to her head with one hand, she snatched up the annoying device. "Wattleford Garden Care, Sara Martin speaking."

"You're back. Good. I'm coming over." Click.

She should have let the call go to voice-mail. Then she could have turned off the lights and pretended not to be home. The last thing Sara needed tonight was a visit from Jackie, especially when her neighbour was in dynamo mode.

Nothing she could do about it now. She gave her damp hair one last rub and raked it behind her ears, letting it hang in dark strings over her shoulders. Jackie would have to take her as she found her, tangled ends and all. She dumped the towel in the laundry and unlocked the French windows.

Golden light spilled out onto the wet brick patio. Sara stood in the doorway for a moment, breathing the cool, moist air and watching the raindrops etch fine, silvery lines against the velvety blackness. Her shoulders relaxed. Maybe Jackie wouldn't stay long.

Turning back to the kitchen, she fetched two glasses and the bottle of Shiraz Jackie had given her for her birthday. Vat 26, declared the looping red letters on the label. "Because you're turning twenty-six. Get it?" Jackie had crowed as she handed it over.

By the time Sara had wrestled the cork out, her visitor was barging into the room, shaking a fine mist of droplets from her springy ginger hair. She halted in the middle of the kitchen, her thin sandy eyebrows arched in surprise. "Why are you in your pyjamas? Are you sick?"

"Just tired," Sara said. "The garden conference was pretty full-on. Actually, I only got home an hour ago. The drive was hideous." She cherished a faint hope that this might give her energetic neighbour the hint to keep the visit short. For good measure, she added a yawn.

As usual, Jackie was oblivious to hints. "Good, because I want to talk to you, and I can't afford to get sick just now. Too much to do." She sat down opposite Sara and picked up the bottle. "Wine — just the thing."

She poured full glasses for them both and lifted hers in a toast. "Confusion to our enemies."

Some of the wine sloshed out and splattered onto the table. Jackie took a generous swig of the rest and sat back with a satisfied look on her thin, freckled face.

Sara frowned. "Do we have any enemies?"

"Of course we do. Melville Barnett is the enemy of every right-thinking human being. And if there are aliens or people living in alternate dimensions, he's probably the enemy of them, too."

So much for a restful evening. If this was going to be a Melville Barnett conversation, Sara already knew two things: it wouldn't be restful and it wouldn't be brief. She gulped a large mouthful of wine to brace herself for the onslaught. Slightly fortified, she sighed and asked the question that Jackie's eager expression was so clearly expecting. "What's he done now?"

"Only got approval for an open-cut mine in the Brogans."

"The *Brogans*?" Shock stiffened Sara's features.

The Brogan Mountains lay only an hour's drive from Wattleford: a landscape of ancient twisted trees, lichened boulders, cool, damp gullies crammed with ferns, dry grassy slopes jewelled with wildflowers every spring. An almost untouched place, magical and strange, wild and beautiful. An image rose in Sara's mind: giant machines ripping at the ground, gouging out massive craters, destroying all that precious, unique life, throwing it aside like so much rubbish. All to make an obscenely rich man even richer. Her jaw clenched and her fingers tightened around the stem of her wine glass until it was in danger of snapping.

Jackie nodded in grim satisfaction at the effect of her news.

Sara forced her fingers to loosen. She found her voice. "But the Brogans are a protected area!"

Jackie snorted. "Protected? That wouldn't stop Barnett. He probably bribed someone. Or maybe blackmailed them. Something, anyway. You know what a crook he is. They had a late-night hearing and pushed it through when there was hardly anyone there. No one knew a thing about it until this morning. And by then it was a done deal."

A pulse beat in Sara's temple. Why did men like Barnett always get their way? Stupid, greedy — she stopped that train of thought in its tracks and deliberately slumped back in her chair, shaking her head. "It's horrible, but I don't see what we can do about it."

"Don't be such a defeatist. There are plenty of things we can do." Jackie drained her glass and clunked it back down on the table. Sara hoped she hadn't cracked it.

"I think—" Sara started, but Jackie rolled right over her. With both hands free to wave about for emphasis, she went on and on, spouting enthusiastically about protest marches and road blockades and lying down in front of bulldozers.

"Yes, but—" Sara tried again, but Jackie just kept going. "If that snake thinks we're going to take this quietly, he'd better think again, that's all."

No one would ever accuse Jackie of taking anything quietly. Just being in the same room with her was exhausting. Would she ever stop talking? Her voice rose and fell, her hands swooping up and down in accompaniment. The extravagant gestures began to threaten not only her empty glass, but also the bottle. Sara quickly moved them to safety. Her own glass was still half full, but she put it down carefully and pushed it away. She didn't want it any more. She'd had enough, and not just of the wine, or even Melville Barnett. Why did Jackie always have to be so over-the-top, so single-minded? So *selfish*? Why couldn't she see — or care — that Sara didn't want to deal with any of this right now?

An almost overwhelming urge to shout at her infuriating neighbour — just yell at her to *shut up* and go home — hit Sara so hard she had to clench her teeth to stop the words forcing themselves out. She wouldn't allow herself to lose control, no matter how much she was provoked.

Oblivious to Sara's struggle, Jackie ranted on, her voice rising even higher. Sara's head throbbed painfully. She pressed the fingers of both hands hard to her temples. A moan slipped out between her teeth.

The flood of words cut off. Jackie stared across the table with her mouth hanging open.

Sara seized her chance. She told Jackie tightly that she agreed with her, but she had a headache and was too tired to talk about it anymore tonight. She wanted to help, but couldn't commit herself to anything specific right now.

It was true enough; Sara did want to help in some way, once her emotions had calmed down. Perhaps she could sign a petition or write a letter of protest to their local Member. Something measured and sensible.

Jackie didn't seem offended as she rose to go, but it was hard for Sara to see anything clearly through the bursts of light that had started flashing in front of her eyes. Blessedly alone again, she fumbled two painkillers from the cabinet and gulped them down with the rest of her wine. Then she tottered upstairs to bed.

Even with her head pounding, it was a relief to be lying flat in the darkness. She wasn't sure what had happened tonight. Where had all that fury come from? She hadn't experienced such strong emotion for years. Not since… She pushed the memory away. She must be even more exhausted than she'd realised.

Damn Jackie and her crusades, stirring everything up like this. All Sara wanted was to live quietly in this small backwater village, minding her own business, literally. Was that too much to ask? She shook her head, wincing as even that slight movement sent daggers of pain shooting behind her eyes. She closed her eyelids, refusing to think about any of it right now — Jackie, Melville Barnett, open cut mines and corrupt politicians. She'd always wanted to be a gardener, and now she was making her dream a reality; focus on that.

She carefully eased the quilt up to her chin and then stilled herself, concentrating on her breathing. Eventually, the headache receded. She was drowsy and comfortable and had no work scheduled for tomorrow morning. She could lie in as late as she wanted. She took several long, slow breaths and let sleep claim her.

At six years old, Sara has never seen roots before.

She reaches out her finger, snatches it back, not sure if the tangled white mass is alive, might suddenly wriggle and give her a fright.

Linda, her foster mother, softly laughs at her. Her laughter isn't like the taunting of the big boys, back at the Children's Home. It doesn't make Sara feel like curling up into a ball, wishing she could squeeze herself so small that no one will notice her at all. Linda's laughter is as warm as the sun on Sara's back. Linda loves her, and Sara loves Linda, fiercely and completely.

"It's alright, Sara, they won't bite. Go on, feel them."

Trusting her, Sara reaches out again, touches the cool furry softness, rubs the gritty dirt between thumb and finger.

"See? This is how plants eat. They reach out through the soil with their roots and drink in water and all sorts of good things. Then they grow big and strong. This little one will be as tall as you by the end of summer."

Linda nestles the little plant in the hole and scoops crumbly dirt around and over the roots until Sara can't see them at all. "Here, you can do this one."

Captivated, she holds out small chubby hands, cupped together to receive the seedling as if it is a rare treasure.

And it is. This is. This moment, kneeling on the ground beside Linda, with the sun warm on her back and the smell of green things all around her. Safe. Loved. Home. She wants it to last forever.

Sara woke and stared up into the darkness with hot, dry eyes. It hadn't lasted forever — she had made sure of that.

Stop it. You're not a child any more.

She hadn't dreamed of Linda for years. She'd put all that behind her, learned to control her emotions, keep them locked away where they couldn't hurt her or anyone else.

Somehow, her anger with Jackie had dredged up memories and feelings that were best forgotten. She closed her eyes, willed her body to relax. *I'm an adult now. I've made my own life, my own home. I don't need a family. I don't need anyone.*

Sara woke to brilliant yellow sunshine filling the bedroom. A blue, rain-washed sky greeted her through the window. It was going to be a perfect autumn day. With winter just around the corner, such a day was a precious thing, and she intended to savour it.

This afternoon, she'd be meeting with a new client, her back-fence neighbour, in fact. Stephen Cooper, Wattleford's new doctor, had just moved into the big overgrown garden behind hers. He wanted her to take a look at it and give him some advice.

But that was later. Right now, this magnificent morning was all hers, and there was only one place she wanted to spend it.

She was halfway down the stairs when the events of last night intruded into her thoughts, stopping her in her tracks. She'd been so incensed with Jackie — over nothing, really. And then the dream. She needed to get a grip. At least the headache had gone.

Shaking the disturbing memories from her mind, she continued down the stairs and into the kitchen. She wished someone could block Melville Barnett's plans, but it didn't seem likely. He had too much money and influence. The mine would probably go ahead, no matter what Jackie or anyone did. Another unique, beautiful place would be ruined by greed.

She thrust the depressing thought aside and made coffee. She was still wearing her pyjamas, but she couldn't wait any longer. She opened the French windows and carried her favourite green mug outside to the small glass-topped table under the cherry tree.

Red and gold leaves hung in perfect stillness against the bluest sky she'd ever seen. Around her slippered feet, the same scarlet and yellow were set against the bright green threads of new grass. The autumn rains had brought her summer-scorched lawn back to life, and now it had decorated itself with fallen cherry leaves to welcome her home. The almost fruity aroma of decaying leaves and rich, moist soil filled her nostrils. She breathed deeply as she sank into her wrought iron chair, heedless of the slight dampness seeping up from the cushion. She sipped strong, hot coffee while her eyes revelled in the colours of her garden.

Beyond the little patio, huge scarlet and orange flowers glowed against finely cut deep green or purple-black foliage. Long wands of pink and burgundy blossom reached for the sky, or leaned drunkenly against each other, almost blocking the narrow brick path. This was Sara's favourite time of the year. Most of her clients preferred spring, with its tiny new leaves and half-open buds, each clump of new growth in its own defined space. Their highest praise for a garden was that it was "neat and tidy". Sara worked hard to give them what they wanted. She weeded, pruned, trimmed and shaped their gardens until they were happy with the results.

But in her own little patch, the first she'd ever owned, Sara let the plants have their way, only interfering when she felt it was in their interest. She pulled out greedy weeds that would have taken over if given the chance. She pruned to encourage healthy growth. If clumps became huge and overcrowded, she thinned them out. But nothing more. Seeds fell everywhere, the resulting seedlings growing together into one joyful, wild, glorious mess. Leaving her empty mug on the table, she rose and pushed her way between the wet plants, careless of the soaking her pyjamas were getting.

She stopped and knelt in front of a dense mat of Stachys, stroking one of its large, grey leaves, enjoying the almost animal softness that had given it the common name of Lamb's Ears. She reached out and gently rubbed the fine silver needles of a nearby Helichrysum, breathing in deeply as the delicious scent of curry drifted up into the warm, still air. It was such a rich, solid smell. She could almost see it.

She blinked.

It wasn't her imagination. The air above the curry plant shimmered like the haze above a bitumen road on a blazing hot day. And the haze was thickening. Now it looked more like wisps of mist or pale smoke. Gauzy tendrils coiled and twisted in the air, right in front of her eyes. Dizziness assailed her. She shook her head, which felt oddly heavy, but that just made the mist swirl faster. It was still getting thicker. She could barely make out the plants in front of her anymore.

Her head was spinning now. She put both hands flat on the ground to steady herself. Maybe she shouldn't have taken those painkillers on top of the wine last night. She closed her eyes and forced a deep breath. The curry smell disappeared, replaced by the sharp, antiseptic scent of pine. Icy air flowed into her lungs. Her throat closed in shock. Her eyelids flew open.

The fog was gone. Her heart thumped as if she'd been running. Her hands felt odd. She looked down at them. They were curled like claws, her fingers half-buried in the dirt.

"Playing with your pets again?"

Sara's heart gave another huge thump. She gasped and swung her head around so fast she almost wrenched her neck.

Jackie was leaning over the low fence between their properties. "Well, I suppose they're easier to look after than a dog. At least you don't have to take them for walks." She tilted her head to one side and raised an eyebrow, a smile hovering. "But do you really think patting them helps them to grow better?"

With an enormous effort, Sara pulled herself together. She took a few more quick breaths, brushed the dirt off her hands and stood. She still felt shaken, but she was pleased her voice came out sounding relatively normal. "I don't know if it helps them, but it can't hurt."

"Well, you must be doing something right. After all this rain, the last few leaves on my roses are covered in black spot and mildew. Yours still look great."

Sara turned her head briefly to see for herself. The billowing rose hedge along the back fence had finished flowering, but the bushes did seem to be green and healthy.

"You, on the other hand, look a bit pale," Jackie said. "Are you all right?"

"Yes, sorry. I felt a bit light-headed for a moment."

It was probably hunger. She'd eaten nothing solid since lunchtime yesterday, just the wine last night and black coffee this morning. "I think my blood sugar's a bit low."

"Well, go and have breakfast, then. I'm off to get some flyers printed. We have to start moving on this mining thing."

After Jackie had gone, Sara headed for the back door, intending to follow her neighbour's advice and find something to eat. But a tendril of thought was nagging at her. The rose hedge along the back fence — it hadn't seemed quite right. She turned to have another look.

The roses were green, as Jackie had said. Greener than they should be at this time of year. The leaves should have begun to change colour and fall by now. Curious, she drew closer.

Something was wrong. The leaves had turned and dropped, as she'd expected — all of them by the looks of it — forming a red and brown carpet beneath the hedge, but they hadn't left the stems bare. Short bunches of twisted, pale green shoots crowded every arching cane from root to tip — hundreds of them, thousands. She recognised them instantly. This was the way rose bushes reacted to certain kinds of weed-killer. And with this much damage, the outcome was certain. The entire hedge was doomed. Tears filled her eyes. She stretched out a hand in an instinctive desire to comfort the plants, then pulled it back. There was nothing she could do.

How could it have happened? She didn't own any weedkiller. Neither did Jackie or Sara's elderly neighbour on the other side, who grew organic vegetables to sell. Only one explanation made sense: someone had sprayed herbicide through the back fence.

Someone? No, not just someone — Dr Stephen Cooper. It had to be him. He must have done it when he moved in. Her beautiful roses. How *dare* he?

Forget waiting until this afternoon. She was going to confront him now. As soon as she'd changed out of these wet pyjamas.

Righteous rage propelled her into the house and up the stairs to the bedroom. By the time she'd changed into jeans, shirt and boots and tugged her hair into a ponytail, the first heat of her anger had died down to a steady simmer. She wouldn't just storm into his house and blast him, much as he deserved it. She would be an adult. She would knock on his door, tell the slimy weasel she knew what he'd done, and ask him what the hell gave him the right to kill her plants. Only more politely than that.

When Stephen opened the door, his eyebrows rose in surprise above his black-framed glasses. Then his lips broke into a smile. His teeth gleamed whitely against his brown skin. His white t-shirt had the words "Trust me, I'm a doctor" printed in big blue letters next to a cartoon of a stethoscope.

Trust him? Huh!

"Sara. You're a bit earlier than I was expecting, but it's nice to see you again."

His pleasure seemed so genuine that Sara caught herself starting to return the smile. She pressed her lips together tightly to suppress the impulse, then opened them just enough to let her words slip out. "Can I talk to you?"

"Of course. Come into the kitchen. It's the only room that's in a fit state for visitors yet, I'm afraid. I'll make us some coffee." Without waiting for an answer, he turned and strode down the hallway. Having lost her chance to confront him on the threshold, she followed him, fuming.

When she reached the kitchen, he was already at the sink, filling a kettle from the tap. Her heart pounded and pain stabbed her temples. She'd burst if she had to hold her tongue any longer. "*Why did you poison my roses?*" The question came out louder than she'd intended.

He turned, still holding the kettle. "What?"

10

"You sprayed weedkiller on my roses. I want to know why." Sara heard the tremor in her voice and hated herself for it. She could feel the blood draining from her face. The kitchen spun around her as she clenched her fists and willed herself to stand her ground. The spinning stopped. She could do this.

Stephen slowly set the kettle down. He wasn't smiling any more. "I don't know what you're talking about. I haven't poisoned anything."

She took a deep breath and forced herself to speak slowly and clearly. "The roses along my back fence are dying because they've been sprayed with weedkiller. It could only have come through the fence from your yard. So, I'd like an explanation. Why did you kill my roses?"

Her voice had risen on the last sentence, and she was glad. To hell with being controlled. She wanted to shout and scream. From deep inside her, something whispered that all this anger was dangerous. She ignored it. "*Answer me!* Why did you do it?"

"I didn't." Flat and unamused.

He was lying. Standing right in front of her and lying to her face. Bitter words rose. She opened her mouth to spit them out, but her throat closed up, trapping them inside her. She couldn't breathe.

He was still talking - she could see his lips moving - but the thundering in her temples drowned out every other sound. She made an enormous effort and finally gasped in a lungful of blessed air. At the same time, words seeped into her brain.

"...I think...estate agent...the spraying. I'm sorry about your roses, no wonder you're upset."

What was he saying? Estate agent? *Oh, no.* She licked dry lips and swallowed. "When did you move in?"

His brows lowered in a puzzled frown. "I just told you, Tuesday."

Tuesday. Six days ago. Not long enough for that much damage to appear on the roses. Why hadn't she thought of that before? *Because I've turned into some kind of maniac in the past twelve hours.*

All the blood that had drained from her face flooded back in a single rush. Her cheeks must be glowing like stoplights. If only the joints between the floorboards would open up, she'd slip down gladly.

Her voice came out as a whisper. "I'm so sorry, Stephen."

He waved her apology away. "Forget it. You have every right to be angry. We should complain to them, make them replace your plants. Hang on, we'd better go and see what damage they've done in my yard first."

He turned and led the way to the back door.

Sara trailed after him, his kindness and understanding somehow making her feel even worse. Outside, she somehow pulled herself together enough to talk to him about the garden, but she was operating on autopilot.

When he went into the house to make the coffee he'd started earlier, she sank down onto a small patch of ground, letting her mind go mercifully blank. A narrow shaft of sunlight slanted down between the trees to warm her. She brushed her hand over plants and soil, the contact with nature making her feel better, as it always did.

Thousands of tiny, emerald seedlings surrounded her, each one reaching for the light, striving for the space it needed. Her fingers began plucking out the weeds, giving the others a chance to grow. Dirt clung to her fingertips and worked its way under her nails. The world shrank to a small patch of earth. Her eyes followed the hand as it dipped down and up, down and up.

The hand found the edge of a clump of larger leaves: deep green, ferny. A straight, dark stem, and above it, a neat pyramid of tight yellow buds, topped with three open flowers. Curved red stamens poked out like tongues licking the air. Words drifted across Sara's mind: Caesalpinia gilliesii.

Linda hadn't called it that. She'd called it her Bird of Paradise Plant. She'd showed six-year old Sara how the stamens resembled the tongues of birds.

Sara shook her head. She didn't want to think about Linda now. She felt bad enough already. But last night's dream seemed to have breached the wall she had built and reinforced over so many years, and now the recollections flooded in, unstoppable.

Sara had been so full of grief and rage, those first days after she'd been sent to live with Linda and Ben and their son, Mark. She had screamed and thrown tantrums and demanded to go home. Linda had absorbed it all, kindly and without fuss. And the little girl had begun to respond, like a wilted flower reviving under a gentle shower of rain.

Sara stretched forward and touched one of the open blooms. Moisture welled in her eyes.

Linda had taught her the names of all her flowers and showed her how to look after each one. They spent hours outside together after school and on weekends. Linda loved all her plants, but the Bird of Paradise was her favourite.

Sara choked and snatched her hand away. The tears spilled over and trickled down her cheeks. This was ridiculous. She should be over it all by now. She had thought she was. It had been twenty years since she'd been banished from Linda's home, and Linda's love. All because of Mark. She clenched her teeth and turned her head away, but it was no good. The memories had their claws in her now and wouldn't be denied.

Eight-year-old Mark had been jealous of his new "sister" from the start, taking any opportunity to pinch her or pull her hair when his parents weren't looking. And then he began lying about her. He would break something and tell Linda that Sara had done it. When Sara denied it hotly, Linda didn't know who to believe. But one day, the last day, Mark went further. He deliberately hit himself on the head with a rock. Then he handed the rock to Sara and started yelling.

When Linda and Ben came running, they saw the blood in their son's hair and Sara holding the red-stained rock. They wouldn't even listen to her side of the story. Linda cleaned Mark's injury and took him to his room to lie down. Ben sent Sara to her room, too, but when she heard Linda going back down the stairs, she crept after her. She crouched, shivering, behind the bannister on the bottom step, and listened to the adults talking in the next room.

"Honey, I think we might have rushed into all this without thinking it through," said Ben. "We've tried, but it's just not working, and we have Mark to think about."

Sara's heart pounded. He meant her — she was what wasn't working.

"I hate the idea of giving up on her," Linda said, "but I didn't think it would be this hard." She sounded like she was crying. "I don't know what to do."

"I don't see how we can keep her," Ben said. "Not after this."

They were going to send her away! Back to the Home that wasn't a home at all. It wasn't fair! It was Mark's fault — horrible, lying Mark; she wished he was dead. She heard a sound from above her and turned to see him standing on the landing, looking down at her, smiling. He'd heard it all. He knew he'd won.

She couldn't stand it. She screamed and bolted up the staircase, grabbed his arm and started kicking him in the shins. He shouted in surprise and pain, wrenched his arm free and twisted past her, trying to get to his parents. They were at the foot of the stairs now, looking up with shocked, pale faces. Sara didn't care. He wasn't escaping from her that easily. She might be smaller than him, but fury made her strong, and he was already off balance. She pushed him in the back as hard as she could.

He had fallen down the stairs, all the way to the bottom.

Sara took a shaky breath and raised her wet eyes to the flowers again. Mark had survived, thank God, with a broken arm and some bruises, but Sara had been banished back to the Martindale Children's Home. She had learned her lesson, and never forgotten it: don't get too attached; don't feel too deeply. Control your emotions. But she hadn't been sent to another foster family.

And she'd never found out who she really was, or where she had come from, or why she had been found at five years old, wandering along a highway in the middle of the night, crying for her lost parents. She didn't even remember their faces any more.

The smug, yellow flowers stared back at her, mocking her pain.

It was too much — the anger, the headaches, the disturbing dream, the dizziness, the dying roses. All of it swirled together in a whirlpool of misery that sucked at her, dragged her down. She had no resistance left. She was a child once more, with her whole world torn apart. Helpless and heartbroken, longing desperately for family and home.

Fog roiled and the world disappeared.

14

TWO
Mena

Rassil was crying again, slumped forward over the kitchen table with her head pillowed on her arms.

Mena felt sorry for the girl, but this was getting to be a habit. If Rassil kept on like this, Mena would have to send her home and train a new serving maid. She didn't want to do that. Rassil's father had died a few months ago, leaving the girl and her mother almost penniless. They were distant relatives; she had a responsibility to do what she could for them. Nevertheless, Soran wouldn't put up with those endless tears much longer. Her brother-in-law liked cheerful faces around him, no matter how dark his own mood had become.

"Rassil, what's the matter?" Mena had spoken mildly enough, but the girl jumped like a startled rabbit. She shot up from the chair and spun to face her mistress, mouth gaping and blonde plaits swinging. Her drowned blue eyes looked huge and tragic.

"It's nothing, Mistress Erdal," she whispered. She brushed the tears away and stood straighter. "I'll be getting back to my work, now." She bobbed her head and turned to leave the kitchen.

Mena's voice stopped her. "Wait, Rassil. I want to know why you were crying. Don't be frightened, just tell me what happened."

Rassil stared at her feet as she answered. Mena caught the word "master" from the low murmur.

"What about the master? Speak up so I can hear you."

15

Rassil raised her head and gulped. "Oh, I'm so sorry, Mistress," she breathed. "I dropped Master Erdal's bottle of brandy, and it broke and ran all over the floor, and he shouted at me."

Mena sighed. Soran had been in a foul temper for weeks, and unfortunately his way of being in a temper involved a lot of brandy and a lot of noise. He was a very big man, and intimidating when he was angry, with his deep voice thundering out from behind his black beard. She understood why Rassil was frightened of him.

But Soran wasn't going to change his personality or his drinking habits any time soon, and the farm belonged to him. Rassil would have to get used to it, just as Mena had, eight — no, ten — years ago, when Soran had offered a home to his brother's widow and nine-year-old son. Mena didn't know what she and Kelan would have done if Soran hadn't agreed to take them in after Veren had died so suddenly. Putting up with his moods had been a small price to pay.

Perhaps firmness would work with Rassil where sympathy hadn't.

"Rassil, if the master shouts at you, that's no reason to cry. You're not a child anymore; you're seventeen years old. You should have apologised, cleaned up the mess and got on with your work. Go and do it now, and don't let me see you crying again."

Rassil scurried out. Mena sat down in the empty kitchen. She was worried about Soran. He was drinking more and more, and he always seemed to be shouting at someone. If it wasn't a clumsy serving girl, it was the farm workers or the neighbours. Although she was worried, she couldn't blame him. She knew what lay behind his filthy moods: deep fear. Fear that the farm would fail, that he would have to abandon it, move off the land. And without his land, who would Soran Erdal be?

More importantly, if they were forced to leave the farm, what would become of Kelan?

Mena clenched her fists on the table. Three years ago, she'd been so sure that her son's future was settled and secure. Soran had made it clear that he intended to leave the farm to his nephew. It was a prosperous place, and if Kelan decided he wasn't suited to farming, he'd be able to sell it for a good price.

Things were very different now. No farm was secure, and Kelan's future hung by a thread. A thread held by the foul Greenhaelen, may Aal curse them.

She hated to think that she'd admired the Greenhaelen once, back in the days when they'd travelled freely around the country, keeping the crops of Algarth flourishing. She'd felt a kind of kinship with them: she used her skal to heal people, they used theirs on plants. She'd also respected them for the way they took the circumstances of their employers into account when they charged for their services: on the poorest farms, they would work in return for meals and lodging alone.

She'd even agreed with their leader, Logen Rush, when he'd been the lone voice on the Council of Six to oppose the new trade agreement with Bregia. She'd believed that clearing wilderness for more farms and doubling the timber harvest from the forests was a bad move for her homeland.

But when Logen had failed to change his fellow Councillors' minds, he'd demanded Chairman Tarn and the Council turn political power over to him, or face the consequences. On their rightful refusal, he'd led the Greenhaelen onto a path that could never be justified, no matter how right their cause. First, they'd descended on the timber-workers' camps, ransacking the cabins and destroying possessions. That had been bad enough, but a week later they'd set fire to several Bregian trading vessels anchored in Eorna harbour. The horrifying thing was they'd done it at night, while the crew slept on board. Many poor sailors had died in their beds, never knowing what had killed them. Others had run out onto the decks, leaping into the water to put out the flames. Only a handful had survived, horribly burned. The day she'd heard the news was the day Mena had lost all respect for the Greenhaelen.

But almost worse, to her mind, was what they'd turned to when the violence hadn't worked. Instead of sustaining the plants under their care, they had chosen to bring death, twisting and corrupting their Aal-given skal. A foul brown stain was creeping across the land, engulfing forests and farmland alike. In its wake, nothing green remained alive.

In response, the Council had declared the whole guild to be

outlaws, but even that hadn't stopped them. Despite arrests and imprisonments, the plant life of Algarth was still dying, the deadly tide still spreading. Where it had passed, farms and even whole villages had been abandoned. Food was running low in many places — Rassil had been practically starving when she'd arrived on the farm.

Mena turned her head to the window. Outside, the last of autumn's golden leaves clung lightly to the branches of the apple trees. Stubble covered the fields beyond, the remnants of this year's exceptional harvest. Would there ever be another on this land? A lifeless farm might be Kelan's only inheritance, destitution and starvation his only future. She bit her lip until she tasted blood. *Aal strike down the Greenhaelen and their ruthless lust for power!*

The terrible weapon they had unleashed had been called many things over the past two years, but one name seemed to have stuck. It was a word that Soran had forbidden to be spoken anywhere on his land, in the superstitious hope that not naming it could somehow keep it away. A short word for something that might destroy an entire country, only six letters: Blight.

The edge of the Blighted area was still some distance away, but it was advancing. If the Blight reached the farm, Rassil really would have something to cry about. They all would.

Mena bowed her head over her hands and prayed. *Aal, have mercy on us. Keep the Blight away. And whatever happens, I beg you, protect my son.*

THREE

Kelan

Kelan stared stonily at his uncle, letting the blast of sound flow right through him, leaving no visible trace. He wouldn't flinch, not this time. He wasn't a child anymore. He was nineteen years old. He was a man. And he would never cringe under Soran's anger again.

Standing in the farmyard while his uncle's booming voice thundered on and on, Kelan felt amazed at the difference a few days could make. This time last week, he had been afraid of Soran, almost in awe of him. Now, examining the large, florid face and noticing with surprise the first signs of grey in the coarse black beard, Kelan almost felt pity. He had found his manhood and his courage, and none of Soran's blustering and shouting could change anything. Rassil loved him, and nothing else mattered.

He had noticed her from the moment she had arrived at the farm, a timid girl, tiny and slender as a sapling, with hair that shone like pale gold in the sun. Everything about her was enchanting, magical. She wasn't at all like the girls he knew, sturdy farm girls with strong muscular arms, or the wealthy young ladies he had seen parading themselves around Eorna as if they owned the city. She was like a fairy creature, shy and delicate and perfect. And last night, after his birthday celebration, she had accepted half of the promise charm he'd bought at last summer's harvest festival.

He had found it on a market stall run by an old woman wearing the black robes of a scholar. The shabbiness and dusty state of the robes suggested she wasn't a wealthy one. The stall was piled high with books and rolls of parchment, and normally, he would have walked right past as his friends had, but for some reason, the charm had taken his eye. It was a flat copper disc engraved with a swirling, interlocking design. When he touched it, the fine lines glowed faintly silver, showing that a Charm Shaper had already activated it. Not that the charm on it mattered to him right then. He hadn't met Rassil and had no plans to split the disc with anyone. He just liked the look of it. The old woman hadn't asked for much money, so he'd ignored the scoffing and laughter of the other boys and bought it. Since then, he'd worn the disc on its double chain around his neck. Under his shirt, naturally. No need to invite more jeering.

But when he'd fallen in love with Rassil, it seemed to him as if the promise charm had been meant for the two of them all along. Last night, they'd whispered each other's names to it and broken it along its centre line. Rassil had even let him kiss her.

So, it didn't matter what Soran thought or said. Kelan loved Rassil and ten months from now, when she was eighteen and of age, they'd be married. He suspected his mother wouldn't approve, and that bothered him more than his uncle's bullying, but she'd get used to it in the end.

Soran had stopped shouting and was trying reason: "Kelan, think! The girl has nothing! Her mother is so poor she can't even support her; that's why she came here in the first place. She has a pretty face, I grant you, but she's no fit match for you, nephew. This farm will be yours when I'm gone, and you'll need a wife who can help you run it. As far as I can see, the girl has no skills at all. What use would she be to you?" His bushy eyebrows twisted in puzzlement.

He's old, and fat, thought Kelan. *If he ever knew what love was, he forgot it long ago.* It was no use trying to explain. His uncle would never understand.

Soran shook his big shaggy head, then, with an abrupt change of mood that was typical of him, he smiled and laid a heavy hand on Kelan's shoulder. "Come on; forget about it for now. I feel like a hunt. What do you say? Time to try out that new bow of yours?"

Kelan felt himself smiling in response. He should have faced up to his uncle years ago. By standing his ground, he'd obviously earned the older man's respect: another reason to be grateful to Rassil. Give Soran time and he'd change his mind about the marriage. After all, he might be past his prime and a bit of a bully, but he wasn't really stupid. Besides, Kelan was eager to test the long ash bow he'd received for his birthday.

Two hours later, he was following a deer through the snow-dusted forest as his uncle watched from cover. Soran wasn't exactly built for stealth, so he left the tracking to Kelan, who was able to move through the familiar woodland like a shadow. His hair, the same red-brown as his mother's, flopped down over his eyes again. He shoved it back impatiently. He had started letting it grow after seeing the city boys on his last trip to Eorna. Hair that almost covered your eyes, so you could hardly see, was the latest fashion there. He wanted to show them he wasn't a farm hick, so he'd refused to let his mother cut his hair ever since. He was pleased at how it looked now, but it was a bit annoying when he was trying to focus his attention on the hunt.

The deer bounded up and away from a clump of bushes, sending a cloud of fine snow particles into the air. Kelan raced after it as it fled towards the Blighted part of the forest. He hated the sight of the blasted trees. Those Greenhaelen should be made to fix what they had done. If Kelan ever got his hands on one of them, he'd see to it himself.

Thinking about the Blight had taken his attention off the deer. He peered between the dead trees. His fringe flopped over his forehead again. He ignored it. His eyes scanned ahead, alert for the slightest change. *There!* A gleam of sun lit up a patch of light brown hair next to a tree trunk. Closer than he was expecting, well within range. The deer must have doubled back. In an instant, he had an arrow on the string. He took aim and let it fly.

A high-pitched, unmistakably human cry broke the silence, followed by the muffled thunk of the arrowhead biting into wood. Horror jolted through Kelan's body. He'd hit someone! What if he'd killed them? The bow dropped from his nerveless fingers. Blood thundered in his ears as he raced over the uneven ground towards the source of the sounds. *Don't let them be dead, please, don't let them be dead.*

FOUR

Sara

Sara was dreaming again. She knew it was a dream, because she was sitting at the base of a tree, and a thin dusting of snow covered the ground. Black trunks marched away in every direction, disappearing into mist. She had been in Stephen Cooper's garden, and now she was in a snowy forest. Definitely a dream. Maybe the whole embarrassing scene with Stephen had been part of the dream, too. She really hoped so. *Of course,* she thought, as relief rushed through her, *that's why I've been behaving so oddly! None of it was real.*

At least this part of the dream wasn't embarrassing, or frightening. It was quiet and peaceful here in the forest. Besides, she'd never seen snow in real life. A little thrill ripped through her as she gazed around. It was like an adventure. Perhaps she could explore a bit before she woke up. Craning her neck back, she peered up through the branches of her own tree. She didn't recognise the species, but it seemed to be a conifer of some kind. Dark green needles clustered in groups, forming a thin canopy. The sky beyond was a dull, almost dirty white. She couldn't see the sun, and she certainly couldn't feel it. Dream or not, she was freezing. She wrapped her arms tightly around herself and watched her breath rise in small white puffs.

It was very detailed for a dream, but she had dreamed in detail before. More than once in the past she had reasoned that she couldn't be dreaming — everything was too vivid and real — only to wake and find herself in her own bed. She had read somewhere that a dreamer can't smell anything, so she drew the frigid air in through her nose. The cold prickled and stung, but she detected something: the aromatic scent of pine, the same odour she'd imagined when she had that dizzy turn in her garden yesterday. So much for that theory.

At least it wasn't a nightmare, not yet anyway, but she was aching with cold. The idea of exploration had lost its charm. Time to wake up. She willed herself to open her eyes. Nothing. She tried twice more before giving up. It didn't always work. And she knew from experience that pinching herself was useless, no matter what you saw in movies. She might have to let this play out. If she kept her dream body moving, maybe she could trick her brain into thinking she was warm.

At the first step, her head began to spin. Nausea rolled through her. She grabbed at the tree with both hands to steady herself, taking deep breaths. The sick, dizzy feeling passed quickly, but she stayed where she was, reluctant to risk triggering it again. With her face only inches away from the shaggy trunk, she noticed an area the size of her palm that looked different to the rest. She wiped away the thin powdering of snow to examine it more closely. A whorled pattern lay on the trunk, too smooth and symmetrical to be natural. Someone had put it there, cutting deeply into the bark. Several spirals, engraved with almost mathematical precision, interlocking to create a single design. She counted as she traced each one with her finger. Six spirals. It was strange and beautiful, but she had no idea what it meant, or why it had appeared in her dream.

Her teeth began to chatter with the cold. Time to try walking again. She took an experimental step away from the tree. No dizziness. She chose a direction at random and set off, glad that she had dreamed she was wearing her sturdy work boots and not something useless like a pair of sandals. After a while, the light grew stronger. Glancing upwards again, she discovered that the blank whiteness hadn't been the sky at all, just a blanket of fog. It was breaking up and streaming away, revealing streaks of blue. Over to her left the sun appeared, pale and sickly behind its veil of mist. She turned her steps towards it, hoping that even a dream-sun might offer relief from the piercing cold. Avoiding the shadows, she darted from one patch of weak sunlight to another like a small, scurrying animal. Every so often, she stopped and made another attempt to wake herself up, but it was no use.

She seemed to have been doing this for a long time when the forest abruptly changed. The trees appeared to be the same kind, but the needles on their branches were shrivelled and brown. Her eyes searched the canopy without discovering a single cluster of green. She knew, with the certainty that often comes in dreams, that every one of these trees had died where it stood, not from age or disease, but as a result of some terrible cataclysm. Untimely death surrounded her. Tears filled her eyes. In her distress at the scale of the disaster, she completely forgot she was only walking among dream trees in a dream forest.

Another few steps, and the broadest trunk she had yet seen rose directly in her path. It loomed tall and solid, but it was dead, like the others. She stopped and stretched out a hand to the shaggy bark in an instinctive gesture of sympathy.

Excruciating pain shot up her arm and exploded at the base of her skull in a blast of white light. She heard her own sharp cry of agony, then fell into nothingness.

FIVE

Mena

The wound was messy, but thank Aal, the arrow had missed the major artery on its way through the forearm. It hadn't splintered the bone either, another blessing. Now that she had cleaned the wound, Mena was confident the damage would heal, although it would leave two small scars: one on top and one underneath. She couldn't do anything about those.

The young woman, whoever she was, didn't seem to be the vain sort, judging from her strange, unfashionable clothing, so perhaps she wouldn't mind the scars. Placing her hands on the torn flesh, Mena willed the wound to close cleanly, without infection. "Be well, my love, be well," she murmured. "Health return to you. Strength and healing be yours."

While she wrapped the arm with a bandage, she studied her unconscious patient. She was a mystery. For a start, the quality of her boots didn't match the rest of her clothing. They were of good leather, with fine seams and sturdy soles, and looked almost new. A rich woman's boots. But her green tunic and blue trousers were of plain, serviceable fabric, without a hint of decoration. And they were far too thin for this time of year, not winter clothing at all. She wasn't wearing jewellery and, according to Soran, they had found no purse or satchel nearby. What had she been doing, all alone, in the Blighted part of the forest?

It was a good thing that Soran and Kelan had gone hunting there today, although of course it would have been better if Kelan hadn't mistaken the stranger for an animal. Mena shook her head. Her son, although he was nineteen now and as tall and broad-shouldered as a man, still sometimes behaved like an impetuous child. Soran, of course, had been furious about the accident, threatening to confiscate the new bow. He was in the next room now, drinking and grumbling. Kelan had taken himself off somewhere or other, no doubt in a huff about being shouted at. As usual, they had left Mena to clean up their mess.

The woman stirred and groaned, but didn't open her eyes. Mena patted her hand. "It's all right, my love. You're safe. Just lie there a moment."

The woman tossed her head from side to side and lifted her arm off the bed. She groaned louder. Mena bent closer, biting her lip. After her ministrations, the arm shouldn't be giving this much pain. Had she missed a second injury? The patient had lifted her hand towards her head, so perhaps she had hit it when she fell. Mena reached out and stroked the stranger's forehead, murmuring again in soothing tones. She would have done this earlier if she'd realised. Compared to physical healing, relieving pain took almost no effort at all.

SIX

Sara

Cool, gentle fingers were stroking Sara's throbbing forehead. They felt good. Perhaps Stephen had found her unconscious in his garden and taken her to hospital. The sharp pain behind her eyes faded. They must have given her something for it.

She half-parted her eyelids, anticipating a white tile ceiling and the unpleasant glare of fluorescent lights. The ceiling was white, but the light wasn't coming from there. No tiles, either. Instead, square sections of rough plaster sagged slightly between lathes of dark timber. She turned her head. A woman of about forty was sitting next to the bed. She was wearing a long-sleeved red dress that might have been made of wool, with a blue apron over the top. Thick chestnut hair hung in a fringe to her eyebrows and tumbled in loose waves to her shoulders. Soft, widely set blue eyes regarded Sara kindly from above lightly freckled cheeks as the woman spoke. The tone sounded friendly, but Sara couldn't understand a word. The woman wasn't speaking English.

Sara was good at languages. Perhaps her skill had been born of necessity: when she had first been taken into care in Australia, she hadn't understood a word that anyone spoke to her. She had been so frightened, surrounded by people speaking nonsense. She had answered their babble with real words, proper words, but they understood nothing. Later, at school, she had been given special lessons so she could 'catch up'. She did more than that: she excelled. Besides English, she studied

27

German, French and Italian. She loved it all. But after learning all those wonderful new words, she couldn't remember a single one from her original language. She didn't even know what it had been.

She listened intently to the woman sitting beside her. The language didn't sound Germanic or Latinate. She was pretty sure it wasn't Chinese or Japanese or Korean, either. Beyond that, her knowledge ended. She levered herself up on her elbows, grateful that the movement didn't start the headache again, swallowed a few times and cleared her throat. "Do you speak English?"

The woman frowned and spoke again. No good. Sara tried French, German and Italian with no better result. The woman had stopped replying and was staring at her in concern. Sara couldn't think of what else to do. Perhaps she was still dreaming and would wake up eventually to her safe, normal life. She lay back, closed her eyes again and drifted off.

She woke bleary-eyed, blinking up at the same plaster ceiling. Memories flooded back and a surge of adrenaline jerked her upright, sending her heart hammering, her hands pushing back the covers, her head swivelling from side to side. Her eyes darted from the empty wooden chair to the single window — flanked by long curtains that didn't meet in the middle — then flicked along the whitewashed wall over the low chest of drawers to the open door. Nowhere for anyone to hide. She relaxed slightly. She was alone, but what the hell was going on? This was no dream — she was wide awake.

Squinting against the light streaming through the gap between the curtains, she made out the bare, knobbly branch of an apple tree. Half a dozen butter-coloured leaves hung from it, curled in on themselves, almost ready to fall. Out beyond them lay a freshly ploughed field, chocolate brown, the horizontal light emphasising the crisp ridges and furrows.

A blackbird landed just outside the window, the twig bowing under its slight weight before springing back, the sudden movement making her jump. The glossy bird opened its beak and poured liquid song into the air, the sound only slightly muffled by the glass. At the same time, a rumble of male voices erupted from below, out of Sara's sight. She strained her ears, but couldn't make out any words.

She shivered suddenly at the chill touch of the air on her bare feet. Someone had taken off her boots and socks and lined them up neatly against the wall near the head of the bed. As she reached for them, she saw the bandage on her forearm. She pressed gingerly on it. Some pain, but nothing like the agony she'd felt in the forest. She ran her hands over the rest of her body without finding any other sore spots. But in the process, she discovered something else: a hard, flat shape in her jeans pocket. *Her phone!* She'd forgotten all about it. She could call someone, figure out where she was and how to get home. She could have cried with relief.

She slid it out, hoping the battery wasn't flat. The screen lit up as soon as she pressed it, revealing first a blinking red circle crossed by a horizontal line and then two words: No Service. It wasn't going to be that easy. She was on her own. So be it.

She swallowed her disappointment, pulled on her socks and boots and tiptoed to the open door. She craned her head around the doorpost, her eyes darting left and right. No one in sight. Taking a deep breath, she stepped into the long hallway.

Halfway along, a stairway opened on her left, leading down. She paused at the top. She had no plan — how could she when none of this made any sense — but somehow getting to the ground floor seemed like a good idea.

Female voices drifted up the stairs, accompanied by the aroma of frying bacon. Despite her fear, saliva flooded her mouth. When had she eaten last? She descended carefully, keeping one hand on the carved banister, heart pounding, hunger warring with caution.

By the time she'd reached the bottom, her heart rate had settled a little, and hunger was winning. After all, the woman hadn't tried to harm her. Just the opposite, in fact — the bandage on Sara's arm suggested goodwill. Besides, now that the idea of food had taken root in her mind, it refused to be dispelled. Her stomach was a yawning cavern. Whatever was happening, she needed to eat. Picking up the pace, she followed the voices and the smell along another hallway, past two closed doors, and into the steamy warmth of a spacious kitchen.

The red-headed woman turned at her entrance, wiping her hands down her apron and beaming a smile in Sara's direction. The other occupant of the room, a slightly-built blonde girl, was bending over an enormous black metal stove, the old-fashioned wood-burning kind.

The woman stepped forward, tapping her chest. "Mena," she said. She raised her eyebrows and cocked her head. Her meaning was clear. Sara pointed to her own chest. "Sara."

The teenager's name was Rassil. She turned her head briefly and bobbed her head to Sara, her cheeks red from the heat of the stove, then returned to her task. She was frying eggs in two cast iron pans and rashers of bacon on a large flat griddle, biting her lip with concentration. Perhaps she wasn't used to cooking. Sara sympathised with that — she wasn't much of a cook, herself.

A scrubbed wooden table occupied the centre of the room, set with earthenware plates and cups. Mena pulled out a chair for Sara and gestured her to sit. Two more people entered the kitchen: a big, scowling man with a black beard and a teenage boy with hair the same mahogany as Mena's. Sara found herself staring. The women's long dresses could have just been a fashion, but the men's clothing was really strange: wide-sleeved shirts under long tunics belted at the waist, loose pants wrapped with leather lacings up to the knee, soft shapeless shoes with prominent stitching. The two of them would have looked at home wandering around a medieval fair. Perhaps they were histor-ical reenacters. Mena introduced them. The big man was called Soran; the boy was Kelan. *Mena's husband and son?* Sara wondered. *And is Rassil her daughter?*

Kelan's hair flopped over his eyes as he ducked his head awkwardly to Sara, then found a seat as far from her as possible. She wondered what his problem was.

Not even glancing at Sara, Soran barked a few sharp words to Mena before throwing himself into the chair at the head of the table. Mena lifted her chin and met his eye as she answered briskly. They locked glances for a few seconds, before the big man growled and looked away. A shiver ran through Sara. Had they been arguing about her?

Rassil brought the last of the food to the table and sat down, shooting a shy glance towards Kelan from beneath her pale lashes. He blushed, but his spine straightened. *Probably not his sister, then.*

The meal was good — soft, fresh bread and creamy butter to go with the eggs and bacon — and Sara ate her fill. She would have preferred coffee to the fragrant herbal tea — a caffeine hit would have been welcome right now — but things could be worse. She felt, if not exactly safe, at least in no immediate danger.

After breakfast, Mena beckoned Sara outside. Not knowing what else to do, Sara followed the older woman all morning while she did her chores. It soon became obvious that the farm wasn't wired for electricity. No washing machine, no vacuum cleaner. But that was just the start. Everywhere they went, people were working by hand or using draught animals. Sara didn't see a single machine or powered vehicle. And no one spoke English. This was more than reenactment. This was a complete lifestyle.

While they were eating lunch, Sara showed Mena the phone. Mena rolled it over and over in her hands, stroking the smooth metal and glass, before handing it back. She'd made no attempt to turn it on, and hadn't even seemed to know the front from the back.

Of course, there were people who chose to live without modern conveniences, but complete ignorance of the existence of mobile phones suggested a cult-like level of disconnection from society. Perhaps they were a foreign religious sect who had brought their language with them, refusing to assimilate in any way. The ugly idea of a cult began to take root in Sara's mind, joined by the possibility that she'd been drugged and brought here to join them. It made a terrifying kind of sense: the snowy forest could have been a hallucination caused by the drug. On the other hand, she didn't feel like a prisoner. They seemed happy for her to go anywhere she liked.

She had to know for sure. After lunch, she left Mena in the dairy and set off across the nearest field. In the distance, a man was plodding behind a heavy horse, guiding a plough. He glanced up and saw her. She stiffened, but he only waved to her and kept going. In the other direction, just beyond the boundary of the field, lay what appeared to be a dirt road. She headed for it, the hair prickling on the back of her neck in constant expectation of a shout of alarm from behind her.

The post-and-rail fence looked easy enough to climb, but as she drew closer, she spotted an open gate. She hurried through, pulse racing, then spun around. No one was paying any attention to her. *Calm down,* she told herself, feeling foolish. *You're panicking for nothing.*

Turning back to the road, she scanned it for clues to her location. There was nothing — no signpost, not even a letterbox — only a dusty ribbon stretching away in both directions, bordered by farms. One way seemed as good as another, so she put the afternoon sun at her back and set out.

She walked for about an hour, as far as she could tell, encountering no one. Despite this, uneasiness grew on her with every step. She tried to convince herself that she should be feeling relief: she hadn't been kidnapped, wasn't being held as a prisoner. But where did that knowledge get her? She had no idea how far it might be to the nearest town, or what she might find there. She hadn't even brought any water. Finally, her feet slowed, then stopped. She shook her head. Perhaps she was a coward, but she couldn't keep heading into the unknown like this. Better to return to the farm, try to work things out from there. Despite the language barrier, there must be some way to find out where she was.

On the long walk back, a possible solution came to her, quickening her steps.

She found Mena in the kitchen, chopping vegetables. The older woman showed no sign she'd even noticed Sara's absence, merely greeting her with her usual quick smile before turning back to her work. Sara waited until Mena had finished and laid down her knife, then gestured her to follow. Mena wiped her hands down her apron and nodded.

Sara led the way outside, where she picked up a stick. She laboriously scratched the distinctive shape of Australia into the soft earth. She made a dot to represent Wattleford, then pointed to herself. Mena peered with interest at the rough map. She held up a hand, as if to tell Sara to wait, and went inside the house. She returned carrying a roll of thick, stiff paper. She unrolled it and stretched it out between her hands to show Sara the hand-painted design covering one side. It was a map. The sea was blue, decorated with waves and tiny drawings of fish and other sea creatures; the land was green, marked with the vein-like branchings of rivers and white-tipped triangles that were clearly mountains. It was beautiful, a work of art.

A single island took up most of the space, but it looked nothing like Australia. Above it, separated by a narrow strait, lay a coastline which ran off the sides of the paper in both directions. Mena touched a finger to the island. "Algarth," she said. She swept her hand across the opposite coastline. "Bregia." She pointed to the ground at their feet and then to a spot on the north coast of the island, to show Sara where the farm was, then raised her eyebrows, as if to ask, "Where is your home?"

The bottom had dropped out of Sara's stomach. *Algarth? Bregia?* Where in the world was she? How could she be standing on an unknown island, off the coast of a nation she'd never heard of? She wasn't dreaming, but she was in a nightmare all the same. Panic rose. She pushed it down. Mena was still waiting for an answer. Sara pulled herself together and gestured vaguely off the map, trying to indicate that her home was far away. Mena nodded, unsurprised. It obviously made sense to her that Sara was a foreigner; it explained why she didn't know the language. But nothing about this made sense to Sara.

She needed time alone to think. She stretched her lips into a semblance of a smile and nodded her thanks. As soon as Mena left to return the map to the house, Sara fled to a quiet corner of the farmyard and sank down on the ground.

She took a tight grip on her mind, refusing to allow emotion to overwhelm her. She could only imagine two possibilities: either she was experiencing some kind of psychotic break, or this was real. If she had lost her grip on reality, there was absolutely nothing she could do. Others would have to find her, get her to a hospital, assess her condition, treat her. Nausea washed over her, leaving her shaking and faint. She dropped her head between her knees and forced herself to take deep breaths until it passed. So much for the first option; it didn't appeal.

So, assume the second one was true: it was all real. *Never mind that it's impossible*, she told herself. *Ignore that for now and focus.* If she was really here, she couldn't rely on anyone else to rescue her; she'd have to find a way home by herself. She stared at the ground, working it out.

The language barrier was the first obstacle. But she could do something about that, couldn't she? A tiny flicker of hope flared inside her. Her head lifted. She was good at languages; she would learn this one. And then she'd find out what was going on, and figure out what to do next.

She rose to her feet and turned her steps towards the house.

SEVEN

Sara

Sara wasted no time putting her plan into action. She was an eager student, and Mena proved to be a willing and patient teacher.

As soon as Sara began to understand a little of what the people around her were saying, she began making herself useful around the house and farm, knowing this would be the quickest way to learn what she needed to know.

One thing she had to get used to was that everyone, including the women, carried knives. The women's blades weren't for fighting or even self-defence, but for practical tasks like cutting vegetables, ripping seams that needed to be re-sewn, or cutting strips of leather for lacing. At first, carrying a blade on a pouch at her waist felt strange, but after a while she realised how useful her little knife was, and came to be quite fond of it.

Mena in her turn was shocked to discover that Sara had never learned to ride, and she set herself to remedy the lack. They took the horses out several times a week, always on errands around the farm, so the time wasn't wasted. Not much was wasted on Soran's farm with Mena in charge. Sara found she loved the freedom of being on horseback, especially as it was the only time she was able to wear trousers rather than a dress and apron. She had never been very fond of dresses, especially ankle-length ones. At least she'd been allowed to keep her boots.

This strange life was becoming a little more familiar and predictable, when something happened that threw her right back into confusion. She and Rassil, who had turned out to be Mena's young maid rather than her daughter, had taken morning tea and a slab of cake out to Dorn, the smith, and were lingering in the forge, watching him work. He was in the middle of shoeing one of Soran's big working horses. He heated a short rod of iron until it glowed red, then hammered it into a rough semicircle. When he laid the hammer down beside it, Sara expected him to pick up the tongs and put the iron back in the fire. Instead, he raised one thickly gloved hand and held it out flat just above the glowing metal. After a few seconds, he lifted the hand. A perfectly shaped horseshoe lay on the anvil, flat and smoothly curved.

Not quite believing what she had seen, Sara watched as he made a second shoe. It hadn't been a trick. The smith was shaping the metal without touching it. She turned to gauge the reaction of her companion. Rassil's small, heart-shaped face was perfectly composed. Her bland expression said that she was simply watching a smith make a horseshoe, in the way that smiths always made horseshoes.

Sara struggled to breathe past the sudden constriction in her throat. She'd been wrong. Algarth wasn't merely an island she hadn't heard of, perhaps on the other side of the world. The truth was so much more insane than that. Dorn had some kind of magical ability. Which meant she was somewhere else entirely: another universe, or an alternate reality. It was ridiculous — she could hardly believe she was even thinking it — but there wasn't any other explanation. Which meant that knowing the language wasn't going to be nearly enough to get her home. She needed someone who could do magic, too, the kind that must have brought her here in the first place.

From then on, she watched like a hawk for signs of anyone using what looked like magical powers. Now that her eyes had been opened, she saw them everywhere. No one made any kind of fuss about them, either. No one cast spells or hurled fireballs. They just went about their business, using their magical skills alongside their mundane ones. Shaping metal with his mind was just another of the blacksmith's tools, like his hammer and tongs. A few of the men, including the bad-tempered Soran, were unnaturally strong, lifting loads that would have needed machinery to move them back home. Mena had a different power. Injuries healed more quickly when she willed it. Watching Mena work, Sara understood that using this ability was as normal to Mena as cleaning and bandaging a wound.

The whole idea began to fascinate Sara. It was incredible, even thrilling, to know that magic was real, and to find herself living in a place that no one else from her world had even heard of. Once or twice she experienced a feeling of envy that she didn't have a superpower, too. But then the seriousness of her situation would intrude upon her thoughts, and the homesickness would rise, and she'd again become desperate to find her way back.

She worked even harder at the language and was pleased at how quickly she became fluent. To her relief, the other women blamed any ignorance she displayed on the fall she'd had in the forest, which must have caused her to lose her memory. They felt sorry for her and were eager to help her remember all the things she'd forgotten. She asked questions and listened to anyone who was willing to talk with her.

They called their strange abilities *skals*. Dorn's skal was Shaping. Metal Shaping, to be precise. Mena's skal was Folk Healing. One talkative young woman, Della, betrothed to a stable hand named Brend, proudly told Sara that her man was a Beast Speaker, which meant animals trusted him and would do what he wanted.

"Last year, everyone knew his skal was coming in because he was in such a foul temper," Della said. "Even the horses didn't like having him around, and I could hardly speak two words without him snapping at me." She smiled broadly. "But it was all worth it — Master Soran says he's going to promote Brend to chief Stableman when old Eric retires."

"So Brend wasn't born a Beast Speaker?"

Della smiled kindly at Sara's ignorance. "No one's born with a skal. They come in sometime between eighteen and thirty. I'm twenty, and I don't have mine yet. I hope I'll be a Beast Healer, and then I can work with Brend in the stables. My mother's one, so I have a good chance."

"Do skals run in families, then?"

"Not always, but a lot of the time."

"Does everyone have one?" Sara wondered what would happen if she couldn't get home and had to spend the rest of her life here. In four years, she'd be thirty, and it would be obvious she didn't have a skal.

But Della shook her head. "Almost everyone. Some people have more than one, but one will be stronger. A few people don't have any, no one knows why. In the olden days, my gran says, if someone turned thirty-one without showing a skal, everyone said they were cursed, and drove them away, but we don't do that anymore."

Sara couldn't help feeling relieved about that. She stored up all the information she came across in case it might be useful. At the same time, she was careful to say as little as possible about herself. She had no way of knowing how these people would react if they knew she wasn't from their world. They followed a religion, or at least Mena did. Her god was called Aal. Sara had never paid much attention to religion, but people who believed in gods often believed in demons, too. If they found out she was from another reality, they might think she was some kind of demon herself and turn on her.

As she listened and learned as much as she could, she soon heard the story of the Greenhaelen and the Blight. Even though Soran had forbidden the word to be mentioned, his workers still whispered it — fearful, but also somehow relishing the sensation. She was horrified that these Greenhaelen had been willing to go so far to get what they wanted. They had started as environmentalists and become terrorists, murdering people without a thought. Finally, insanely, they'd begun to destroy the natural environment they said they wanted to protect. All of Algarth might become like those dead trees she'd seen in the forest, unless the Greenhaelen could be forced to reverse what they'd done.

But despite all the different kinds of skals Sara was seeing and hearing about, no one could tell her of anyone who could move even the smallest object with their mind, let alone transport a person from one world to another.

EIGHT

Sara

It was lunchtime on a hot day at the tail end of summer. Sara was sitting under a tree, picking at a plate of food and feeling dissatisfied with herself. Almost nine months after her inexplicable arrival in Algarth, she was no closer to finding a way home.

She might have had more success if she'd relocated to the capital city, Eorna. But the truth was, as week had followed week and her language skills had improved, life on the farm had begun to feel familiar and secure, until it was almost like a second home. In Eorna, she would have had to start all over again — discover a way to earn money, find somewhere safe to stay, make new friends and connections. It had all seemed too hard, too complicated, too frightening. And so, the months had slipped by.

But today, sitting under that tree, none of those excuses seemed adequate any longer. Enough of being a coward. If she didn't want to be stuck on this medieval farm for the rest of her life, she had to find the courage to pack up and go. She took a deep breath and nodded. She would do it.

But not quite yet. Mena and Soran had fed and clothed her, given her a roof over her head. She owed them for that. And right now, they needed every spare hand to finish bringing in the harvest. When all the crops were safely gathered, she'd say goodbye and be on her way. No more excuses or delays. Satisfied with her decision, she attacked her lunch with a renewed appetite, watching the activity around her with interest.

Over in the fields, men were cutting grain, their scythes swinging rhythmically, dazzling sunlight flashing off the blades. Gleaners followed them, collecting the fallen stalks and loading them onto carts to be taken for threshing. Youngsters swarmed in the trees near the house, gathering fruit, while their grandparents shuffled along underneath, filling baskets with nuts to be stored for the winter and spoiled apples for cider.

They all worked feverishly, because they had a deadline. In less than a week, the whole of Algarth would celebrate a holiday — the Festival of Ripening, always held over the final two days of summer. In past years, Mena and her family had travelled to Eorna, where every kind of entertainment could be enjoyed. Many revellers would stay up all night, eating, drinking and dancing. But this year, Soran had decided they should stay home and celebrate privately on the farm.

Mena had seemed disappointed, but now that Sara had made her own decision, she was quite happy to be staying here. It would give her a chance to rest and spend a few final days with her friend before heading off to her new life in the city. She swallowed the last mouthful of bread and headed for the field where she and Mena, together with several other women, were harvesting vegetables. She grabbed a basket, moved to a fresh row of leafy greens and knelt, making sure her apron was tucked under her knees to protect her dress from the dirt. She had only been working for a few moments when a great shout boomed out from the other end of the field.

"Blight!"

Sara froze, her heart thudding. Dropping her knife and the bunch of cut leaves, she rose to her feet. The other women were doing the same. They were silent, but their faces were grim as they squinted into the sun, trying to see who had called out. Shading her eyes, Sara could make out a small group of men. Standing beside them was the unmistakable silhouette of Soran himself, legs apart and shoulders bowed. His massive arms hung loose at his sides. Then, as if his legs had been cut from under him, he dropped to his knees. Several of the women cried out and began running towards the fallen figure. Sara followed them, fearful of what this would mean for all of them, including her.

Before she was halfway there, Soran was on his feet again, shouting orders with his usual authority. There was no sign of his momentary collapse, unless perhaps his voice was harsher and his expression even angrier than usual.

Arriving first, Mena placed her hand on his arm as if to comfort him. He paid no attention. His eyes were fixed on the neat rows of plants stretching from his feet to the edge of the field.

Sara followed his burning gaze. She frowned and took a step closer. These were summer spinach plants, the same as the ones she'd been harvesting. But the dark green corrugated leaves were blemished by a rash of black spots, each one surrounded by a large yellow blotch. Some leaves had barely any green left on them at all and hung twisted and shrivelled. Sara didn't know what she had been expecting to see, but it wasn't this. The mystical Blight, supposedly created by the powers of the Greenhaelen, didn't appear magical at all. On the contrary, it looked suspiciously familiar.

She crouched for a closer inspection. She was right: the plants were infested with Black Spot, the same fungus that attacked rose bushes back home. The Blight was just an ordinary disease. The Greenhaelen hadn't created it at all, they'd just taken credit for it. And no skal was needed to cure it. At home she'd used a simple solution of milk and baking soda, sometimes seaweed solution. There must be natural fungicides on Algarth, too. Had anyone even tried something like that?

Sara's pulse sped up. This could be her answer. If she helped them control the Blight, the authorities would be grateful enough to do anything she asked. They'd help her get home.

Giddy with hope, she stretched out a finger and stroked a large yellow leaf, as if to comfort it. Behind her moving fingertip, a streak of fuzzy green appeared. As she watched in bemusement, it spread quickly across the surface, engulfing the yellow. A moment later, she gasped and snatched her hand away from the now completely green leaf. A huge voice boomed out from overhead:

"Greenhaelan!"

Heart racing, Sara scrambled to her feet and whirled to face the man towering above her. Shaking her head, she stammered, "No, no, I'm not —"

Soran didn't let her finish. His hand shot out, grabbed the front of her tunic, and hauled her up until her face was level with his. Black brows contorted and his lips pulled back from his teeth, reminding her of a vicious dog. For one terrified moment, she thought he was going to bite her. She closed her eyes and tried to wrench her face away. Her chest was tight: she could barely breathe. Something hit her on the cheek, making her jump. Her eyes flew open. Wet goo slid down her face.

He had spat at her.

She glared at him, but the sight of his face had her cringing back, the words of outrage dying on her lips.

He dropped her and she landed hard, one ankle twisting beneath her, making her yelp. She was helpless, terrified of what he might do next.

But Soran had already turned away. She heard the rumble of his voice as he stalked off: "Bring her."

Two men grabbed her arms and hauled her to her feet. One of them was Brend, the Beast Speaker stableman. He'd often spoken to her in a friendly way while he was saddling her horse. She pleaded wordlessly with him now, but he ignored her. The other man was Dorn the smith.

They stretched her arms out to the side, gripping her by the wrists, avoiding letting her hands touch them. Her shoulders began to burn. She could still feel the residue of Soran's spittle on her face, making her gag. She was afraid to speak again, but her eyes darted around the silent crowd of farm workers, begging for help. She didn't know the men very well, so she looked to the women. They had been kind and patient with her when she first arrived. She had begun to think of them as friends.

But now in each face she saw only hostility. Their eyes were like stones. Their lips were pressed into thin, straight lines or else twisted in fear and anger. Some of them had even turned their backs, refusing to look at her. Timid little Rassil hadn't turned away. She appeared rooted to the spot. Her mouth gaped and her blue eyes bulged in fright. No help there.

Sara's ankle throbbed and her arms felt like they were being yanked from their sockets. Where was Mena? Sara let out a sob as she recognised the straight back of the woman who had been her first and closest friend on the farm.

"Mena?"

Sara could see by the way Mena's shoulders slumped and the sudden droop of her head that her friend had heard the hoarse whisper, but she didn't turn.

Brend and Dorn pulled Sara into motion. She tried to keep up with them, to ease the pressure on her arms, but her ankle screamed every time she put her foot to the ground, until she was forced to give up and let herself be half-dragged. She could hear others following, but no one spoke. She moaned, overcome with pain and terror, all the way to the enormous barn where the livestock spent the winter.

They hauled her inside and across to the far wall, where they wrenched her around to face the open doorway. Now that she wasn't moving any longer, the pain eased a little, enough to let her mind start working again. She had to find a way out of this.

The silent workers entered behind them, spreading themselves around the other three walls. They wanted to see everything that was going to happen, but they were staying as far away from Sara as they could. She thought it was the way people might behave around a wild beast, fascinated and terrified in equal measure.

It was cool and dim inside the barn. But even when they dragged the heavy door shut, the windowless building wasn't plunged into complete darkness. Sunlight lanced through gaps between the wall boards, striping the dusty floor with gold. She focused her attention on the motes that sparkled and danced in the beams, finding a tiny moment of relief in the simple beauty of light slicing through darkness.

Without warning, someone jerked her wrists together behind her back. She almost screamed at the agony in her wrenched shoulders. A spark of anger flared inside her, growing swiftly as it fed on her pain and fear. She bit down hard on her bottom lip to stop the cry forcing its way out. She straightened her back, lifted her head and looked Soran squarely in the face. Her eyes blazed into his as Brend tied her wrists together. The pain had receded to somewhere where it didn't matter. So had the fear.

"Let me go! I haven't done anything wrong!" Her furious shout echoed around the barn.

The crowd flinched and pressed themselves closer to the walls. Even Soran took an involuntary step backward.

He's afraid of me, she realised. *Because of what he thinks I am*. Her anger flared even higher. "I'm not a Greenhaelan! I'm not even from this world!" She twisted her shoulders, straining against the ropes. They bit into her wrists as she struggled to free herself, but still she felt no pain.

Without warning, she felt the constraints part and drop away from her wrists. Soran must have sensed something. His face went ashen. Chin up, holding his gaze, she slowly brought her hands out from behind her back. Gasps echoed around her.

Soran seemed frozen in place, but out of the corner of Sara's eye, she saw a movement to her right. She half-turned, but it was too late.

Brend's fist came towards her, filling her sight. At the last second, she twisted her head away. Pain exploded, followed by darkness.

NINE

Kelan

Kelan was hiding in a hay wagon, struggling to hold back a sneeze. It wasn't a very dignified position to be in — he felt that keenly — but he was doing this for Rassil, making a noble sacrifice for the sake of love. The reflection cheered him but didn't help with the sneezing.

He'd been furious when his uncle had ordered Rassil to go to Eorna with Kelan's mother and that Greenhaelan woman. But one glance at Soran's face had shown him the futility of argument. Brend and Dorn would do whatever Soran told them to, of course. They'd take Rassil away — and who knew what might happen to her in the city? Kelan had despaired at first, until a brilliant plan had come to him. He'd met Rassil that night and explained it to her.

Rassil would join Mena on the farm cart in the morning, as Soran had ordered. Kelan would stow away on the larger hay wagon that was due to leave for Eorna in two days' time. The driver was an old man named Peddar. He didn't seem very bright, but how smart did you need to be to drive a hay wagon? He was working for a group of merchants from Eorna, who'd bought all the hay Soran and his neighbours could spare this year. Their plan was to ship the fodder to Bregia, where it would feed farm animals during the northern continent's longer, harsher winter. There'd be no reason for Peddar to examine his load until he reached the docks at Eorna; that was the brilliant part.

As soon as the wagon entered the city, Kelan would slip away and use his half of the promise charm to find Rassil. He'd rent a room for them in another part of the city for two months, until she came of age. Then he'd find an Aaldan to marry them. Kelan would have been happy to forget about the religious fuss — any official in the Town Hall could perform the ceremony — but he knew his mother wouldn't accept Rassil as his wife unless their marriage had been blessed by a holy man or woman.

Rassil had gazed up at him with shining eyes as he'd explained all this to her. She believed in him completely. He wouldn't let her down.

The first part of the plan had worked perfectly. After the cart had left with Rassil and the others, he'd spent the day making sure lots of people saw him around the farm, chatting casually so no one would suspect anything. He even helped Peddar load the hay. He was a bit surprised when the old man had trouble lifting the bales. He'd assumed that a carter would have the skal of Strength. Otherwise, why choose to spend your life loading and unloading cargo? But perhaps Peddar was one of those unfortunates who had no skal at all.

Just before first light, while Peddar snored in the barn, Kelan climbed onto the wagon. He shoved the bales out to the sides, opening a space for himself in the centre. It was a very small space, and he could only fit into it curled up. Stacks of hay towered over him, hiding him from the ground and the driver's seat. With nothing more to do, he tried to sleep, but he was too keyed up. It was almost fully light when he finally heard Peddar bring out the horses.

The hours since then had passed slowly. The hay tickled his nose, and the stifling air was full of dust. His eyes watered continuously; he kept them closed for most of the journey. His cramped position was becoming more and more uncomfortable. He needed to stretch and breathe some fresher air. Should he risk burrowing his way through to the outside? Surely he could take the chance, just for a moment. The wagon rumbled to a stop.

Kelan froze. Was Peddar going to check the load, after all? A deep voice split the sudden silence. The speaker was somewhere off to the right, but Kelan couldn't make out any words. A loud cry of fear — or maybe pain — burst from the front of the wagon: Peddar. The floor rocked violently under Kelan and then was still.

Kelan's blood pounded in his ears, loud enough to drown out any other sound. Someone could be coming to attack him right now — he had to see what was happening.

Staying low, he squeezed his way between the bales, gripping his nose tightly whenever a sneeze threatened. When he was only a single bale away from the side of the wagon, more voices rose, freezing him again. He detected at least three of them, all men. They must be bandits. He lifted his head slowly, breathing as silently as he could, and squinted through a narrow gap.

The first sight of full daylight blinded him. He blinked hard until the scene became clearer. A sliver of blue sky above dark green treetops. Below that, nothing but trunks and branches. The wagon's high side blocked his view of the ground. No sign of the bandits.

He was wondering what to do next when heavy footsteps sounded, trudging towards him from the back of the wagon. He ducked as low as he could and held his breath. The footsteps came to a halt right in front of him. Had he been seen? He strained his ears. A single grunt of effort, and then — shockingly — the bale in front of him shot straight up into the air. He lifted his head to find himself staring into a round, red-bearded face. What happened next would have made him laugh out loud if his situation wasn't so dangerous.

At the sight of Kelan, the man's eyes bulged and his mouth opened in a wordless yell. He stumbled a few steps backwards, the hay bale wobbling wildly above him, before his middle-aged legs gave up the struggle. As he sat down abruptly in the dirt, his hands flew apart and the bale fell right down on top of his head, making him yell again. It was better than a play.

But the shout had brought others running. There were three of them, all young and fit-looking. They skidded to a halt beside the older man, who had now scrambled back up to his feet and drawn a short sword. Two of the new arrivals were tall and broad-shouldered. They gripped their wooden staves as if they knew how to use them.

The final man was slim and dressed in black. His hand rested lightly on the hilt of a half-drawn sword. He looked Kelan over, and then slid the blade back into its sheath. The ghost of a smile lifted one corner of his mouth. "Put up your arms, friends. It's only a little mouse hiding in the hay." His voice was an amused drawl.

The other three obeyed him, but their expressions were still wary. It seemed they didn't share their companion's sense of humour. The older man in particular was scowling like a bulldog.

The one in black stepped closer. "What's your name, little mouse?"

After everything Kelan had gone through this morning, this was too much. It was one thing to be attacked or even killed; it was quite another to be laughed at and called a mouse. He knew he might be in danger, but he didn't care. He lifted his chin and glared at the insolent man. "What's yours?"

The stranger laughed. "So, the mouse has teeth." He bowed low to Kelan, with that infuriating smile quirking one side of his mouth. "I beg your pardon, Sir Mouse, for my poor manners in not introducing myself. I have the honour of being Niall Crawley, Lord of these woods. He inclined his head graciously. "You may call me Sir Niall. And these, my noble courtiers, are Sir Tulley, Sir Adric and Sir Bram." He waved a languid hand at each in turn.

Tulley was the one who'd dropped the bale on his head. He was shorter than the others, with a crop of wild red hair to match his beard. He wore a dirty cream woollen tunic and brown trousers. The short sword was tucked into a wide leather belt slung below his generous stomach. Adric and Bram were alike enough to be twins: tall and broad-shouldered, with yellow hair and thick beards. Their clothing was strange — green and brown mixed together in random splotches. Their eyes scanned their surroundings continuously.

Although Kelan had never seen a courtier, he was sure they didn't look like Tulley, Adric, or Bram.

Niall Crawley himself was a puzzle: he didn't seem to belong with the others at all. His short, smooth hair was as dark as midnight, and it looked as though he'd chosen all his clothing to match. Even his scabbard, belt and boots were made from black-dyed leather. A flamboyant cape hung from his shoulders, its hem almost reaching the tops of his boots. But the oddest thing was his facial hair. The thinnest arc of ebony moustache curved above his lips, dipping low at the ends to merge with the narrow black strip that edged his jawline from one ear to the other. Kelan had never seen or heard of anyone who shaved like this.

Perhaps Crawley was a foreigner. He'd called himself a Lord. Kelan was almost certain that the title had been a joke, yet it fitted somehow. Crawley's speech was that of an educated man, and his weapon and clothing must have been expensive. What was someone like him doing out here, waylaying travellers on the road?

"Now that the demands of courtesy have been satisfied," Crawley drawled, "May I know who I have the honour of addressing? Or must I continue to call you Sir Mouse?"

Kelan rose to his feet and answered with as much self-respect as he could, considering he was standing in a hay wagon. "My name is Kelan Erdal, and I am on important business for my uncle, Master Soran of Erdal Farm."

"Hiding in the hay?" Tulley guffawed.

They were all laughing at him now. Kelan felt his face warm, but before he could speak again, Crawley gestured lazily at him to get down. "Well, young Master Erdal, you had better come with us." Again he flashed that lopsided smile that said the world had been created for his private amusement. "It would be remiss of us to leave you here. Who knows what kind of scoundrels might be lurking on this road?"

With a chuckle, he turned and strode off along a broad path that led into the trees, his long cloak billowing after him.

Kelan climbed down to the ground and brushed the hay and dust off his clothing as best he could. There was no sign of Peddar, either dead or alive. Hopefully the old man had just taken fright and run away. After all, it wasn't his hay or his wagon, and he probably wasn't willing to risk his life defending either of them.

The big blonde twins entered the woods next, leading the horses, with the wagon bumping along behind them.

That left Kelan alone with the older man, Tulley. He didn't look as fit as the other three, but there was something about the solid way he stood that suggested he knew how to handle himself in a fight. "Come on lad," he growled, still scowling. "We don't have all day." He stumped off.

Kelan's mind raced. What if he just turned and ran away? He judged he'd travelled about twenty reaches from the farm, meaning he was almost halfway to Eorna. If he kept walking through the night, he'd reach the city some time tomorrow. If he met another vehicle on the way, he might even be able to beg a ride. Or he could offer to pay — he'd brought a purse of his uncle's coins with him, hidden inside his tunic.

But would the gang just let him go? It didn't seem likely, not when he'd seen them steal the wagon and could describe them to the authorities. Tulley might be old and slow, but what if the others were hiding just inside the trees to see what Kelan would do? He wouldn't put it past Crawley to be playing with him like a cat with a mouse, setting him free just to pounce on him again. If he tried to escape, they might tie him up or knock him on the head, putting him in an even worse position.

Besides, Crawley had been right about the kind of people he might meet on this road. Bandits preyed on lone travellers, sometimes leaving them for dead. The Council had done their best to make the roads safer, but as soon as Commander Renn's Warrant Guards cleared out one group of outlaws, another took its place. On foot in the dark, armed with nothing but his knife — he hadn't thought he'd need his bow in the city — Kelan would be easy prey. Even fully armed, he doubted he could hold his own against a group of desperate thieves.

Crawley's group were thieves too, of course, but at least they hadn't attacked him. All they'd done so far was steal a wagonful of hay. Kelan frowned. That was a strange thing. What would bandits want with fodder, anyway?

The answer came to him in a surge of excitement — they must have horses with them. Not only the two carthorses they'd stolen, but at least one trained mount; Niall Crawley had been wearing heeled riding boots. That was Kelan's way out. He'd escape on horseback and be in the city before morning. He'd ridden the farm horses many times, and hardly

50

ever fallen off. He was sure he could evade or outstrip any bandits he might meet, as long as he chose a fast horse.

For now, he'd do whatever they told him to. He'd pretend to be the little mouse that Crawley had called him. Then, in the darkest part of the night, when they were all asleep, he'd steal a horse from right under their snoring noses. That would show Crawley that Kelan wasn't someone to be laughed at.

Smiling to himself as he imagined their faces in the morning, Kelan squared his shoulders and followed the red-haired man into the woods.

It took a moment for his eyes to adjust to the green dimness under the trees. The air felt cooler here. He breathed in the scent of pine as he hurried along behind the stocky man. A soft layer of brown needles covered the path and silenced his footsteps. This was perfect for his purposes. No one would hear him fleeing on horseback along this thickly carpeted ground. Rounding the next bend, he saw Tulley's broad back about twenty strides ahead and hurried to catch up. He had a plan now, and he didn't want to raise any suspicions.

When he was still a few steps away, Tulley spoke. "Took your time."

The man hadn't even turned his head; he had good hearing for his age. Kelan resolved to move more noiselessly tonight. Tulley was also fast for a fat man, but Kelan could have outpaced him. Instead, he chose to stay a few strides behind, as if cowed into obedience.

From long habit, his eyes roamed his surroundings for signs of game. On several rough-barked trees, patches of smooth, pale wood spoke to him of young bucks rubbing the velvet from their antlers. Here and there, vertical gashes marred the bark: the signs of climbing beasts. Squirrels had made those short, shallow ones, but a wild cat was responsible for the longer, deeper furrows. The cats were Algarth's largest predator, although legend said that bears had once roamed the island.

It would be amazing to see a bear. They still lived in the wild forests of northern Bregia and were supposed to be ferocious, with no fear of humans. Wild cats could be fierce, too, and very quick, but Kelan had shot his first one at thirteen years of age and killed almost a dozen since. Whenever his mother's chickens started disappearing, it meant the wild cat population was growing out of control again. Then Kelan would take his bow into the woods for a few days and reduce their numbers. They no longer presented much of a challenge. But a bear would really test his courage and skill.

Maybe he and Rassil would travel to Bregia one day. He had no intention of spending the rest of his life on the farm, no matter what his uncle thought — or what Kelan's skal turned out to be. Swiftness would be his first choice — speed and good hand-eye coordination were essential for a hunter. But he wouldn't mind being a Beast Speaker like Brend, either. As long as it wasn't something boring like Reckoning or Remembering, or even worse, Charm Shaping. Charm Shapers had to spend years in the Academy in Eorna, wasting their lives away inside four walls, poring over musty old books.

Deep in dreams of the future, he strode around a corner and ran face first into Tulley's unyielding back. He bounced off and raised a hand to his already throbbing nose, his mind snapping back instantly to the present.

Tulley whipped round like a snake. "Watch where you're going, fool of a boy!"

This was unfair: Tulley had stopped without warning, even though he knew that Kelan was right behind him. Kelan opened his mouth to say so, and then shut it again. If his plan was going to work, he had to convince Tulley and the others that he'd meekly accepted his situation. His mashed nose hurt horribly, but he swallowed his anger.

"Sorry," he muttered.

Tulley grunted and set off again. It seemed that was all the reply Kelan was going to get. He followed, holding his sore nose and paying closer attention.

The path led to a sunlit clearing. It wasn't natural: someone had felled dozens of trees to create the large open space. Right now, some of the remaining stumps were serving as chairs. Kelan counted six people, seated in a rough circle.

He noted with satisfaction that he'd been right about the horses: several were picketed alongside the ones from the wagon. He switched his attention back to the people, who had all turned to face him: Crawley,

Bram and Adric, another man and two women. One of the women had long grey hair lying in a plait over one shoulder. The other was younger, with glossy dark hair rippling down her back.

As Tulley started forward, the remaining man rose to his feet. He was tall, with coppery hair that reached to his shoulders, and a short beard of the same tone. He clapped Tulley on the back as if he was glad to see him. They spoke for a moment, but Kelan was too far away to hear what they were saying.

Tulley looked up and beckoned.

"Come on, lad, no one's going to harm you here."

Kelan's legs were reluctant to carry him forward, but he was among a group of armed men who seemed determined for him to join them. Holding tightly to the memory of his secret plan, he stepped forward and crossed the clearing.

Close up, the copper-haired man looked about thirty years of age, with tanned skin that argued his life was spent mostly outdoors. He was dressed like Bram and Adric, in patterned green and brown tunic and trousers. But it was his eyes that held Kelan's attention. They were a clear, piercing blue, like chips of sky come down into the forest. They gazed gravely at Kelan as the man held out a hand. "My name is Logen, and Tulley tells me yours is Kelan. Welcome to our temporary home."

Logen's grip was firm and Kelan made sure his was the same.

"You've already met Niall, Bram, and Adric."

The twins just stared at him, but Crawley gave him a smile and a wink.

Logen gestured towards the grey-haired woman.

"This is Finath, Tulley's wife."

She was wearing a soft dress of cream wool and a motherly smile. She clasped her small hands together.

"Please, call me Fin. Everyone does."

Logen turned to the final member of the group. "And Cahira, who is married to Bram."

For some reason, the stunningly beautiful dark-haired young woman had dressed herself like a man, in deep blue tunic and trousers. She frowned at Kelan, but not in a hostile way like her husband. Instead, she regarded him with her head on one side, as if he was a problem she was trying to solve.

Kelan nodded to both women, but he was confused. What were all these people doing here in the forest? Bandits wouldn't have women with them, would they? At least, he corrected himself, warmth flooding his cheeks, not these kinds of women. Little grey-haired Fin looked the essence of respectability. And, while Cahira's clothing wasn't exactly conventional, nothing about her indicated the kind of, well, *professional* woman he'd heard the farm workers discussing on their return from town. Anyway, Logen had said Fin and Cahira were both married. It didn't make any sense.

At least Kelan didn't seem to be in danger right now, but it was a fact that these men had stolen the horses, hay and wagon and maybe harmed poor old Peddar. They weren't law-abiding citizens, and whatever they were up to in this forest, Kelan couldn't afford to get mixed up in it. He had to reach Eorna and find Rassil.

He'd stick to his plan, steal a horse tonight and leave them all behind.

Kelan lay on a makeshift bed of branches, staring at the sky and cursing himself for an idiot. He'd forgotten about the moon. It was two nights before the full, riding in a cloudless sky. It lit up the clearing like a lantern.

He'd waited patiently to make sure they were all asleep, and had been thinking it was time to make his move, when that wretched moon had risen above the trees and flooded the area with cold, white light. This late in summer, it wouldn't set until after sunrise. There'd be no more darkness tonight.

What should he do now? He could move stealthily enough, but if one of the gang happened to wake for any reason, they'd see him straight away. Should he risk it? They'd treated him well so far, but that could change if they caught him escaping. On the other hand, there was no point in waiting for better conditions: tomorrow night would be just as bright. Unless it clouded over, but he couldn't depend on that. And he had no idea of these people's plans. Anything could happen to him by tomorrow night.

Then there was Rassil. She'd be expecting him tonight or tomorrow at the latest, and she'd be scared and worried if he didn't come. That decided it — no matter the risk, he had to try tonight. And he'd better do it now, before he lost his nerve.

Holding his breath and moving an inch at a time, he eased himself off the blanket and onto the ground. He lay prone for a moment, breathing softly and listening. Nothing. So far so good.

He crept towards the horses, taking a route that wouldn't lead him too close to any of the sleepers. His careful movements were making very little sound on the thickly carpeted ground, but his heart was pounding so hard and fast that he was afraid someone would hear it. His blood roared in his ears.

Fighting the urge to get up and run, he forced himself to stop and take a few deep breaths to slow his heart luckrate. He told himself this was just another hunt. He was tracking, as he had done many times before, moving slowly and silently so as not to scare his prey. That helped. Finally, he was a few paces from the last horse in the picket line.

He'd noticed the fine-boned bay mare earlier in the afternoon. She looked well-bred and fast. She'd been unsaddled for the night — too risky to do anything about that now, but he'd ridden bareback before. He considered going back for the blanket, but his body was buzzing with the need for action; he couldn't face another agonizingly slow crawl.

The mare was dozing and hadn't noticed him. Kelan eased slowly to his feet, murmuring comforting sounds to the sleepy beast as he approached her head. She was tethered by a long rope threaded through a ring below her headstall. Luckily, her legs hadn't been hobbled. She nickered as if in greeting. Kelan grasped the rope just below the ring. The mare didn't seem to mind. The other end of the rope was tied around a tree trunk, at least four paces away. Kelan didn't want to let go of the horse now. He'd lead her to the tree.

The mare stepped willingly, almost as if she knew Kelan's plan and was eager for a midnight adventure. The rope was loosely knotted and he freed it in a few seconds. He had to move fast now — he'd only get one chance at this. He bunched the rope in his fist and leapt onto the mare's back. The startled horse shied, but Kelan was ready for that. He hung on and dug in his heels. The mare snorted and tossed her head, almost smacking him in the face. She stamped her front feet.

Fear shot through Kelan. This was taking too long; someone would notice. He pounded his heels on the stubborn horse's flank, at the same time using the free end of the rope as a whip. *Come on, you stupid beast. Move!*

The mare tucked her legs under her hindquarters and leapt forward, almost unseating him. He fell forward onto her neck and banged his sore nose again. Tears sprang to his eyes. His sweat-slick hands grabbed blindly for the mane, his fingers finally catching in the coarse hair. He had to slow this stupid horse down, but the rope was dangling loose, out of his reach, slapping against her legs and maddening her further. All he could do was stay low, hold on, and pray it didn't tangle around something and bring the mare crashing down, killing them both.

He clung on, somehow, as the horse swerved left and right, over and over again, following the track through the trees. The musty scent of horse sweat filled his nostrils. His heart thumped as if it would burst out of his chest.

They rounded another bend and Kelan caught his first glimpse of the road, still some distance ahead. How would the mare react once she'd left the shelter of the forest? Would she turn onto the road and speed up even more? Or would she stop dead, flinging Kelan over her head? There was no way to know, nothing he could do to prepare himself. He closed his eyes and prayed he wouldn't die.

And then, thank Aal, he felt the horse slowing. She dropped to a canter, and then a trot. Kelan opened his eyes, sucked in a deep breath and pushed himself upright. A sob rose in his throat. He'd survived.

The mare trotted to a halt in the middle of the broad, moonlit road and dropped her head, her sides heaving. Kelan forced his stiff fingers to uncurl from the mane. With a trembling hand he reached for the dangling rope.

"Get. Down." The low voice was thick with anger.

Kelan's head whipped around. Niall Crawley was striding up the road, sword in hand.

Feeling like his body belonged to someone else, Kelan half slid, half fell off the slick horse and collapsed on the ground. He cringed as Crawley leaned over him, but after one long, contemptuous look, the man straightened up, sheathed his sword, and turned his attention to the mare.

He stroked her face, murmuring. Then he walked around her, running his hands over her to check for injuries. Kelan scrambled up and lurched to the side of the road, where he pressed his back to a tree. His eyes followed Crawley mechanically.

When Crawley had finished examining the horse, he gently removed the headstall and rope. He carried them to Kelan and shook them in his face. Crawley's mouth was twisted in disgust, and his bared teeth gleamed white in the moonlight. "I should put this on *you* and force *you* to flee in terror." He almost spat the words.

Kelan shrank back, wishing he could push himself all the way into the tree trunk.

"That mare is worth ten idiot boys," Crawley hissed, his eyes blazing. "Your stupidity might have *killed* her."

Kelan's mouth gaped — he couldn't seem to close it. The rough bark dug into his back as Crawley leaned even closer, his black gaze fixed on Kelan's face.

After what seemed an eternity, the man abruptly backed away, throwing up his hands

"All right, no need to look as if you think I'm about to eat you. Sit down before you fall down."

Kelan obediently sank to the ground. Crawley watched him for a few moments in silence, and then spoke again. The anger was gone from his tone.

"I do believe Sienna frightened you almost as much as you frightened her. Can you walk?"

Kelan still seemed to have no will of his own. He licked dry lips and nodded. Crawley helped him up and they trudged back towards the camp. After a few moments, Kelan's mind began turning again. How had Crawley managed to be on the spot when the mare stopped? And where was she now? Kelan glanced behind. Sienna was following them, without headstall or rope. The truth burst upon him: Crawley must be a Beast Speaker.

Kelan hadn't factored a Beast Speaker into his plans. He'd worried about being seen in the moonlight or heard in the silence, but the real risk had been taking the horse itself. Crawley must have sensed its distress and woken up.

No, that was wrong. Crawley was on foot — he couldn't possibly have reached the road before the bolting horse. He must have been waiting there already. But why? In a flash, the answer came: Crawley had been on guard. While the other thieves slept, he'd been watching the road, ready to raise the alarm if any Warrant Guards came searching for them.

Things were even worse than Kelan had feared: he'd fallen in with wanted criminals, on the run from the authorities. And now they'd caught him trying to escape, they'd make sure he didn't get a second chance. His fate was in the hands of a gang of desperate outlaws.

They were up and waiting when he stepped into the clearing. This time, there was no polite chat. Bram or Adric — he was in no state to tell them apart — searched him, removing his knife and purse. They found his half of the promise charm, too, on its chain around his neck. Logen examined it briefly then tucked it away in his pocket. He questioned Kelan while the others stood listening. Who was he? Where had he come from? Who had sent him? Where had he been running away to?

Kelan didn't see any point in lying — the truth couldn't make things any worse. He told them about the farm, the discovery of Blight, and the foreign woman who'd turned out to be a Greenhaelan. He explained that Rassil had been sent to Eorna with the Greenhaelan and Kelan's mother, and described how he'd stowed away in the hay wagon to follow her.

As he talked, the gang kept shooting glances at each other. His story meant something to them, but no one spoke until he'd finished.

"Stay here," Logen said, and walked a little way off, followed by the others.

Kelan shifted from one foot to the other. What would they do with him? He couldn't decipher any of the low-voiced conversation, and even the occasional gesture gave him no clue.

The sky was lightening; dawn was almost here. Would it be the last one his eyes would ever see?

TEN

Sara

Something was dripping. Sara tried to ignore it and return to the dark, warm fuzziness of sleep, but the "plink, plink, plink" was relentless. She mustn't have turned the bathroom tap off properly last night. She'd have to get up, but maybe she could go back to sleep afterwards. What time was it, anyway? She groaned and opened her eyes to check the bedside clock.

She came wide awake. This wasn't her bedroom. Shock pushed her to her feet, her heart racing.

Then reality crashed in. Of course it wasn't her bedroom — she was in Algarth. But — she'd been in the barn, hadn't she? She'd freed her hands, but then Brend had — Sara raised a hand to her head. She couldn't feel any bruising. Had he missed? It seemed impossible. As impossible as waking in this small, almost square room, surrounded by walls of rough grey stone. The blocks fitted so tightly against each other that she couldn't see any mortar between them. The floor was stone, too, but the blocks were large, flat and smooth. A thin mattress lay in one corner, with a dark woollen blanket crumpled at the foot. This was where she'd been sleeping. The room contained nothing else, except a black-barred window and a closed door.

They must have carried her to one of the stone outbuildings on the farm while she'd been unconscious. Heat rose in her cheeks. Enough was enough. This was the second time she'd woken in a strange place with no memory of how she'd arrived there; she was tired of being carted around like a suitcase. Her chin lifted. *Well, this piece of luggage has a mind of its own.*

She listened at the door for a moment, then pushed against it. It didn't move. The door was of plain, thick wood, without a lock or handle on her side. She pushed harder, then with all her strength. The door remained stubbornly shut. She turned her attention to the window.

The bars were thick and solid, but it was the view between them that caused Sara to stiffen in dismay. She'd expected fields or a farmyard; instead, a broad grey cobbled street met her eyes. Across the cobbles, purple shadows slanted diagonally across the face of a building of amber stone. A multitude of chimneys rose from its tiled roof into the pale blue sky. It must be either early morning or late afternoon; Sara couldn't tell which. At least she'd solved the mystery of the plinking: fat drops were falling from a water pump just under her window and splattering into a metal bowl beneath.

Sara unclenched her hands and sucked in a long, slow breath, then another. There was no reason to panic. Farm or town, what difference did it make? She was a prisoner either way and the solution was the same: find a way to escape.

There were no street signs and nothing about the chimneyed building to indicate its identity. Three archways cut through it at ground level. Two of them were blocked by closed doors, but the other appeared to be a walkway leading into the structure and out the other side — she could see glimpses of another street and more buildings. A possible escape route, if she could get to it.

A line of windows indicated the presence of a second storey. They were shuttered, meaning it was more likely to be morning than afternoon. *That's it,* Sara urged herself, *gather as much information as possible. You never know what might come in handy.* Besides, thinking was keeping the fear at bay.

The level of technology she could see fitted with what she'd experienced on the farm: shaped stone and timber for building, fireplaces for heating, hand-woven woollen blankets. So it was likely that she was still in Algarth. But how long had she been unconscious, and how far had they brought her?

The skin on her wrists, which had been rubbed raw by the ropes, appeared completely healed. She couldn't even detect any scars. She explored the side of her head again, where Brend had hit her. There was no trace of tenderness, even when she pressed hard. The events on Soran's farm must have happened weeks ago, yet somehow, that didn't feel right.

Unless, she suddenly realised, someone like Mena had used magic to speed up her healing. The thought of her former friend almost brought everything inside Sara crashing down again, but she bit her lip and forced the emotion down. She couldn't afford it now.

A loud scraping from outside made her jump. Across the road, the shutters were being pushed open, timber grating against stone. Then, a new sound, this time from right behind Sara. She caught her breath and spun around.

Mena stood in the open doorway, as if conjured by Sara's thoughts, red hair, long blue apron and all. "Sara! Thank Aal you're awake."

Sara couldn't speak past the lump in her throat. Mena stepped into the room, and the door closed behind her. Her smoky eyes searched Sara's face, then she pulled her into an embrace, murmuring in her warm, comforting tone: "There, there, my love, don't fret. We'll sort it out. I'm here. You're not alone."

Sara leaned against the older woman, her eyes closing in sheer relief.

They stood like that for a moment, then Sara stiffened. What was she doing? She pulled away, bitter words rising to her lips. "Why did you turn your back on me? I thought you were my friend. But when I really needed you, you acted just like all the others." Tears threatened, but she swallowed them down.

"Oh, my love, I'm so sorry." Sara was surprised to see moisture glistening in Mena's eyes, too. "When I saw you heal that plant, I was as shocked as Soran. I didn't know what to think. I could hardly believe you could be a Greenhaelan, but I had just seen the proof with my own eyes. You were one of them, and you'd brought the Blight to our farm."

Sara threw her hands up. "I didn't—"

Mena rushed back into speech. "I know, I know. I was wrong and I'm so sorry. I've been doing everything I could to make up for it."

"Was it you that healed me, then?"

"Yes."

"And—"

Mena held up a hand. "I promise I'll tell you everything. But it's going to take a while, so we'd better get comfortable." She returned to the door and knocked twice. When it opened, Mena murmured to someone Sara couldn't see.

They waited, not speaking. A man came in, wearing a blue shirt with a yellow shield-shaped patch on the chest. He kept his face turned away from Sara as he set down the two chairs he'd brought with him.

As the door closed behind the man, Mena took one chair and gestured to Sara to take the other. "They'll bring us a meal in a little while, but I thought your need for answers might be more urgent than your need for food right now."

Sara nodded.

Mena smoothed the apron over her knees and began. "We're in Eorna. We've been here for two days. I know, you don't remember any of it. I've been healing the wound on your head, and it was safer to keep you asleep while I was doing it." She clasped her hands tightly. "I've been so afraid that you might die, or that even if you lived, your mind might be addled."

A note of anger entered her voice. "Brend hit you much too hard. Soran wanted to let you die right there and then, but I couldn't let that happen, not once I had a chance to think about it. You might have the power of a Greenhaelan, but I knew you weren't one of them. I healed you and taught you to speak our language and spent eight months with you. I couldn't have been fooled. I knew you meant us no harm. I told Soran that if you were hurt any further, I would never heal anyone on the farm ever again. He knew I meant it. Oh, he was angry! I don't think he'll ever forgive me." Her face crumpled momentarily and she bent her head, wiping her eyes.

Then she straightened up and continued in a voice of steely determination. "Even if he doesn't, I had to do what was right. How could we call ourselves children of Aal if we murdered a stranger, lost and far from home, who had never done us any harm? It would have been an evil deed, one that would have stained our lives forever. It was the hardest thing I ever did. But it was *right!*" Two red spots burned on her cheeks.

"Soran let me have my way. He sent the others outside and watched me begin work on you. Then he spoke. Four words only, in a voice he has never used to me before. Hard and cold as stone. 'She goes to trial.' He hasn't spoken to me since."

"I'm sorry," Sara said. The words didn't seem adequate: Mena had been a far better friend than Sara had any right to expect, risking her home and maybe even her life. Soran was a bully, but to Mena he was family. And now the rift between them might never be repaired. Sara felt responsible, although she didn't know what she could have done differently.

Gazing at the locked door, the barred window, Sara's thoughts snapped back to the present. She was in deep trouble, about to be tried as a Greenhaelan. If she was found guilty, she faced life imprisonment, maybe even execution.

Perhaps Mena shouldn't have fought for her but just left her to die peacefully. Sara was so sick of this world with its stupid, incomprehensible magic. She desperately wished she was back in Wattleford, where her biggest problem had been trying to keep her temper because someone had poisoned her roses. That seemed so petty now.

A rattle at the door. It opened to admit a girl carrying a tray, followed by the same blue-shirted man who'd brought the chairs. This time, he was bearing a small table. He set it down, keeping his eyes averted as before, and the girl placed the tray on it. Her head was bowed, and her long pale hair fell like curtains, concealing her face. It seemed that only Mena was brave enough to face Sara eye to eye.

It was all so ludicrous. She wasn't a Greenhaelan. True, the leaf had turned from yellow to green when she'd touched it, but there must be some other explanation. She didn't have a skal. How could she? She wasn't even from this world. She glared at the timid serving girl, who was setting out cups and dishes from the tray onto the table, willing her to lift her head.

Sara frowned. There was something familiar about this girl. Just as she realised what it was, Mena spoke. "Thank you, Rassil."

The teenager bobbed her head quickly and scurried out, followed by the Guard.

"What on earth is she doing here?" Sara asked.

"Soran ordered her to come with me. I think he wanted to get her away from Kelan. I don't suppose she'll be much use to us. She's never been to a city before and she's terrified of everything." She smiled at Sara. "Especially you. But I couldn't abandon her, so I told her to help out in the kitchen. Speaking of which, you've been fasting for a long time and you need to eat."

The food was plain but plentiful, and Sara did feel better once she had something inside her. They didn't speak during the meal, but afterwards, Sara had more questions. The conversation lasted through that day and into the evening. Twice more, Rassil brought in meals for them. Worried as she was for herself, Sara spared a thought for the frightened young girl who'd been forced to leave her home and the life she knew. She hoped the little maidservant wasn't being mistreated here.

In answer to Sara's questions, Mena explained the procedure for the trial. Tomorrow, the Guards would transport her and Sara to the City Hall. The Council of Six would hear the evidence against Sara and then pronounce their verdict.

Mena had volunteered to be her friend's Speaker, which meant she could question witnesses and speak directly to the Councillors. Sara wouldn't even be allowed to open her mouth. She would have thought this outrageous, but given that she didn't know the laws of Algarth or the rules of the trial, it was probably best. She doubted that Mena knew much about them either, having lived her life on a farm, but there didn't seem to be any alternative. No one else would be willing to Speak for Sara. In fact, the reason she was being held in a private house rather than the official prison was the fear that if the people of Eorna knew her location, there might be an attempt to harm her.

Sara felt even more grateful for her friend's support. It would have been so much easier for Mena to wash her hands of Sara and abandon her to her fate, which seemed inevitable anyway. How could they prove she wasn't a Greenhaelan, when the evidence said she was? Imprisonment for life in a medieval gaol was the best she could hope for.

Scenes from historical movies marched relentlessly across Sara's mind, refusing to be dispelled: rat-infested dungeons, starvation, torture chambers. All the food she'd eaten churned in her stomach, threatening to come back up.

Execution might be a mercy after all. But Mena made it very clear that she had no patience with such talk. "Don't you dare think about giving up," she said fiercely. "Where there's life there's hope, and we are very much alive. I intend both of us to stay that way, and so should you."

Towards evening, Sara made a decision. There was no point in keeping secrets any longer. She told Mena the truth of who she was and where she came from. To her surprise, Mena accepted her story immediately, which gave Sara a glimmer of hope that the Council might believe it, too. But it was only a very small glimmer.

ELEVEN

Kelan

After what seemed like an eternity to Kelan, the group broke apart and scattered in different directions.

Logen strode up to Kelan. "We're going to Eorna today for the festival. If you give me your word of honour that you won't try to steal another horse — or anything else — we'll take you with us. When we arrive, you'll get your money and your promise charm back, and you can go and find your girl. What do you say?"

Kelan was dumbfounded. Was it a trick? It was hard to believe, after everything that had happened, that things were going to work out so easily. But if Logen meant him harm, why bother to trick him? All he had to do was tie Kelan up and leave him, or worse.

He'd take the offer at face value and hope for the best. He gave Logen the promise he'd asked for.

In a short time, they were on the road to Eorna. Kelan was back on the hay wagon, but this time he sat on the driver's bench, beside Tulley. The others were on horseback. The older woman, Fin, rode beside the wagon, leading a spare horse that Kelan guessed belonged to her husband. It was a big, bony gelding with an ugly head and it kept nipping spitefully at Fin's smaller grey mare. Fin scolded the gelding half-heartedly, but the mare just ambled along, ignoring her tormentor as if he was beneath her notice. It was pretty funny.

Tulley, who seemed to be in a better mood this morning, noticed Kelan's smile. The red-bearded man leaned towards him and whispered, "Just watch."

Sure enough, after a few minutes, the sturdy little mare wheeled without warning, stretched up, and sank her teeth deep in the gelding's shoulder. The big brown horse tried to back away, but the lead rope was too short. Finally, the mare released him, turned her head calmly away, and walked on as if nothing had happened. Fin hadn't even moved in her seat. Kelan laughed out loud.

"Aye, lad," chuckled Tulley. "Pearl's like her mistress. Calm as a millpond most of the time, but full of surprises. Brick's not the smartest horse in the world, or he would have learned his lesson by now." He locked eyes with his wife, and she smiled sweetly at him. She included Kelan in the smile, then turned back to face the road. Brick seemed to be sulking.

Kelan twisted around to look behind, where Adric and Bram were riding. He had no trouble telling them apart today. They'd exchanged their green and brown for violently-coloured trousers and shirts with slashed sleeves that showed flashes of other colours beneath as they moved. Adric was in shades of red and orange, while Bram wore blues and purples. Kelan thought the two of them looked like clowns. They were riding chestnut horses, not as big as Tulley's Brick, but well-muscled and in good condition. Thinking about horses reminded Kelan of Sienna. He hoped she'd recovered from last night's wild ride. If she pulled up lame today, he wasn't sure what Niall Crawley might do to him.

Logen was in the lead, on a big grey stallion. Behind Logen, Crawley and Cahira rode side by side.

Cahira had replaced her tunic with a split-sided riding dress of the same royal blue, trimmed at the neck and sleeves with wide bands the colour of red wine. Her trousers were wine-red, too. She was mounted on a mare with hair as black and satiny as her own. She and the raven-clad Crawley rode close together, inclining their heads toward each other as they talked.

Kelan was relieved to see that Sienna was stepping out willingly, apparently none the worse for her adventure. Although he couldn't hear what the riders were saying, they laughed often and were clearly enjoying each other's company. Niall Crawley seemed like a better match for the beautiful woman than the stolid Bram, with his huge shoulders and long rough beard. What did he think about Crawley riding with his wife? But when Kelan turned to look, Bram and Adric were deep in conversation, too.

Soon they began to pass, and be passed by, other travellers. Just a few at first, then more and more as the day wore on, until the road was packed with all kinds of people heading for Eorna and tomorrow's festival. Some were on horseback, others in carts or on foot. They were in a good mood, laughing and talking in the sunshine, obviously looking forward to the holiday and the sights of the city. Many called out greetings and a few even rode alongside the wagon for a while and chatted with Kelan.

Children jumped down from their family carts and ran around together, racing forwards and then back to their parents. They would have travelled much further than the adults by the end of the day. On Kelan's own boyhood visits to Eorna, he had done exactly the same thing and arrived in the city more than ready for bed, tired out from all the exercise and excitement.

This time, he would enter Eorna physically rested but just as filled with anticipation. Every reach was taking him closer to Rassil. If Logen kept his word and gave him back the promise charm, he might even find her tonight.

The gang's behaviour on reaching Eorna did nothing to ease Kelan's suspicions of them. Darkness was falling as the wagon wove its way through a maze of narrow, crooked back streets to reach a shuttered building with a closed door. Although no sign hung from the building, Tulley told Kelan it was an inn. With only one night to go before the festival, most hostelries would be trying to attract travellers. This one was dark and eerily quiet. Logen knocked on the door. It swung open on oiled hinges, spilling light and noise onto the street. The shutters and doors must fit very tightly to keep all this hidden inside. And why hide it anyway? As the door shut behind him with a muffled thud, Kelan's heart began to beat faster.

Logen was already speaking to a foreign-looking woman with long curly black hair and dark eyes. They pitched their voices too low for Kelan to overhear their conversation, but they seemed to know each other.

Soon the travellers were sitting down to supper in a private room on the ground floor. Kelan had no intention of staying any longer than he had to, but Logen refused to give back the money or the promise charm until Kelan had eaten something. Kelan was forced to agree. He was willing to leave the money behind if it meant they'd let him go, but he needed the charm to find Rassil. Niall Crawley ate quickly and slipped out on some errand of his own. Logen and the others took forever to finish. Kelan was too jittery to eat much.

Finally, the dirty plates were cleared away. And then Kelan's companions surprised him. Adric handed over his belongings as promised, Logen wished him luck, and Tulley slapped him on the back. Almost afraid to believe they were letting him go, Kelan gingerly walked out. He kept glancing over his shoulder, but no one came after him. He reached the front door and hauled it open. Another glance behind him. The hallway remained empty.

He was about to step outside when he noticed the hand that he was using to hold the door open. It was filthy. So was the arm attached to it. After a morning spent in a dusty hay wagon, a night lying on the ground and riding a sweaty horse, and a further day on the road, he was covered in dirt. He smelled pretty ripe, too. He could hardly bear to wait any longer to find Rassil, but did he really want to meet her like this? He didn't. There was a bathroom upstairs. He would clean himself up before he set out.

Easing the door shut again, he headed for the stairs. He trod lightly, not wanting to push his luck.

He did his best in the bathroom, although there wasn't much he could do about his clothing. He sniffed at his arm and thought it smelled better. A bit better, anyway. It would have to do. He crept down the stairs, testing each step before he trusted his weight to it. The inn was old. If a creaky board gave him away to the gang in the room below, he still wasn't sure what they'd do.

As he reached the ground floor, he heard footsteps coming along the hall. He spotted a small space under the stairs and squeezed into it. The maid whose footsteps he'd heard hurried past, carrying a tray of drinks. She disappeared through a doorway at the end of the hall.

A low murmuring rose and fell from the private room. Kelan was about to emerge from his hiding place when he caught a few words.

"first light…scout…plan…"

Intrigued, he waited to hear more.

"Bram and Adric can…"

A mumble he couldn't make out, followed by Tulley's deep voice. "…sell the wagon…another horse…she ride?"

"…have to…only chance…her out of the city."

Who were they talking about? He strained to hear.

Logen's voice rose, loud and emphatic enough for Kelan to understand every word. "We have to try. She's a Greenhaelan and I won't leave her here to be murdered."

The hairs rose on Kelan's neck. They were planning to rescue the foreign woman! They must be Greenhaelen, too! And Logen — Kelan cursed himself for a fool. He'd shaken hands with Logen Rush himself and hadn't suspected a thing.

If Rush caught him spying now, Kelan was as good as dead. His body screamed at him to run, but that would be suicide. He eased himself from his shelter and crept along the hallway, holding his breath. Thank Aal, raised voices were still coming from the room, covering any sound he might make. He yanked the front door open, slipped through, and closed it noiselessly behind him.

Heart pounding, palms sweating, he ducked around the corner of the building and crouched, listening. No sounds of pursuit. He pulled out the chain. Grasping the charm, he rubbed it and whispered, "Rassil." The silver lines in the copper began to glow. He made a full circle, watching the charm to see which direction shone the brightest. Staying low and keeping to the darkest shadows, he set off at a run.

The charm led him twisting and turning through dark back streets, a perfect haunt for thieves, but he wasn't thinking of anyone but Rassil. She would've been expecting him last night. She must be very worried about him by now. He had to get to her as quickly as he could.

After a while, the streets broadened and more people appeared. Kelan smelt the sea and knew he must be close to the waterfront. The charm glowed brighter. Nearly there. He turned down a cobbled street lined with stone buildings. As he approached the far end, the charm seemed to dim. He retraced his steps, pinpointing the exact spot it had changed. There! She must be somewhere in that building.

What now? He couldn't just knock on the front door and ask to see her. She was a servant. He should try the back first. He slipped around the corner and along an alley, counting the buildings until he was sure he was behind the right one. As he entered the yard, he spied a slim figure beside the back door. It raised its head and the moonlight fell on a familiar face. Rassil! For a moment, she looked almost alarmed to see him, but it must have been a trick of the light, because an instant later, she smiled and held out her arms. Kelan ran to embrace her.

Her body trembled against his. "Oh, K-Kelan," she breathed, "I thought you were never coming!"

"I got here as soon as I could. There's so much to tell you. But are you all right? No one hurt you?" He held her at arm's length. She was as pretty as ever, especially with her cheeks so pink with excitement.

"No, I'm fine. I was frightened of the Guards at first, but they've shown me nothing but respect. Because of your mother, I think."

Guilt prodded at Kelan. He'd been so focused on tracking Rassil, he'd almost forgotten his mother was here. "How is she?"

"She's in good health but not very happy."

Well, she shouldn't have taken that Greenhaelan's side, Kelan thought, but didn't say it aloud. His mother often grew over-fond of the people she'd healed. He supposed she couldn't help it.

Dismissing Mena from his mind, he took out the coin purse and showed it to Rassil. "Look, I've brought plenty of money for us. Come away with me now. Mother doesn't really need you here. Uncle Soran only made you come because he wants to keep us apart."

But Rassil was shaking her head even before he'd finished. "Oh, Kelan," she gasped, "I couldn't do that to your mother. She was so kind to me, taking me in after my father died."

To Kelan's horror, Rassil's wide blue eyes swam with tears. "Oh, it was such a terrible time; I didn't know how I was going to survive. You have no idea how scared I was." She gulped. "And then, Mistress Erdal rescued me. It was like a miracle. She helped me when I needed her. I can't abandon her now."

She laid a gentle hand on his arm and shook her head sadly. "Kelan, she's so worried about that Greenhaelan woman. The trial is tomorrow and they're bound to find her guilty. Mistress Erdal will be so upset. I can't leave her until I'm sure she'll be all right. She has no one else here but me. Oh, please let me stay until after the trial."

That was all very well, Kelan thought, gazing down into the small, pleading face, but shouldn't Rassil care more about his feelings than his mother's? The two of them were finally together again, and he didn't want to be separated from her so soon. Of course, it was nice that Rassil was so fond of his mother, and it was good that they were getting along...

Kelan brightened. When his mother saw how devoted Rassil was to her, she'd change her mind about the betrothal. And once she was on their side, Uncle Soran would come around eventually. Of course, Kelan was going to marry Rassil with or without his family's approval, but it would be easier if they didn't make a fuss about it.

Poor little Rassil was still waiting for his answer, biting her lip in anxiety. He lifted her soft hand and clasped it in both of his. "You can stay with my mother until that Greenhaelan woman is in prison. Then, my mother will go home to my uncle and you'll come with me."

Rassil's face cleared. "Oh, thank you, Kelan. I knew you'd understand."

"Listen, Rassil, I've found something out: there's a plan to help the Greenhaelan escape."

Rassil's eyes widened. "How do you know?"

"It's a long story, but I heard the gang talking about it. I have to tell one of the Guards."

Rassil's brow furrowed for a moment, and then she gazed up through her long lashes. "I know Sergeant Oren, just a little. He's in charge. He went out earlier, but I heard him say he'd be back in two hours. It must be almost that now. If we wait here, we'll see him coming back."

This seemed to be the best plan, especially as it meant Kelan could spend some more time alone with Rassil. He wanted to kiss her again.

The time passed too quickly. It seemed only a few minutes later that a burly man, wearing the blue shirt of the Warrant Guards, stepped from the back alley into the yard. He stopped for a moment at the sight of the two of them outside the back door, and then came on.

As he approached them, Rassil called out softly, "Oh, Sergeant Oren, this is Kelan. He has something to tell you."

Oren listened to Kelan's story, and then rapped out a few crisp questions. Kelan was able to name and describe each of the conspirators, but when Oren asked him where they were now, he realised, to his dismay, that he had no idea where the inn was or how to get to it.

The Sergeant seemed to find this ignorance suspicious. Kelan was forced to confess that he'd found his way here by following a promise charm. Oren glanced from Kelan to Rassil and back again, running an absent hand over the dark stubble that covered his head. Kelan finished the explanation and faltered to a stop. The Sergeant shook his head and sighed, and Kelan felt his cheeks flush with heat.

Oren uttered a few brisk words thanking Kelan for his information, and then strode into the house. Even before the door closed, he began barking orders. "Never mind, Kelan," Rassil said. She seemed to understand how he was feeling. "I think you were very smart to overhear their plans. And very brave." She kissed him on the cheek. "It's late. You'd better go and find a room for the night. I'll see you tomorrow." She opened the door and slipped inside.

Kelan's spirits had risen. Thanks to him, the plan to rescue the Greenhaelan woman would fail. He might even get a reward. Then he could find a really nice place for them to live, and buy Rassil some fancy dresses and jewellery. She'd like that.

He hadn't told her, but he had no intention of leaving this yard tonight. If it came to a fight tomorrow between the Greenhaelen and the Guards, innocent bystanders could be in danger. He needed to be on the spot, ready to protect his girl. He looked around for somewhere to get a few hours' sleep.

For a moment, he thought he could make out a dark figure standing near the entrance to the alley. He blinked, trying to adjust his vision to the darkness after the brighter light of the open doorway. No, there was no one there, just his imagination.

A low shed stood in a corner of the yard, and the door was only secured with a wooden latch. Bales of hay filled the interior almost to the roof, but a small clear space lay just inside the doorway. Kelan pulled a bale apart, spread the hay on the ground, and settled down for the night.

TWELVE

Sara

The twin torments of cold and anxiety had woken Sara again and again throughout the night. Finally, as the first pale fingers of dawn crept through the window, she gave up the struggle. Wrapping herself in the thin blanket, she paced the stone floor, trying to warm up.

They were coming for her today. She shuddered with more than the cold. Less than a year ago, life had made sense. She'd been doing well in a job she loved. She'd made a home for herself. She'd had friends. No one had been threatening to kill her.

Dread rolled through her, leaving her trembling. She pulled the blanket tighter and forced herself to focus on what Mena had told her. There must be a loop hole, a way out. But no matter how she looked at it, she couldn't see one. Everything was stacked against her. The people of Algarth hated the Greenhaelen too much to give her a fair hearing. Teeth chattering, she stopped pacing and faced the truth. She couldn't risk the trial. She had to get out of here.

She checked the window first, but a single glance told her the bars were set too close to allow anyone to squeeze through. How strong was the metal? She gripped and pulled, bracing her feet against the base of the wall and leaning back with all her weight. They didn't budge. She had nothing she could use to chip away the stone; Rassil had even removed the cutlery each time she'd cleared away the meals. The door then? Even if Sara could pry it open, Mena had told her a Guard was stationed outside around the clock. Sara's mind raced. Could she lure the Guard inside and hit him with something? All she had was a mattress and this blanket.

Strangle him with the blanket? Her mind shied away from the grizzly image. It was ridiculous anyway. She'd never learned any kind of fighting, not even self-defence. She was fit and strong, but no match for a trained Warrant Guard, probably twice her size.

No, if she was going to escape, she'd have to wait until they took her out of this room. They wouldn't relax their security, probably just the opposite. But surely there was a greater chance of something unpredictable happening once she was out on the street, on her way to the City Hall. All she could do was stay alert for any small opening, any chance to get away. It wasn't even close to a plan, but strangely, she began to feel a little better.

While she'd been thinking it all out, the sun had broken free of the horizon. The scene outside looked much the same as it had yesterday morning. Again, she heard the soft scrape of wood on stone as a pair of shutters across the road began to open.

At that moment, two men came walking through the open archway, their voices shockingly loud in the early morning hush. Both were tall and yellow-haired, wearing garishly coloured clothing. They strode confidently through the arch and across the cobbles, talking and laughing. They were so alike, apart from their clothing, that she guessed they must be brothers. The one in eye-searing red and orange plucked three balls from his pocket and began juggling them as he walked. They must be performers of some kind, in the city for the Festival.

As they turned and passed her window, the one in blue and purple suddenly flicked a small object between the bars without turning his head. Both men continued around the corner. Gradually, their voices faded.

Sara bent down and picked up the thing the man had thrown into her room. It was a piece of paper, crumpled into a ball. She unfolded it and smoothed it out. Several lines of writing above a hand-drawn map. Was it an advertisement for a performance? After so many months, she spoke the local language very well, but she hadn't yet learned to read it.

She peered at the map. It showed streets and buildings, some labelled. A cross inside a circle had been placed at the intersection of two streets near the centre. Perhaps that was where the performance was to be held. Well, she wasn't going to a performance today, unless her trial counted as one.

She was about to screw up the useless piece of paper, when the door burst open. A Guard strode up to her and levelled his sword point a few inches from her throat. "Don't move!"

Sara froze. A second Guard followed the first. This one darted forward, tore the piece of paper out of her hand and ducked back behind his sword-wielding companion. If she hadn't been so frightened herself, Sara might have found his obvious fear of her amusing. Their task accomplished, both Guards backed towards the door, the first keeping the sword pointed at her the whole time. They left, slamming the door behind them. Sara sank to the floor, shaking and gasping.

After an interval, the door opened again. Not ready to have another sword pointed at her, Sara scrambled to her feet and shrank back into a corner. Four Guards entered this time, but they were followed by Mena. Eyeing Sara warily, the Guards took up positions, one in the middle of each wall.

Ignoring them, Mena made a beeline for Sara, guiding her over to the mattress and sitting down beside her. She murmured reassuringly until Sara began to feel calmer. She wanted to tell Mena about her intention to escape, but she couldn't risk the Guards overhearing. The men stood like statues, showing no sign of interest in the two women, but no doubt they were listening and would report every word.

Nothing else happened for a long time. Eventually, Mena turned to the closest Guard. "Excuse me, how much longer do we have to wait?"

He didn't respond. After another nerve-wracking interval, a fifth Guard entered the room. How many men did they think they needed to keep Sara under control?

But something about this Guard was different. He appeared younger than his companions, yet they came instantly to attention. He acknowledged each of them with a nod, and then directed his gaze to Sara. She stared back, curious about this man who wasn't afraid of her like the others. He was only about medium height, but solidly built and strong-looking, with a round, serious face. His dark hair was shaved close to his scalp — back home, Sara would have called it a buzz cut — and his beard and moustache had been trimmed to little more than shadows. The yellow shield on his chest was enclosed by a thin red border.

After a long moment of scrutiny, he turned away and addressed one of the other Guards. "Everything secure?"

"Yes, Sergeant Oren."

"Good. Take them down now."

Despite Mena's protests, they tied Sara's hands and blindfolded her. So much for her escape plan. If a chance came, she'd never even see it. Someone grabbed her around the waist and lifted her off the ground. She was slung over a shoulder, head lolling downward, and then carried down the stairs like a rolled-up carpet.

The creak of a door, a jumble of voices, the clatter of hooves on cobbles. She was out in the street.

Her stomach rose unpleasantly as she was hauled down from the shoulder and dropped onto a yielding surface. The hands released her. She squirmed, trying to right herself, but whatever she was lying on was slippery. She couldn't get any purchase with her wrists tied together like this.

A touch on her shoulder made her flinch. "It's all right my love. I'm here. I'll help you."

With Mena's assistance, Sara sat up. She was surrounded by the sounds of men's voices, horses stamping, and harnesses jingling. She guessed she was in a carriage of some kind, surrounded by riders. Mena confirmed it and added that Rassil was with them.

Without warning, the vehicle lurched, pressing Sara against the back of the seat. They were moving.

As the carriage rumbled along, Sara brooded in silent misery. There was nothing she could do. No chance to get free. No possibility of running. She'd been a fool to think she might escape. She would be tried and sentenced, either to death or permanent imprisonment. Her life was over. And no one back home would ever know what had happened to her.

The vehicle jerked to a stop, almost throwing Sara off the seat. She braced her feet hard against the floor and managed to stay upright. She could hear shouting and the pounding of hooves.

Someone screamed; she couldn't tell if it was Rassil or Mena. Had there been an accident? "What's happening? What is it?" No answer. Blind and panicked, she flung her head from side to side, not sure where the danger was coming from. She twisted her wrists, desperate to free her hands, but the bonds had been tied too tightly. "Mena? Rassil?"

With another lurch, the carriage started forward again. It quickly gained speed and began to sway from side to side. Unable to keep her balance, Sara toppled sideways. Above the thunder of hoof beats and the rumbling of the wheels, she could hear someone whimpering. Perhaps it was her.

The swaying carriage swerved viciously once more, juddered and tipped up. Sara slid head-first along the seat, crumpling into the side wall. She was sure the carriage was going to roll over, but it miraculously righted itself with a bone-jarring thump. Sara's head banged the wall again, drawing a yelp of pain.

Back on four wheels, the carriage picked up speed. Several horrifying minutes later, it shuddered to another stop, dumping Sara onto the floor. Bruised, blind, and terrified, she desperately tried to right herself, but she was wedged in place.

Something touched the back of her head. She screamed. The blindfold slid from her eyes, exposing them to a painful glare. She blinked furiously to clear her sight but could make out nothing beyond a looming shadow surrounded by light. The carriage door must be open. She blinked some more. Someone was leaning in through the opening, but she couldn't even tell if it was a man or a woman.

"Are you badly hurt?" The deep, clearly male, voice sounded worried. Sara tried to answer, but her throat was as dry as dust and nothing emerged. She shook her head.

"Good." The owner of the voice seemed relieved. "I'm going to pull you out now. We need to be quick."

He lifted her out and set her down on the ground before freeing her wrists. Sara sat up. She could see him clearly now. He had a bright copper beard and long hair the same colour. His clothes were green and brown, patterned like army camouflage.

Sky-blue eyes gazed into hers. "Can you stand?"

Sara nodded. He grasped her hands and pulled her to her feet. They were standing in a narrow alley, with no Guards in sight. Sara's arms and shoulders ached, and her head hurt where it had hit the carriage wall, but she seemed in good shape, considering.

"This way. Hurry." He took her arm and urged her towards a group of horses and riders further down the alley.

Sara didn't resist. She had no idea who these people were, but she'd have more options on horseback than tied up and blindfolded in that carriage.

Two men and two women were already mounted. Sara's rescuer boosted her up into the saddle of a bay horse. "Do you know how to ride?"

Sara finally found her voice. "Yes."

He handed her the reins and turned towards a big grey. As he mounted, two men tore around the corner beyond the carriage and raced up the alley. From their colourful clothing Sara recognised them as the ones she'd seen from her window this morning. They reached the group and skidded to a halt, panting hard.

The one in red and orange called up to the man on the grey horse. "Logen, they're only a few blocks behind us! They know there was a Greenhaelan in the carriage, and they're in an ugly mood. We need to get moving."

The man he'd called Logen snapped out orders: "Tulley, Niall, take the lead. Sara, you and me next, then Cahira and Fin. Bram and Adric, bring up the rear, arrows on strings." He stared hard at the man who'd given the warning. "And Adric, don't hit anyone. Just discourage them from getting too close."

The two men vaulted into the last empty saddles, and the riders urged their horses into motion. About to do the same, Sara froze. Mena and Rassil! She'd almost forgotten them. Logen circled his own mount and came back to her. "What's the matter?"

"My friends are still in the carriage!"

He shook his head. "We can't wait. If that crowd catches up to us, we won't be able to keep you safe from them."

"Then my friends won't be safe from them either! I'm not going without them!" She slid from the horse and pelted down the alley.

By the time she reached the carriage, Logen had caught up with her. He reached for her arm. "There's no time!"

She twisted away from him and peered in through the open door. Rassil was crouched on the floor, looking up in fright. Mena was nowhere to be seen.

"Rassil, are you hurt?"

The girl shook her head without speaking, her blue eyes huge in her small pale face.

"Where's Mena?"

"She told me to stay here." Rassil's voice was a whisper.

Sara spied a flash of movement from the corner of her eye and spun around. Mena was advancing on Logen from behind, a thick piece of wood raised in one hand. Grim determination marked her features.

"Mena, no," Sara screamed. Logen whirled and grabbed Mena's wrist, twisting it until she cried out and dropped the wood.

Sara tugged hard at Logen's arm. "Let her go!"

Logen stared back over his shoulder at her in disbelief.

It was then that Sara began to notice the sound. It was like the distant roar of surf crashing onto a beach. At first, she couldn't imagine what it might be. It grew louder and more distinct. There were voices in it. Fear twisted her stomach. It was the crowd that Adric had warned them about. "We have to get to the horses!"

"I'm not going anywhere with these criminals, and neither are you!" Mena snapped, still struggling to break Logen's grip on her arm.

"If you stay here, they'll kill both of you," said Logen. "They're out for blood. Can't you hear it?"

"Please, Mena." The clamour was raising the hairs on the back of

Sara's neck now, sounding more like some unstoppable force of nature than anything human. Mena finally seemed to understand. She gave Logen a sour-faced nod. He released his hold on her.

Rassil emerged from the carriage. "What is it? Oh, what is it?" She appeared, if possible, even more terrified than before.

Sara stared straight into Logen's eyes and shouted loud enough to be heard above the appalling noise. "We're taking them both!"

He lifted his hands in exasperated surrender. "All right, but we have to go. Now!"

They raced to the horses, Sara expecting to hear the crowd thundering into the alley any second. She reached the bay and mounted. Logen boosted Mena and Rassil up behind Adric and Bram before springing into his own saddle.

They fled through the city, taking one turn after another until Sara had lost all sense of direction. The sound of the pursuing mob gradually diminished. Finally, it disappeared completely.

Even then, Sara didn't allow herself more than a sliver of hope, until they'd left the narrow, crowded streets far behind them and were galloping along a broad, empty road, heading deeper into the countryside.

THIRTEEN

Kelan

Waking at first light, Kelan brushed wisps of hay off his clothing and considered his next move. Should he steal a horse from the stable attached to the house? It would make following Rassil easier, but a few minutes with his eye to a crack in the shed door showed him it was too risky. An almost constant stream of armed Guards passed through the yard, many of them already mounted. He'd never slip a stolen horse past them. He'd just have to do the best he could on foot.

Choosing his moment, he wormed his way out of the shed, and, keeping to the shadows, snuck around to the front of the building. A four-wheeled carriage waited outside, with horses already harnessed. He hadn't woken a minute too soon. He crossed the street and kept watch from the shelter of an archway until he saw Rassil and the others emerge from the house and enter the carriage. It set off, and Kelan followed.

Sergeant Oren had obviously taken Kelan's information seriously, because he'd chosen to drive the carriage himself. Only four Blueshirts rode alongside, but they wore swords and their eyes constantly scanned for trouble. All the other Guards must be stationed along the route to the City Hall.

Despite the early hour, the streets were packed with festival goers. They spilled past the curb and onto the road, and were slow to step aside, even for Oren and his Blueshirts. Kelan wove his way through them, managing to stay level with the carriage.

A pair of acrobats appeared up ahead, tumbling along the street, their bright clothing flashing in the sun as they jumped and spun. The crowd surged forward for a closer look, but Kelan slowed and stared. His heart gave a thump of shock. He recognised those costumes: Bram and Adric. And there, keeping pace on the opposite side of the road, were Niall Crawley and Logen Rush himself!

Kelan shouted a warning to Sergeant Oren, but he couldn't make himself heard above the crowd. He tried to muscle his way through to the carriage, but the press of people hemmed him in and carried him along. The human tide swept him up the street and hard against the trunk of a tree. Afraid of being crushed, he swung himself onto the lowest branch. From this vantage point, he waved his arms wildly, trying in vain to catch Oren's eye.

It was too late. Kelan watched helplessly as disaster unfolded right in front of his eyes.

It began with the horses flanking the carriage. One moment, they were carrying their riders calmly. The next, all four reared up and spun around. Cries rose as people scrambled madly to avoid the flailing hooves.

Having cleared a space around themselves, the horses ignored the shouts and kicks of their riders and bolted in different directions, scattering the rest of the crowd from the roadway onto the footpath. At the same time, the two carriage horses stopped dead in the middle of the street.

Kelan held his breath. This was Niall Crawley's doing. Rassil was in terrible danger. He had to go to her. But dozens of people were packed as tightly as salted fish in a barrel around the base of his tree. He could do nothing but watch, his heart in his mouth.

Deserted by his men, Oren rose from the driver's seat, drawing his sword. The red acrobat vaulted up behind him. They struggled for a moment, but Adric was too strong. He pinned Oren's arms, lifted him off his feet, and threw him to the ground. Bram and Logen climbed up to join their fellow outlaw, all three sharing the bench.

Crawley was already perched on one of the carriage horses. He leaned forward. The beasts raised their heads and stepped out, straining against their harnesses until the carriage jerked into motion. The horses leapt to a canter. The carriage careered past Kelan, swaying dangerously. Curtains at the window prevented him from seeing anyone inside.

In the wake of the speeding carriage, the crowd surged back onto the roadway, but Kelan stayed in his tree. He had to see where they went.

At the end of the street, the horses made a sharp turn to the right, without slowing. The carriage lost traction, all four wheels skidding across the cobbles, then the vehicle tipped up. Kelan gasped. It was going to roll over. For one agonising instant, the carriage held its precarious balance, two wheels on the ground, two in the air. Then, teetering wildly, it swung around the corner and disappeared.

They'd stolen Rassil! Kelan jumped down from the tree, his legs carrying him forward as soon as his feet hit the ground. He was halfway to the corner when he stopped. He had no chance of catching them on foot. He glanced back. Sergeant Oren was rising slowly to his feet, but without a horse the man was no use to him.

An angry voice yelled, "They took the Greenhaelan! After them!" The cry was taken up by others, spreading through the crowd like flames through a pile of kindling. Shouting and shaking their fists in the air, the mob began to move.

Kelan didn't wait any longer. He ducked and wove his way through the growing mass of people, then sprinted back to the deserted stable.

Wonder of wonders, there was one horse left, a medium-sized grey gelding. It stood calmly as he hefted a saddle onto its back and buckled the girth strap with shaking fingers. In the gloom, he spotted something long and narrow hanging from a hook. It was a battered leather scabbard with a sword hilt sticking out of the end. He lifted it from the hook and took it with him.

Outside in the light, he drew the sword. It looked old, and the blade was spotted with rust, but it was better than nothing. He strapped it on and walked a few steps. He was hunting desperate men now, and it felt good to be armed. The sword had been a lucky find. Or maybe it wasn't just luck. Maybe it was a sign that Aal was with him, as his mother always said, and that he'd succeed in rescuing Rassil. He wasn't sure if he really believed that, but it was a cheering thought.

He took out the promise charm and activated it by speaking Rassil's name, then began turning in a slow circle. When he was facing almost directly south, it began to glow brightly. He took another step, and it faded again. They must be heading for the ford over the Eder River. It made sense. From there they could continue south to Edervale and the mountains, or lose themselves in the Greenwood Forest to the east. He tucked the charm back inside his tunic, next to his heart. Then he mounted the horse and rode out of the yard.

By the time Kelan had found his way out of the city, he had grown to hate the grey gelding with a passion. It was unkempt and it smelled bad. Worse, it refused to be hurried, keeping to the same slow, lazy canter no matter how much he kicked it or swore at it. He wasn't surprised that the Blueshirts had left it behind. He only wondered why the useless animal had been in the stable in the first place.

He was tormented by the thought that Rassil was getting further and further away all the time. No doubt the outlaws were travelling as fast as they could. But he had the promise charm. He'd be able to track Rassil, no matter how far away she was. And something might happen to help him catch up. He only prayed that Rassil would be safe until then.

He drummed his heels against the grey's flanks again. The beast gave no indication it had even noticed. With a sigh of disgust, Kelan slumped down in the saddle. The horse kept up its steady pace along the southern road.

FOURTEEN

Sara

Sara clutched the front of the saddle with both hands, hoping the galloping horse would follow the others without any guidance from her. It seemed to be working. She was staying on but still lurching back and forth with every stride. She clamped her thighs to the horse's sides and held on grimly. She was going to be very sore the next day. Assuming she lived that long.

The road had been running along the edge of a forest for some time when Logen finally raised an arm to halt them. He turned his horse onto a narrow track under the trees and led them in single file. The hooves made no sound on the soft litter of the trail, but the blowing of the spent horses reverberated through the quiet wood. The trail led slightly downhill, curving slightly as it went.

For the first time on this wild ride, Sara had the chance to look around her. The woodland was lovely. The sun slanted down through narrow gaps in the thick canopy, creating alternating bands of golden light and purple shadow. It could hardly have been more different to that other forest, from her first day here, and not just because of the Blight. The other had been a wood of dark green conifers, with needles clustering on the branches. The trees surrounding her now carried broad, lobed leaves, similar to maples or oaks. Although it was almost autumn, every tree was still in full, verdant leaf.

The undergrowth on both sides of the trail grew thick and tall.

She breathed deeply, savouring the fragrance of sun-warmed herbs, spicy above the ever-present smell of her horse's sweat. Underneath everything, she detected the deep earthy note of the forest floor as the horses churned it up. A wave of quite irrational happiness flooded over her. She wished she could stay in this beautiful forest forever.

She only knew she had fallen into a doze when she jerked into wake-fulness with her nose an inch from the horse's neck. They'd stopped on the bank of a small stream that crossed the trail. The others dismounted and began leading their mounts down the shallow bank. Sara tried to do the same, but her legs were so stiff she almost toppled over as she reached the ground, only saving herself by grabbing the stirrup leathers. Straightening up and stepping carefully, she led the bay to the water. Free of their riders, the horses moved eagerly into the stream, lowered their heads, and drank with long sucking swallows. Sara struggled back up the low bank, wincing as her abused muscles protested even this small exertion.

Logen was looking around. "We won't find a better place before nightfall. We'll camp here and go on in the morning."

A pang of fear hit Sara. Go on to where? What were they planning to do with her? For a crazy moment, she considered getting back in the saddle and taking off again, but she couldn't bear the thought of any more riding today. And where would she go? The only place she was familiar with was Soran's farm, and she could hardly return there.

Besides, her only friend in the world was right here, sitting under a tree with Rassil. Both women were slumped over, staring at the ground. This was so unlike Mena, who usually preferred to meet trouble head on, that Sara was alarmed.

She hobbled over to them. "Are you all right?"

Mena tilted her head back at Sara's approach. Her generous mouth was pinched and her eyes were like chips of slate. "Who are these people, Sara? How did you meet them?"

Sara gaped. "What? I didn't - I don't - you think I had something to do with this?"

Mena sent her another long, searching look. Then her face relaxed and she shook her head. "No, I don't suppose you did." She sighed and patted the ground. "I'm sorry, Sara. Come and sit down."

Sara eased herself to the ground and gingerly stretched out her legs. Rassil's blonde head was still bent low over her drawn-up knees. She appeared very small, sitting that way, and she seemed to have withdrawn into herself. The shy teenager had been caught up in something that had nothing to do with her, and Sara's heart went out to her. If she could protect Rassil somehow, she would.

"Do you know where we are?" Sara asked. She kept her voice low, hoping not to draw unwanted attention.

"The western part of the Greenwood Forest," Mena said. "The largest forest on Algarth. I'm not surprised they came here. They could stay out of sight of the Guards all the way east to Gadara, if they wanted to take a ship, or south, and lose themselves in the White Mountains." She cocked her head at Sara. "What I don't understand is why they brought us with them. What do they want with you?"

Sara shook her head. "I don't know, but Logen said—"

"*Logen?*" Mena caught her breath. She shot a glance towards the copper-bearded man and her face stiffened again. "It must be Logen Rush!" she hissed. "That's why they kidnapped you — he knows you're a Greenhaelan, and he's trying to build up the guild again. He wants you to join him."

Sara's mouth dropped open. Could Mena be right? Just then, the chief kidnapper himself arrived, bringing them cups of water and a small sack of dried berries and nuts, similar to trail mix.

"Rest yourselves while we set up camp," he said. "Then we can all introduce ourselves properly."

At his friendly tone, Rassil looked up and smiled shyly at him, but there had been a touch of irony in that pleasant voice that made Sara wonder if he'd overheard what Mena had been saying.

Mena eyed the food and water with suspicion. But Sara didn't see why Logen would have risked his life to get her out of Eorna, just to poison her now. Besides, she was hungry. She scooped up some of the trail mix. After a moment, Mena and Rassil followed suit. As soon as she began to chew, Sara realised she wasn't just hungry; she was ravenous. She hadn't eaten anything since last night, and not much then. She hoped they'd be getting more for dinner than a handful of nuts and berries.

Logen's group set up camp quickly and efficiently. Sara leaned back against the tree trunk, watching them put up tents, picket the horses, make a fire, and prepare a hot meal from their supplies. There were seven of them: five men and two women. Logen, Bram and Adric looked to be about her age, and so did two of the others: a man dressed in black and a young woman in blue with long dark hair. The remaining man and woman were older, maybe in their late forties or early fifties.

As the outlaws went about their homely tasks, they chatted together, relaxed and comfortable, joking back and forth as they worked. It was puzzling. These people didn't fit Sara's ideas about how violent criminals behaved. Besides, they'd saved her from being tried for treason. Despite Mena's hostility, Sara owed them some benefit of the doubt for that. But if they were Greenhaelan, she wasn't going to help them, no matter what they thought.

After a while, feeling restless, she got up and limped over to the horses. No one tried to stop her. The bay she'd been riding nickered at her approach, and she felt absurdly grateful for the friendly greeting. Now that she had a chance to really look, she saw that her mount was a mare, and a very pretty one, with four white socks and a diamond-shaped blaze on her forehead.

A voice spoke from right behind her. "She likes you." Sara froze, and then turned to face him. It was the man dressed in black. What did he want with her? But he only stepped around her and laid a gentle hand on the horse's neck. The mare nuzzled at his short black hair. He laughed. "You're a very forward lady, Mistress Sage."

Sara's heart settled back to its normal rhythm. She cleared her throat. "Sage? Is that her name?"

He stroked the mare's nose. "That's what her owner said. We only met today, but she's a fine girl. She'll carry you well." He turned to face Sara. "My name is Niall, by the way."

Sara was at a loss how to reply to this. *Pleased to meet you?* Ridiculous. *Who cares?* Closer to the truth, but it wasn't in her interest to antagonise her captors by insulting them.

She settled for nodding quickly and turning away. Embarrassed by her own awkwardness and angry at him for causing it, she felt the blood rising up her neck as she made her slow way back to Mena and Rassil.

As dusk fell and the air cooled, Logen invited the three of them to join the others around the fire. The meal was a thick vegetable soup, flavoured with a smoky dried meat. It was delicious, and Sara had two helpings.

After dinner, Logen made the introductions he'd promised. Sara already knew that the tall fair-haired brothers were called Adric and Bram. They had changed out of their colourful clothing into camouflage outfits like Logen's, making them hard to tell apart.

The younger, dark-haired woman's name was Cahira. She was dressed in wine-red trousers and a bright blue tunic that set off her green, almond-shaped eyes. She was remarkably beautiful, and so was her voice as she greeted the newcomers. She was married to Bram.

The older woman's name was Fin. Tulley, the older man, was her husband. They seemed an odd couple, the tiny, soft-spoken woman with her neat grey plait and sweet smile, and the stocky man with his wild red beard, dirty rumpled tunic and gruff, scowling manner.

Finally, Logen introduced Niall, whom she'd already met. His clothing was a puzzle. It wasn't just that the man had chosen black. Anyone might do that. But this seemed more deliberate, as if he'd gone to some trouble to make sure that every single item he was wearing was a deep, jet black, even his belt and boots. She wondered if he was in mourning or if it was a kind of fashionable affectation.

When Logen asked for Sara's story in return, she stuck to what she'd originally told Mena: she'd been visiting Algarth from another land far away, when she'd had an accident and lost her memory. She'd been recovering and starting to remember a few things when she'd somehow healed a Blighted plant and been imprisoned as a Greenhaelan.

Logen stared at her. "You healed a Blighted plant accidentally?"

"Yes." Had she said something wrong already?

Logen and the others exchanged glances.

"Your skal must be very powerful," Fin said. Her delicately lined face broke into a smile. "We have a real chance now, Logen."

"I won't help you destroy any more trees or crops, if that's what you're thinking," Sara said bluntly, her heart hammering.

The older woman shook her head, her grey eyes serious again. "No, no, my dear. You don't understand. We didn't cause the Blight. We want to heal it. But there are so few of us. That's why we risked our lives to rescue you. Logen and I tried to do it on our own, but we could only heal a few plants before we became exhausted. When we met Bram, we hoped that three of us together would have more success. We were on our way to try again, when we heard about you." She smiled on Sara as if she was a favoured child. "And now, with your help, we might actually be able to do it."

So only three of the group were actually Greenhaelen. And if Fin was to be believed, those three wanted to cure the Blight, not spread it. Sara glanced at Mena, wondering how she was taking this. Her friend was looking thoughtful, but said nothing.

"If you didn't cause the Blight, who did?" Sara asked. "And why does everyone think it was you?"

"We think it might be a natural disease," Logen said. Sara was surprised. That had been her hypothesis, too. With everything that had happened, she'd almost forgotten.

"We can't imagine any Greenhaelan deliberately causing it" Logen went on. "We believe that Chairman Tarn just took advantage of the situation to silence opposition and increase his political power. He's a Mind Wender, so people are inclined to believe him, as long as they don't think about it too much."

"A Mind Wender?" Sara asked.

"Don't they have Mind Wending where you come from?" Logen asked.

"Um, no, I don't think so. I mean, they might, I don't really remember much." Sara mentally kicked herself for her curiosity. She had to be more careful what she said, or she'd give herself away, and who knew how these people might react?

93

"It's a rare skal, not surprising you haven't remembered it yet," Mena put in quickly. "A Mind Wender can influence another person's thoughts, persuade them to their point of view."

"You mean they can control someone's mind?" That was a horrifying thought.

"No, not control, just have some influence," Logen said. "You can fight it, especially if you know the person is a Mind Wender. But if you're not paying attention, or you're in a weakened or confused state, it can have a stronger effect."

"But there are old stories and songs about Mind Wenders who were far more powerful than the ones we have today," Cahira added. "They could control people's minds and make them do anything they wanted."

Niall smiled. "They're just stories to frighten children, Cah."

The beautiful young woman frowned at him. "I'm not so sure. Some historians, like Adara Domben, think there's a lot of truth in the old legends. If life ever goes back to normal, I'd love to spend some time digging into the Memorer archives and trying to make more sense of them."

"We'll go together one day, I promise," Bram said. Cahira smiled brilliantly at him.

"I'm sure that will be absolutely fascinating for you both," Niall drawled. "But sadly, I'll have to leave it to you. I have an allergy to musty old papers. They make me break out in severe boredom."

Cahira laughed.

"Well, Tarn can't control minds, thank Aal," Logen said. "I've been in Council meetings with him, and he never managed to persuade me to his point of view. Or Adara Domben for that matter. When the Blight appeared, he just saw it as an opportunity to get me off the Council and turn people against the Greenhaelan cause."

It sounded plausible, but Sara wasn't completely convinced yet. "What about the attacks on the timber camps and the boats?"

Logen shook his head. He looked angry. "We have no idea who did that. It wasn't us, or any Greenhaelen we know. You have no reason to believe me, Sara, but I swear it's the truth. We had nothing to do with it, or with starting the Blight."

"But you do think it would be possible for a Greenhaelan to cause something like the Blight, if they wanted to?" It mightn't be wise to press him like this, but she had to know the truth.

"Perhaps. We don't know everything about how skals work. But look at it this way, Sara. Would you deliberately create a disease that kills plants on this sort of scale?"

Sara recoiled. "No, never. I've always loved growing things, even as a child."

"Of course you have, dear," Fin said. "You're a Greenhaelan. Even before a skal manifests, our natures are already set towards it. My Tulley spent his boyhood making models from clay and wood and wire long before he became a Shaper." She smiled wryly. "I myself was always in trouble for staying out in the garden long after supper time, and coming inside with mud on my hands and face." She turned to the man in black. "Niall dear, where did you spend most of your childhood?"

He smiled crookedly at her. "Why, Fin, dear, I spent as much as I could of it in the stables with the horses, and in the kennels with the hounds."

"Exactly," the little woman said with satisfaction. "Because you're a Beast Speaker. Aal knows what gifts he intends for each of us, and shapes us accordingly. That's why I can't believe any Greenhaelan would have done this. It goes against everything we are."

She had a good point, but there was still a problem. "Even if everything you're saying is true," Sara said, "I don't think I can help you. I've only just discovered I'm a Greenhaelan. I don't understand anything about it yet."

Logen leaned forward, an eager light in his blue eyes. "That doesn't matter. I'm the strongest Greenhaelan here, perhaps the strongest of my generation, and I've had years of practice using my skal. And still, it's an effort for me to heal even one Blighted plant. It takes complete concentration. Yet you did it without any training, without even meaning to. How did you feel afterwards? Were you tired?"

Sara thought back and answered honestly. "No. It surprised me, and

I was frightened and shocked by the reaction to it from the others, but it didn't take any effort at all. It just happened."

He nodded in satisfaction. "That's why we think you might be able to help. Your skal must be very strong to manifest like that. There are legends about two Greenhaelen from long ago whose skals were especially powerful, right from the moment they appeared. They needed no training or practice. The other Greenhaelen called them Master Healers."

"If you're going to start talking about legends," Niall said, "I'll be off to stand guard. Old stories make my teeth ache." He sauntered away.

Fin rose, too. "I should be off to bed," she said, "I'm not as young as I used to be." Tulley snorted and slapped his leg. "I'd still bet on you against any of these youngsters, lass." But he stood and went with her.

Logen continued his story. "One Master Healer was a man and one was a woman. In each of their lifetimes, Algarth was damaged by a disaster that devastated the natural world. In one case, it was a flood that covered the land for more than a month and drowned most of the plant life. In the other, it was a fire that raged for weeks, leaving nothing behind but ashes. In both stories, the Master Healer somehow linked their skal with the skals of their fellow Greenhaelen."

"There's a song about it," said Cahira, "but it doesn't say anything about how they did it, just that they joined their skals and sent out a wave of healing. Even huge trees regrew in seconds." She sighed, raking a hand through her long hair. "I wish we knew more."

"Many people think these stories are just tales that have become exaggerated in the telling," Logen said. "But, like Cahira, I believe there is truth in them."

He leaned forward and Sara could see the firelight dancing in his clear blue eyes. "Perhaps, Sara, you have been sent to Algarth in this generation for the same reason they were sent in theirs: to heal the land and save our people."

Sara was too appalled to speak. They thought she was some sort of saviour? A superhero? A Chosen One, for heaven's sake? They must be insane. And she was stuck here with them, completely in their power.

That night, as she lay awake in the tent she was sharing with Mena and Rassil, she went over the conversation again and again, trying to tease out the truth. Logen and Fin had seemed open and honest, and she had a strong instinct to trust them. And yet, what did she know about them, really?

Mena was her friend, a good and honest person, and she believed Logen and the other Greenhaelen had attacked timber camps, set fire to the boats, and deliberately caused the Blight. But then, Mena had been living on a farm, far from the places where those things had happened. She only knew what she'd been told, and perhaps what she'd been told wasn't true. It could all be politically motivated lies, as Logen had claimed. She turned over onto her other side, wrestling with the problem of who to believe.

Logen and the others had risked their lives to save her; that was a fact. The only reason she could imagine for them to do that was the possibility that she could help them cure the Blight. She certainly couldn't be of any other use to them. So, she would accept for now that they wanted to cure it. Did this mean their motives were pure? Not necessarily.

The people of Algarth were desperate for a cure and might be willing to do almost anything in return, even giving amnesty to Logen and the Greenhaelen.

Logen could be planning to use her for his own ends, as a means to gain back some political power. That made sense, if he was as ruthless and ambitious as Mena believed. On the other hand, he might be telling the truth: that they had had nothing to do with the violence or the Blight, and that the Council Chairman had cynically used the appearance of the disease as an opportunity to remove his biggest political rival. But Tarn hadn't stopped at ruining Logen's political career; he had started a campaign to capture all the Greenhaelen and try them for treason. He'd even executed some of them. If he knew they were innocent, it was an almost unbelievably evil thing to do. And yet, in Sara's own world, many politicians and dictators over thousands of years had done unbelievably evil things to hold onto power. Tarn could be one. But then, so could Logen.

She flopped onto her back and stared into the darkness. This wasn't helping at all. Her thoughts were going around in circles. No matter how much she worried at the problem, there was no way to know who was lying. Her heart told her that Fin and Logen were sincere, even if their ideas about her were mistaken, but she couldn't be absolutely sure. She lay listening to Mena's slow, steady breathing and the little whispers of air that came from Rassil, wishing she could fall asleep as easily. Wishing she knew what to do.

A thought came to her, clean and sharp, cutting through her confusion like a knife. It didn't matter who was telling the truth. Because there was one thing she knew with absolute certainty. The Blight was a terrible, wrong, sickening thing, and it had to be fought and stopped. Trusting or not trusting Logen Rush had nothing to do with it.

Master Healer or not, she was a Greenhaelan. At some point in that long conversation, they'd convinced her of that at least. She'd be a Greenhaelan, then. She'd do everything she could to cure the Blight and worry about the rest later.

The morning light shining through the tent woke Sara. She rolled over and saw Mena already sitting up. How would her friend take the news that she'd decided to help Logen and the others?

"Um, Mena?"

Mena turned. "I'm glad you're awake. I wanted to talk to you."

Sara propped herself on her elbows, every muscle tense. She knew that clipped tone. It was the one Mena used with Kelan when she thought he needed firm guidance about something. Mena had made up her mind. She was going to tell Sara they had to escape and turn the outlaws in to the authorities.

But Mena surprised her. "I was wrong about these people," she said. "I had a talk with Fin last night. She's a good woman, with a strong faith, and she vouched for the others. I don't believe they hurt anyone or caused the Blight. I was too ready to listen to Chairman Tarn's lies. We all were." She closed her mouth and stared hard at Sara, as if daring her to argue.

Sara sank back in relief. "It's all right, Mena, I agree with you. I want to help them."

Rassil was propped up on one elbow listening to them, her eyes going from one to the other. She'd hardly said a word to anyone yesterday, but she didn't appear to be so frightened this morning. "I'm sure you're right, Mistress Erdal," she said. "They seem like friendly folk."

Mena nodded her approval. "I'm sorry you've been caught up in all this, Rassil. When it's over, I'll find you a place on another farm. One of our neighbours is sure to need a serving girl."

Rassil ducked her head. "Thank you, Mistress Erdal."

As the three of them left the tent, blinking in the sun, Tulley and Fin approached them.

"Thought you could use these," Tulley said gruffly, holding out his big hands. Three knives lay across the calloused palms. The sunlight revealed rippling patterns in the blades, just like the ones on Mena's best and most prized knife. The handles were of smooth, curved wood.

Sara reached for one. It fitted her hand as if made for her. "Thank you," she said, surprised at how good it felt to have a knife again. "It's beautiful."

"You won't find better in all of Algarth," Fin said. "My Tulley is a Master Shaper." Tulley's broad face flushed as red as his beard, but he looked pleased.

Cahira came over next, with a thick bundle draped over her arm. "We didn't know what you'd be wearing in the prison, Sara, so we brought clothing for you." She shook out a long-sleeved green tunic of similar design to her own blue one, a pair of loose grey trousers, and a soft, grey cloak. "I had to guess the size of the tunic and trousers. I hope they fit."

Sara accepted these additional gifts with heartfelt expressions of thanks. She'd decided yesterday that Cahira's style of clothing was much more practical than the long, bulky dress she herself was wearing, and she'd envied the other woman's freedom of movement.

Cahira turned a rueful expression on Mena and Rassil. "I'm sorry, we didn't know you were coming, or I'd have brought something for you, too."

"A dress and apron have always served me well," Mena said with a certain tartness — she'd never really approved of Sara's fondness for riding trousers. "I see no need to abandon them now."

Rassil merely bobbed her head as if in agreement with her mistress.

Cahira flashed a brilliant smile. "Well, that's all right, then. Better get changed fast, Sara, Logen wants to make an early start."

The trousers were a little long in the legs, but when Sara had rolled them up a few times she was more than satisfied with her new ensemble.

After a quick breakfast, they broke camp and mounted up, with Mena perched behind Adric and Rassil behind Bram. Logen's plan was to make their way to a large area of Blighted trees in the far south-eastern part of the forest, where there were fewer trails and not many people passing through.

For the first few hours, they followed narrow, winding tracks that crossed small streams. Occasionally the path was wide enough for two to ride side by side. Whenever this happened, Sara took the opportunity to question Logen further. If she was going to be any use, she had to know as much as possible.

As they talked, she began to understand that it wasn't just farmers and Greenhaelen who'd been hurt by the Blight. For a start, the lives of Tulley, Niall, Cahira and Adric had been turned upside down, because they'd refused to abandon their Greenhaelen friends and loved ones, fleeing with them instead. But Logen's words made it clear that many others had been affected, too.

"Algarth is dying, Sara. Before we met the others, Niall and I spent months travelling around, trying to find other Greenhaelen. We saw what the Blight does, not just to plants, but to people. In places, the roads were choked with them, men and women, old folk and children, all forced to leave their homes. No one can survive long where the Blight takes hold. It kills every growing thing. When their stored food ran out, they had to abandon their farms and villages. Many of them were starving. We saw some of the elderly fall and die on the road. And in the healthy areas, the farmers and villagers were afraid of taking in so many strangers. They tried to turn them away by force. The refugees were desperate and kept coming. There was bloodshed."

He paused, his eyes haunted. "We saw terrible things." He shook his head. "The Blight is still spreading. If we don't stop it, thousands will die."

The further they penetrated into the forest the more overgrown the way became, until the trails vanished and the riders had to choose their own way. More than once, Logen called a halt while Niall went ahead to scout. When the sun was almost overhead, they emerged from the trees onto a wide, dirt road.

"It was built for the wagons carrying timber to Eorna," Logen said. "It cuts through the whole forest and joins the highway east of the city."

They crossed the wide road quickly, and pulled up in the shelter of the trees on the other side. While Niall quested for a way forward, the rest of them listened for any sound of pursuit. There was none. Sara wondered aloud about that.

"We still have a few friends in Eorna," Logen said. "They're laying a false trail, leading east to the port of Gadara, as if we intended to escape by ship. After the Guards get there, they'll have to search the streets and check all the vessels in the harbour. And even when they finally realise they've been tricked, they won't look for us in the forest."

"Why not?" Rassil asked timidly. "It seems like a perfect place to hide."

"They still think we caused the Blight; they don't know we're trying to reverse it. In their minds, we'd want to put as much distance between ourselves and Eorna as possible. That means taking the southern road towards the White Mountains." His lips twisted in a wry smile. "It's where I'd go if I was actually leading some sort of rebellion, as Tarn claims. There are plenty of places to hide in those foothills. Besides, the people there value their independence. They have no love for authority, and they've been known to harbour outlaws before."

Niall returned, having found a suitable trail. Sara tried to relax and enjoy the ride like she had yesterday, but her brain wouldn't stop churning over everything that had happened, trying to make sense of it. She'd accepted she was a Greenhaelan, but she still didn't understand how she could be. The people of this world took their skals for granted, but she wasn't from this world.

101

Mena and Fin believed that the skals were a gift from their god, Aal, but Sara didn't believe in Aal. Could the skals be caused by something in the environment? Maybe magic was invisibly floating around everywhere, like pollen. As you breathed the air and drank the water and ate the food, it just seeped into you.

Whatever the reason, she was committed to this now, like a character in a fantasy story who has to complete her quest before she can return home. And how was she going to return home, anyway? If this was a story, she might have come through some sort of magic door, like the wardrobe that led into Narnia. She'd loved those books as a child and wanted to be Lucy Pevensie. Narnia had seemed like such a wonderful place compared to the Children's Home. Even the dangers the Pevensie children faced seemed exciting rather than horrible. And of course, there was always a happy ending. But they were just stories. This was real.

She was still committed to do what she could to heal the Blight. But after that, she'd leave the future of Algarth to the people who belonged here and concentrate all her energy on finding the way home.

After supper that evening, in another makeshift forest camp, the group were entertained by Cahira. Logen had told Sara that the beautiful dark-haired woman was a Skalsinger, but Sara hadn't risked asking what that meant. Now she found out.

With the velvety darkness of the forest at her back and the firelight flickering in her green eyes, Cahira parted her lips and began to sing a lilting, wordless melody. Her voice was true and clear, a pleasure to listen to. Sara relaxed back against a log and closed her eyes to enjoy the music.

A second voice joined in, deep, resonant, singing a harmony. Someone else had talent; Sara opened her eyes to see who it was. She glanced around the circle of rapt faces, but they were clearly listening, not singing. Yet that second voice rolled on. Sara's pulse quickened. Someone else was here! She jerked upright, her eyes scanning the darkness beyond the circle of firelight. Mena, seated next to her, touched her arm lightly. "It's all right," she whispered, "it's her skal."

A third voice arose, and a fourth, each singing in a different register. Mena was right; all the music was coming from Cahira. The voices dipped and rose around each other, blending and separating. Pleasure thrilled through Sara. Cahira's skal was incredible.

She was so entranced that it took a moment to realise the singer had begun to weave words into the melody. At the same time, the air above Cahira's head began to shimmer and coalesce into faint images, translucent at first, but solidifying moment by moment. They were moving like a video. Sara found that if she focused too hard on the pictures, they faded back into translucence, but if she relaxed her eyes, they firmed up again. Once she had the hang of it, she sat back and listened to the song.

Cahira was singing about a king from long ago, called Tana Lossil. In his time, ships from Bregia crossed the strait and landed at Eorna. Sara was surprised to hear the song describe the city as a small fishing village. The Bregians put the village to the sword and marched south towards Edervale, the capital city, burning and looting as they went. King Tana mustered his forces at Edervale Castle, intending to march north to meet the invaders. Just before they set out, an old holy man, an Aaldan, begged an audience with the King. The Aaldan spoke to King Tana, telling him that Aal had sent him a prophecy and a vision.

"My King," Cahira sang in the high, trembling voice of an old man, "Join not in battle with the fierce invaders. Defeat and death will be your portion. Use the gift to shape the Gateway. Step between the worlds. Find the stone."

At the words "step between the worlds", Sara's heart began to beat faster. This could be the clue she was looking for, the way to get home. She listened and watched closely as the rest of the story unfolded.

King Tana shaped a Gateway and stepped through it into a strange land, where he found a charmed stone. Following the old man's instructions, he wedged the stone into the base of the castle wall, gathered all the people of Edervale inside, and shut the heavy wooden gates.

The enemy arrived with siege engines, and bombarded the castle with enormous boulders. But every missile halted in mid-air just short of the wall, then flew back to fall among the invaders themselves, wreaking havoc on them. The survivors raced forward to scale the walls, but the stone blocks became as slick and smooth as glass. The ladders and grappling hooks could find no purchase.

The Bregians tried to burn the wooden gates. The fire blew back at them in such a fierce storm of smoke and flame, they were forced to retreat. When the flames died down, the wood was undamaged, not even blackened by the smoke. The terrified remnant of the invading force fled north to their ships. All of Algarth praised Aal and the King.

"This is the chronicle of King Tana, Gate-Shaper, the Strider of Worlds." Cahira had discarded all the voices except her own clear, pure alto. It rang like a bell as she concluded the song. "From that time to this, Algarth has not seen his like. His fame spread as wide as the oceans, and peace and plenty marked the many years of his reign."

The song ended to soft applause around the circle. Cahira bowed her head gracefully in acknowledgment.

The words and images had told the story in great detail, except for the part Sara needed to know: how did King Tana shape the Gateway? She asked Cahira, but the Skalsinger said she didn't know anything more than the words she had sung. "It's one of the problems of Skalsinging," she said, raking her dark hair back from her forehead. "We learn these songs, our own history, but they never tell the whole story. And no one knows how much is true and how much has been embellished over the years. It's very frustrating."

"Not to me," Bram said solemnly. "I don't care if it's true or not. I just love hearing you sing."

Cahira smiled fondly at him and took his hand.

"But you know how our Cahira hates a mystery," Niall drawled.

"Only one I can't solve." Cahira sniffed, tossing her head.

Sara had been thinking. "Is Edervale Castle still standing?" If it was, she might find the answers she needed there.

"Oh, it's standing all right," Niall answered her. "Villembelt Tarn owns it now. He claims to be descended in a direct line from King Tana himself. He says that over the centuries the name Tana was changed to

Tarn." Niall's tone made it clear what he thought about that. His lips quirked in a sly smile. "His seven-times great-grandfather was probably King Tana's privy cleaner."

"But have you ever heard of anyone else with the skal of Gate Shaping?" Sara pressed. Neither Cahira nor any of the others had. They weren't even sure how much of the story was true. King Tana, Gate Shaper, had faded into folklore.

Still, a renewed sense of hope lightened Sara's steps to the tent that night. For the first time, she'd heard of someone who could move between different worlds. Maybe she was deluding herself, but it felt like progress.

FIFTEEN

Sara

Sara woke to a dim, foggy morning. She crawled from the tent, trying to make as little noise as possible. Cold, damp air struck at her as she emerged, raising goose bumps beneath her clothing. It didn't matter. She had an urgent need to be alone.

Tulley was already at the fire, his stocky silhouette unmistakable even in the thick mist. Thankfully, he was facing the other way. Sara crept behind the tent and tiptoed to the edge of the clearing. No one in sight. She picked her way into the trees, being careful not to step on any twigs that might snap and give her away. She had no destination in mind. She just needed time and space to think.

The optimism of last night had drained out of her, leaving queasiness in its wake. She wasn't a superhero; she wasn't even Lucy Pevensie in Narnia. She was just Sara Martin, the same person she'd always been. A good gardener, but otherwise ordinary. She'd never wanted to be more than that and she still didn't. Enough of this stupid world, its problems and its magic, its people who expected too much from her. It was none of her business. She didn't even belong here.

Logen's plan wasn't going to work. Supposing they reached the Blighted trees without getting caught, there was no way she'd be able to do what he wanted. She'd try, because she'd made a promise to herself, but she'd fail. She wasn't a Master Healer; the whole idea was ludicrous.

Hopefully, once Logen and the others realised she wasn't going to be any use to them, they'd let her leave. Mena and Rassil, too. But then what? She had nowhere to go.

Her stomach churned. She leaned against a tree, drawing a little comfort from the touch of the rough bark under her hands. She tipped her head back. A drop of water splashed onto her face, then another. High above, the broad trunk rose through layers of dripping foliage before disappearing into the dense whiteness. Sara's mind flashed back to another foggy morning, another forest.

She caught her breath. There was her answer: she'd ask Mena to take her back to the Blighted trees where Kelan had shot her. From there, she'd make her own way to the place this whole mess had started. She'd been following the sun that first morning. If she reversed her steps, with the rising sun at her back, she should be able to find the exact spot, the tree with the spiral carvings on the trunk. There must be a Gateway there, like the one Tana Lossil had made. It was the only explanation for how she'd come to Algarth. She'd keep looking until she found it.

The queasiness had receded. It was time to head back to the camp before anyone missed her.

As she stepped into the clearing, a shout rang out. "He's gone!"

Her head snapped around. It was Niall Crawley, over by the horses.

"Who's gone?" Tulley's deep voice bellowed back.

"Arrow! He's not here."

Arrow was Bram's chestnut gelding, the one who'd carried Rassil out of the city.

The noise had roused the others. Bram ran over to Niall at the picket line. "Can you sense him?"

"No, nothing. I'm sorry, Bram."

Bram stroked his beard. "I don't understand. He's never run away before."

"He didn't run away." Mena emerged from the tent. "Rassil's missing, too. She must have taken him."

"Rassil?" It was the last thing Sara would have expected from the timid girl. Ride off on her own, into a dark forest at night? "Why would she do that?"

107

"She's gone to betray us to the Blueshirts." Bitterness tainted Niall's voice. "I should have stayed awake. We had no reason to trust her. If I'd sensed Arrow leaving—"

"It's not your fault," Logen said. "Any one of us could have guarded the horses and prevented this. Blaming anyone is a waste of time we don't have. We have to decide what to do next. And we have to decide fast."

The whole group had gathered now. "Can we catch up to her before she reaches the Guards?" Sara asked.

"I'll chase her down," Adric said. He patted the bow already slung over his shoulder. Sara glared at him. Rassil was only a frightened child. The idea of shooting at her was barbaric.

But Niall was already shaking his head at Adric's offer. "It's too late. I can't sense Arrow at all. They must be far away."

"She probably headed straight back to the logging road," Logen said. "If she left soon after we went to bed, she'd have reached it hours ago. We'll never catch her before she makes it to the highway. She's gone."

"Does she know where we're headed?" Tulley growled.

Mena nodded, her lips pressed together in a grim line. "She was sitting next to me the whole time we were talking about it. She knows everything." Her voice was harsher than Sara had ever heard it.

They'd all made up their minds, but what evidence did they have of Rassil's intentions? Sara knew firsthand what it was like to be falsely accused and have everyone against you. "We don't know that she's gone to tell the Guards," she protested. "Maybe she just got scared and ran away."

Tulley snorted.

"Perhaps," Logen said, "but we can't take the chance. We have to assume the worst. The plan was only ever going to work if no one had any idea where we were going. We can't be sure of that now."

"So, what do we do?" Bram asked.

Silence greeted the question.

"We abandon the idea for now," Logen said at last. "And we head for the mountains, as fast as we can go."

They packed in silence and mounted up. With one horse down, they rearranged themselves. Bram rode Sage, and Adric boosted Sara up behind Logen on his big grey stallion, Ash.

The sun was burning through the fog as they made their way south through the forest. They hadn't been riding long when they came upon an area where the trees had all been felled. The timber cutters had constructed broad trails for their log carts, so the riders made better time than the day before. But the easy chatter and camaraderie were gone.

So much for Sara's plan to find the Gateway that would lead her home. With every step, they were getting further away from where she needed to be. But she had no choice. None of them did. Survival was all that mattered now.

As the morning wore on, the sun chased away the last remnants of fog and lit up the forest, but it couldn't brighten Sara's thoughts. Eventually, the trail they were following joined the main logging road, much further south than where they had crossed it yesterday.

Niall was in the lead. As they reached the intersection, he raised a hand, and then waved them all further back into the trees. "I've been sensing a horse. It's less than half a reach away and coming down the road towards us. There's only one."

They hid themselves among the trees as best they could, remaining mounted in case they needed to make a run for it. After a few tense minutes, Sara heard hoof-beats approaching. A pulse in her throat pounded in time with their rhythm.

A rider came in sight, on a loping grey horse. For a moment Sara thought he would pass them by, but as he drew level, he pulled up, gazing into the trees. The strong sunlight sparked red highlights from his hair as he appeared to stare directly at Sara. To her surprise, she recognised him.

At the same time, Mena let out an astonished cry. "Kelan! What are you doing here?" She slid from Briar's back and ran towards her son.

Logen urged Ash back onto the road. Kelan had dismounted and was submitting to being hugged by his mother, but when he saw Logen and Sara on Ash's back, he disentangled himself, pushed Mena behind him and drew out a sword. He waved it through the air in front of him. "Stay there!" His rusty fringe flopped over his forehead, and he shoved it back with his free hand. He looked determined but slightly ridiculous. "Where's Rassil? What have you done with her?"

Logen halted the horse. "Put your blade away, Kelan, and we'll explain everything. Rassil isn't with us. She left last night."

Confusion clouded Kelan's eyes. The sword wavered. "B-but she has to be here. I followed the promise charm right to you!"

"See for yourself," Logen said, motioning the others onto the road.

"It's true, Kelan," Mena said, coming out from behind him and laying a hand on his sword arm. "Rassil took a horse last night and left us. Put the sword away, before you cut yourself."

Kelan looked doubtful but obeyed his mother. He took something from his pocket and stared down at it, before stepping forward. Switching his attention between the riders and the object in his palm, he passed the horses, frowned, and then turned back. Finally, he stopped beside Ash. The big grey stallion swivelled his head curiously towards him, but at a word from Logen, stood steady as Kelan opened a saddlebag and drew out a small trinket on a chain.

"I don't understand," Kelan said, as if to himself. "Why is it here?" He tilted his face upwards, glowering at Logen. "Did you take it from her?"

"No, Kelan." Logen shook his head. "I never even saw it. If it's Rassil's, she must have put it into Ash's saddlebag before she left."

Mena sent her son a look of sympathy. "She didn't want you to follow her, Kelan." She squeezed his arm. "I'm sorry."

Kelan stood frozen for a moment, gazing down at the two charms in his hand. His hair had flopped forward again and his eyes were hidden, but Sara saw his jaw clench, before he lifted his head and shoved the charms roughly into his pocket. He glared up at the riders. "Will someone tell me what's going on?"

His voice was harsh, but a hint of moisture glinted in his green eyes. Behind his brave front, he was fighting tears. Mena gently tugged her son aside and began speaking to him in a low voice.

"What are we going to do with him?" Adric asked.

Logen frowned but didn't answer.

"Well, we'd better decide soon," the blond-bearded man burst out. "This has taken long enough already. I say we leave him here, and his mother, too. They'd be nothing but a liability in the mountains."

Fin shook a finger at him. "Shame on you, Adric. If the Guards find Mena, do you think they'll just let her go? They know she's been with us, and we have a responsibility to her. Besides," she finished firmly, "she's a Folk Healer and that might come in useful."

The big archer's heavy brows lowered in obstinance. "Maybe, but the boy's useless. He doesn't even have a skal yet."

"None of us are here because someone thought we were useful, Adric," Bram said in his slow, solemn way. "We each made our own decision to come. Kelan should be given the choice, too."

His brother snorted, but turned his horse away.

Mena and Kelan returned. The teenager was looking mutinous, but when Logen asked if he wanted to come with them, he nodded sulkily.

"Has your mother explained the danger we'll be in?" Logen asked.

"I've tried," Mena said, shooting her son an exasperated look. "But he won't go home without me."

Kelan raised his chin proudly. "I'm coming along to keep my mother safe, and no one's going to stop me."

"Touching as this reunion is," Niall drawled, "perhaps we could resume our desperate flight from the authorities now? I for one feel rather exposed, standing here on the road."

"Wait," Kelan said suddenly.

"What is it?" Logen asked.

Kelan's face flushed red. "It's just…my horse won't go very fast. It's old and stupid, but it was the only one I could find."

Adric threw up his hands and Tulley chuckled, but, to Sara's surprise, Niall dropped his facetious tone and spoke kindly to the embarrassed youth. "I may be able to do something about that." He paused for a moment. "There, I think you'll notice a difference now. He only needed a bit of encouragement. You should give him a name, too. It's important to bond with your horse."

"Sure," Kelan said, throwing the grey a dirty look. "I'll call him Lightning."

Now it was Niall's turn to chuckle. "Trust me, Kelan, he might just surprise you and live up to that name. He's not as old as he looks."

Kelan shrugged, unconvinced, but mounted up.

They set off down the logging road, quickly pushing the horses to a gallop. Niall had been right. 'Lightning' was keeping up with the rest, his short legs working hard as he gamely followed Niall's mare.

They rode for the rest of the morning, encountering no other travellers. In the early afternoon, Logen called for a break. They dismounted and led the tired horses to graze under the trees. Sara was thankful for the respite from the glaring sun.

Fin shared out bread and dried meat from the saddlebags. Sara's chunk of bread was stale but still edible and she tore at it hungrily, but the dry bread and tough salty meat made her thirsty.

Logen and Niall had been standing a little way off, talking together as they ate. Now they returned to the others. Logen passed a leather water bag to Sara. It felt light, less than half full, so she restricted herself to a few swallows before giving it back. After the simple meal, they mounted up and kept going, with Niall in the lead again and Logen and Sara bringing up the rear.

After the morning's exertions, they kept the horses to a walking pace. Sara sat tensely behind Logen, torn between utter thankfulness that her abused leg muscles were getting some relief and fear that they were going too slowly, giving their pursuers time to catch up with them.

It was late afternoon when they finally left the forest behind. The road narrowed, meandering along the floor of a spacious valley. Farmland stretched out to the hills on either side. To Sara, it all felt very exposed. As their surroundings changed, so did the weather. The sky clouded over and a cool breeze sprang up. The plodding horses pricked up their ears and stepped out with more energy.

Sara started to notice the occasional farm house or cottage, set back among the fields. They became more numerous, springing up closer to the road. Nervous that people might be watching from inside the houses, Sara peered around Logen's shoulder as they rounded the next bend, hoping to see a clear road ahead. Instead, even more buildings met her eyes. They'd reached the outskirts of a town.

What was Niall thinking, leading them here? Shouldn't they be avoiding population centres? She had no choice but to trust that Logen and Niall knew what they were doing, but an itch developed between her shoulder blades as the group made their way along the main street, flanked by tall timber buildings. Directly ahead, just beyond the last of these, the land rose steeply to rolling foothills, with glimpses of higher peaks behind.

At least there weren't many people on the street, and the few pedestrians didn't seem overly interested in the riders, merely glancing at them before continuing on their way. Perhaps they'd make it to the hills without any trouble.

Just as Sara was beginning to breathe more freely, Niall brought Sienna to a halt outside a dilapidated two-storey building. A wide verandah ran along the front, bordered by a hitching rail. This whole town was like a set from a cowboy movie, although Sara assumed there'd be no gunslingers here. Above her head, a faded sign creaked in the cold breeze, depicting a white bird standing on one leg. Below the illustration, wobbly lettering spelled out the name of the place: *The Lame Goose*.

At Niall's signal, they dismounted and tied the horses to the rail.

Logen gathered them together. "We're in the town of Fortune Creek. Niall and I have been here before. We're going to try to make contact with an old prospector called Garst. He knows the hills better than any man alive and if he's willing, he can lead us by ways the Guards will never find."

"Why not head into the hills as fast as we can?" Adric glanced around, his hand on his sword hilt. "I don't like the feel of this place. It's too quiet."

Logen shook his head. "I know it's a risk, but it's worth it if it means we can pick up a guide. We won't stay long. We'll get a hot meal while we have the chance and try to buy some provisions, but we'll leave at the first sign of trouble." He looked around at all of them. "Stay alert. Let Niall and me do the talking. Don't answer any questions about yourselves."

He crossed the veranda and pushed open the door. Sara and the others followed him inside.

The room was plainly furnished: half a dozen wooden tables, chairs, a brick fireplace in the middle of one wall and a counter along the far end. Most of the chairs were empty, but two men sat talking in a corner. Sara and the others settled themselves at a long table while Logen and Niall approached the counter.

Sara found herself seated next to Bram. She hadn't really spoken to the big fair-haired man before, but she'd already realised he was much gentler and calmer than his brother. He seemed to have taken the loss of Arrow hard, and Sara felt a strange desire to cheer him up. Maybe it would help her forget her own fears for a while.

"How long have you all known each other?" she asked, gesturing around the table.

Bram's eyebrows lifted slightly as if in surprise at Sara addressing him, but he answered readily enough. "Adric and I grew up with Cahira, on her parents' estate. Our father is Land Steward there, and our mother worked with him. She was a Greenhaelan." He paused, gazing down at his hands, and Sara wondered if he was going to continue. Then he sighed and gave her a sad smile. "She died four years ago. When my skal came in and I found out I was a Greenhaelan, too, I started travelling around the district, wherever I was needed. Cahira and I were married by then, so she came with me, singing in the towns."

He shook his shaggy head, brown eyes distant. "We were so happy. I had never imagined I could be so happy."

"And then?" Sara prompted.

"When the trouble started, we came home. Cahira's parents hid me

114

for almost two years. But a lot of people knew about my skal, and word leaked out in the end. Adric got me away." He smiled fondly across the table, where his brother was having a subdued but apparently heated discussion with Tulley.

"It must have been a terrible time," Sara said.

Bram nodded. "I wanted Cahira to go back to her parents, but she wouldn't. She said being married meant staying together no matter what." He gazed further down the table to where Cahira was talking to Mena. "She can be very determined, you know." He sounded proud of the fact.

"Where did you go then?" Sara wasn't sure this was the way to cheer him up, but she was interested in the story now and wanted to hear the rest.

"East, to the forest. We lived by hunting. And then, about a month ago, we came across the others. Cahira and Niall knew each other as children, and Fin is an old friend of my mother, so we knew we could trust them. And none of our family ever believed Logen was guilty, anyway. We've been together ever since, trying to stay one step ahead of the Guards." He fell silent again, his expression glum.

Sara cast about for a less depressing topic. "What skal does Adric have?"

"He has some Strength, but his main skal is Swiftness. I have a small amount of it, too. It means we're both good shots with a bow, but after we met Tulley, he started training us to fight with swords as well, to be ready if we ever needed to." He stroked his bushy blond beard, his eyes far away again. "Adric loved it. Before all this happened, he wanted to be a Guard." He paused, and added in a voice so low that Sara had to strain to make out the words, "But I hope I don't ever have to kill anyone."

His face had fallen again, so Sara asked something she'd been wondering about since she met the brothers. "Are you and Adric twins?"

"Yes, but not identical. Our family and friends could always tell us apart."

Sara realised she could tell them apart, too. She'd known from the start that she was sitting with Bram, rather than Adric. How? She examined him closely, comparing his features to his twin across the table. "Your hair and beard are lighter."

"Yes, and Adric's temper is quicker." He smiled at that, and Sara smiled back, deciding she liked Bram. He was just a kind, ordinary man who didn't deserve what had happened to him. None of them did. She was sure of it now. And they had risked entering Eorna, just to rescue her.

Logen and Niall returned from the bar, carrying mugs of dark ale for everyone.

"The meal's coming," Logen said. "And we're in luck. The bar keeper said Garst came into town yesterday. He sent a message for us."

Sara had never cared for beer, but she was thirsty enough by now to drink anything. She sniffed dubiously, steeled herself, and took a swallow. She blinked, drew in another portion, rolled it around her mouth. The flavour was a revelation, more like food than drink. Christmas cake, she decided, and yeast, and honey, all tinged with the slight, pleasant bitterness of molasses. She wrapped both hands around the pewter mug and leaned back with a happy sigh. Whoever had invented this stuff was a genius.

While they waited for the meal to arrive, Sara and Bram continued their conversation between sips of ale. He asked her about herself and seemed genuinely interested in her answers. But something else was niggling at her.

"Bram, what was that piece of paper you threw into my room back in Eorna? And how did you know I was there, anyway?"

Adric heard the question and grinned. "The fake rescue plan? That was Logen's idea. When Kelan went after Rassil, Niall followed him, right to where you were being held. Kelan told one of the Guards all about us, and Niall overheard that, too. So Logen drew a map that showed we were going to attack the carriage halfway along the route to the Council building, and Bram threw it into your room for the Guards to find. The idea was to draw most of them away to the spot marked on the map. It worked, too. There were only a few around the carriage when we ambushed it."

"Kelan betrayed you to the Guards?" Sara's heart sank. What if the outlaws wanted to take some sort of revenge?

But Bram was shaking his head. "I don't see it like that. Kelan had no reason to trust us. He was just doing what he thought was right. That's all any of us can do."

The meal came then: succulent slices of steaming pink meat flooded with dark gravy, golden-brown roasted vegetables, fresh crusty bread with yellow butter. It all smelt amazing, and tasted even better. Sara almost swooned at the first mouthful. With ale and food this good, the Lame Goose should be full of customers.

The two men in the corner had left a few minutes before, and the bar keeper was nowhere in sight. The ten of them were alone in the room. Despite the fire burning in the hearth, Sara felt a sudden chill. She stopped eating, her loaded fork halfway to her mouth.

"Look out!" Tulley's chair crashed backwards as he bellowed the warning.

Everyone leapt to their feet. Swords scraped as the men spun outward. The tramp of booted feet sent Sara whirling to face the open doorway. Blue-shirted men poured into the room, swords drawn. More boots were coming from behind. Sara's head twisted to see two Guards vault over the counter.

She dropped to all fours and crawled under the table. Mena and Fin were already there. Mena must have dragged Kelan down with her — he was struggling to break her hold on his arm. "Let me go," he rasped, but Mena's grip must have been like iron. After a few seconds, he subsided.

Sara peered out between a chair and a pair of brown-clad legs. The Guards were lined up several metres away, facing the defenders. There were at least eight, maybe more. Their swords were in their hands, and they were blocking the way to the door.

Sara's heart drummed a rapid tattoo through her whole body. Her throat closed up until she could barely breathe.

For a few moments, no one moved. Then a deep voice spoke. "Logen Rush, you are under arrest. Surrender and the women won't be harmed."

"That's a lie," Fin whispered. "They execute Greenhaelen women as well as men."

Sara clenched her fists and concentrated on making herself breathe.

Before Logen could reply, a humming noise arose from somewhere out of Sara's view, building quickly to a buzzing, discordant melody that pressed on her eardrums as if the atmosphere of the room had thickened. A second voice joined in, twisting through the first, a kind of shrieking whine that slithered up her spine and raised the hairs on her neck. She shuddered and clapped her hands to her ears. It must be Cahira. What was the Skalsinger doing?

She soon found out. As the disturbing sound swelled, one of the Guards began mumbling. He shook his head as if he was trying to clear water out of his ears. A moment later, he froze, and then jerked his head upwards. His face twisted. A shout burst from him as he lurched backwards, raising his sword and slashing at something above his head, out of Sara's sight. One by one, his companions did the same.

Sara had to see what was happening. She shuffled forward, craning her neck out from under the table. A swarm of ghostly figures, with vicious, demonic faces, was swooping down at the line of Guards, clawed hands outstretched as if to tear out their eyes. Her flesh crept, even as she told herself they weren't real. This was a whole other side to Cahira's gift, and Sara didn't like it at all, even if it was working in their favour for now.

Only one of the Guards wasn't fooled. "Stand firm!" he bellowed. "It's a trick!"

The others ignored him, yelling in fear and anger as they slashed at their imaginary attackers.

The outlaws took their opportunity, charging the distracted Guards. Sara shrank back under the table. Cries of pain and the clash of metal warred with the shouting of the Blueshirts and the spine-chilling music still spilling from Cahira.

Sara had never been so terrified. In all the noise and confusion there was no way to tell who was winning. She stifled a scream as a Guard reached the table, only to topple right in front of her. Contorted in an agonised grimace, his face lay centimetres from hers. Blood soaked through his shirt, turning his yellow badge red.

She let out a sob and closed her eyes, but that didn't stop the sounds. Her eyelids flew open as someone shoved past her. Kelan was crawling out from under the table.

"No!" Mena cried, reaching desperately for him.

Kelan evaded her grasp and stood up. He managed two steps, then stumbled and fell headlong. Mena screamed. A cry of horror escaped Sara's throat. Cahira's song cut off.

In the sudden absence of that hair-raising sound, two Guards closed in on the table. A figure flashed into view between them and Sara. He straddled Kelan, roaring and swinging his sword to keep the attackers away from the fallen boy. From this angle, she could only see him from the shoulders down. Green and brown camouflage. Logen, or one of the twins. In the middle of a swing, his sword arm dropped, the weapon clattering to the floor. He staggered backwards, collided hard with the edge of the table, and slid down until he was seated on the floor, his broad back blocking her view. Blond hair, matted with blood. Adric, or Bram. Sara swallowed a hiccupping sob. Was he dead? Was Kelan? Cahira?

The sounds of fighting died away. Only the cries and moans of the injured punctuated the silence.

Without warning, a head appeared under the table. Sara bit back a scream before she recognised Logen.

"It's safe to come out," he said, offering her a hand. She was shaking almost too much to take it. He pulled her up to her feet.

Not one Blueshirt was standing. Two sat in a corner with Tulley's sword pointed at them. He had a bloody cut across one forearm but seemed otherwise unhurt. The other Guards lay on the floor. Some were twitching and groaning, but a few lay still. Sara's eyes slid away from them. If they were dead, she didn't want to know.

Mena knelt beside Kelan, who slowly sat up, looking dazed. "Thank Aal, you're alive!" she said and burst into tears.

Niall and Adric were on their feet, sheathing their swords.

So, Bram was the one who had fallen in front of Sara, protecting Kelan. She turned to him. He sat unmoving, with his shaggy head

119

drooped forward over his chest. Below it, blood darkened his tunic. Tears filled Sara's eyes as Adric crouched in front of his brother.

"Bram?" he asked blankly, as if he couldn't believe what he was seeing.

No answer. Adric tenderly lifted his twin's head. Bram's eyes were closed, and Sara couldn't tell if he was breathing. Like a child pleading for help, Adric peered up at them, his eyes like dark holes in his white, desolate face.

Mena knelt beside him. "Let me see," she ordered. She laid a hand on Bram's forehead. She was very still for a moment. She sighed and turned wet eyes on Adric. "I'm so sorry. There's nothing I can do. He's gone."

The tears spilled down Sara's cheeks. It couldn't be true; it was too horrible. Bram couldn't be dead. Big, gentle Bram, who had hoped he wouldn't ever have to kill anyone, who had only wanted a life of peace, caring for plants and loving his wife.

Sara's heart jolted. Where was Cahira? She scanned the room, dreading what she might see. The Skalsinger was slumped in a corner with Niall bending over her. A pit opened in Sara's stomach, but then Cahira raised her head. Niall helped her to her feet and led her to Bram.

When she reached him, the sound that came from her made the hair on the back of Sara's neck stand up all over again. It was an animal howl of pure anguish. Cahira threw herself across her husband's body, still keening in that terrible voice. The air above them shimmered and turned a murky grey. Something started to take shape in the centre, and Sara felt a chill of fear, although she didn't know why.

"Hush, hush, sweetheart," Fin crooned, stroking Cahira's hair. Cahira quietened, and the grey cloud dissipated.

Tulley raised his voice from across the room. "We need to go, Logen. Someone betrayed us to them. More might be coming. This place isn't safe."

Adric had been crouching with his shoulders bowed. At Tulley's words, he lifted his head. Hatred blazed in his eyes. Springing to his feet, he drew his sword and started across the floor towards Tulley and the prisoners.

"Adric, no," shouted Logen. He and Niall leapt forward and grabbed the enraged man, but he shook them off as if they were children. When he reached Tulley, the Metal Shaper threw his brawny arms tightly around him, pinning his sword arm. Adric struggled and swore, but he couldn't break the older man's hold. Finally, he dropped the sword. Logen picked it up and used it to cover the two men still cowering in the corner.

Tulley released Adric, who whirled on Logen with a snarl. "Let me kill them!"

"No," Logen repeated. He stood toe to toe with his furious friend. Compassion etched his face but his voice was hard as granite. "We swore an oath. We fight only in self-defence."

"They killed Bram!"

"I know," Logen said. "But we will not become the murderers they believe us to be. We won't turn lies into truth."

Adric growled again, but turned and stalked away.

The eyes of the two prisoners stared up at Logen from faces as pale as paper. Their beardless chins trembled below bloodless lips. For the first time, Sara realised that they were both very young, probably not much older than Kelan. Bram's words came back to her: "He was just doing what he thought was right. That's all any of us can do." These young Guards had only been doing what they thought was right, too, helping to arrest a group of dangerous outlaws. And Bram would have been the last person to wish them dead because of it. Logen had made the right decision. Sara hoped Adric would understand that one day.

"Find something to tie them up," Logen told Tulley. "Mena, would you check on the others, please?"

Niall and Kelan took up watch at the doors as Mena went quickly from Guard to Guard. Sara counted: there were ten altogether. Two were badly wounded and unconscious, but Mena assured Logen they would survive, as long as they obtained help soon. Tulley found some rope in a back room and tied up the other eight, whose injuries were comparatively minor. They seemed dazed more than hurt. Then the subdued company gathered around Bram.

Logen laid a hand on his friend's shoulder and bowed his head. Cahira was weeping. Fin urged her to her feet and supported her as they all trailed outside after Logen.

Sara was afraid there might be another group of Guards waiting for them, but the street was deserted. The weather had shifted while they'd been inside the tavern. The cloud cover had thickened, and a blustery, biting wind picked up the dust and tossed it around in little flurries.

The horses stamped uneasily. Sara mounted Sage, trying not to think of Bram riding the mare just a few hours ago. But she couldn't prevent the sobs that shook her as they galloped the length of the street and out of Fortune Creek.

The plan was in tatters. They had no guide and hardly any food and water left. More Guards would be coming with orders to capture or kill them. They were heading further away from where they needed to be. Worst of all, Bram was dead. What hope was left for them? But with hope or without it, they had no choice but to keep going. Despite Sage's warm body beneath her, Sara shivered in the chill wind. Charcoal clouds pressed down on her. The light was almost gone.

The first peal of thunder rumbled around them as they pounded over a wooden bridge, and then headed up a narrow track into the foothills, desperate to put some distance behind them before nightfall.

SIXTEEN

Sara

They rode until darkness and driving rain forced a halt, and then made a rough camp in the lee of a tangle of tall shrubs. Too tired to even think about food, they unsaddled the horses, set out pots to collect rainwater, and settled down as best they could to get some sleep.

It was still raining the next morning when they packed up and headed off again. For the next two days, they plodded through the soggy hills while water fell in sheets from a steel-grey sky. The mood of the company mirrored the miserable weather.

Bram's death had hit all of them hard, but especially Adric and Cahira. Adric took refuge in anger. He desperately wanted revenge for his brother's death and was furious that Logen didn't want it, too. He alternately stormed and sulked, until no one knew what to say to him.

Cahira reacted differently. The bright, confident young woman, whom Sara had just begun to know, had disappeared completely. In her place was a pale wraith, who barely seemed to have the strength to stay on her horse. She hardly spoke. Niall rode as close to her as the terrain allowed, shooting frequent glances at her from the corner of his eye.

On the second night of this, sheltering in the back of a cave, they gathered close around the tiny campfire that was all they'd allowed themselves. Even this small fire could be dangerous — the glow might be seen by the searchers who must already be in the hills — but they were all soaked through and chilled to the bone. They craved warmth and light and agreed it was worth the risk.

Fin shared out the last scraps of the salty, dried meat. The rest of the food was already gone. After the meagre supper, Logen spoke soberly to them. "It's time we made some decisions. We've been lucky to evade capture so far, partly thanks to the rain, but that could change at any time. Renn's men aren't going to give up looking for us. Without a guide, it's going to take a miracle to get Sara safely through these hills and into the Blighted area. Even so, I still plan to try, if she's willing."

Sara nodded, too weary to speak, and he continued. "But the rest of you should think about going home or finding somewhere safer to hide." He gazed around the circle of tired faces. "I can't tell you how grateful I am for every single one of you, and for everything you've done, but I won't put you in any more danger than I have already."

No one answered him. After the silence had drawn out for an uncomfortably long time, Logen turned to Adric. "My friend, you and Cahira only came with us in the first place because of Bram. There's no reason for the two of you to stay."

At the mention of his brother, Adric's expression grew dark and thunderous. Logen held up a hand. "Please, Adric." He lowered his voice. "Cahira can't keep doing this, it's hurting her too much. She needs to be with her parents. They can hide you both, better than I can."

Sara looked towards Cahira. She had bowed her head, and her whole body was shuddering - with cold or grief, or maybe both. Logen was right. Adric seemed to see it, too. His face softened. "All right," he said gruffly. "I'll take her home. For Bram's sake."

"Cahira?" Logen asked. "Will you go with Adric?" A curtain of wet hair hid her face, but she nodded, once.

"I think I'd better go, too," Niall said suddenly. "There could be more Blueshirts between here and Edervale. Adric fights like two men, but still, another sword might come in handy."

"And your skal may be just as useful," Logen said, smiling at the black-clad man. "We couldn't have succeeded in Eorna without it."

Niall shrugged off the compliment as if it made him uncomfortable. "As soon as Cahira's safe, I'll come and find you again," he said to Logen. "I told you I'd help clear your name, and I intend to keep my word." He twirled his hand with an elaborate flourish and put on an exaggeratedly noble voice. "The honour of the Crawleys, you know."

There was a bitter, self-mocking flavour to his play-acting that raised Sara's curiosity, but Logen simply nodded and turned to Mena. "I'm sorry you and Kelan got caught up in this. I think you should both leave, too."

Mena shook her head. "It was my brother-in-law who reported Sara to the authorities. Now that I'm an outlaw too, he won't take me back. My only chance of ever going home is for you to cure the Blight and clear all our names. Besides, I won't abandon Sara now."

Sara was immensely grateful for this. She didn't even want to think about going on without Mena.

"Of course you're welcome to stay, if you're sure," Logen replied. "And I won't deny that we might need a Folk Healer on this journey. But at least Kelan should go. He's only a boy. Surely his uncle won't blame him for any of this?"

"I don't care if he does or he doesn't," Kelan broke in loudly, "I'm not going anywhere."

"Kelan," Mena began.

He didn't let her finish. "Bram gave his life to save me! You can't expect me to just forget about that and run home, like a-a *mouse*." He flicked his eyes towards Niall, and then turned to Logen. "I have to pay my debt, help you do what he wanted. I'm not a Greenhaelan, or a Healer, but I'm a good tracker and hunter. You could use me."

Mena tried again. "Please, son—"

"No, Mother. I'm not a child any more. I'm nineteen years old and I've made my decision." His jaw jutted out with determination. "It's a matter of *principle*."

He infused so much portentous solemnity into the final word that Sara felt a sudden, awful urge to giggle. But he would never forgive her if she did. Besides, she scolded herself, he was being completely sincere and didn't deserve to be laughed at. She pressed her lips together, resisting the urge even to smile.

Fin and Tulley also insisted on staying, as Sara had guessed they would.

Now that each of them had made their decision, the talk died down. The die was cast: in the morning, three of the company would be turning back and six would be going on.

They rode for four days through intermittent showers and increasing periods of sunshine. They were still one horse short. Sara was back on Sage, while Mena took turns riding behind Logen on Ash, and Tulley, on his big gelding, Brick.

Logen was trying to reach a town on the far eastern edge of the foothills, a place called Deep Lake, hoping to find a safe way north from there into the Blighted area. They couldn't risk following the marked trails, so they picked their way around the hills as best they could, using the cover of shrubby bushes and small stands of trees.

They discovered that Kelan always seemed to know what direction they were facing, even when the sun was completely hidden. He also had the keenest hearing, signalling to the others to get under cover long before anyone else heard a thing. Three times now, he had saved them from riding straight into a group of Guards. After the first of these near misses, Logen had put him in the lead.

The teenager had been right when he'd claimed his skills could be useful to them, and Sara was glad she'd resisted the temptation to laugh at him. But it was very slow going, slogging their way over this crumpled landscape, repeatedly doubling back to avoid the Guards. Sara was constantly tense, always anticipating the shout that would mean they'd been found or the sudden agony of an arrow in her back.

Little streams, swollen by the rain, ran everywhere through the hills, slowing them even further, but also providing an abundance of drinking water. There was plenty of grass for the horses, too. But there hadn't been much for the humans to eat.

In this too, Kelan had turned out to be the most useful of them. Adric had unexpectedly gifted him with Bram's bow, and he'd shot several rabbits. Mena had also recognised a plant with starchy roots that grew here and there along the streams. But they couldn't afford to sacrifice too much time hunting for food. They weren't starving, but they were hungry most of the time.

They took turns standing guard at night. Last night it had been Sara's turn for the first watch. To her shame and horror, she had fallen deeply asleep, to be woken hours later by Logen, coming to relieve her. The others seemed just as exhausted, all except Tulley, who appeared impervious to everything: rain, hunger, anxiety and tiredness. He was taking double shifts at night, but even he wouldn't be able to keep it up forever.

Sara was beginning to wonder how long they could go on like this, even if they weren't caught by the Guards.

SEVENTEEN

Sara

On a dull, grey afternoon, Kelan was leading them through a narrow clearing in the centre of a large stand of trees. Although autumn had barely begun, many of the leaves had already fallen, clothing the ground with a colourful tapestry that lifted Sara's flagging spirits. The horses moved almost soundlessly, their hoof-beats muffled by the leaf litter. Ahead, Sara could see Kelan's head nodding towards his chest as he rode. She was half asleep herself.

The sun broke through the clouds, and light speared through the threadbare canopy. A warm breeze blew up. Sage tossed her head and snorted, startling Sara into wakefulness. Kelan jerked upright and flung up a hand. They halted.

At that moment, while they were all strung out in a line, blue-shirted figures stepped out from behind the trees. "Hands in the air! Don't move or we'll shoot!"

At least twenty Guards surrounded them, with bows drawn. Sara raised her hands and the others did the same. It was over. They were caught.

The Sergeant of the Guards wasn't taking any chances with his prisoners. First, he barked at them to dismount. When they were safely on the ground, he ordered some of his men to keep arrows pointed at their targets, and the others to disarm the captives and bind their wrists behind their backs.

Waiting her turn, Sara laid a trembling hand on Sage's flank and wished desperately that Niall was still with them. The Beast Speaker could have set the horses against the Guards, as he had in Eorna. In the confusion, at least some of the group might have had a chance to escape. But Niall was gone.

A young Guard with a nasty grin on his face gripped Sara's shoulders, spun her around, and jerked her arms behind her. There was nothing she could do. The rough rope scratched her skin, and she winced in anticipation of the Guard pulling it tight. Instead, shouts of alarm went up all around her.

A Blueshirt dashed past, yelling and slapping at himself. Another followed, doing the same. Sara risked turning her head. Her own Guard had vanished. The length of rope lay abandoned on the ground. What was going on?

The Sergeant bellowed, but his men weren't listening to him. They were on the move, racing in different directions, in and out of the trees, shouting and waving their arms.

Spooked by the frenzy around her, Sage whinnied in fear and wheeled around. Sara threw herself out of the way, only just escaping being trampled as the mare galloped off.

Sara found herself prone on the ground, bruised and shaking. As she pushed up onto her hands and knees, swinging her head around for more signs of danger, a low drone met her ears. It was familiar, but she couldn't think what it was until a Guard tripped and fell headlong in front of her. Dozens of huge yellow and black wasps dove at the fallen man, buzzing fiercely. Red welts blotched the Guard's exposed neck and the backs of his hands where stings had already found their targets.

Sara scrambled to her feet, back-pedalling and waving her arms, but none of the insects came near her. The moaning Guard lurched to his feet and shambled off, followed by the angry wasps.

All five of Sara's companions stood huddled together near the centre of the clearing, apparently unharmed, as the wasps pursued the few remaining Guards. She staggered over to join them, her legs like jelly. Reaching Logen, she stumbled and almost fell. He steadied her with his arm, and together they watched the incredible scene around them.

The last of the tormented Guards disappeared from sight. The wasps were gone, too. The clearing was suddenly, blessedly, quiet. They were free. But their mounts were gone — the other horses had bolted like Sage.

It was Tulley who broke the stunned silence. After the insanity Sara had just witnessed, his flat, gruff tone proved incredibly comforting. "Well, that was a sight to see, and no mistake."

"Why didn't the wasps attack any of us?" Kelan asked. He sounded none the worse for the adventure, although the whites were showing around the edges of his eyes.

"Maybe they don't like blue," Tulley said. He was joking, but it was true that none of them happened to be wearing blue today.

"It was Aal," Fin said, tapping her husband's arm in rebuke. "He used his creatures to protect us." Her voice rang with certainty, but her words made Sara uncomfortable. If Fin's god had chosen to save them from these Guards, why had he let Bram die in Fortune Creek?

Logen might have been feeling something similar, because he spoke up briskly. "The question is, what do we do now?"

No one answered. They were already exhausted, and their food was gone. Without horses, they had even less chance of making it the rest of the way through the hills.

At that moment, a new sound arose, coming from the direction the Guards had fled. What now? The men drew their swords and turned to face it. At first all Sara could hear was a meaningless jumble of noise, but as it drew closer, she realised it was the voice of a man, singing.

The words of the song began to resolve themselves just as the singer came in sight. An old man, riding a mule, singing at the top of his voice about a tavern where the ale was so good, even the angels came down to have a taste. He made his way through the trees towards them, until he was only a few metres away. Then he suddenly seemed to notice he had an audience. He pulled up, breaking off his song. He swung a leg over the mule's neck and slid to the ground, showing no dismay at the three swords levelled at him.

His teeth flashed white through his wiry grey beard as he smiled and stuck out a hand like wrinkled brown leather. "Logen Rush, glad to see you."

The point of Logen's sword didn't waver. "Don't step any closer, Garst. I have some questions for you and you're going to answer them."

"Of course, son," the old man nodded. Light blue eyes under brows like hairy grey caterpillars flicked over the group and came to rest on Sara. She held his gaze and stared back.

He was a small man, no taller than Tulley, but with none of Tulley's solid bulk. He was slight, almost scrawny, although the ropey muscles in his forearms argued that age hadn't sapped all his strength. He was dressed in a leather vest over a dirty brown shirt, and even dirtier trousers. His hat fascinated her. It was crumpled and stained, and the brim had more ups and downs than the hills they had been riding through. It looked as though it had been trampled by the mule and then buried in a compost heap.

The newcomer turned his eyes back to Logen. "Made some new friends, I see."

The high, cracked voice suggested frailty, but Sara hadn't forgotten the robust sound of his singing. Logen must have been thinking the same thing.

"Don't try that 'weak old man' act with me, Garst, I know better. Someone betrayed us in Fortune Creek. Was it you?"

Garst shook his head. "Not me, son. By the time I got to the Goose, you were gone."

"Who, then?"

"A stranger, travelling through." He had shed the 'weak old man act', as Logen had called it; his voice held no trace of a tremor now. A hard note entered it. "Shoulda kept travelling, curse him. He recognised you in the tavern, ran off to tattle to the Blueshirts." He took a step forward. "No soul from Fortune Creek woulda told them a thing, son, least of all me."

Logen stared at him for a moment, as if judging his sincerity, then slowly sheathed his sword and gestured for Kelan and Tulley to do the same. "So, how did you find us?"

"Well, now that's a funny story. Lucky and me been chasing our tails through these hills for days, dodging Blueshirts, trying to pick up your trail. Then today we see the strangest thing." His wrinkled face twisted into a grin. "It seems some o' them Blueshirts decided to go swimming in the creek. In their uniforms, too, making a racket fit to raise the dead. Me and Lucky followed their tracks. And here you are."

"It was wasps," Kelan said. "I suppose they jumped into the water to get rid of them. The wasps left us alone, though."

"Wasps, eh?" said Garst, scratching vigorously under his beard. "Chancy creatures, wasps. Only Aal knows who they'll take against. Well, we better get moving."

"*We?*" Logen asked. "I don't remember inviting you to join us."

"Course you did, son. Back at Fortune Creek. You wanted a guide, didn't you?" He scratched his chin again. "A little late, maybe, but better than never, eh?"

"That remains to be seen," Logen said. "And things have changed. Back then, we had horses."

"Don't fret yourself, son. Too hard for horses anyway, the way I'm taking you. Too hard for Blueshirts to track, too."

He turned to the mule and cupped his hands around her face, gazing into her big, liquid eyes. The animal wasn't wearing a bridle or even a rope headstall. Sara's gaze travelled along the mule's sturdy brown body. No saddle or stirrups, not even a rug on her broad back.

"Home, Lucky," Garst said, affectionately. "Go home, girl." The mule nuzzled him, knocking his hat off in her enthusiasm. Then she swung around and trotted off between the trees.

Garst bent and picked up the hat. He slapped it against his leg a few times to get rid of the dust, although Sara wondered why he bothered. He jammed the disreputable object back onto his head and rubbed his hands together. "Well, that's that. Long way to go before sunset. Come on." He strode off without looking back.

"Do you trust him?" Tulley asked.

"Not completely," Logen said. "But I think we have to take the chance. If anyone can guide us through these hills safely, he can. He's an old man and he's unarmed. There are six of us and three swords, not to mention Kelan's bow. We'll keep an eye on him in case he tries anything."

EIGHTEEN

Sara

Over the next few days, the prospector proved to be as good as his word, but the journey through the hills on foot wasn't easy. The agile old man led them scrambling over boulders and squeezing through rock crevices that looked too small to admit a child. They splashed across shallow streams and crawled along dim tunnels of tangled briar.

Sara soon found it was all she could do to keep putting one foot in front of the other. Garst himself was tireless, not only vigorously leading the way, but also disappearing at the end of each day's effort to gather food for them all. He seemed to have a knack for finding nuts, fruit and berries. Kelan hadn't come across any more rabbits or other game to shoot, so Garst's finds were very welcome.

The nights were cold, but the rainclouds had blown away and the sun beat down on them whenever they were out in the open. Sara panted along, hot, filthy, and bleeding from numerous scratches, thoughts of Sage playing on her mind. She had bonded quickly with the quiet bay mare who had carried her so willingly from the start, and it felt wrong to have abandoned her and the other mounts somewhere in the woods. But Garst had been right that the horses couldn't have made it through this terrain. It seemed he'd also told the truth about being the only one who knew these ways through the hills. So far, even Kelan's sharp ears hadn't detected any sound of pursuit.

On the fourth afternoon, Sara was trudging along a winding track hemmed in by enormous boulders, almost asleep on her feet. She negotiated another bend and abruptly emerged onto a small, windblown plateau above a narrow valley. Her companions had gathered in a little group not far from the edge. She pushed her aching legs into one final effort and joined them.

Only a few metres ahead, the land plunged away, down a stone-covered slope. Far below, a cluster of ramshackle buildings hugged the shore of a body of intense blue water. Sara closed her eyes for a moment, savouring the cool caress of the breeze on her sweltering face.

"Deep Lake," said Garst. "Told you I'd bring you through safely."

"We're not there yet," Logen said, "and we can't risk going down in daylight. We'll try tonight."

Sara opened her eyes again. "How far are we from the edge of the Blight?" She couldn't detect any sign of it in the lush, green valley.

"About fifteen reaches," Logen said.

Sara's heart sank. At least four hours on foot, and considering how tired they all were, probably nearer six. It was impossible. She couldn't do it.

Logen smiled at the expression on her face. "Don't worry, I'm not planning on walking. Look." He pointed. "See the river running north from the lake?" Sara nodded. "That's the Tal. It flows all the way through the Blighted area and on to the coast. All we have to do is get to the water and borrow a couple of boats."

"Borrow?" Fin raised her eyebrows. "Are we going to take them back when we've finished with them, Logen dear?"

Logen grinned back at her but didn't answer. In the glaring sunlight, Fin's normally pink cheeks were almost grey, the soft wrinkles carved deeper than usual. She looked even more exhausted than Sara felt, if that was possible. And yet she hadn't complained once since this whole thing started. She displayed a quiet strength that Sara admired more each day.

Kelan spoke. "It's only two days to the dark of the moon, so it's a good night to try for the boats. Will they be guarded?"

"I've visited Deep Lake before," Logen said, "and I never saw anyone guarding a boat. It's a small town. The people trust each other. As long as we don't make too much noise, we should be fine."

"What if there are Blueshirts down there waiting for us?" Mena asked.

Logen pursed his lips. "It's a risk coming out into the open anywhere, but we have to get to the Blight somehow. I'm hoping they'll be guarding the roads and won't think of the Lake."

"What you need is a diversion," Garst said, tipping his disgusting hat back and scratching his head. "Don't fret yourselves, I'll make sure they're too busy to notice any of you."

"But what if they catch you?" Sara asked. She'd grown fond of their little old guide and didn't like the idea of anything bad happening to him.

Garst tapped a finger against the side of his nose and closed one clear blue eye. "No need to fuss about me, daughter. Never been caught yet and don't intend to start now. I'll be in and out of the place before they know a blessed thing about it." He jammed the hat back down on his forehead. "And then it's home for me. Lucky will be wondering where I've got to."

Logen glanced around the circle, but no one seemed to have anything more to say. He nodded. "It's decided, then. Get some rest. We leave in the darkest part of the night."

The wind had risen while they'd been talking, whipping up the dust, and they retreated back to the shelter of the boulders. Small stones littered the hard ground, but no amount of discomfort could have stopped Sara from dropping off to sleep.

I hope someone's on watch. The brief thought floated through her mind, before slipping away into the depths. Her eyelids closed.

She woke to darkness and a large stone pressing into the centre of her back. She winced and sat up with a groan, rubbing the sore spot. The world was etched in black and grey. At the feet of the dark masses of the boulders she could just make out the prone bodies of the others, still sleeping. No one seemed to be on guard.

She got up, wrapping her cloak tightly around herself, and then made her way to the top of the slope. Below her, yellow light spilled from the windows of the town, creating a warm, homely glow around the settlement. She couldn't detect any movement. Even so, she backed away from the edge, unsure if her silhouette would be visible to an observer looking up, but not wanting to take the chance.

The black bowl of the sky hung over the valley, sprayed with glittering silver stars, distant and cold. She shivered despite the cloak. It was cold down here, too. As she turned away, something caught her eye, a deeper patch of shadow to her right. She didn't remember any large rocks this close to the edge. She stared, trying to make it out. The mass suddenly resolved itself into a seated figure, topped by an unmistakable hat: Garst. He sat, unmoving as a statue, facing outward as if gazing across the valley.

The appearance of a companion when she'd thought she was alone was unsettling, to say the least. When her heart rate had returned to normal, she cleared her throat. "How long was I asleep?"

The old man shook himself like a dog coming up out of the water. She wondered if he'd been dozing, but his voice was as lively as always. "About five hours, I reckon, and you could have a bit more if you want. You won't be heading off for a while yet."

Deciding she wanted company more than sleep right now, Sara fetched her blanket and sat down beside him. The truth was, she was scared stiff about the prospect of leaving the shelter of the hills and deliberately entering a town. The last time they'd done that, Bram had died. After everything they'd all gone through together, she couldn't bear the thought of losing anyone else.

"A nip of frost in the air tonight," Garst said casually.

"Yes."

"Another fine day on the way."

In a few hours, someone might be dead, and the old man was talking about the weather. But perhaps he was right; there was no point dwelling on things she couldn't change. She cast around in her mind for something else to say and came up with a question. "Garst, are you a Beast Speaker?"

Garst laughed. "No, daughter, not me."

"But your mule understood you when you told her to go home."

"Ah, well, me and Lucky, we been together a good long time. Gotten to understand each other pretty well, I'd say. No need to be Beast Speaker for that."

Sara wanted to ask something else, but wasn't sure if it was polite. She was still learning the customs of this world. Garst seemed to sense her thought. "And now you're wondering what skal I do have." He leaned close, as if about to impart a secret. "Well," he whispered, "I don't have none at all." He straightened up and let out a bark of amusement. "Ha! Surprised you, haven't I?" He shook his head. "Never had any, and never felt the lack of any, neither. I do what I have to do, and I do what I want to do. What would I be needing with a skal?"

Della, back on the farm, had said that some people never developed a skal. The conversation seemed like a lifetime ago, so much had changed since then. For one thing, Sara had found out that she had a skal of her own.

"I'm glad I'm a Greenhaelan." She'd spoken without thinking, but it was true. Even though her skal had led to trouble and danger, she couldn't imagine being without it now. It was a part of who she was. An important part. When had that happened?

Garst abruptly stood up. "Time for me to go," he said. "I need to be setting up that distraction." Had she offended him? Before she could say another word, he began picking his way down the slope.

"Good luck," Sara called softly after him.

"No such thing as luck," she heard faintly, as he disappeared from her sight into the shadows below.

NINETEEN

Sara

Hours later, Sara crouched behind a wooden shack on the Deep Lake waterfront. Navigating the rocky gradient in the dark hadn't been as bad as she'd feared, but she'd been glad to reach level ground again. The whole town seemed to be asleep. Nothing broke the silence except the water lapping the shore and the occasional bark of a dog. If Guards awaited the outlaws here, they didn't appear to have set a lookout. Logen's plan might work even without Garst's distraction, but there was no way to contact him and call it off.

The dark silhouette of Logen motioned Sara forward to the water's edge, along with the others. "Tulley says this is the boat we should take," he whispered. "The rest of you get in, and we'll push it out as far as we can. Once we're all on board, I'll steer us into the current and let it carry us away from the town."

"What about Garst?" Sara breathed.

"We're not waiting. Fishermen wake up early, and I want us to be far away by then. We're going now, diversion or no diversion."

Tulley had chosen a long, low vessel built of wooden planks, with crosswise rows of benches. Sara felt her way along a seat, making room for Mena beside her. In the darkness, she could just make out the thick base of a mast rising from the deck a short distance in front of her, fading into blackness a few metres up. She couldn't tell if it held a sail or not.

A slight splashing came from the stern, and she quickly laid a hand on the gunwale to steady herself, but the push was smoother than she'd expected. The boat scraped along the muddy lake bottom, briefly resisting the men's efforts, then glided forwards. The vessel rocked briefly under her as Logen and Tulley scrambled in over the stern.

It was a strange sensation, moving silently along like this. It felt almost as though the boat was swimming through the water of its own volition, carrying her to safety. *Faster,* she thought, gripping the gunwale. The cold night air blew into her face, whipping back her hair. Their speed was increasing; Logen must have steered them into the current already. Rushing through the velvety blackness, Sara felt strangely at peace. It was going to be all right.

The night was shattered by the boom of an explosion somewhere behind her. She twisted around on the seat. Faint shouts reached her over the water. Moving blurs of orange light appeared — people running along the shore, carrying torches. If this was Garst's diversion, it was doing more harm than good. Between the explosion and the shouting, the whole town must be awake by now. She only hoped the light from the torches would blind the men on shore to anything on the water.

As the minutes passed, it did seem as though they'd made a clean escape. The stolen vessel cleaved through the water, the commotion fading away as the distance increased. The flames shrank to pinpricks of light, then disappeared.

The wind poured its rushing song into Sara's ears, the water slapped the planks below her hand, and the boat sped on.

"Now we row," came Logen's voice from the darkness. "Turn around, find your rowlocks, and lift the oars." Scrapes and rattles told Sara the others were moving to obey.

She'd done some rowing at school, but that had been years ago. Still, she was suddenly tired of being a mere passenger. Since this whole mess began, she'd been rescued, clothed, fed, and guided by other people, as if she was a child. Even Kelan, still in his teens, had contributed more to the welfare of the group than she had. She swung her legs over the seat and faced the stern, feeling along the gunwale until she encountered a rowlock and the rounded end of an oar. Using both hands, she drew the oar up through the iron ring and into position against her stomach.

"Pull," Logen called.

Sara leaned back and strained with the others, keeping in time with Logen's instructions. The boat responded.

Sara's shoulders began to burn. She ignored them.

They rowed for hours, taking turns at the oars. The wind had switched around a hundred and eighty degrees and was buffeting their faces again, and the sky had paled to a pearly grey that signalled the approach of dawn, when they discovered they weren't alone on the water.

It was Kelan who spied the danger and gave the warning. A broad, high-prowed vessel was following their craft, gaining rapidly as the wind bellied out its big square sail.

"It's a cog," Tulley said. "Probably a cargo ship. Might be nothing to do with us." But he didn't sound convinced.

Last night, Sara had thought their own boat might be equipped with a sail. But the mast was bare. All they could do was keep rowing and hope that the cog would ignore them. As it drew closer, she saw a large number of crew moving around on the deck. None of them wore the blue shirts that marked out the Warrant Guards — perhaps they were just traders, as Tulley had suggested, crossing the lake on business of their own.

The light grew. The distance between the vessels shrank even further. As the larger boat began to overhaul them, sailors lined up along the closest side. Some of them gripped sticks or poles. Others raised bows.

"Look out," Tulley shouted.

Arrows arched over the narrow channel between the hulls. Sara flinched and ducked. The bolts hissed and thwacked all around her, sending shards of wood flying. A stab of pain — she gasped and snatched her hand from the gunwale. Blood oozed from the back of it where a jagged splinter had struck home. She slid from the seat and curled up in the bottom of the boat, making herself into as small a target as possible, before gritting her teeth and yanking the sliver of wood from her flesh. A scarlet globe welled up from the wound. She lifted the hand to her mouth, tasting salt and metal.

The barrage ceased.

"Logen!" Fin cried into the sudden silence.

Sara raised her head. Logen slumped sideways. A feathered shaft protruded from his chest.

A man shouted from across the water: "Show them what we do to thieves, boys!"

Another flight of arrows pelted around Sara's huddled form, followed by Tulley's booming voice: "Into the water! Swim!"

She crawled across the deck and launched herself over the side and into the lake. The water closed over her, and the cold stole her breath. She struggled upwards until her head broke the surface. A tight band squeezed her chest and she fought for air, thrashing her arms to keep her nose above the waves. The saturated cloak was dragging her down; she fumbled to untie it from her throat. Finally, she freed herself from its heavy folds and regretfully watched it sink into the depths.

Two heads bobbed up further along the boat. Impossible to recognise them from here. The tightness in Sara's chest eased. She gulped in air as she trod water.

"*Swim!*" Tulley's voice thundered from above. She struck out from the boat. Her arms were jelly, but terror gave her strength.

When she couldn't lift her arm for one more stroke, she paused and looked around her. No one in sight. She gasped and almost went under again, flailing to keep herself on the surface. She scanned the choppy expanse of water between her and the distant boats. Correction: boat. She could only see one of them now: the oar-powered craft they'd stolen. The cog had already sailed away, its mission completed. How long had she been swimming?

She was alone, and she couldn't detect any movement on the remaining boat. Her friends were gone. A sob forced its way up into her throat. She wanted to scream and shake her fists. What had she done to deserve this? What had Kelan or Mena, Logen, Fin or Tulley? What was the point of anything? Why not stop struggling and let the lake take her?

Only the realisation of what Mena would say to that stopped her. And Mena would be right. Giving up now would be pathetic and ungrateful. Mena and the others hadn't given up on her, not for a moment. She wouldn't either.

She thought she could make it to the boat, after she'd rested for a bit, but it was too big for her to control alone. And what if the attackers had left someone on board to deal with anyone who made it back? The more she considered this possibility, the more likely it seemed. Why else would they have abandoned the stolen vessel? She could be swimming straight to them. Then everything really would be over.

There was no way to help the others right now. Even if they were still alive — please God let them still be alive — she couldn't rescue them from a group of armed men. But there was one thing she could do for them, if she was brave enough. She could continue on alone, following the river into the Blighted area, and complete what they'd started. If she failed, at least she'd know she'd tried.

She floated on her back for a while, gathering her strength, then turned her face away from the boat and began stroking.

Reaching the current, she turned over and floated again, buoyed up by the embrace of the lake. The rising sun dazzled her eyes and she shut them, letting her thoughts drift.

Warm sun caressed Sara's face and even the water around her had ceased to feel cold. It cradled and soothed her, like a hot bath at the end of a long, tiring day. She luxuriated in the feeling of peace and well-being. Somewhere, far away, a faint warning bell clanged, but she was too comfortable to move. Someone else could take care of it.

Soft fingers brushed her hand, jolting her awake. She splashed wildly, twisting around to see who had touched her. The sun flung spots of light into her newly-opened eyes, blinding her. Something snagged her foot and dragged her down. She gulped a breath and held it, waiting for

143

the water to engulf her. All she felt was the heat of the sun on her hair and face, and an unexpected heaviness anchoring her body. The world came into focus. She was kneeling in clear shallow water, surrounded by broad patches of swaying brown weed.

She exhaled and rubbed the remaining water from her eyes. The lake stretched away in front of her, blue and empty. After a few tries, she rose to her feet and slowly turned around. A headland came into view, then a curving shoreline. A long stretch of coarse yellow sand emerged from the water, sloping up to a line of scrubby trees.

She forced her numbed legs to carry her through the weed and onto the land. She was less than halfway to the trees, slogging through the dry sand, when she spotted movement up ahead.

Two men loped down the beach at a frightening speed and grabbed her arms. She struggled in their grip, but her strength was almost spent. Another two men emerged from the trees. One of them carried a pole with a big ugly hook on the end. *Stay calm,* she ordered herself. Maybe this was some kind of misunderstanding. They might just be angry because she was trespassing on their private fishing spot.

"Don't try nothing, Greenhaelan," the man with the gaff shouted. "We'll get the reward if you're in good condition or not. Makes no difference to us."

So much for misunderstanding.

The reward was bad news. Now ordinary people would be on the lookout for the outlaws, too. She didn't even know if it was *the outlaws* any more, or just her. An image of Logen with the arrow sticking out of his chest flashed across her mind.

Stop it, she told herself fiercely, *that's not helping.* She lifted her head and glared at the man who'd shouted at her. It had no visible effect on him, but it made her feel better, so she kept it up while they found her knife, tied her wrists and ankles with a length of stinking rope and carried her to a boat anchored just around the headland.

They slung her into the bottom of the boat and pulled up the anchor. She closed her eyes and tried to ignore the stomach-turning stench of the turbid water sloshing around her. She'd rest and restore some energy while she had the chance. She had no intention of meekly helping these men collect their blood money. As soon as the smallest opportunity for escape presented itself, she'd be gone.

Back in the town of Deep Lake, they dropped her to the floor of a small wooden shack and left, barring the door on the outside. She struggled into a sitting position with her back to a wall. It could've been much worse. Beyond binding her, they hadn't tried to harm her in any way. She was hungry and thirsty and tired but — except for a few bruises — unhurt.

The door opened and a leather water bag and a hunk of bread were tossed inside. One of the men entered and approached her. He drew out a long-bladed knife and she shrank away. But he only sawed through the ropes on her wrists, before retreating back outside. She flexed her hands and reached eagerly for the water. When she'd slaked her thirst, she ate the hard, tasteless bread, down to the last crumb.

Her legs were still bound, but now that her hands were free, she might be able to do something about that. But the man who'd tied her had known what he was doing. She couldn't budge the knots at all. It made sense that a fisherman would know how to securely tie a rope.

There must be something else she could try. Once before, she'd been tied up and managed to work the ropes free. Facing Soran in the barn, her bindings had just fallen away. She hadn't thought about it again, but it was strange how easily she'd managed it.

Brend had tied her up that time, and a stable worker must be just as used to ropes as any fisherman. Had he deliberately left the knots loose? No, that didn't make any sense — Brend had been the one who hit her on the head to make sure she couldn't escape. So why had the ropes let go? She gazed at the coils around her ankles. Could magic have been involved? But she was a Greenhaelan, with power over plants, not rope. Hang on, rope was made from plants, wasn't it? Dead plants, but still…

Her pulse sped up. Could it be true?

Another flash of memory: her hand on the gunwale of the boat, and the feeling that it was some kind of live thing. Yes, and when she'd urged it to go faster, it had. She'd assumed that Logen had steered the

145

boat into the current, but what if the wood had actually responded to her touch?

Tingling with excitement, she gripped the knots in both hands and concentrated. *Loosen, untie.* She felt silly giving mental commands to a rope, but so what? There was no one here to laugh at her if she was wrong. But if she was right...

The knots began to slide under her hands.

Holding her breath in wonder, she watched the rope uncoil, slither across her trouser legs, and fall free. Exultation sang through her.

As she rubbed the feeling back into her ankles, she came back to earth. She wasn't free yet. She'd be able to walk around, and perhaps use this new power to unbar the door from inside the shed, but what then? She'd still be alone in a town full of hostile people who would jump at the chance to claim the reward. And if they caught her again, they might beat her, even knock her out, to ensure she couldn't escape a second time. Her knife was gone and she wasn't at all sure she'd be able to use it on a living, breathing human being, anyway. She had no way of travelling except on foot. She'd be recaptured for sure. She sank back against the wall, her resolution draining away.

Even if she evaded them, where would she go? All this time, she'd been thinking that she needed to get back to the place she'd first arrived in this world, to use the same Gateway that had brought her here. But how likely was it that a Gateway existed between Algarth and Stephen Cooper's back garden? Now that she thought about it, it seemed wildly improbable.

Could she have somehow made it happen herself? How? She tried to remember exactly what she'd done. She had been angry with Stephen, and somehow it had all got mixed up with her feelings about Linda and Mark and Ben. She'd been miserable and longing for — what? Home? Yes, but Algarth wasn't home. So maybe it was just the misery and the desire to be somewhere else that had triggered the Gateway.

It was tenuous at best, but something inside Sara whispered that she was on the right track. If misery and longing opened a Gateway, could she form one here? She was miserable enough and she certainly longed to be somewhere else. Perhaps she could open a way directly to the Blighted area.

But her mind twisted away from that like a fish wriggling to free itself from a hook. In the lake, she'd been determined to let the current carry her into the forest, but now, faced with the possibility she might be able to open a Gateway to anywhere she wanted, there was only one place she really yearned to be: home in Wattleford.

It was cowardly — she knew that — but she couldn't pretend she felt any longing for this world, where innocent people were stabbed with swords and shot by arrows, where there was no peace or rest, only running and fear and grief.

Surrendering, she clenched her eyes shut. *I don't want to be here anymore*. Tears forced their way from under her eyelids and trickled down her cheeks. Her fingers dug into the dirt floor. Home. *I want to go home*.

TWENTY

Sara

Dizziness swept over Sara. When she opened her eyes, the interior of the shed was gone. She was sitting on a hard floor beside a bed, in a stone-walled room. Not home, then.

Even so, she paused for a moment to reflect on her accomplishment. She had created a Gateway, just like King Tana Lossil. She was a Gate Shaper; it was incredible. She was tempted to try again immediately, but she was still woozy, and a headache was throbbing behind her eyes. It might be wiser to rest for a while. The good news was that she wasn't locked in this time — the door of the room stood half-open.

Where was she? She pulled herself to her feet, clutching the bed for support. Her legs wobbled, but the dizziness receded a little. She made her way slowly to the narrow window and looked down.

A long, sheer drop met her eyes, ending in a grey cobblestoned yard enclosed by a curving outer wall. Constructed from enormous blocks of stone, the wall had clearly been built for defence. A thickly barred metal gate reinforced the impression of a fortress. Fortunately, it didn't seem to be a fortress under siege. No army massed against the gates, and not a single soldier or Guard was visible in the yard.

Outside the wall, a broad dirt road meandered lazily into the distance. On either side of it, peaceful fields of golden stubble lay dreaming in the sun, each one bordered by a fringe of trees. The green and gold patchwork reminded Sara irresistibly of an enormous quilt laid over the land, stretching all the way out to a row of blue hills.

The medieval fortress, the uneven stubble of fields harvested by hand, the absence of any sign of a bitumen road, argued that she was still in Algarth.

She lifted her eyes to the horizon, where her attention was captured by a group of three peaks, standing slightly apart from the others. The central one resembled a cone with the top neatly sliced off. It rose above its two round-shouldered companions as if they were suppliants bowing at its feet. The distinctive appearance of the three hills nagged at her — there was something familiar about them — but she couldn't recall where she'd seen them before.

Her legs felt stronger now. Turning from the window, she tiptoed to the half-open door and listened intently for any sound that might indicate someone was coming her way. Hearing nothing, she turned back and examined the room for clues about exactly where in Algarth she might be. *A map with a cross to mark the spot would be first choice,* she thought wryly.

The single bed was covered by a counterpane that had been pieced together from fabric dyed in many shades of green, and then embroidered with images of trees. The dark timber headboard was carved with an intricate border of flowering vines. Beautiful objects, but not useful to her right now. The same carvings decorated the tall cupboard and the edge of a shelf holding leather-bound books. A small round table and a chair stood in a corner. The tabletop was even more elaborately decorated than the rest of the woodwork, being inlaid with a composition of birds, leaves and fruit, constructed from segments of variously coloured wood.

She opened the cupboard. It was empty, apart from a neatly-folded bundle of sage-green cloth. The fabric was closely woven, smooth to the touch. She lifted it and shook it out. It was a hooded cloak. She closed her eyes and rubbed its softness against her cheek, breathing in the comforting scent: lavender, rosemary, thyme.

Her heart thumped. Her eyes flew open. She shook her head. What was she doing? She was supposed to be searching for clues. She shoved the garment back onto the shelf and closed the cupboard door.

The books seemed her best bet. Keeping her ears open, she crossed to the shelf and took one down. The pages were made of thick paper, like Mena's map, and the lettering appeared handwritten. She couldn't read it, but the shapes reminded her of the writing on the map and the twins' note in Eorna. She was still in Algarth. Even though she'd been almost sure of it already, the confirmation was a slightly bitter blow. She'd shaped a Gateway, but hadn't succeeded in leaving this world. She returned the book to the shelf and quickly flipped through the others, just in case, but found nothing helpful.

What she needed was a safe place to hide and regain her strength. Then she'd try again. Now that she knew it was possible, she wouldn't give up until she'd shaped a Gateway that would take her all the way home.

No sound from outside. She risked a glance around the edge of the door. An empty corridor stretched in both directions. She hesitated, unsure which way to choose.

The tapping of approaching footsteps made up her mind for her. She bolted in the opposite direction, running along the stone-flagged corridor as swiftly and silently as she could. She whisked around the first turn she came to, desperate to be out of sight before the owner of the feet came around the corner. She found herself in a narrower hallway, lined with closed doors that might open at any minute. Adrenaline kept her going, down passages and around corners, pausing briefly at each new intersection to choose the way that seemed darkest and quietest, least used.

The place was a maze; it was impossible to keep any sort of map of it in her head. She encouraged herself with the thought that it didn't matter, as long as she could find somewhere to rest and recover in peace. After that, she'd simply shape a Gateway and be gone. Panting and dripping with sweat, she dropped to a walk but kept moving, desperate to find a hiding place before exhaustion forced her to a stop.

An alcove opened on her right, empty save for a narrow iron staircase spiralling upwards. An unblemished layer of grey dust coated the bannister. She was trying to decide whether going up would be worth the effort, when the silence was broken by the mumble of voices coming from the corridor she'd left.

No choice. She climbed as quickly as she could, hauling herself up by the banister to keep her feet from stumbling. Two turns, three, four, and the stairs dead-ended on a small landing in front of a wooden door. Unbroken walls curved away on either side: a tower. There was nowhere else to go, other than back down. The voices sounded as though they were right below her now, only a turn or two away. Still no choice. She steeled herself, inhaled a deep breath, and pushed the door. It swung open, emitting a low creak.

The grey-haired man in the centre of the room spun around and glared at her. "Who are you? How dare you come in here?"

He was tall and spare, dressed in a long scarlet tunic embroidered at neck and wrists with gold thread. His long, thin face with its tightly clipped salt-and-pepper beard was twisted in anger.

Despite the clothing, a shock of recognition jolted through Sara. Her knees threatened to buckle. She grabbed at the edge of the door to steady herself.

"Well? Who are you? Answer me!" His dark eyes were almost black as they bored into her.

"I'm Sara Martin," she gasped. "And you're...you're Melville Barnett!"

The momentary shock on Barnett's face was swiftly replaced with an expression of even greater fury. "How could you know that?" he hissed, striding up to her and gripping her chin with one hand. His nails dug painfully into her skin as he stared down into her eyes.

"I've seen your picture," Sara whispered, "in the papers and on TV."

Nothing made sense to her. How could Barnett be here in Algarth?

He released her and she sagged against the door. He backed a few steps, frowning and running his fingers over the gilded cuff of one sleeve.

The frown lifted, and his expression grew smug. "So," he murmured, "that's who you are. Well, well, this is an unexpected family reunion."

Family? What was he talking about? Sara was calculating her chances of edging back out of the room and slamming the door between them, when a voice spoke from behind her, shredding her nerves even further.

"Is everything in order, Sir? We heard shouting."

Barnett waved a hand airily. "A misunderstanding, that's all. Close the door and set a guard to make sure no one disturbs us."

"Yes, Chairman Tarn." The man bowed and retreated.

Chairman Tarn?

"Confused?" Tarn/Barnett sounded pleased with himself. "Come and sit down, Sara…Martin, was it? Perhaps I can make things clearer for you."

Sitting down sounded good, right then. She followed him to a table set under a window. It was bigger than the one in the bedroom, but its top was inlaid with the same design. He pulled out a chair and Sara seated herself. Avoiding him, her gaze roamed around the cylindrical room. Tapestries along the curving wall; rugs covering the floor; shelves holding books; a second closed door. And then something that snagged her attention: a slatted wooden bench, its surface crammed with potted plants. They grew in a jungle-like profusion, some of them reaching almost to the ceiling.

"What do you think?" Tarn/Barnett asked. "Have you ever seen healthier ones?"

To be honest, Sara hadn't — the plants looked magnificent — but she wasn't about to pay him any compliments, whether he was Tarn or Barnett or somehow both. She tore her eyes away from the display and fixed them on his face. "Who are you, really?"

He took a moment, as if considering his answer. Then he inclined his neat grey head in a parody of a formal introduction. "I am Villembelt Tarn, direct descendant of King Tana Lossil, and Chairman of the Council of Six of Algarth."

He leaned closer. The corners of his mouth turned up in an unpleasant smile. "But sometimes, I take a little trip. And then, I am known as Melville Barnett, successful Australian businessman."

When Sara didn't reply, Tarn's smirk widened. "And I'm not the only one with two identities. Sara *Martin?*" He shook his head. "No, my dear. You are Sara *Loren*, the daughter of my younger sister, Elana. You and your parents also took a trip when you were very young, with my help. It seems that, after all these years, you have finally come home. Welcome, niece, to Edervale Castle, where you were born."

Sara became aware that she was gaping at him and closed her mouth. Was he telling the truth? She couldn't think of a reason for him to lie about it. But then, she wasn't thinking very clearly at the moment.

Tarn seemed to realise it, too. "Enough for now," he said, leaning back. "You must be tired and hungry. His nose wrinkled. "And in need of a bath and more suitable clothing. We'll talk again tomorrow."

In stunned silence, Sara watched him walk to the door, open it and give low-voiced instructions to someone outside. She stayed where she was until two women came in through the other doorway and led her out, down a wide staircase, along several corridors, and into another bedroom.

She didn't try to resist any of it. There was nothing she could do for now. And by allowing her to rest, Tarn was giving her what she most needed, whatever his intentions were. Not only that, she was desperate to hear more about her parents, even if it was from him. She comforted herself again with the knowledge that she wasn't trapped here, no matter what he might think. Locks and guards couldn't keep her in the castle. She could leave any time she wanted, once she'd regained her strength.

The women were kind to her. They waited while she removed her damp, stinking tunic and trousers, and then helped her into a large, metal bathtub filled with warm, scented water. After weeks of travelling and sleeping rough, it was heavenly. She soaped herself all over and slid under the water, then lay back with her head resting on a cushion. She was almost asleep by the time the water cooled and the women returned with towels and a night dress.

Clean and dry, she climbed between blessedly soft sheets and closed her eyes.

TWENTY-ONE

Kelan

Kelan surfaced and shook the wet hair out of his eyes. Thank Aal, there was his mother, just a few strokes away. The water had darkened her thick mass of wavy hair and plastered it close to her head, making her face peculiarly small and vulnerable. He mentally renewed his promise to protect her. She gave him a wan smile, as if guessing his thoughts.

A splashing sound drew his attention: someone else in the water, already some distance from the boat, and swimming hard. He couldn't tell who it was, but it didn't matter right now. He had to get his mother away before the archers discovered them.

"Can you swim with me?" he asked.

She nodded. They set off, Kelan glancing back occasionally to make sure they were keeping the two boats lined up. That way, their own vessel would be at least partially blocking the attackers' view of them.

But after only a few minutes, his mother was gasping for breath, her face white with strain. She probably hadn't swum in years. Her long, waterlogged dress would be weighing her down, too. Why did women wear such impractical clothes? Cahira had had the right idea, and Sara too. He wished his mother had made the same choice. He slowed down and supported her as well as he could while she recovered a bit.

The sailors should have secured the stolen boat by now, but there was no sign of them on board. In fact, by some trick of the pre-dawn light, he couldn't even make out the cog any more. A movement in the water — something had broken away from the smaller vessel and was swimming towards them. A big animal of some kind, with a long, low hump along its spine. Kelan tensed. He had nothing to defend them with.

The animal drew closer. Suddenly it resolved itself into Tulley, with Logen on his back. The older man's burly arms powered through the water, creating a wake on either side. And the two men weren't alone: Fin clutched her husband's trouser leg with one hand and stroked with the other. It must have been Sara he'd seen swimming away.

Tulley and the others arrived. Not a single arrow had been fired at them, and there was no sign of pursuit; it was strange. Logen's eyes were closed, but his arms were clamped tightly around Tulley's barrel chest, so he must be alive. Fin asked about Sara, and Kelan told them what he'd seen. His mother thanked Aal, but Kelan had been thinking, and he didn't see much reason for optimism.

Tulley was a strong swimmer, but even with his help, they couldn't outdistance a boat, and the shore was too far away to offer any hope. The sailors could come after them any time they liked and pick them out of the water one by one. They were probably just taking their time tying up the second boat, ready to be towed back to shore as soon as the job was finished. Why should they hurry? Their quarry wasn't going anywhere. Sara might have a long enough start to get away, but the rest of them were doomed, defeated by a gang of fishermen.

Tulley let out what sounded like a bark of laughter. Kelan stared at him. What was there to laugh about?

Tulley grinned back at him through his beard. "Watch, lad" he said, pointing towards the boat. Long, narrow shapes were floating out from behind it. Some of them had strange, rounded lumps on top of them. As each one cleared the hull, the current swung it around and carried it away. Kelan squinted across the water, trying to make out what he was seeing.

"What are they?" his mother asked.

Tulley chuckled. "The planks from the cog."

Kelan could see it now. The strange humps were the heads and shoulders of the sailors, using the planks to keep themselves afloat.

"They'll come ashore further north," Tulley said, "and then they'll have a nice long walk back to town."

Kelan was relieved that the men weren't going to drown, even though they'd been trying to kill everyone. But he was also glad about the long walk. He hoped they all got blisters. Big, painful ones.

He turned back to Tulley. "How did the boat come apart?"

"With a bit of help from my talented husband," Fin said, patting Tulley's arm proudly. "When we went overboard, he swam behind the other boat and used his skal to shape the rivets that were holding the planks together."

"Made them long and thin and drew them right out," Tulley said with satisfaction.

"My Tulley can do anything with metal," Fin said.

"Thought they might swim to our boat," Tulley said, "and I'd have to pull it apart, too. Lucky they were too spooked to think straight, swearing about demons and curses. They couldn't get away quick enough."

"But we know it wasn't a demon," Fin said, "it was just you. So we can get back on the boat and keep going."

Kelan's head was spinning at how quickly their luck had changed. The attackers were gone and they were all together again. Except Sara, of course. But if she followed the plan and headed north in the current, they'd catch up with her eventually. He suddenly had a feeling that things were going to work out after all.

They didn't encounter any other boats as they rowed their way northward, but they saw no sign of Sara, either. Around the middle of the morning, they came across a small island and searched it thoroughly, hoping she had come ashore onto the beach, but there was no trace she'd ever been there. Kelan agreed with Tulley's assessment that Sara couldn't possibly have come further: either they'd missed her in the water, or she'd drowned.

After some discussion, they all agreed that it made no difference to their own options. If they went back to look for her, they'd be captured.

All they could do was keep following the current all the way to the north end of the lake. If Sara was still alive, she'd be heading that way too. Fin insisted they should keep hoping, but personally, Kelan didn't believe they'd ever see Sara again.

There was some good news: Logen had woken up. Kelan's mother had been working on him, and his wound was healing nicely, although he still wasn't strong enough to take a turn at the rowing.

Kelan did his best at the oars, determined to contribute his fair share. His mother and Fin helped, but it was Tulley who ended up doing the most. He rowed for hour after hour, despite the growing lines of strain on his face and the grey pallor under his tan. Tulley was as exhausted as the rest of them; he just had no intention of giving in to it.

Up until today, Kelan hadn't really paid much attention to Tulley. At their first meeting, he'd just been annoyed at the old man for laughing at him. But back then, he hadn't thought much of any of them, believing they were criminals and up to no good. So much had changed in the past few weeks. He'd come to admire these men: Logen, who was a good leader, and Niall, who might have a strange sense of humour, but who'd used his skal to keep them safe while he was with them. And Adric, who'd generously given him his brother's bow — the brother who'd died saving Kelan from the Warrant Guards. They'd all turned out to be so much more — well, so much more than he'd expected.

But he hadn't felt the same about Tulley. As far as he could see, the older man hadn't contributed anything special to the group or done anything particularly heroic. He'd just been tagging along. Until today.

If it hadn't been for the red-bearded Metal Shaper, they'd all be dead. When Logen had been wounded, Tulley had taken charge and commanded them all to jump into the water. And then he'd pulled the rivets out of the other boat, a quick-witted move that Kelan wouldn't have thought him capable of. And now, he was using his physical strength, and even more, his strength of will, to get them all to safety.

Kelan couldn't help comparing this new Tulley with his uncle, who was about the same age. Soran was broad and imposing, with muscles built by hard work on the farm and enhanced by his skal of Strength. But, for the first time, watching Tulley, Kelan realised that his uncle was weak in other ways. He ranted and shouted to get his own way. He drank too much. And he'd never have been willing to stay in the background and follow a younger leader, as Tulley had followed Logen. Soran always had to be the big man, the man in charge.

Kelan's mother had been right in what she'd said to Logen. His uncle wouldn't take them back, now that they'd sided with the outlaws against Tarn and the Council. Soran would be afraid it would damage his reputation and make him appear weak in front of his neighbours.

Kelan was young, and he had no doubt he could make a new life for himself, with or without Soran's help, but what about his mother? He squared his shoulders. It was up to him to take care of her now. He would be like Tulley, and like Bram, strong in the ways that counted. He went forward to take another turn at the oars.

They dropped anchor at sunset and tried to get some sleep. It should have been easy, considering how tired they all were, but Kelan's stomach was complaining. They'd only been able to bring a small amount of food down from the hills, the last of the nuts and berries Garst had found for them. It was all gone now, eaten earlier in the day to give them the energy they needed for rowing.

He wondered if there were any fish nearby and if he might be able to catch them. There'd be no way to cook them, of course, not on the boat. Could he eat raw fish? The empty gnawing in his middle suggested that he could. He had the bow and a quiver of arrows. Perhaps he could shoot a fish. He wished he'd thought of that earlier. It was almost dark now and there'd be no moon tonight. The fish would have to wait until the morning. He settled down with his back against the rowing bench and tried to sleep. If he was lucky, he might dream about food.

He was woken by a violent rocking. The wind had risen and the boat was tipping from side to side, wallowing as the waves strove to break it free from its anchor. Kelan heard the others murmuring together but he couldn't see them. There was no light anywhere.

The wind was getting stronger. The boat tipped so far that Kelan grabbed onto the gunwale to stop himself falling overboard. He heard cries and gasps around him in the dark. Then a massive gust struck them like a hammer. He gripped the wood as the craft bucked wildly under him.

"Help...pull...anchor!" Logen shouted from behind him, half his words snatched away by the rushing air.

"No time," bellowed Tulley's voice. "Cut the rope!"

The boat rolled again. It was about to overturn. The wind filled Kelan's head to bursting, roared through his shaking body. Yet it was outside him, too, batting at him like the paw of an enormous beast, crushing him against the seat. His stomach convulsed. His heart fluttered like a wounded bird. This was the end. He would drown in the black water, and no one would ever know what had happened to him.

The wind eased slightly. Kelan's ears unblocked and he lifted his ringing head. An enormous wave tossed the vessel high and slammed it viciously down, leaving Kelan's stomach on the crest. The heavy hull pitched. Spray hit him in the face. A black wall rose before his stinging eyes. He ducked. A second later, the wave smashed into him, flattening him to the planks. Drenched and gasping, he used all his strength to haul himself out of the freezing water and onto the seat. His whole body was shaking and his teeth chattered violently.

A savage lurch, almost jerking him to the floor again. Another. Then the boat shot forward, scudding up and over the next wave. Someone had cut the anchor rope.

They raced through the darkness, with no way to tell where they were heading. They might smash into hidden rocks or run aground on the shore. Kelan didn't even know if everyone had managed to stay on board. Where was his mother? His eyes strained but he couldn't see anything. No point in shouting to her: the wind was back, drowning out every other sound.

And then the rain came, huge drops at first, splattering on Kelan's scalp, driving against his back. He bent forward and wrapped his trembling arms around his head, covering his ears. The rain became stinging needles of sleet. Kelan bent lower.

He had no idea how long he stayed like that, his body numb, his mind blank, but he finally became aware that the onslaught had stopped. The wind was still blowing, but the roar had changed to a moan. Kelan unwrapped his stiff arms and lifted his head. Was that a slight brightening in the sky? Or were his eyes playing tricks? No, there was definitely a lighter patch there, and it was spreading. Soon he could make out shapes in the boat. The wind dropped further.

"Mother?" his voice came out in a croak.

"Kelan! Are you all right?"

A shadow rose and clambered towards him. They hugged. Hot tears ran down Kelan's stiff cheeks. He hoped it was still too dark for his mother to see them.

"Tulley? Fin?" came Logen's voice.

They both answered. All five of them had survived. They were wet and freezing, but alive.

They were being carried along by the current. As the sun rose, the lake narrowed, the shores on either side drawing closer every minute. Finally, they were no longer floating on a lake at all, but along a wide river, bordered with reeds. The wind blew the last tattered shreds of cloud away, and then fell to a gentle breeze. Sunlight sparkled and danced on the water. The river flowed calmly between green banks. It was as if the storm had never happened.

They were riding low, weighed down by all the water in the bottom of the boat. Tulley began bailing with his hands, and the others followed, splashing as much water on each other as over the side. No one seemed to mind. Their spirits had risen with the sun. When the boat had been emptied, they sat in silence, basking in the sunshine as it dried their clothes and eased their shivering. They were alive and safe, at least for now. To Kelan, eyes closed and face upturned to the warmth, that felt like enough.

After a while, they began to talk about what to do next. Logen, who seemed to be completely recovered from his wound, wanted to keep

160

to the original plan. "We're on the Tal River, and it flows right into the Blight," he said. "All we have to do is let it carry us there."

Kelan's mother was rubbing her hands over her apron, trying in vain to smooth the wrinkles. "But what about Sara? We don't know where she is." Her hands clutched at the fabric and she bent her head. "Or even if she's still alive. What can you do without her?" Kelan had never heard his brisk, matter-of-fact mother sound so sad and defeated. It gave him an odd, uncomfortable feeling.

Logen was silent. Perhaps, deep down, he knew that she was right. Perhaps they all did. Then Fin spoke up, and her quiet voice held a note of fierceness that surprised Kelan.

"Stop it!" she said. "Where's your faith? Your gratitude? Look at what Aal has brought us all through so far. Do you think he's going to abandon us now? Sara's very existence, exactly when Algarth needs her, is a miracle." She gestured to their surroundings. "And now, not only have we lived through that storm, but it brought us to where we need to be, much faster than we could have come on our own.

"If Aal can do all that," she finished triumphantly, "he can keep Sara safe, too, and bring her to us at the right time. We just have to keep going." She glared around at their startled faces, as wild as a little falcon.

Tulley nudged Kelan. "What did I tell you, lad? Calm as a millpond most of the time, but full of surprises." Fin huffed, but didn't say any more.

In the end, no one had any better suggestion to make, so they agreed to stay on the river. Kelan didn't share Fin's certainty that Aal was looking after them, but he hoped she was right about Sara. If the Greenhaelan had somehow survived the storm, they had a chance, and a chance was better than nothing.

He wondered what Sara was doing right now, and if she was as hungry as he was.

TWENTY-TWO

Sara

Pale light was streaming in through the window when Sara woke. She yawned and stretched experimentally under the covers. A bit stiff, but not too bad. Actually, she felt pretty good, considering. She threw off the bedclothes and stood up, stretching again.

The table under the window held something covered by a cloth — food, hopefully. She lifted it: thickly sliced bread and a pot of creamy cheese, a cup of amber fluid and another of water. The yeasty smell of the still-warm bread mingled with the sharp, fragrant scent of fresh apple juice, bringing saliva springing to her mouth. She sat down and finished it all. For a few moments she felt utterly content and ready for anything.

Outside the window, the sun was rising, above the same group of three hills she'd noticed yesterday. Tarn had said she'd been born here. Was that why the formation seemed familiar? Had she really spent her early years in this castle? If she wanted to find out more, she'd better get dressed.

Her tunic and trousers had been taken away, and a dress was laid out on a chair. It was much like the ones the servant women had been wearing last night, made from undyed cloth the colour of oatmeal, and clearly not new. So, this was what Tarn considered "suitable clothing" for his niece? The richness of his own garments revealed how much he cared about status; she guessed he'd ordered this to humiliate her. If that had been his aim, he didn't know her at all. The only thing that bothered her was that the length and fullness of the fabric would be a hindrance if she had to do any more running. Her faithful boots were gone, too, replaced by soft leather shoes. A worse loss, but nothing she could remedy now. She dressed quickly, but couldn't find anything to tie her hair back. She teased out the tangles with the comb the women had left for her and decided she was ready.

She padded to the door and tried the latch, but it was locked from the outside. Not really surprising. Well, she had plenty to think about while she waited for Tarn to send for her. If she could believe what he'd told her, he was not only Tarn and Barnett, but also her uncle, her mother's brother. Her parents were from Algarth, and she'd been born here. Yet she'd ended up in a different world, in the country of Australia. The same place Melville Barnett owned a mining company and bribed politicians to let him destroy the environment.

How did all that fit together?

She needed answers, but she dreaded them, too. Tarn had said her parents had taken the 'little trip' with her. Where were they now? Had he harmed them? What would she do if he had?

The sun hung high overhead, when a servant finally came in with another meal. The morning had gone. How much longer would Tarn make her wait? She wasn't really hungry, but she forced herself to eat the thick stew: she might need the energy. Following the same reasoning, she lay down on the bed and tried to rest, but disturbing thoughts nagged at her. Maybe Tarn had changed his mind about sending for her today. Perhaps he planned to keep her imprisoned in this room forever. She wondered how long she could stay sane, locked between these four walls, with only herself for company.

Only herself for company. Her mind snagged on that. This was the situation she'd been looking for. She was well-fed and rested, and she was alone. She could shape another Gateway right now. But if she did that, she might never know the truth. What did she want more right now: freedom, or answers? Unable to decide, she swung her legs over the side of the bed and stood, hoping to clear her head.

At that moment, the door opened to admit a Guard: a grizzled older man, with a hard face. "Chairman Tarn wants to see you," he growled. When she didn't move immediately, he grabbed her roughly by the arm and pulled her towards the doorway.

The Guard set a fast pace along the corridors, his grip like iron. He yanked her up the staircase and deposited her in the tower room without ceremony, releasing her and backing out without a word. She stood there, panting and rubbing her arm, feeling flustered and already at a disadvantage.

Tarn was wearing emerald green today, with the same gilt-embroidered trim. He invited her to sit, which she did, but remained standing himself. "No doubt you have many questions, Sara, and I intend to explain everything to you."

As she opened her mouth to reply, he raised a gold-ringed hand to silence her. "It is a long story. It will go faster without interruptions." He stared into her eyes. Discomfit prickled along her spine. "You will not repeat anything you hear in this room."

He held her gaze for a moment longer, and then continued. "My father's name was Mendo Tarn. He was a direct descendant of King Tana Lossil and Chairman of the Council of Six for many years, as was his father before him. From childhood, I knew that I, too, was destined for the Council. But my father had other ideas." Anger coloured his deep voice. "He chose my sister, Elana, instead."

He directed his attention to the landscape outside the window. "I suspect my father was jealous of me, afraid I would outshine him. Elana, naturally, was no threat; she was only a Greenhaelan. Or, perhaps that very fact blinded him. Our mother was a Greenhaelan, too, you know. She died when Elana and I were quite young. My father was very fond of her. Perhaps Elana reminded him of her."

Still gazing out the window, he clasped his hands together behind his back, rocking on the balls of his feet. "Whatever the reason, he thought more of my sister's talents than she deserved. And of her judgement. She was beautiful and should have married well, but instead she chose a nobody, another Greenhaelan, named Serd Loren. They married and had a child."

He stopped rocking and spun around, pointing at Sara in what was clearly meant to be a dramatic gesture. "You are that child."

As he'd already told her Elana was her mother, the revelation fell flat as far as Sara was concerned. She felt nothing but impatience at his posturing.

He dropped his arm and continued. "All three of you lived here in Edervale until you were five years old, when my father announced he would be stepping down from the Council and recommending Elana take his place." He shook his head slowly, a solemn look on his face. "I knew what a disaster that would be."

He was ridiculous, with his acting and his self-importance. A stupid, melodramatic, pompous man. In any other situation, she would have been tempted to laugh at him. But however idiotic he was, he had power here. She schooled her face into polite interest.

He began pacing up and down in front of the window. "For the sake of Algarth, I had to act." His voice had grown louder and more agitated. He seemed to be working himself up to something. She hoped it wouldn't be something violent towards her.

"You may have heard that I am a Mind Wender," he went on, "but I am more than that. Like King Tana, I discovered I could shape Gateways. I knew I was his natural heir, the first Gate Shaper for generations."

He halted in front of Sara and stared at her with wild eyes. "It was a sign, don't you see?"

Still wary of provoking him, she nodded. That seemed to satisfy him, and he started pacing again. "I tried to explain to my father, but he refused to understand. So, I did what I had to do. Right in front of your parents, I shaped a Gateway and pushed you through it. I knew they would follow you. Then I closed the Gateway." He stopped and bent his burning gaze on Sara. "You understand, I could have just taken your mother, stranding her alone, but I acted out of kindness, as a brother, and an uncle. I sent all of you together, so you could start a new life as a family."

Fury boiled in Sara. The incandescent heat of it rose up her neck and set her cheeks flaming. She wanted to tell him exactly what she thought of his *kindness*, but she mashed her lips together tightly. First, she'd hear the rest.

Tarn sat down opposite her and shrugged. "I know it didn't work out for you as I planned. The Gateway opened onto a busy road; your parents were run over and killed instantly. Somehow, you escaped serious injury and wandered away. It wasn't my fault; I had no way of knowing that would happen. And I could hardly go after you and bring you back here; there would have been too many questions to answer." He smiled complacently and spread out his hands. "And see, here you are, all grown up, and home again. No harm came to you."

No harm? Sara's nails dug into her palms so deeply they must have been drawing blood. She swallowed, forcing down the words that were trying to claw their way up into her throat. She had to know all of it now. "Why did you keep going back," she rasped, "pretending to be Melville Barnett?"

He shrugged again. "I became fascinated by that world. All the things that people could do there, everything they had invented. And I found that they had no resistance to Mind Wending at all. None! It took no effort to make them do what I wanted. I considered staying there, but after all, this is my home. The Chairmanship was my birthright, my destiny. But I realised I could use the other world to help me achieve it."

Keep him talking, Sara thought. *Find out as much as possible.* "How did you become Barnett?"

He sat back and smiled, apparently delighted at the question. "First, I found a language teacher and made her teach me English. I'm very quick at learning languages. Then I recruited other people: managers, lawyers, accountants, all kinds of experts. There was no need to pay them." He chuckled, enjoying himself. All this time, he must have been dying to tell someone how clever he'd been. It poured out, more detail than she wanted to know.

"I persuaded wealthy people to invest and politicians to smooth the way. It was so easy. All I had to do was meet someone, tell them what I wanted, and it was done. The money started rolling in. I had it converted to gold and precious stones and brought it here. And I began importing trade goods, too, superior products the people of Algarth have never seen before. The merchants pay a premium price for things I can buy for a few dollars."

Sara understood how he'd managed the double identity now. Melville Barnett was a famous man, but the newspapers always referred to him as a recluse; he wasn't seen in public very often. And with other people "persuaded" to manage every aspect of his business, Tarn wouldn't need to be away from Algarth for long on his visits. It was frightening what a Mind Wender with no conscience could achieve in her world.

No, not my world. Algarth was the world she'd been born into, the place she should have grown up, in a real home with two loving parents. Rage rose up once more, and again she choked it down. The longer he talked, the greater chance she'd have to learn something she could use to destroy him. And she wanted to destroy him, more than she'd ever wanted anything. More than she desired to save Algarth from the Blight. More than she yearned to be back in Wattleford, pretending this had all been a dream.

The odious man was gazing expectantly at her, as if waiting to be congratulated on his success. She asked another question, searching for some kind of leverage. "What about the Blight? I know the Greenhaelen didn't cause it."

"Well, that is another interesting story," Tarn purred.

The man would be twirling the ends of his moustache next. He was a living, breathing, caricature, a Bond villain, eager to explain all his actions and plans to the captive hero. *And we know how that always turns out, don't we?* Sara thought viciously. *The hero escapes and annihilates the villain.*

"It was a pure accident at first," Tarn went on, oblivious to her scorn. "I always shape my Gateway from the same place in the forest, a tree at the junction of two trails. After a few visits, I began to notice some dead grass around the tree. Each time I returned, the dead area was larger. I must have brought some sort of disease back through the Gateway. I needed to fix it, before it began to draw unwanted attention. I used some garden chemicals from the other side, but none of them had any effect. I finally realised I would have to heal the plants myself."

Sara frowned; what did he mean, heal them himself? He leaned forward again, and lowered his voice, as if he was speaking confidentially. She had a strong urge to slap the smile off his stupid face, but she resisted, moving back far enough to remove the temptation.

"Did I mention that I have the skal of Green Healing, too?" He nodded at her surprise. "Yes, I have three skals — almost unheard of, you know." He stroked his short beard, preening himself. "I suppose the Green Healing came from my mother. I never saw any use in it, but it is strong, like my other talents, and I was sure I could cure the plants. But Logen Rush and the Greenhaelen were making trouble for me by then, and that gave me a better idea. I began to spread the disease on purpose, blaming them. It worked perfectly. Almost all the Greenhaelen are gone." He leaned even closer. She could see the ugly pores of his nose and feel his disgusting breath on her cheek. "Except you, of course, and you won't be doing anything I don't want you to." As his dark eyes bored into hers, Sara began to feel slightly dizzy.

Tarn pushed his chair back and stood without breaking eye contact. "I've enjoyed our talk, niece," he said. "But I'm afraid you're capable of causing me a lot of trouble. The only way you could have found your way to Algarth is by shaping a Gateway of your own, and one Gate Shaper in the family is quite enough. Listen carefully. You will return to your room and wait until I tell you to come out. You will not try to escape, speak to anyone or plan anything against me in any way. In two days, the Council meets in Eorna. You and I will travel there together for your trial, where you will confess to being one of the Greenhaelen who helped Logen Rush spread the Blight. I will prepare a little history for you to memorise. After your conviction, I will reveal that I am a Green Healer myself."

He gestured at the bench of plants along the wall. "I've been practicing for months, and I've finally succeeded in curing a Blighted plant. I will cure the rest." He waved his arm in a grand, sweeping arc. "After I save Algarth from the Blight, nothing will be beyond my reach. One day, I will be hailed as King Tana the Second."

He pointed a bony finger at her. "Now go, and do exactly what I told you."

Desperate to get away from this maniac, her mind spinning with everything she'd heard, Sara bowed her head meekly and hurried from the room.

Outside the closed door, she paused for a moment, considering her next move.

If she was lucky, she might have a few hours before Tarn found out that his Mind Wending hadn't worked on her. Perhaps being related to him, hateful as that thought was, gave her some kind of immunity. The important thing was, she had some time.

A part of her still wanted nothing more than to shape a Gateway straight back to Wattleford and forget all about Tarn and Algarth. But now a bigger part couldn't bear the thought of him winning. He'd murdered her parents, imprisoned and killed other innocent people. He'd spread the Blight on purpose, without knowing if it could ever be stopped. He should pay for all of that.

She wasn't going back to Wattleford, not yet. She'd stay here and do whatever she could to bring him down, even though she didn't know what that might be. He'd admitted everything to her, but she had no proof to show anyone.

She'd stood here long enough. She needed somewhere to hide and work out what to do. Choosing a direction at random, she set off down the hallway, alert to any sound, staying on the balls of her feet. After a few minutes, she came to a flight of stone steps, spiral-ling down out of sight. Candles in metal holders, fixed at head height on the wall, shed a soft, golden light, somehow inviting. Following the other staircase upwards hadn't turned out too badly in the end. True, she'd been caught, but now she was free again, with much more information than before. She paused to listen for footsteps, and then started down the stairs.

There were more of them than she'd first imagined, winding around and around, taking her deeper at every turning. She wondered briefly why she didn't feel more nervous, heading into the unknown like this, but every step was taking her further from Tarn, and that had to be a good thing. She was beginning to suspect she was on her way to an underground dungeon — castles had dungeons, right? — when she caught a glimpse of someone in a black robe whisking around the bend just ahead. Whoever it was, they seemed to be in a hurry.

She stopped for a moment to put more distance between them, and then kept going, keeping her ears open for any sound. Two more turns of the staircase, and she found herself at the bottom, abruptly blinded by strong, white light. Instinctively, she shrank back against the wall and hunched down, making herself as small as possible, willing her eyes to adjust and show her where she'd ended up. Eventually, they did.

She'd reached a cavern, or rather a long, narrow room that had been formed from a cavern, with uneven rock walls and stalactites still hanging from the high roof. Instead of the friendly orange light of the stair candles, a line of torches marched the length of the room, burning with a pure white flame. They illuminated hundreds of barrels and crates, stacked along both long walls, with a narrow passage down the middle. This must be some kind of storage area for the castle.

Crouching at the base of the stairs, she could see straight down the centre aisle. About two thirds along, a short, slight individual in a black robe and flat black cap was trotting briskly away from her, towards an archway cut into the far wall. Thankfully, the figure hurried through the archway without looking back.

Sara had been lucky so far, but she was completely exposed here: anyone coming down the steps or up that aisle would see her immediately. The strange composure she'd felt on the staircase had abandoned her; she recoiled from the thought of climbing all the way back up, not knowing what might be waiting for her around each new bend. The mere idea of it was tying a knot in the pit of her stomach. But the only other exit she could see was the archway. Logically, that could be just as dangerous as going back up the steps, maybe even more dangerous, considering she knew there was at least one person on the other side. Unfortunately, logic was powerless to stop the trembling in her knees. She simply couldn't make herself go back up those stairs.

Before her growing fear could paralyse her completely, she clenched her jaw and set off down the long aisle, walking as quickly as she could.

She was glad of the soft-soled shoes now. Her progress was marked by nothing but a whisper against the smooth stone. She reached the archway and passed through into a broad corridor with openings along both sides. They led into other rooms, some large, some small. There were no doors on any of them. She sped past, heart thumping, hoping any occupants would assume she was a servant on an urgent task. The first five rooms were empty of people, but there was also nowhere in them she could hide. She went on.

She'd almost reached the next room on the right, when a small figure in black rushed out of it, turned and ran head-on into her. Sara sprang back with a startled cry, which seemed to distress the other.

"Oh dear, I am sorry, yes I am," the woman said breathlessly, straightening her squashy cap, which had been knocked over one eye. "Please forgive me, I was not watching where I was going, no I was not."

Light blue eyes anxiously peered up at Sara from a tiny wrinkled face with round red cheeks. Wisps of white hair stuck out from under the cap. Whoever this accidental assailant was, she didn't seem aggressive or dangerous. Sara's heart rate began to settle down.

"I do hope I haven't hurt you, so I do." The old woman's voice was high-pitched, like a bird, and she spoke very quickly, as if she was anxious to get all the words out before someone stopped her.

"No, I'm not hurt," Sara said, wondering what to do now.

"Oh, that is good, yes, it is. Were you looking for me?"

"I'm - not sure," Sara said. "Um, who are you?"

"Oh, of course, that was foolish of me, so it was. Enge is my name. Are you here to see the archives?"

Sara hesitated. This Enge seemed harmless, but if she started wondering what Sara was doing here, she might raise the alarm. It seemed best to play along for now. "Yes, I'd love to see them," she said.

Enge clasped her hands together. "That is wonderful, yes, it is," she twittered. "Hardly anyone cares to visit the archives any more, hardly anyone at all. Follow me, follow me."

She popped back into the room she'd come out of, and Sara followed as bidden. Enge led her across the empty room and through yet another archway. Unlike the others, this one was neatly outlined in blocks of stone. Sara stepped through and halted in amazement, confronted by a seemingly impenetrable wall of books and papers, crammed together higgledy-piggledy. The mass of paper, taller than Sara's head, loomed precariously, as if ready to topple at any moment.

A smooth, domed ceiling soared high above, painted with a panorama of wispy white clouds floating in a blue sky. The artist had feathered some of the clouds into shapes that resembled outstretched wings. Considering the size of the dome, the room underneath must be enormous. Was the whole space filled with documents? If these were the archives, it was hard to imagine anyone doing research here. Sara couldn't even see a way in.

Her guide, however, didn't hesitate. She had turned sharp right on entering the room, and now she veered abruptly left, seeming to disappear straight into the wall of paper. Hurrying to catch up, Sara spied the opening and plunged in. She found herself following the small black figure along a narrow path that wound between the stacked manuscripts. It twisted and turned and doubled back on itself, but Enge trotted along at a surprising pace, looking as much in her element as a dusky fish darting through a coral reef. Sara, a clumsy land-animal who'd fallen in by accident, pressed her arms tight against her sides, watched where she put her feet, and tried desperately to avoid brushing against anything. Some of the mounds appeared ready to collapse at the slightest contact, and she didn't want to be the cause of a paper avalanche.

When the archivist finally halted, Sara breathed a sigh of relief. No avalanche, and the old woman had brought her to a relatively clear space, holding a large table and two chairs. It might be somewhere near the centre of the room, judging by the dome overhead, although it was hard to tell for sure when she could only see a few metres in any direction.

Enge swept the chair seats clear with her hands, sending the ubiquitous pages fluttering to the ground like autumn leaves. "Sit down, sit down. It is so nice to have a visitor down here, yes, it is."

Sara obeyed, trying not to crush the fallen pages with her feet. "You certainly have a lot of books and papers down here."

A smile bunched Enge's cheeks. "Yes, indeed. I have gathered together every book, scroll, and scrap of parchment I could find about the history of Edervale Castle. Historians nowadays, they think the skal of Remembering is all they need, so they do. But skals come and go, my yes. Memorers die, memories are lost. Written knowledge is precious, yes, it is. I have collected these documents from all over Algarth, and I can now say with some certainty, yes, with much certainty, that I have not missed one, not even one. What do you think of that?"

She gazed eagerly across at Sara, like a dog who has done something clever and is expecting to be praised and patted on the head. Sara wasn't about to pat the old woman — close up, the black cap was unpleasantly grimy and moth-eaten — but Sara was prepared to give Enge some praise if it kept her happy, yes, she was.

"I think it sounds like a great achievement," she said firmly.

Enge clapped her hands together and beamed. Her unclouded blue eyes sparkled with enthusiasm. "It is, it is, but not many people seem to think so. Chairman Tarn isn't interested in history, you know, not interested at all. His little sister, Elana, now, she always wanted to know about all the old stories and histories, especially those about the ancient Greenhaelen. She was already the strongest of her own generation, yes, she was, and she was still young when she disappeared. Who knows how powerful her skal might have become?" She sighed, and then brightened again. "But now, you are here, and I am at your service, yes I am. What information are you seeking?"

Sara had been distracted by the mention of Elana — her mother, according to Tarn. But now she had to come up with some reason for visiting the archives, and fast. Enge had said they contained the history of Edervale Castle. A memory surfaced in Sara's mind: sitting by a fire in the forest, listening to Cahira singing about a king. Yes, and Tarn had mentioned him, too.

"Do...do you have anything about King Tana Lossil?"

Enge nodded vigorously. "Oh, I have much about him. He was a collector of histories himself, so he was. Some of the earliest parchments here were gathered by him. And he was a great writer too, oh yes indeed. He wrote a detailed account of his life and many other works. Was there anything in particular you wanted to know about him?"

Sara had already thought of her next question. The answer might even be useful to her. "Did he write anything about Gate Shaping?"

"Oh yes, yes he did, now where did I put that?" Enge disappeared into the stacks and Sara could hear her rustling around for some minutes. She reappeared triumphantly, holding a bound set of parchments. "Here we are. *Some Observations on the Skal of Gate Shaping*, by Tana Lossil, King of Algarth."

Sara reached out eagerly before realising there was no point — unless she could persuade the little archivist to help. "Would you be willing to read it aloud to me? I haven't been in Algarth long, and I can't read your language, yet."

"Oh, of course, of course, I would be delighted, young lady, delighted. To tell the truth, even if you had been born here, you would have difficulty with this. Our language has changed since King Tana's days, you know, yes it has. I will translate as I go so you will understand, yes you will."

King Tana had a formal and flowery style, but once Sara grew used to it, the document was fascinating. He'd obviously had a scientific type of mind. As soon as he discovered that he had the skal of Gate Shaping, he began to conduct experiments to find out as much as he could about it. And then, helpfully, he wrote down all his results. Sara listened hard and tucked away every nugget of information that seemed useful.

One thing King Tana had proved was that strong emotion assisted Gate Shaping. That made sense to her: she'd been caught up in loneliness, anger, and despair that first time, when she accidentally made a Gateway here to Algarth.

He also found that he could shape a Gateway more accurately if he formed a detailed image of the destination in his mind. When he tried to reach a place he'd heard about but never seen with his own eyes, his results were mixed.

But hadn't Sara been picturing her house in Wattleford when she'd tried to go there? Yet she'd ended up in Edervale Castle. She'd been longing for home, and the Gateway had brought her to her first home, one she didn't even remember. For her, unlike the king, emotion, or perhaps even the words she spoke, had a stronger influence than imagining the destination.

It was all very interesting, but time was passing, and it might be time she didn't have. Tarn could have already discovered she was missing and sent people to search for her. She felt fully recovered now, and if she could just be alone for a few moments, she could shape a Gateway. But first, she had to decide where to go. No, not just decide. She had to feel strong emotion about going there, otherwise she would end up somewhere else again.

Where did she most want to be? Some place that would help her defeat Tarn. She knew that he was a murderer and a liar, and that he had started the Blight, but who would believe her? It would be the word of the Chairman of the Council against the word of an outlaw no one had ever heard of. How could she get them to listen to her? She could only think of one way: cure the Blight herself. They might be grateful enough to listen. Even if they weren't, at least Tarn wouldn't receive the credit he wanted. It was a sketchy plan at best, but with time ticking away, it would have to do. She'd try to shape a Gateway to the Blighted forest, the place Logen had wanted her to go from the beginning.

She would be fighting the Blight alone, but Logen and Fin had thought her skal was strong. Enge had said Sara's mother had been the most powerful Greenhaelan of her generation, and Sara knew now that her father had been gifted with the same skal. So, it was possible that she could be even stronger than her mother. Perhaps even a Master Healer.

Enge was still reading aloud in her fluting voice. *"I have also found, through exhaustive trials, that it is less wearisome to return to destinations to which I have already travelled by Gateway. That is, those marked with the characteristic pattern of six interlocking spirals that Gateway travel creates. They are far easier to reach than fresh destinations, even ones already familiar to me through more mundane means of transport. I do not know why this should be so, but I have tested it many and various times and have no doubt it is a correct observation."*

Enge closed the book and balanced it precariously on top of the pile already on the table. She opened her mouth to say something, but Sara never found out what it was. There was a sudden rustling noise, followed by the sound of sliding paper. Enge jumped to her feet. "Oh dear!"

Sara leaped up in alarm as a stack to her right shuddered, wavered, then slowly toppled sideways into another, sending a fountain of pages into the air. It didn't end there. All around her, the archives surrendered to gravity with sighs and rustles of defeat. Loose pages fluttered around her head and flapped at her face like live things. She dropped to the floor.

Through the storm of flying paper, she made out a figure approaching, too tall to be Enge. A few seconds later, a blue-shirted man stepped into full view, followed by another. They had swords in their hands and a wild, staring look in their eyes that said they were ready to use them on the first person they saw.

Sara sprang up and ran, slipping and sliding on the literary debris covering the floor. Where was the archway? When the last stack gave way and the paper settled, she'd be able to see where she needed to go, but the Guards would spy her, too. Her only chance was to get out of the room before the avalanche ceased.

A dark opening in the far wall. She didn't know if it was the same one she'd come in by, but she struck out for it with all her strength. More volumes slid down around her, until she was wading knee-deep through them. They caught the folds of her dress and dragged at her, spitefully holding her back. Progress became agonisingly slow. She was gasping and sweating; her thighs were burning with the effort of moving forward. She only hoped the Guards were having as much trouble as she was. She urged herself on as if encouraging a child: *Come on. You can do it. Almost there.*

A flash of blue in the corner of her eye; she flung herself down. A silver blur streaked through the air above her: too close. She dived the other way. The blade missed her head again, but sliced horribly into the flesh above her right elbow. She screamed in agony and clutched her arm. Her body curled itself around the wound, her gaze angling upwards to keep the Guard in sight. He raised the sword again. No escape this time. One final burst of defiance lifted Sara's head, until she was staring her executioner full in the face. His lips pulled back from his teeth in a feral grimace.

Time slowed. The sword reached the apex of its swing and began its ponderous, unstoppable descent. The moment stretched out.

A black bundle hurtled into the Guard from one side. Sara's heart gave a massive thump; time sped up again. Thrown off balance, the big man lurched, the sword swinging wildly. Sara pushed herself up onto her knees and one hand, and scrambled awkwardly out of the way. Just in time. The Guard's arms windmilled, and then he toppled backwards and crashed full length onto the floor. Half a second later, the black bundle collapsed on top of him.

The little archivist lifted her head from the Guard's chest, revealing a red-flushed face with a worried expression. "Oh, dear me, I do hope you are not hurt, yes I do. Let me help you up, sir. I am always forgetting to look where I am going, yes I am."

She tugged vigorously on the Guard's arm, as if trying to pull him to his feet, but as she was sitting on his stomach, she achieved nothing except to infuriate him further. He snarled and began to rise, shaking his arm violently to dislodge her. With a heave, he gained his feet and his freedom from the squeaking archivist at the same time. Enge slid to the floor in a flurry of black, but somehow the Guard's sword became entangled in her long robes. Swearing savagely, he bent to extricate the weapon.

The papers had all settled now: across the wreckage of the archives Sara could see the exit; she'd almost made it there. But the second Guard stood squarely in front of it, legs solidly planted, sword pointed straight at her. In a few moments, his companion would be untangled from Enge, and Sara would be caught between them.

She dropped her head, panting, and tried to think past the shock and exhaustion. A nauseating stream of gore flowed down her wounded arm and dripped from her fingers: the sword had done serious damage. The arm would be useless, and the spots swimming in front of her eyes told her she was close to passing out from the pain and blood loss.

She'd run out of time and almost out of options. Her only chance was to shape a Gateway right now and disappear. She was probably too weak to do it, but maybe desperation counted for something.

An image appeared, unbidden, in her mind. It wasn't what she'd planned, but it loomed larger and larger, refusing to be dispelled. It would have to do. At least it was somewhere other than here.

She closed her eyes and focused all her fear, all her yearning for safety, on that one memory: the tree she'd found herself beneath on her arrival in Algarth. The huge trunk, the dark, shaggy bark, and the intricately whorled carving — the distinctive mark that King Tana's book had told her was created by the shaping of a Gateway.

"The spiral tree," she gasped, and, to her intense relief, felt the dizziness consume her.

TWENTY-THREE

Tarn

Tarn was furious. He felt the rage almost like a living thing inside him, hot and red, clawing to get out. If he had been wearing his sword, the two Guards who had brought him the news would already be spilling their lifeblood onto the floor. The fools deserved death for letting her get away.

How had she done it? He had ordered her to stay and she had disobeyed. The stupid, treacherous little girl had disobeyed him! How? And where had she gone? The fury rose again, but this time he forced it down. He needed to think. And he needed every Guard searching for her, no matter how satisfying it might be to kill these miserable failures cowering in front of him.

"Find her," he grated, glaring into the men's frightened eyes. "Find her, or I'll make you wish you had never been born."

TWENTY-FOUR

Sara

Sara opened her eyes. Disoriented and faint, she staggered and fell against the rough bark of the trunk in front of her.

The agony that shot through her body was so intense that she reeled back with a hoarse scream. She lost her footing and crashed to the ground, landing on her back. She lay there, winded, shocked and afraid to move. Waves of nausea rolled through her. Tears overflowed her eyes, blinding her. Had she been shot again?

It took an enormous effort, but she dragged in a ragged breath, then another. She knuckled the wetness from her eyes and sat up. The pain was already receding, only her arm still burned and throbbed where the sword had slashed it. She gripped the wound with her other hand, trying to stem the blood. It oozed out slowly between her fingers, thick and red. She swallowed against the nausea and surveyed her surroundings, alert for any threat.

She was alone, but not in a forest. The tree stood in a browned field. Blankly, not understanding, she struggled to her knees and peered at it more closely. The trunk was rough and fissured, like the one she'd been picturing when she made the Gateway, and the pattern of six interlocking spirals was identical, as far as she could tell. But it wasn't the same tree. The Blighted remnants that hung from its branches weren't conifer needles, but the dry, curled remains of what had once been large, flat leaves. Her Gateway had brought her to the wrong place. She had no idea where she was.

Even worse, she knew instinctively she was in no state to try again. She was stuck here.

Now that she could think again, she recognised the agony that had sent her to the ground. It was the same sensation that had hit her when she'd touched another Blighted tree, almost a year ago. She'd assumed then that it had been caused by Kelan's arrow, but now that she examined the memory, she was almost sure the pain had come before the whirring sound of the shot.

Tentatively, still on her knees, she reached out one fingertip to the trunk. Even that slight contact made her wince and snatch back her hand. She didn't know what it meant, but touching the Blighted trees caused her physical pain. Although the sensation quickly subsided, she was still bleeding, dizzy and sick. She slumped back into a sitting position, her head spinning.

All she wanted was to lie down and sleep, somewhere safe and comfortable, with no one trying to hurt or manipulate her, and no one relying on her to save anyone or anything. But that was a childish wish. She had to face the situation she was in and go on from here. She took a deep breath and steeled herself to examine her injury.

Beneath the veiling blood, a long dark incision was visible, laying diagonally across the inside of her right arm, just above the elbow. As far as she could tell, the wound was clean, but it was also deep. She needed to stop, or at least slow down, the blood loss before she did anything else.

It was fortunate that Tarn hadn't provided her with fancy clothing. The simple dress, worn thin from many washings, was exactly what she needed now. Clenching her teeth against the pain and nausea, she found an especially worn spot, just above the hem, put one foot on it to hold it down, and began ripping with her good hand.

A few minutes of that and she had a long bandage, of sorts. She wrapped the strip of cloth around the cut, making sure it was tight but not cutting off her circulation. When she had almost used up the entire length of her makeshift dressing, she tucked in the end as firmly as she could. It wasn't a professional job, but her arm did look better with the gory wound covered.

Sara watched for a while, until she was sure the blood wasn't seeping through. She felt a small glow of achievement, but she was under no illusions. She was still in a very bad situation. If the cut became infected, she could die. She had no food or water, and she doubted she had the strength to stand, let alone walk.

If only Mena was here, with her amazing power of healing. But Mena was gone, most likely dead by now. Logen, Kelan, and the others, too. Tears dripped onto the bandage. Sara averted her face to keep it dry and squeezed her eyes shut. She couldn't afford to give way to grief.

Eventually, the tears stopped flowing. She wiped her eyes again and tried to concentrate on what she could do, instead of what she'd lost. But thinking was hard when she was so tired and so dizzy. Her thoughts kept circling back on themselves.

Perhaps if she gave in and slept for a while, she'd be restored enough to make another Gateway. Her head swimming, she stretched out on the carpet of dead leaves.

TWENTY-FIVE

Kelan

They'd been on the river for two days now, and they still hadn't reached the Blighted area. At least the weather had been kind. With only the occasional nudge of the rudder from Logen or Tulley, the boat glided through the sun-freckled water, past low banks lined with willows.

Perhaps it was the influence of Fin's continuing optimism, or simply that they were in a beautiful place on a warm autumn afternoon, but to Kelan it felt almost like a holiday. Almost. If it was a holiday, he wouldn't be so hungry.

Everything around him was conspiring to worsen the empty feeling in his stomach. Glittering blue-green kingfishers knifed into the water from the willow branches, emerging with small, silver fish struggling in their beaks. Swallows looped and spiralled through the air almost faster than his eyes could follow, snatching their meals on the wing. Storks waded through the reed beds, ignoring the boat as they went about their own business, stabbing their long beaks into the mud and throwing their heads back to gulp their catch. On both sides of the river, beyond the trees, fields of stubble, studded with huge golden haystacks, alternated with untouched pastures where sheep or cows wandered, grazing the last of the summer's grass.

Every living creature along the river seemed to be stuffing itself with food, and Kelan envied them all. He had offered to shoot something, if they'd stop the boat long enough for him to retrieve the kill, but Logen reminded him that the storm had taken their anchor.

"We'd have to steer into the shore and deliberately run aground," he said. "I'm sorry, Kelan, it's a good idea, but it's too risky."

"He's right, lad," Tulley said. "If anyone found us, we'd be helpless, stuck like a rat in a bog."

Kelan thought they were both being ridiculously cautious. "There's no one here," he pointed out. "We haven't seen another soul for days."

This very reasonable argument fell on deaf ears.

"Look," Logen said, "just hold on until tomorrow. We'll be close to the Blighted area by then, less chance of being spotted by anyone." He gazed ahead as he spoke, as if trying to peer around the next bend and into the future. "You can shoot us some lunch, and we'll carry the leftovers in with us." His eyes returned to Kelan. "We've come so far; I don't want to take any chances now."

Kelan thought there was a good chance he might collapse from hunger before tomorrow, but Logen didn't seem to care about that.

So they stayed on the river and let the slow current carry them, all through the long afternoon and into another hungry night.

His grumbling stomach had woken Kelan early, while it was still dark. He sat alone in the bow and watched the dawn light slide slowly over the landscape, his hunger giving way to a creeping dismay.

Every trace of green was gone. The grey skeletons of dead willows rose from the riverbanks, the wet tips of their branches dipping in and out of the water like knobbly black fingers. Beyond them stretched expanses of bare, cracked earth, broken here and there by dry sticks and more dead trees. The reed beds were a brown, slimy, stinking mess. There were no grazing animals and no birds, except the occasional one flying high overhead. Logen had miscalculated. They had passed into the Blighted area during the night. So much for his promise that Kelan could shoot something before they went in.

The other four were awake now. No one spoke. There wasn't anything to say. Kelan had heard people talking about the Blighted farmlands, but the reality was overwhelming. He turned his gaze back to the river. At least the water looked the same.

No, that wasn't right. Up ahead, even the river was changing. It was beginning to narrow, and small patches of white floated here and there on the surface. He wondered what they were. Surely the water couldn't be Blighted? He stared as the boat carried him closer, trying to work out what he was seeing. Suddenly, with an awful jolt of recognition, he knew.

"Rapids ahead!"

"Everyone to an oar!" Tulley roared. "Row for the left bank!"

Kelan spun around to face the stern. His mother appeared beside him. He slid along the seat to make room for her. They took up the oars and began to row in response to Tulley's shouted commands.

Despite their efforts, they didn't seem to be making any progress. Every time Kelan glanced over his shoulder, the rapids were closer. He could see the white patches of foam clearly now, the grey backs of the rocks emerging from the water, the glittering mist of spray. Further ahead, the rocks crowded together more thickly, the spume rose higher. There was no gap wide enough for the boat to pass through.

Tulley was right. They had to get to the bank. Kelan gritted his teeth and dug his oar deeper, grunting with the effort. He kept one eye on his mother, whose face had gone almost as red as her hair. She was panting and looked ready to drop. Kelan's own heart was thumping. Sweat ran into his eyes, plastered his shirt to his body.

After an age, the boat began to respond. Sluggishly, it turned diagonally across the current.

"Keep going," Tulley shouted. "We're almost there!"

Kelan's shoulder muscles were screaming. Finally, the boat came free, shooting out of the current and rushing towards the bank. Tulley yelled more orders. After a few heart-stopping moments, they managed to steer the vessel into a pool of calm water between two of the dead willows. It floated there, held in place by an eddy. Kelan dropped his oar and sat gasping, head down, sweat dripping off him onto the deck.

When he'd caught his breath, he raised his head, only to see Tulley already on the move, clambering over the gunwale closest to the shore.

The stocky man landed in the shallow water and offered a hand to his wife, who was leaning over the side. She climbed down. Together they waded to the shore. Without a word, Logen followed their lead. Kelan helped his mother off the boat and gestured to her to go ahead of him. They splashed through the water and slogged up the muddy bank, Kelan keeping his eyes on her in case she slipped.

At the top, they all sank to the bare, dusty ground and discussed what to do next. Blighted land lay as far as Kelan could see in every direction, only relieved by the glinting silver ribbon of the river winding its way north and south. As he'd already guessed, the rapids were truly impassable. The rocks multiplied, and the channels between them narrowed, until there was almost as much stone as water. Far ahead, a misty line hung in the air, suggesting the presence of a waterfall.

Their journey by boat was over. From now on, they'd be travelling on foot, and with no provisions.

They talked back and forth for a while, but no one really wanted to return south, retracing the distance they'd already covered. Besides, that way only led back to the lake, and there could already be pursuit coming after them from that direction. They needed to keep moving.

"If we head north, along the river, we'll come to the town of Talford," Logen said, sketching a simple map in the mud with his finger to show them what he meant. "It's on the highway, about thirty reaches east of Gadara. It's inside the Blighted area, so most of its people were forced to leave some time ago, but if anyone is still living there, or passing through on the highway, they might cause problems for us. There could even be Guards still stationed in the town."

"Then that just leaves west," Tulley said. "Do we know what lies that way?"

"More Blight," Logen said. "The forest begins about twenty reaches from here, and it's Blighted for another thirty or so after that. It's where we were originally trying to get to with Sara. If she's alive and able to choose her path, she may make for it. I think it's our best bet."

"What about food?" Kelan asked. "We can fill our water bags from the river, but where in this Blighted place will we find anything to eat?"

"There won't be much anywhere in this country, it's true," Logen said. "Even if we come across a farmhouse or two, the owners will have picked them clean before they left. We'll just have to tighten our belts."

Kelan groaned and Tulley slapped him on the back. "Cheer up, lad. A bit of hunger won't kill you."

It was all right for Tulley; the man could live off his stomach for a month. Kelan's own middle felt hollowed out. Soon his front would be touching his back.

Fin was looking up at the sky. "Kelan, I've been seeing birds flying overhead. Do you think you could shoot one down?"

Kelan warmed to her. "Maybe. If it's low enough."

"One of those?" Fin asked.

Kelan followed her pointing finger and saw the v-shaped formation of a flock of geese heading their way, probably flying south for the winter. He readied the long bow he'd been carrying on his back all this time, and waited. Soon he could hear the birds' weird, honking cries. When the leaders began passing overhead, he put an arrow on the string and drew it back, aiming for the centre of the flock, where the bodies were massed the thickest. He didn't know the range of the bow, but if his arrow reached the geese at all, it should hit something.

He heard his mother and Fin murmuring prayers to Aal as he inhaled a breath, held it, then loosed the arrow. He had another on the string before the first one reached the geese, released it too. He sent four arrows speeding upwards before the migrating flock was out of range. Then he lowered his eyes to see if he'd brought any of them down. With a surge of joy, he spotted two birds spiralling out of the sky. He had missed with half his shots, but the other two had found their marks.

For a few heart-stopping moments, it appeared as if the geese might fall in the river and be lost, but as he watched in agonised suspense, they dropped to the ground a short distance away. Both birds were already dead, shot through the breast. Kelan's heart swelled with pride as his companions congratulated him.

With no sign of anyone else in the area, and plenty of dry material all around for fuel, even Logen agreed they could risk a fire.

While his mother took charge of the geese, Kelan searched for the other two arrows and found them, undamaged. He returned them to the quiver with satisfaction. The two successful ones were already there, having been washed in the river and dried on his shirt. A good hunter looked after his equipment.

By this time, the smell of the roasting meat was tormenting him, filling his mouth with water. He swallowed again and again, staring at the birds as if he could speed their cooking by sheer force of will.

At last they were done to his mother's satisfaction. Kelan crammed his mouth with hot roasted goose and bit down. The grease spilled out over his chin and the warm savoury juices trickled down his throat, making him groan again, this time in utter bliss. He chewed, swallowed and reached for more. It was the best breakfast he'd ever tasted.

When even Kelan had had his fill, they wrapped the rest of the meat, collected all the water they could carry, and set off with the morning sun at their backs.

They walked for most of that day on dirt roads, following the fence lines of what had once been farms, without encountering a single other person or any sign of animal life. Apart from the five of them, the only movement was from the occasional dust-devil, snatched up from the road and whirled around by a gust of wind. This had once been the same kind of country Kelan had grown up in; this was what Soran's land might become, now that the Blight had reached it.

They passed several abandoned farmhouses, but as Logen had predicted, they'd been stripped of any food. They found a couple of abandoned packs in one, and filled them with objects they thought might be useful, including a small cooking pot that merely taunted Kelan with the probability that it would remain empty for the foreseeable future.

By late afternoon, Kelan had begun to feel they were the only living creatures left in the world, condemned to trudge forever through this eerie, deserted landscape.

The high-pitched cry shocked him to a standstill. It was a human sound — someone calling out in pain — and it came from the base of a huge dead tree up ahead. Logen and Tulley had drawn their swords, and Kelan hastily followed suit. The group cautiously moved forward, until Kelan could make out a lone figure lying under the tree, writhing on the ground. Before he could tell any more than that, his mother dashed past him, her skirts flying. She reached the tree and dropped to her knees. "*Sara!*"

Kelan was already sprinting to join her. He skidded to a stop and saw that she was right: against all the odds, they'd found their lost companion. Sara was wearing unfamiliar clothing — an old, worn dress instead of the tunic and trousers he'd last seen her in — but it was her. She didn't look in very good shape. Her eyes were closed, and she was grimacing and twisting on the ground as if in the grip of a nightmare. His mother put a hand to the sweat-beaded forehead. "Sara! Wake up!" There was no response.

The others arrived. "She's injured," Fin said, pointing to the strip of cloth bound around Sara's right arm.

"She's running a high fever," his mother replied. "The wound must be infected." She undid the knots and unwound the cloth, to reveal a long, ugly gash surrounded by dried blood. The edges of the cut had closed, but they were red and angry. The skin all around was swollen and dark, like a bruise. "I need a fire and a sharp knife," she said firmly. "I have to reopen this wound and let the infection out, before it poisons her whole body."

Everyone got to work. Kelan and Logen gathered dead wood and started the fire, protecting it with their bodies as well as they could from the fitful breeze. Tulley took out his knife and began sharpening it on a stone, passing his hands over the blade to shape it to a fine edge. Fin filled the newly-acquired cooking pot with water, dropped the strip of stained bandage in it and set it over the fire.

By the time the water boiled, the wind had dropped to a whisper, and the sun was close to setting. Fin removed the pot from the heat and set it aside to cool, fishing out the bandage with a stick and hanging it over a low branch to dry. Then she held the blade of the sharpened knife in the flames for a few seconds before handing it to Kelan's mother, who was bending low over her patient, murmuring soothing words.

As Kelan and the others held Sara down, his mother skilfully ran the hot, sharp blade along the line of the cut. Thick liquid spurted out, greeny-yellow and foul smelling. Kelan turned his face away, swallowing convulsively and hoping he wouldn't be sick in front of Logen and Tulley. Then, embarrassed by his weakness, he forced himself to keep watching.

His mother squeezed Sara's arm again and again, pressing out as much of the disgusting discharge as she could. Her patient writhed more violently against the restraining hands, moaning and crying out hoarsely, but her eyes remained closed.

Finally satisfied, Kelan's mother bathed the arm with the freshly boiled water and re-wrapped it in the now dry strip of cloth. "It should really be stitched," she said, "but I don't have the means. I pray that my skal will be strong enough."

As the last rays of the setting sun flooded golden light across the field, she bowed her head and stroked Sara's arm from shoulder to elbow, murmuring words as familiar to Kelan as her voice and face. He'd heard them from as far back as he could remember, listening as his mother tended farm workers who'd been injured by scythes or thrown from horses, and villagers who were sick. On many occasions — whether he'd broken an arm falling out of a tree or just scraped his knees while playing — she'd uttered the very same words over him: "Be well, my love, be well. Health return to you. Strength and healing be yours."

As she stroked and whispered, her patient gradually calmed. Finally, Sara's face relaxed and she lay still, breathing slowly and deeply, as though she was simply sleeping.

Kelan's mother sat back and gave a long sigh. "I think she'll be all right now," she said, sounding exhausted. "I'll need to do more healing, but the worst danger is over."

"How in Algarth did she come to be here anyway?" Kelan asked. No one had an answer.

"Who do you think attacked her?" Fin asked.

"And are they coming back?" Kelan put in. It seemed the most important point.

"We'll set a guard tonight," Logen said, "and see if she's able to travel

190

in the morning." He insisted on taking the first watch himself, urging the others to get some sleep.

Kelan already knew his mother wouldn't lie down tonight — her patients always came first. In fact, her strong connection to anyone she'd healed was the reason they were both here now. If she hadn't insisted on protecting Sara against Soran, none of the events of the past weeks would have happened. Kelan would still be living on the Erdal farm, trying to get out from under his uncle's thumb.

He lay down on the hard, dry ground, remembering the last time he'd seen Soran. It felt so long ago, like a different life. Back then, his highest ambition had been to marry Rassil and perhaps become a hunter after his skal came in. The Kelan of those days seemed like a stranger now. He'd been so annoyed at his mother for taking Sara's side against Soran, leading to Rassil being sent away with her.

But he was the one who'd got it wrong. Sara had been innocent, and his mother had done a very brave thing standing up for her. And now, because of her actions, they'd both been caught up in something much bigger than themselves. Kelan was a bit surprised to realise he was glad about that, in spite of the danger. All of Algarth was depending on the six of them now, even if nobody else knew it. Compared to that, the ambitions of his boyhood felt very small and unimportant.

He rolled over, trying to get more comfortable. Really, coming across Sara again was an incredible coincidence. Could Fin be right to believe that Aal was helping them? Kelan had always believed that the god existed, the same way that he believed the sun, the moon, and the stars existed, but he'd never imagined Aal taking an active interest in his life, any more than the sun, the moon, or the stars. The idea was somehow comforting and pretty unsettling, both at the same time.

He blew out a sigh and flopped onto his back. He'd think about it tomorrow. Right now, he needed to get some sleep, before his turn came to take the watch.

TWENTY-SIX

Sara

Sara woke to a fresh, cloudy morning. The breeze felt good on her upturned face. She breathed the cold air in deeply, feeling better than she had for ages. The dizziness and nausea were completely gone. Her arm still throbbed, but it was nothing like the agony of before.

A faint whisper whipped her head around.

Mena was sitting cross-legged beside her with her eyes closed and her lips moving. Choking back a cry, Sara extended a trembling hand to make sure her friend was really there. At her touch, Mena opened her eyes. "Sara! You're awake!"

Right then, Sara had never seen anything as beautiful as Mena's smiling, freckled face. Something bubbled up in her throat, and she couldn't tell if she was about to laugh or cry. It came out as a kind of sobbing hiccough. Mena seemed to understand. She helped Sara to sit up, and they hugged each other tightly.

It was unbelievable. She had gone to sleep ill and alone, expecting to wake the same way, if she even woke at all. She had hoped desperately that Mena and the others were still alive, but it had been a very faint hope. And here they all came, crowding around her, apparently as glad to see her as she was to see them. If a miracle like this could happen, anything must be possible.

She was eager to find out what had been happening to them while she'd been at Edervale Castle. And of course, everyone wanted to know how she'd come to be here, alone and wounded. To her surprise, they told her she'd been unconscious for a whole day and night, and that Mena had saved her life, yet again. She heard about Tulley's amazing destruction of the attackers' boat on Deep Lake and her friends' journey since then.

In turn, she explained about shaping a Gateway to Edervale Castle, Tarn's part in bringing the Blight to Algarth, and his insane plan to cure it himself once the other Greenhaelen were gone. She also mentioned King Tana's book. But she kept back her most personal discovery.

She felt bad about it, but she just couldn't bring herself to reveal her true identity. She knew Mena wouldn't reject her, but how would Logen, Fin, and Tulley react if they knew she was Tarn's niece, and that she'd been deceiving them all this time about where she was really from? Unless Mena had already told them. But no, Mena wouldn't do that. As a healer, she must be used to keeping other people's secrets, and as a friend, she wouldn't gossip about Sara behind her back.

But even Mena didn't know the whole truth. Sara's entire being shrank from the idea of sharing the story of how Tarn had murdered her parents and stranded her in another world. It was too private, too painful. She didn't want to face all those feelings again right now.

The questions and answers went on and on until her head began to swim with tiredness. Mena noticed and sternly ordered them all to leave Sara alone to rest.

As they stood to go, Sara surreptitiously laid a hand on the Blighted ground beside her. She concentrated, willing the brown remnants of plants to come alive again, but nothing happened, except that a dull ache began throbbing behind her eyes. Mena was right, she wasn't recovered enough.

The others had gone a little way from her and sat down together to talk some more. She knew that her newfound ability to shape Gateways had stunned them all. She wondered again why she'd ended up here when she made that last Gateway, instead of in the forest, where she'd intended to go. She tried to recall exactly what she'd thought and felt to make that happen, but her head felt like it was stuffed with cotton wool.

She was too tired to think properly. She closed her eyes and slept again.

When she woke, the others were all standing around a wagon, talking to an old man. He was stooped, and his short, bandy legs were bare below a ragged tunic that seemed to be tied around his waist with knotted string. A faded green felt hat — shaped like a squashed bag and looking as though it might have been handed down through several generations — was jammed down over his ears. Beneath it, bits of dirty white hair stuck out in all directions.

Glancing her way and seeing she was awake, Logen left the group and came over. He squatted beside her. "The old man's name is Peddar. He's heading for Gadara, looking for carting work on the way, but we're hoping he'll sell us his wagon and one of the horses instead."

"Why do we need a horse and wagon?" Sara levered herself up on her good elbow.

The diffused light from the overcast sky dimmed the amazing blueness of Logen's eyes, shading it slightly towards grey. Lines that Sara hadn't noticed before etched his forehead. Whatever he'd been through over the past few days, it had taken a toll. "We're too easy to spot in this open farmland. It'll be safer for all of us if we can get to the shelter of the forest a few reaches further west. The trees are Blighted, but they'll still provide more cover than we have right now. Mena says you aren't fit enough to walk that far yet, but if you ride in the wagon, we'll be able to start out straight away. The rest of us can take turns riding and walking. Once we're there, you, Fin, and I will work together to heal the trees."

He'd spoken firmly, but Sara sensed anxiety behind his words. Logen wasn't as optimistic about the outcome as he was pretending to be.

He switched his gaze back towards the wagon. "Poor old Peddar is practically a simpleton — no one with any sense would be looking for work in Blighted country — but luckily he used to cart hay for Soran, and he seems to have a lot of respect for Mena. She's trying to persuade him now."

Sara couldn't hear what Mena and Peddar were saying, but she could see that Logen was right about the carter's respect for her friend. As she watched, the old man took off his bag-like hat and clutched it against his chest with both hands. Each time Mena spoke, he ducked his head and bowed to her as if she was royalty. Finally, still ducking and bending, he took something from Mena's outstretched hand. Then he went and unhitched one of the horses. Clapping his hat back on his head, he scrambled up onto the horse's bare back and trotted off.

Mena and Kelan came over.

"Well done, Mena," Logen said. "I didn't seem to be getting anywhere with him."

"He's an old idiot," Kelan said. "And he's disgusting. Did you see that hat? It looked like rats had been nesting in it."

"He was scared of you," Mena said to Logen, shooting a frown of disapproval towards her son. "He's a good soul but easily frightened by strangers and big words. As soon as he understood what I wanted, he agreed straight away. He offered the horse and wagon for free, but I made him take some money. Tulley and Kelan both had a few coins, but I still feel we cheated him. If we ever get back to normal life, we have to pay him properly."

"We will, Mena, I promise," Logen said. "I was already indebted to Peddar before this. I'll do my best to make it all up to him."

Mena frowned. "What do you mean? How were you already indebted to him?"

Logen smiled faintly. "It was the day Kelan and I met for the first time."

"I was hiding in the hay wagon, trying to get to Eorna to see Rassil," Kelan broke in. "Hey, what happened to Peddar that day, anyway? I thought they attacked him when they stole the wagon, but I guess not."

Logen shook his head. "They didn't exactly steal it, or at least not intentionally. Niall stopped the horses, and Tulley went to ask Peddar if he could buy a bale of hay, because we were on our way to the Blighted area. But the poor man took one look at them, yelled, and ran away. Adric and Bram went after him, but he was gone. So, we took the wagon with us and left it at Bella's inn, to be returned to the docks. It had an owner's brand on the side, just like this one. It might even be the same wagon. Maybe Peddar got it back later."

Kelan laughed. "And now he's left it behind again. They're not going to be happy with him!"

Seeing the expression on Mena's face, Logen spoke quickly. "We'll pay our debt to him if we can, Mena, I swear. But for now, let's put Sara on the wagon and be on our way."

"I can get myself onto it, thanks," Sara said tartly, and stood up to prove it. After everything she'd learned at Edervale, she was done with being a passive participant. Her old self, the one who'd wanted nothing more than a quiet, safe little life, was almost incomprehensible to her now. It was as if she'd been sleepwalking for the past twenty years. She'd finally woken up, and she had no intention of drifting off again. She might not be fully recovered, but she could certainly climb onto a wagon without help.

Logen looked surprised at her sharp reply, but not offended. "I'm sorry, Sara. Of course you can. After you."

The bed of the wagon was mostly empty, except for one small bale of hay in a corner and a litter of ropes covering the floor. Sara sank down with her back against the bale. Even the slight exertion of climbing up had left her a little out of breath. Her arm was almost healed, but she certainly didn't have her full strength back, and she was quite glad she'd be riding rather than walking for now. Not that she would have admitted it.

A few hours later, Sara spotted the edge of the browned forest. More broadleaved, deciduous trees — her Gateway had taken her a long way from where she'd planned. She tried to work out what had gone wrong. She'd been picturing the huge, living conifer with the spirals. Ah, but she'd also been thinking about the Blight and wanting to cure it, hadn't she? So, her skal had taken her to a Blighted tree about the same size and with the same markings. It might even be a place that King Tarn had used hundreds of years ago; its size suggested it was old enough. This new ability she'd discovered was amazing, but it would take some practice to get it right.

"Just a little further," Logen said as they reached the tree line. "If anyone comes along, I want us hidden from sight."

"Wait a minute," Kelan said suddenly. "What about food? The goose is all gone, and we don't know how much longer we're going to be here, do we? You won't be able to cure the Blight if we all starve to death."

The yawning emptiness in Sara's stomach agreed. Her last meal had been the bowl of stew in the castle, two days ago.

"What do you suggest, Kelan?" Tulley asked, waving a brawny arm around to show the lack of anything resembling food nearby. "Have you seen any more geese?"

"No." Kelan's beardless chin jutted out defiantly. "But I've been thinking. We've been travelling through farmland, right? Some of these plants might've been root crops. Even though they're Blighted, won't the roots still be there under the ground?"

Appreciation replaced the scepticism in Tulley's broad face. "You might be onto something there, lad."

"Yes," Mena agreed, smiling at her son. "I don't know why I didn't think of it myself. Let's have a quick look before we go into the forest. Even Blighted, we should be able to recognise the leaves."

"It's certainly worth a try," Logen said. "But we should get the wagon into the trees first. And someone should stay with Sara. I don't like the idea of any of us being alone."

"I'll stay," Fin said. "To tell you the truth, I'm feeling a bit tired myself."

Tulley took a step towards her, his brow furrowed, but Fin just smiled at him. "Go on," she said. "I'll be fine. Sara and I will have a nice chat while you're gone."

When the others had left, Sara peered more closely at her companion. She'd never heard the little woman complain of tiredness before, or of anything else. Fin was usually so quiet that it was easy to forget she was there and just assume she was all right. But she wasn't as young as most of them, and this journey must have been very hard on her.

Sitting opposite her now, Sara felt a pang of guilt as she noticed the lines of strain on the older woman's face. Her cheeks, normally plump and flushed with pink, appeared sunken and almost grey.

Disquiet shivered through Sara. "Are you really all right?"

"I must say, I've felt better," Fin said. Seeing the look on Sara's face, she shook her head and smiled. "Now don't worry, Sara. Aal will make sure I get to where I'm meant to be. Perhaps Mena can do something to help. We'll ask her when she gets back."

"And from now on, you stay here with me and rest." Sara wasn't going to accept any argument about that. "No more walking."

"Yes, Sara," Fin agreed humbly, but at the same time her lips quirked in a smile that made Sara chuckle, despite her anxiety.

"All right, all right, I won't order you around anymore."

Fin nodded in satisfaction. "Good."

They began to talk of other things, but Sara's uneasiness wouldn't be dispelled. It wasn't only Fin. Logen seemed worn down by the strain of responsibility, and Sara herself was hardly at her best.

Right now, the plan for the three of them to cure the Blight before the Guards caught up with them seemed about as feasible as an assault on Mount Everest. And as likely to end in their deaths.

TWENTY-SEVEN
Sergeant Oren

"We're still searching, Commander Renn, but we haven't had any luck finding them."

"*Luck?*" Chairman Tarn hissed.

Sergeant Oren tried to keep the apprehension from showing on his face. He'd never been inside the Chairman's office before, and all these rich furnishings, not to mention the gilding that seemed to cover every hard surface, were making him nervous. He usually reported only to Commander Renn, whose own office was small and without decoration, a place of work rather than display.

Oren pulled himself together and continued, addressing both the men in front of him. "We think they had help getting away, sirs. The Guards they left tied up in the tavern said they'd been attacked by demons."

"Demons?" Tarn scoffed. "Don't be an idiot, Oren! There's no such thing! They're just trying to cover up their own incompetence. Ten armed Guards and they couldn't arrest a rabble of outlaws, including four women!"

He stood and began pacing, his long face red with anger. He was a tall, imposing man, whose bearing befitted his high position. His iron-grey hair and beard were neatly trimmed, and the sight of his high, prominent cheekbones made Oren even more aware of his own round, peasant face and bulbous nose. Each time the Chairman changed direction, his deep blue cloak swirled around his legs. Gold embroidery, on the neck and hem, glittered in the early morning sunlight that streamed through the tall windows.

He halted in front of Oren. "I should make an example of you, Sergeant, and promote someone who can get the job done. First," he held up a furious finger right in Oren's face, "you allowed your men to be ambushed in the heart of my capital city. Second," another finger shot up, "you went on a wild goose chase to Gadara, letting them get further away. Third, the debacle in Fortune Creek. And now," the fourth finger raised with such violence it actually hit Oren's nose, "fourth, you have had dozens of men searching for more than two weeks, without finding so much as a trace of them."

"The Chairman flung himself back onto his chair. "Why am I surrounded by fools who can't do the simplest job?"

"I, too, am eager to learn how Logen Rush was able to snatch the Greenhaelan woman from you and your men, Sergeant, right in the centre of Eorna," Renn said. "I understand that you had advance warning of the ambush and yet were unable to prevent it. How is that possible?"

He hadn't raised his voice, but Oren was under no illusion that the Commander was any less angry than the Chairman, or that his anger carried less threat for Oren's future. Commander Asher Renn, Deputy Chairman of the Council, wielded almost as much power as Tarn, although you wouldn't know it to look at him.

He was a slight man, of only medium height, dressed — like Oren himself — in a simple Guards' uniform of blue shirt and black trousers. The only sign of his rank was the Eagle of Algarth picked out in dark blue thread on his yellow Guards' badge. His hooded blue eyes bored into the Sergeant's brown ones, and his bony nose jutted out from his pale, beardless face, like the beak of the eagle on the badge. His head was completely bald, although none of the Guards knew if this was its natural state, or if the Commander shaved it.

Oren swallowed. His only chance was to tell them everything and hope they would decide it hadn't been his fault after all. "The Erdal woman's maid, Rassil Yar, and the boy, Kelan Erdal, brought me infor-mation that an attempt would be made on the way to the trial. The boy was able to name and describe each of the outlaws in detail."

It had been a good idea, befriending the little maid. Oren had found her crying in the kitchen, on her first night in Eorna. She was a simple, naïve girl, scared of the big, noisy city, and worried she would get in trouble for associating with the Greenhaelan woman. Oren had reassured her and, seeing his chance, offered her a reward for doing her duty and telling him everything she overheard in the prisoner's room. She'd been pathetically grateful and eager to help. Her information had been useful up to a point, but the time he'd spent with her had really paid off on the third night, when she'd brought the boy to him.

He went on with his report. "I made my preparations early in the morning, sending archers to the rooftops lining the road and Guards on horseback along the route, all of them with descriptions of the outlaws. I planned to drive the carriage myself, surrounded by mounted Guards."

He paused. Renn nodded to him to continue.

"I had also posted one of my men to watch the prisoners through a spy hole in the door until it was time to move them. He saw the Greenhaelan prisoner reading a piece of paper. He confiscated it and brought it to me. It outlined a plan to attack the carriage as it reached the market square, about halfway to the Council building. The spot was marked on a map drawn on the paper. I kept four good men with me and sent the rest to the ambush spot, hoping to apprehend them before the carriage arrived."

He swallowed again. This was the tricky part.

"And?" Tarn waved a gold-ringed hand impatiently.

"They attacked us almost as soon as we left the building. The paper was a ruse." Hot blood surged up Oren's neck. He'd been taken for a fool and he knew it. It wouldn't happen again. He'd bring them to justice no matter how long it took.

But first he had to get through this interview, hopefully with his Sergeant's badge intact. "The Erdal boy neglected to mention that one of the outlaws is a Beast Speaker, sirs. He sent the horses mad. They bolted with my Guards, leaving me to defend the carriage alone."

"A well-thought-out plan," Renn mused. "One of them is intelligent.

I suppose sending you to Gadara was another of their ploys?"

"It seems so, sir. The word came from a long-time informant, a stableman in the inn where they had been staying. He had never given us bad information before."

The man in question had disappeared by the time a furious Oren had ordered men after him, but he saw no need to volunteer this additional failure.

"You sent out their names and descriptions to the Tellers?"

"Yes, Commander, and the offer of twenty silver coins for the capture of each of them, as you ordered. The news should be all over Algarth by now. They cannot elude us much longer."

"No? And how did they *elude* you at Fortune Creek?" The Chairman's deep voice dripped with sarcasm. Oren felt his cheeks burn as he answered.

"The same young maid escaped from the outlaws and found me and my men, on our way back to Eorna. When she told me that Logen Rush was heading for Fortune Creek, we set off as fast as we could ride."

Little Rassil had proven herself braver than he'd expected, escaping in the night and setting out to find him. He'd given her a few coins and sent her back to Eorna with one of his men, but he should probably do more for her. The city could be a dangerous place for a pretty, young woman on her own. She'd need someone to look after her, and she certainly couldn't depend on that foolish boy with his promise charm. Oren's sister-in-law owned a dress shop. Perhaps he could persuade her to give Rassil a job.

Lost in thought, he suddenly realised that the Chairman and Commander Renn were staring at him. He rushed back into speech. "As soon as the prisoner escaped, before I heard that Rush was heading for Gadara, I sent troops of Guards to watch the main roads. One troop was stationed in a farmhouse, near Fortune Creek. They discovered the outlaws were in the tavern and set out immediately.

"By the time I arrived, Rush and his men had already defeated all ten Guards and tied them up. One of the outlaws was killed in the fight, but the others fled into the foothills. It was raining heavily and too dark to see, and I had to wait until first light the next morning to continue the

202

pursuit. By then, all traces of their trail were gone."

Tarn and Renn regarded him for long moments in silence, and then stepped aside to talk privately. Oren stood at attention, eyes forward, resisting the urge to run his hand over his bristly scalp. One word from either of his superiors, and his career would be over.

He'd always taken pride in being a Warrant Guard, upholding the law and keeping the people of Algarth safe. Almost from the day he'd left his parents' farm to enlist, it had been his ambition to rise as high in the service as he could. He'd even dared to believe he might be Commander one day.

Now, at only twenty-eight years old, he was already Sergeant of the Garrison in Eorna. When the Commander had announced that, due to the increasing need for Warrant Guards, he intended to promote two of his Sergeants to a new rank, Captain of the Guard, Oren had resolved to be one of them. He was dedicated and hardworking, and — despite his skal being the physical one of Strength — he was also smart. He deserved the promotion, and had been fairly confident of getting it, until this disaster. He had to redeem himself. He'd do whatever it took, within the law, to prove himself worthy of his Commander's confidence.

"Come here, Oren," the Chairman said at last. Oren stood stiffly in front of him. "Where are the ten Guards from Fortune Creek now?"

"In the farmhouse, Mister Chairman, recovering from their injuries. They should be ready to ride out and join the search soon."

Tarn stroked his beard, pursing his lips. "I shall not demote you, Sergeant, not yet, although you richly deserve it. Instead, I will give you one last chance. Listen closely."

As those dark eyes stared deeply into his, a strange dizziness came over Oren. He couldn't move a muscle. The Chairman's words seemed to be reaching him from a long way off, yet at the same time tunnelling right into his brain, echoing inside his skull.

"When you arrived in Fortune Creek, Sergeant, you discovered all ten of your Guards already dead. The outlaws had captured them, tied them up and then murdered them in cold blood. You saw the evidence with your own eyes. Do you understand?"

Oren found he could nod. He did.

"In consequence of this barbaric act, the Council of Six has voted that no trial is necessary. The outlaws have all forfeited their lives. The reward for each of them will be increased to one hundred silver coins, dead or alive. You will send this news immediately to all the towns and villages of Algarth. You are dismissed."

Oren found himself in the corridor outside the Chairman's door, with no memory of how he had got there. It didn't matter. He'd been given his second chance. He knew what he had to do, and this time, he wouldn't fail.

TWENTY-EIGHT

Tarn

After Oren had left the room, Tarn regarded his Deputy. "What do you think, Renn? Will that dolt finally be able to catch them now?"

"Sergeant Oren is not incompetent, sir, he merely lacks imagination. With the extra…ah…incentive you gave him, it is only a matter of time."

"I hope so, Renn. Now, something must be done about those Guards in Fortune Creek. We can't have them turning up alive when I've just told Oren they're all dead." He stared intently into his Deputy's eyes, reinforcing his words with all the mental force at his command. "Send some reliable men to take care of them — quietly. Make sure no one ever sees them again."

"Yes, sir. I suggest the same men we employed at the timber camps and the harbour. They are professionals, and if they are paid sufficiently, they will not talk."

Tarn nodded. He smiled as a further thought occurred to him. "And organise a public memorial service to honour the fallen Guards' noble sacrifice. After that, Logen Rush and his Greenhaelen won't have any support left."

"I shall arrange it, sir." No trace of doubt or defiance in Renn's dull blue eyes or flat, nasal voice. There never was. A boring man, but useful.

"Good. And now, what about the Blight?"

"The disease continues to spread. It appears unlikely to die out naturally."

"Excellent. As soon as Rush and my niece are out of the way, I will step in. Afterwards, no one will challenge my position ever again."

Renn bowed his bald head. "Is there anything else, sir?"

Tarn waved a hand. "No, no, just go and get on with it. I'll see you in the Council Chamber in an hour."

After Renn had left, Tarn poured himself a glass of brandy and stood at the window, sipping it slowly. His city lay spread out below him. He always thought of it that way — as *his* city — even though he hadn't grown up in Eorna, but in Edervale Castle, like generations of his family before him. He visited the castle often — it was the perfect place to relax and rest from his responsibilities. But Eorna was his home. And of all the buildings in the city, he belonged most truly in this one, the City Hall, steering the nation as he had been born to do. His father had been too blind to see it, the stupid old fool.

Tarn gulped a mouthful of brandy, slopping some over the rim. His hand shook as he set the glass down on a nearby table. The memories could still affect him, even after all these years.

As the third in his line to rule the Council of Six, Mendo Tarn had naturally educated and trained his only son to follow him into the "family business" of government. Villembelt had been more than willing — in fact, his own secret ambition had been to become the youngest Chairman ever, eclipsing the achievements of his ancestors. That was, until the day Mendo had called his twenty-eight-year-old son into his study and told him that it was all over.

"You are only interested in power, Villem, power over others." Father's face was even sterner than usual, his expression set like lines carved in stone. "You have no desire to work for the good of our nation and its people. You value shallow flattery and the slavish obedience of your inferiors over your responsibility to Algarth. I had hoped that you would grow out of this before my time on the Council was done, but you have not." He paused and bowed his grey head.

Villembelt wished his father would get on with it. He was bored with these endless lectures about duty and responsibility. He shuffled his feet loudly.

Father lifted his head and gazed into Villembelt's eyes, the same deep brown as his own. "The family are not supporting your bid for a seat on the Council, Villem. Your sister will be the one to continue our legacy. Elana is young, but she is intelligent and hard-working, and she understands the concepts of duty and service. With guidance, she will make a fine Councillor and one day, perhaps, Algarth's first female Chairman."

For long moments, Villembelt was too stunned to speak. Then an anguished squawk of protest burst from him. "But she's a Greenhaelan! She has no trace of Mind Wending at all!"

Father frowned darkly. "You place too much value on such things, Villem. No skal is superior to another." His voice grew harsh. "Your own mother is a Greenhaelan. Or had you forgotten?"

"N-n-no," Villembelt stammered, taking a step back. "It's just that you and Grandfather are both Mind Wenders, and so am I…" He heard the whining note enter his voice, and despised himself for it. Why couldn't he ever stand up to Father?

Mendo's gaze flicked over his son's twisted face. When he spoke again, the harshness was gone from his voice. "It is true that you are a Mind Wender, my son, although your skal is weak. But that would not matter, if you truly understood what it means to lead and govern." He heaved a sigh and dropped a hand onto Villembelt's shoulder. "Enough now, son. The decision has been made. We will not speak of it again." He squeezed the shoulder. "Take some time to consider what you wish to do with your life. I will provide sufficient funds to support you in any enterprise you wish to undertake."

The mere memory of that long-ago conversation made Tarn burn with fury and shame. Father had not only been unjust, but completely wrong. Mind Wending was far more useful to a ruler than Green Healing; Tarn had proved it. To persuade others to your point of view, to motivate them or frighten them into obedience, that was the way to get things done!

He'd always known he'd be a Mind Wender, long before his skals came in. The Green Healing had come as a shock, but he'd chosen to ignore it and concentrate on his mental abilities. That shot of his father's

— your skal is weak — had hit home, but he'd been sure that if he trained and practised long enough, he'd grow stronger.

And he'd been right. Oh, not at first, he admitted that. For years he seemed to be making almost no progress. But he'd persisted and finally achieved success. Over the last four years, his control had become more and more sure. His skal had risen from mere persuasion to an irresistible compulsion, as long as he concentrated on only one person at a time, as he'd just done with Oren and Renn.

Everything had gone according to plan, except for the return of his cursed niece. She could rob him of everything he'd worked for, everything he deserved. He slapped his palms down on the windowsill in frustration.

But then, Renn's words came back to him: *it is only a matter of time.* He was worrying for nothing. With a hundred silver coins on each of their heads, none of the outlaws stood a chance, not even Sara.

And afterwards? Sara and Rush, at least, must be put to death. He couldn't risk leaving either of them alive. He might show clemency to the others and imprison them for life. That would demonstrate to his people that he was a merciful ruler as well as a powerful one.

He straightened and turned away from the window. He had work to do. His only regret was that his father hadn't lived long enough to see his triumph.

Thirty minutes later, Tarn swept into the Council Chamber. His fellow Councillors rose at his entrance, then resumed their seats. He scrutinised them one by one as he sat down.

Renn, as Deputy Chairman, sat on Tarn's right. His bald head and gaunt face had always reminded Tarn of a skull, and he had a peculiarly stiff and formal way of speaking. A dreary little man, made for standing in the wings while those with greater gifts took their place on the stage. It was entirely due to Tarn's influence that Renn was on the Council at all. He had only one skal, a weak one of Remembering, but he was an excellent organiser and very efficient at taking care of details. Tarn had seen his potential when no one else had and used his traditional right as Chairman to appoint his own Deputy four years ago. He hadn't regretted it.

Next to Renn sat Forn Geralt, looking, as usual, as if he had come straight from the stable. It was offensive that a man like that was allowed to be a member of the Council of Six. Geralt was barely literate, a complete peasant, from his haystack of dirty-blond hair to his frayed leg wrappings and old goat-skin shoes. Even his skal lowered the prestige of this body. He was a Beast Healer, specialising in horses, and only moderately talented at that. Surely the farmers and agricultural workers could be persuaded to choose a more suitable representative, someone from the land-holding class, who knew how to dress and behave in polite society. The ridiculous old man was actually sitting there picking his teeth!

At least Dania Malath, next to Geralt, was dressed fittingly, in a costly red hooded cloak over a yellow silk gown. She wore a thick gold necklace, and her fingers were covered with rings holding precious stones. Her brown hair hung loose on her shoulders today, which was unusual for her. Perhaps she was trying to project a softer image. If so, she would fool no one here. They all knew she was as hard as nails, caring for nothing except the accumulation of wealth.

As long as Tarn kept the business opportunities flowing her way, he could count on her loyalty. She'd already made a fortune from the first sale of timber to Bregia, after he'd given her advance notice of his export plans. As Council Treasurer, with a strong skal of Reckoning, she probably had some scheme of embezzlement of Council funds going on, but he didn't care about that, as long as she didn't grow too greedy. No, he wasn't worried about Dania Malath.

The other woman on the Council was another matter entirely. Adara Domben cared for neither money nor power, although she came from a family rich in both. Her skal of Remembering was very strong, her memory almost eidetic. At fifty years old and in her third term on the Council, she represented her fellow Memorers, who were Algarth's teachers, historians, archivists and Tellers. She also spoke for the Skalsingers, most of whom had Remembering as a secondary skal. She managed Algarth's growing civil service, a task she performed efficiently enough, and no doubt with unimaginative honesty.

She was wearing a leaf-patterned shawl over a simple rust-coloured dress, with no jewellery. Her grey-streaked hair was parted in the middle, with two long plaits hanging down the sides of her plain, round face. Tarn didn't care for her, and he knew that the feeling was mutual. Not that she was ever openly rude. On the surface, her words were always courteous, but they often carried a sting in the tail, usually directed at him.

The tiresome woman also seemed to have an unusually strong resistance to Mind Wending. Tarn had rarely been able to persuade Adara Domben to his point of view. She had argued strongly, if futilely, against outlawing the Greenhaelen.

Bander Frey sat beside her, his head bent towards her as she spoke under her breath, their faces close enough that one of his coarse red plaits touched her hair. Tarn had suspected for a while that there was something going on between them, although Frey was at least five years younger and very much her social inferior. They were both in for an unpleasant surprise today, one they richly deserved.

The two of them, along with Logen Rush, had once formed a bloc on the Council, posing a real threat to Tarn's plans. That was over now, of course, but he still hoped to remove the other two from office. And now a way to do just that — to one of them at least — had dropped right into his lap, thanks to Oren's report. Picturing their reactions, he smiled at them. Frey quickly straightened, his light eyes staring at Tarn out of his broad, freckled face. He looked apprehensive, as well he might.

Tarn called the meeting to order, and then sat impatiently through all the tedious routine business. Finally, it was time for Renn to present his report on the activities of the Warrant Guards, including the intelligence obtained from Oren that morning. Tarn sat up.

As Renn repeated the names of the outlaws now known to be travelling with Logen Rush — including one *Tulley Frey* — Tarn fixed greedy eyes on Bander Frey's face. He was rewarded with exactly the expression of dismay he had hoped to see. When Renn reported that the outlaws had killed ten Warrant Guards in Fortune Creek, both Frey and Domben appeared absolutely stricken. Delighted, Tarn schooled his own face to show only grave concern.

He was about to speak when that oaf Geralt beat him to it. "What's wrong with those good-for-nothing men of yours, eh, Renn?" he growled. "Why can't they catch these blasted outlaws?"

Renn replied as calmly as always, ignoring Geralt's rudeness. "We believe the criminals are being assisted by a small number of misguided people who are still loyal to Logen Rush. However, when news of the massacre at Fortune Creek spreads, that will change. Chairman Tarn has also generously offered to increase the reward for the capture of the outlaws from his own funds. It will not be possible for Rush and his followers to remain free for much longer."

That was Tarn's cue. He lowered his eyes to a spot on the table directly in front of him and spoke slowly and solemnly, as if he regretted the need to say anything at all. In fact, he was enjoying himself hugely. "Thank you, Deputy Renn. Unfortunately, this brings up a rather, ah, *painful* matter. There now seems no doubt that Master Shaper Tulley Frey has joined Logen Rush, and that he was heavily involved in the atrocity at Fortune Creek. Ten good men, while attempting to do their duty to Algarth and this Council, were wounded, disarmed and then cold-blood-edly killed. I believe several of them left widows and children behind."

He paused for effect. Complete silence filled the room. They all knew what was coming now. He raised his head and skewered the shrinking Frey with a piercing gaze. "I believe this Tulley Frey is in fact related to a member of the Council?"

Above his red beard, the dark freckles stood out in sharp relief against Frey's ashen cheeks. "He's my older brother." He pressed his lips tightly together and said nothing more.

"It can't be true," Adara Domben said fiercely. "I've known Logen Rush and Tulley Frey for many years. They would never do such a thing, never."

"We are all shocked, Madam Councillor," Renn replied, "but the truth of the matter is not in doubt. We have taken witness statements from Sergeant Oren and others who were present at Fortune Creek. The outlaws resisted violently when the Guards attempted to arrest them in the tavern. All ten Guards are dead. When they were discovered, their hands and feet were tied with rope. Rush and his men bound them and then executed them."

"History has taught us time and time again that witnesses are not always to be relied upon," Adara insisted. After the first shock of the news, her usual composure was already back in place. Tarn almost admired her. The woman didn't know when she was beaten.

"Men may tamper with the truth for all manner of reasons," she continued. Her hazel eyes slid sideways to meet Tarn's, and suddenly he knew her words were meant for him. With an effort, he stared back blandly, but inside he was seething with anger at her impertinence.

After a moment, she shifted her gaze back to Renn, and her chin lifted in challenge. "I for one do not believe a word of it."

Renn merely raised his sparse eyebrows, as if to say, *I cannot help what you choose to believe.* Her eyes blazed at him but she said nothing more.

"The facts do seem clear, Councillor Domben," Tarn said. "And that being so, Councillor Frey has a decision to make. Can he, in good conscience, retain his seat on the Council of Six, knowing that the deeds of his brother have brought shame and disgrace on his family, tainting not only his own good name, but, by virtue of his high position, the good name and reputation of this Council?" Tarn was quite proud of that question. He had practised it several times to get it just right.

Adara opened her mouth to speak again, but Frey laid a hand on hers. She turned her head sharply towards him.

Here it comes, thought Tarn.

"You're right, Mister Chairman," Frey said slowly. "I don't believe Tulley committed this horrible crime, but it's not fitting for me to be on the Council, not until my brother's name is cleared." He bobbed his head to Tarn, stood, tipped his chair forward against the edge of the table, and left the room.

It was all over very quickly after that. Adara Domben voted against accepting the resignation, but she was the only one, as Tarn had known she would be. Bander Frey was gone. Of Tarn's three original enemies on the Council, only one remained. He adjourned the meeting in high spirits.

Back in his quarters, he wasted no time. His monthly trip to the other world was scheduled for today. There would be papers waiting for his signature and some decisions only he could make. It shouldn't take more than a few hours. He changed into Melville Barnett's suit and tie, and, after a moment's thought, buckled on his sword and added a knife. The Blighted area was large, and he had no real reason, beyond a vague intuition, to think she might have gone there, but if the opportunity came to rid himself of his inconvenient niece, he intended to take it.

The trip through the Gateway left him momentarily dizzy as always, but he was ready for it and waited for the feeling and the mist to pass. Yes, he was standing beneath the tree with its familiar whorled pattern, at a spot where two trails met. Despite the existence of the trails, it had been a lonely place — he'd rarely seen anyone else here. Since the Blight had taken hold, it had become even more deserted, the perfect junction to come and go unseen.

He'd taken a small risk today, shaping a Gateway from Eorna, rather than riding out here as usual, but he wanted to be away for as short a time as possible. The gamble had paid off. After a short rest, he'd be on his way to Melville Barnett's apartment in Sydney.

He shook off the last of the haziness and shot a quick glance over his shoulder to make certain he was alone. His breath caught. He spun around. A horse and wagon had been standing behind him this whole time, only a dozen steps away. Thankfully, the wagon seat was empty. He let out the breath. No one had seen his arrival.

Even so, he'd had a shock, and his heart was still beating too fast to reliably shape his Gateway. He tried to calm it down, but it was no use. First, he needed to be sure he was safe. He approached the cart, his sword half drawn, his eyes scanning the trees for any sign of the owner returning. Barnett's black business shoes crunched loudly over the dry, Blighted leaves that covered the trail.

Someone sat up in the back of the wagon and stared straight at him. The hair lifted on the back of his neck. In his fright, he didn't even recognise the apparition for a moment. Then he drew his sword all the way out and broke into a run.

She was already on her feet when he reached the lowered tailgate. He leaped up, landing almost on top of someone else, who was lying between him and Sara. With a cry, the grey-haired woman reached out and snatched the loose cloth of his trousers, as if to hold him back. Recovering from his surprise, he knocked her on the head with the hilt of his sword, thrust her aside, and kept going. He was only a few strides from his target when a shout of outrage rang out from behind him.

Pointing his sword straight at his niece, he briefly turned his head. A young man was running towards them, stringing an arrow to his bow as he came. Tarn swore and made a grab for Sara, intending to swing her around and use her as a shield. To his astonishment, she fought him like a wildcat, twisting, punching and kicking. Her strength was no match for his, her blows too feeble to hurt him, but her wild flailing made it impossible to get a grip on her.

The sword was no use in these close quarters. He tried to back away, give himself room to take a swing, but she followed him, grabbing at his sleeve. He abandoned the sword and reached for his knife. She kicked him in the knee. Hot pain buckled his leg under him.

With all his strength, he threw his weight onto the other foot. Hopping backwards on one leg, his arms flung out to the sides, he tried desperately to recover his balance. For a moment, he seemed to be winning, and then his foot came down on a coil of rope. His ankle twisted awkwardly and he went down, striking his head hard against the side of the wagon.

Agony and rage exploded, and with them a further burst of strength. He had kept hold of the knife. Quick as a snake, he was back up in a crouch, ignoring the throbbing knee. He swept his free arm behind Sara's legs and, with a mighty heave, pulled her towards him. Her feet shot out from under her. A split second later, her back slammed onto the floor of the cart.

She cried out once, and then lay gasping for air, all the fight knocked out of her. Like a flash, he set the knife blade against her throat, pressing just hard enough to draw a fine line of blood along the edge. At the touch of the knife, she stiffened, staring up at him in terror. The breath rasped through her motionless lips.

He bared his teeth. "One move and I'll slit your throat."

A grunt sounded behind him. His head jerked around. The young archer landed on the rear of the wagon, only a few strides away. Tarn's heart yammered in shock. His fist tightened on the handle of the knife. "Stay back or she's dead!"

The boy froze, his own hand gripping the hilt of his sheathed sword, his eyes switching between Tarn's face and the blade at Sara's throat.

Tarn's mind raced. He couldn't see the bow. The boy must have dropped it when he'd jumped up onto the wagon.

"Let her go!" The voice was high-pitched, betraying fear.

Tarn took a deep breath. No need to panic. He had control of the situation now. He shook his head. "No, I don't think so. If you want her to stay alive, you'll do exactly as I say. Sara and I are going to take a little trip. If I see you following, I'll kill her."

He suddenly remembered the grey-haired woman, who had so foolishly tried to stop him from getting to Sara. There she was, lying crumpled against the opposite side of the wagon, very still. Served her right for getting in his way. He briefly wondered if she was dead or merely unconscious. It didn't matter. She would just be an inconvenience, either way.

"Wait," he ordered the boy, who had slowly begun to climb down from the back of the wagon. He gestured towards the slumped figure. "Take her with you."

The whelp snarled but obeyed. He picked up the limp woman and carried her to the tailgate, then jumped off and lifted her down.

"Good boy. Now go. And remember what I said about following me."

The youth's face was full of baffled fury. "If you harm Sara, I will find you and kill you."

"Get walking," Tarn growled. He stared into the insolent green eyes and tried to add a little mental force to the command, but the effort made his head ring with pain. He must have a concussion from hitting his head on the side of the wagon. Damn Sara! He wouldn't be able to Mind Wend until he'd recovered.

Still, the threat of the knife seemed to be enough. The boy edged backwards, carrying his burden. When Tarn judged he was far enough away, he ordered Sara to tie her ankles together with the rope, holding the knife at her throat the whole time to make sure she didn't try anything.

Her expression was as sullen and rebellious as the boy's had been, but like him she bent her head and obeyed. Tarn made sure the knots were tight, and then tied her hands together behind her back himself. He retrieved his sword and climbed onto the driver's seat.

A single glance behind showed that the youngster was still keeping his distance. He had deposited the woman on the ground and was bending over her.

Time to go. Tarn picked up the reigns. Two men and a woman emerged from the trees. Tarn recognised the taller man instantly. Logen Rush! The sight of his enemy filled him with such fury that he wanted to leap off the wagon and cut him down right now, but he knew it would be suicide — three against one, and him with his head pounding so hard he could barely think. Another item to add to his niece's account. Once they were out of sight of the men, he would take great pleasure in slitting her throat.

Then he'd rest and recover just long enough to shape a Gateway back to Eorna. He could tell Renn exactly where the outlaws were. Dozens of Guards would ride out immediately and surround them. Logen would finally be captured and executed.

Murky swirls of colour twisted around the edges of Tarn's vision, but they didn't matter. All that mattered was that he'd won. His head didn't even hurt any more. With an effort, he focused his gaze on the outlaws.

They stared back at him, but none of them seemed inclined to come any closer. He slapped the reins and headed west.

When he pulled up the horse about half an hour later, his head was still free of pain and his vision had almost completely cleared, but he was beginning to feel sleepy. He stood. His injured knee was swollen but he could take weight on the leg. He scanned the dead forest around him, listening intently at the same time. No sign of movement and no sound of pursuit. He didn't let this fool him. He was sure that Logen, at least, was following — the man wouldn't give up on Sara so easily when he'd gone to so much trouble to rescue her in the first place — but he wasn't close enough to cause Tarn any trouble, yet.

His niece was lying bound and helpless in the bed of the wagon, just as he'd left her. He drew out the knife, but then an unwelcome thought occurred to him. It might not be wise to kill his only hostage before he was sure he could shape a Gateway and escape. He'd better check. He closed his eyes and concentrated hard. Nothing. And now his head was aching even worse than before. He couldn't shape a Gateway until the effect of the concussion had worn off. He needed a new plan.

He returned to the drivers' seat. A trail branched off to the right not far ahead. He read the signpost: *Talford*. That would do nicely. The town was almost deserted because of the Blight, but a small troop of Guards were still stationed there. He'd send them after Rush and get a message through to Renn at the same time.

It was disappointing that he couldn't kill Sara yet, but it wouldn't be wise. The outlaws would be coming after him, and he was in no shape to fight them off if they somehow caught up. He still needed his hostage. He glanced down at her — no change. It seemed she had given up. Good.

With his head pounding like a drum, he urged the horse back into motion.

TWENTY-NINE

Sergeant Oren

Sergeant Oren gave ex-Councillor Frey a generous head-start before nudging his own horse into a walk. There was no need to keep his quarry in constant sight, not yet. He knew where Frey was heading.

It had been a stroke of luck, overhearing Frey and Councillor Domben after the Council meeting. He hadn't been intending to listen to their private conversation. At first, he hadn't even known they were there.

After his meeting with the Chairman and Deputy Renn, he'd spent an hour in his office, sending instructions to his various troops and ordering new reward notices to be posted in villages and towns. He had also written personal messages to the parents and widows of the men who had been killed in Fortune Creek, assuring them their loved ones had died in the line of duty, and that the perpetrators would be caught and punished. It had been a necessary task, but not a pleasant one, and he'd been taking a short break in the open air when he heard a woman's voice coming through the open window above him.

"Bander, don't let Tarn throw you off the Council. Not for this. You know Tulley and the others are innocent."

"Don't you see, that's exactly why I need to go." The man — presumably Councillor Frey — sounded apologetic. "I can't help them from here. But if I join them, at least they'll have another sword to protect them. Don't look at me like that, Adara. I have to do this."

"Do you even have any idea where they are?" Exasperation coloured her voice.

"I know they were in Fortune Creek fifteen days ago, and then headed up into the foothills. It's somewhere to start."

Councillor Domben's sigh was loud enough for Oren to hear from outside. "It sounds like a wild goose chase, but I won't try to stop you. Just promise me you won't take any foolish risks."

"I promise, love."

The Sergeant listened in amazement. Frey was going after his brother! He didn't seem to know where the gang was, but Oren privately agreed with him that the hills were the place to start looking. If they'd come out into the open countryside, his men should have found them by now.

It was just possible that if Tulley Frey spotted his brother, seemingly alone, he would break cover to meet him. It was an outside chance, but Oren had no other leads, and he believed in luck. He'd had a run of the bad, up until now. Perhaps this conversation was the first sign that his fortune was changing.

Now, less than an hour later, mounted on his favourite mare from the Garrison stables, Oren decided that he could safely pick up the pace. He would have to judge his pursuit perfectly: stick close enough to Frey to catch regular glimpses, but far enough behind that the man never realised he was being followed. To aid this deception, Oren had changed out of his distinctive Warrant Guard shirt into a nondescript brown tunic. It felt odd to be doing his job out of uniform, but needs must. He pushed the mare into a canter and headed for the southern road out of Eorna.

It was late afternoon and Oren was about five reaches west of Fortune Creek, when he rounded a bend and saw his quarry, halted in the middle of the road. Oren hurriedly guided his mare into the shelter of some bordering trees. Why had the man stopped here?

Peering between the branches, he soon had his answer. A rider emerged from the tree line adjacent to Frey, trailed by several riderless horses. The two men dismounted and clasped forearms. Oren was too far away to make out the newcomer's features, but his build and clothing fitted the description of one of the outlaws: a slim man of medium height, wearing a long, black cloak. Yes, and now Oren could see there were no lead ropes on the horses. This must be the Beast Speaker, Niall Crawley.

As the two men mounted up again, Oren knew his gamble had paid off. Crawley and Frey were going to lead him straight to the other outlaws.

He followed as closely as he dared, all the way to the outskirts of Fortune Creek. He expected them to turn south and head up into the hills, but they kept to the road, passing straight through the town. The horses trailed after them. So did Oren.

Only about a reach further on, they pulled up opposite an open farm gate. The two men put their heads together for a few seconds, then drew their swords and galloped through the gateway, leaving the riderless horses behind.

What were they doing? Surely the outlaws weren't hiding out here, so close to the town. And why the swords? Oren cantered to the gateway. Up a tree-lined drive, past the two galloping horses, lay a large farmhouse. In front of it, blue-shirted men were engaged in furious fighting against a large number of opponents. The light breeze carried the faint clashing of swords and screams of pain to Oren's ears.

The outlaws! A troop of his Guards must have found them here. And there were more of them than the eight Logen Rush was supposed to have with him. Oren's men were outnumbered at least two to one. Abandoning caution, he drew his own weapon and galloped to their aid.

Crawley and Frey reached them first. Still mounted, swinging their swords, they waded in. Two men wearing brown went down before them. Why were Crawley and Frey attacking the other outlaws, instead of the Warrant Guards?

The outlaws regrouped and came at the riders en masse, slashing at the horses' legs.

Crawley felled three more, but Frey's mount went down with a scream, throwing its rider free. He landed hard, and the outlaws were on him in a second. Crawley wheeled his horse, sweeping his blade in broad arcs, forcing the attackers away from his downed companion. But they were severely outnumbered. Frey would be killed. He was no longer a Councillor, but he was a respectable citizen of Algarth, not an outlaw like Crawley. Oren's duty was clear.

He rode one man down to clear his way to Frey, who was already back on his feet. But the mare was fighting Oren now, maddened by the smell of blood and fear. He slid off and saw Crawley doing the same. Their mounts plunged and kicked, then bolted. Oren stood back-to-back with Frey and Crawley, forming a tight circle against the men surrounding them. The attackers closed in, taking their time, confident of the outcome. Their fellows were still keeping the Guards busy, off to one side.

A blur of silver to Oren's right, and one outlaw was down, a dagger hilt protruding from his chest. His companions halted in shock, and then one of the biggest men Oren had ever seen growled and charged straight at him. From the corner of his eye he saw a second dagger leave Crawley's hand, and then the sword slashing at his head captured his full attention. He blocked the blow with his own blade, his arm juddering with the impact but holding firm. A look of surprise crossed the big man's face, and then he disengaged and swung again. *Too slow,* Oren thought, *too used to relying on your weight and reach, instead of brains and skill.* He ducked and thrust the point of his sword into the man's exposed gut. He yanked it out again, as fast as he could, and saw the giant drop like a huge sack of potatoes. Another man was coming at him already: smarter, more wary. He went for Oren's shoulder, and Oren only just twisted away in time, their swords clashing. His skal of Strength saved him again, as he clenched his jaw and shoved the man backwards by sheer force on the blade. But the effort cost him his balance. He stumbled forward, just as a third man thrust at him from the other side. Crawley stepped out and parried that one, using some kind of complicated twist to flip it right out of the attacker's hand. But now their tight circle of three was broken, their backs exposed.

As Oren struggled to raise his sword in time to meet another, coming at him fast, his eye was caught by a flash of blue. The man directly in front of him shrieked and staggered to one side, a sword point bursting out from between his ribs, followed by a gout of blood. Oren lifted his gaze. Warrant Guards were attacking the outlaws from behind. Forced to turn and defend themselves, the villains exposed their flanks to Crawley and Oren. Frey, too was doing his part. In moments, the tables had turned. The outlaws broke and ran. Oren, Crawley, Frey and the Guards pursued them, picking them off one by one. The last enemy still standing threw down his sword and raised his hands in surrender.

Only then did Oren have a chance to check on the Guards. Seven stood upright, and the other three lay on the ground, wounded but alive. Oren stared at one of them, a youngster with a cut across his upper arm. The wound wasn't serious, but something about the young Guard was bothering Oren. He searched the injured man's face, trying to pinpoint what was wrong.

Oren knew every one of Eorna's Warrant Guards by sight, could name most of them. He made a point of it. You can't command men you don't know. And surely that young man nursing his arm was Pinder, a new recruit, only two months at the Garrison. And the Blueshirt standing beside him was Donard, who'd joined the Guards at the same time as Oren. They'd patrolled the streets together — gotten drunk together, too — in the days before Oren had been promoted to Sergeant and Donard to Troop Leader.

But Donard was *dead*, wasn't he? And Pinder, too — murdered by Logen Rush in the tavern at Fortune Creek. Oren had written letters of condolence to their families just this morning.

He passed a hand over his eyes, his thoughts mired as if in thick mud. They stirred sluggishly, and a memory rose from the murky depths: Oren finding Donard's troop tied up in the tavern and ordering them to the farmhouse to rest and recover. How could he have forgotten that? Why had he been thinking they were all dead?

He shook his head and a second memory surfaced: his dizziness in the Chairman's office, and Tarn's words to him: *The outlaws had captured them, tied them up and then murdered them in cold blood. You saw the evidence with your own eyes. Do you understand?*

An enormous shudder travelled through Sergeant Oren from the top of his head to the soles of his boots. His mind snapped into complete clarity. He knew exactly what had happened: Chairman Tarn had lied to him — used *Mind Wending* on him! — to convince him the outlaws had killed his men in cold blood. A hard lump of anger lodged itself deep in his gut. He took Donard aside. "What happened here?"

The Troop Leader eyed Oren's civilian clothing curiously, but answered in his usual phlegmatic tone. "We were camped in the house, Sir, as you ordered. About an hour ago, an old man tapped on the back door. I thought he was a tramp begging for food — he was scrawny enough, and in filthy old clothes. But he only wanted to pass on a message. He'd been riding past on his mule and had seen a large group of armed men hiding in the trees near the road. He said he didn't like the look of them, and thought we should know. I put the men on alert and prepared to send scouts to check out the story." He gestured to the young Guard lying on the ground. "Pinder was watching the front window and saw armed men sneaking up the drive. We charged out and took them by surprise." Donard's face flushed slightly. "They fought better than I expected."

That had surprised Oren, too. The men hadn't been dressed like a trained force, more like scruffy bandits. But bandits preyed on weak and lonely travellers — they wouldn't have attacked a group of armed Warrant Guards. Unless there was more to them than there seemed.

Fortunately, at least one of the assailants was still alive and able to answer questions: the man who had surrendered. Oren strode over to where he was being held. Crawley, Frey, and the uninjured Guards came with him.

The young man must have sensed that Oren was in no mood to be crossed. It didn't take much persuasion to get the whole story out of him.

If Oren had been angry before, he was incandescent with rage now. His own Commander had sent mercenaries to kill his men! What Tarn had done was bad enough, but he was a rich man and a politician, and

Oren didn't expect much from either. But Commander Renn was a Warrant Guard himself! There was no excuse for what he'd tried to do. He was a disgrace to the uniform, a contemptible, dishonourable worm of a man.

He deserved nothing less than death, but Oren wouldn't sink to personal vengeance. His treacherous superior would answer to the law. With the prisoner as his witness, Oren would go straight to the Chief Magistrate and demand an arrest warrant for Renn. Tarn, too. The Chairman had wealthy and powerful friends, so the charges against him mightn't stick, but Oren would be damned if he wasn't going to try.

Donard interrupted his musing. "Sergeant, there's something else you should know. Earlier today, before we were attacked, we received word about Rush and the other outlaws. They were sighted three days ago on Deep Lake, heading north into Blighted country. The troop at Talford were alerted. They'll be searching up there now."

It was a measure of his outrage at Renn's betrayal that Oren had almost forgotten about the outlaws, even though he had one of them right here. He turned to Crawley. "Where are they going?"

"I'm sure I don't know, Sergeant." The man in black smiled. "I left them in the foothills twelve days ago, and I haven't seen them since."

Oren had already had a gutful of liars today. "Do you take me for a fool? Who are the horses for, then?"

"Well, now, friend, that's a funny thing." The way Crawley spoke, the two of them might be drinking ale in a tavern, swapping stories. "I admit I was on my way to find my companions again, when what should I come across, but their horses? They were wandering around near Fortune Creek, and I heard them." He tapped the side of his head and smirked patronisingly. "In my mind, you understand. I'm a Beast Speaker."

Oren discovered that he was grinding his teeth. "I know. You stole the carriage in Eorna and sent my Guards' horses mad."

"And I sincerely apologise for that, Sergeant, but it did seem like the only way. I do hope your men and their horses are fully recovered now from their fright?" Now he was talking like a nobleman sipping tea in a lady's drawing room. Whatever idiotic role Crawley was playing, Oren had had enough of it. Renn would have to wait.

He turned back to Donard. "Take one of your men and escort the prisoner to Eorna Garrison, then send a Healer back for the wounded."

"Yes, Sir. And the other men?"

"They're coming with me. We're going to track down those outlaws once and for all."

He pointed to Crawley. "Tie him up too and I'll take him along." It might be useful to have a hostage when they found Rush.

"Sergeant, is that really necessary?" put in Frey. "He did help to fight off the attackers, when he could have just ridden away and left us all."

Frey might have been a Councillor yesterday, but he wasn't one today. He had no authority to tell Oren what to do. "He's still a wanted man, sir, and I don't intend to let him escape."

As if sensing that the Sergeant wouldn't be moved on this point, Frey fell silent again.

While Crawley was being bound, Oren took a moment to think everything through, checking that he hadn't forgotten anything. *Oh, yes.*

He stepped up to the dandy in the fancy black clothing and stared him straight in the eyes. "And if I see even one of the horses acting the least bit funny, I'll start killing the others until it stops, understand?"

Crawley's black eyes blazed. "I understand perfectly, Sergeant."

THIRTY

Mena

Waves of dread vibrated through Mena's body as the wagon disappeared into the trees, carrying Sara away from them. Why had that man taken her? Was he after the reward? Or something worse?

You're wasting time, she rebuked herself. She couldn't do anything for Sara now, and Fin needed her. *Focus on the one you can help.*

The roots she'd gathered tumbled from her apron as she dropped down beside the older woman. The head wound looked nasty, but at least Fin was still awake, gazing at Mena with her grey eyes unclouded. Even so, Mena didn't like the shallow raspy sound of her breathing or the yellow parchment tone of her skin. As she made her examination, fear for her other friend clawed at her again, ripping and tearing at her attention. If she didn't subdue it, she'd be useless here.

Using all the self-discipline at her command, she swept all thought of Sara from her mind. Taking a few deep breaths and murmuring a quick prayer, she placed both hands on the blood-soaked grey hair and set to work. The damage was worse than she'd thought. It was a miracle that Fin was conscious at all.

"What happened?" Logen asked from somewhere above her bowed head.

"That man— I-I tried to stop him," Kelan said earnestly, "but— he had a knife at Sara's throat. I should've shot him as soon as I saw him." Bitter shame at this failure filled his voice. "I wasn't quick enough."

Mena's heart ached for her son. She longed to reassure him, but Fin's life hung by a thread, demanding all her skill.

"It's not your fault, Kelan," Logen said. "You did the right thing."

"Why did he take her?" Kelan asked.

"Because he's Villembelt Tarn," Logen said grimly.

Mena's head shot up. *Tarn* had Sara?

"*What?*" Tulley roared. He had been kneeling beside her, holding Fin's hand. He rose as if on strings, almost knocking Mena sideways, and took off. Logen sprinted after him.

Her concentration shattered, Mena strove to clear her mind again, this time without success. The best she could do was to maintain a fine thread of healing between her and her patient, while her heart pounded and her eyes stayed glued on the two running figures.

Tulley was fast for a heavy man, but Logen had longer legs. He grabbed his friend's shoulder and jerked him to a stop. "Tulley! Let him go!"

Tulley twisted in Logen's grip. His broad face was suffused with blood, the familiar features distorted by anger. Logen took a step back but didn't release his grasp. Tulley raged up at him. "*Let him go?* What's wrong with you? He ruined all our lives, for his own stinking ambition. Have you forgotten Bram? *And now he's hurt Fin!*"

That bellowing voice, that contorted brick-red face, reminded Mena of Soran in one of his rages. Tulley tried to break Logen's hold on his shoulder, but Logen hung on grimly.

"*Let me go!*" Tulley bellowed.

"No," Logen gasped. "Tulley, listen to me."

In the few seconds of charged silence that followed, Mena saw that Tulley was poised on a knife-edge. He hadn't shown it until now, but the stress and frustration of months on the run must have been eating away at him, day after day. He'd been helpless to change the situation, powerless to fight back, unable to ensure the safety of the woman he loved. For a strong man, so like Soran in some ways, and even her own Veren, that must have been intolerable.

Now, finally, he'd found an enemy he could fight. And not just any enemy, but the one man who was to blame for all of it. The same one who'd just attacked his wife and left her for dead.

And Logen was standing in his way, trying to hold him back.

Fear had its talons deep in Mena now. Tulley was beyond reason. He was going to attack Logen. Nothing and no one could prevent it. Even so, she opened her mouth to shout something — anything — in a desperate attempt to stop the unstoppable.

Another voice spoke first. "Tulley, please."

Only two words, whispered so softly in that thin, pain-filled voice, yet they dropped into the moment of silence like a stone, bearing the weight of all the years and all the love that Fin and Tulley had shared.

And Tulley bowed his head without a word and returned to his wife. She smiled up at him. He crouched and took her hand.

Tears obscured Mena's vision as she went back to work on her patient. Some of them were born of sheer relief, but not all. As Tulley and Fin had joined hands, a sliver of pain had sliced into Mena's own heart.

She'd lost so much, the day that Veren had died. So many moments of love they should have enjoyed. She'd expected to grow old with him, never imagined for a moment that they would have so little time together, that he wouldn't even live long enough to see the birth of his son.

Veren had been a Shaper like Tulley, but of wood rather than metal. He'd loved most of all to build houses, and he had died doing the very thing he loved, falling from a half-completed roof and cracking his skull. Dead as soon as he hit the ground. When they'd brought her the news, Mena had thought her life was over. She'd been wrong, but at times like this the loss still hurt unbearably.

But Fin and Tulley were depending on her now, and they needed her to be at her best. As she'd done many times before, she swallowed the tears and tucked the precious memory of her husband safely away in a corner of her mind.

Ten minutes later, Fin had fallen into a peaceful sleep. Mena sat back with a sigh and flexed her hands. "She's out of immediate danger. She still needs care, but I believe she'll make a full recovery."

"Thank you," Tulley said gruffly, then stood and faced Logen. "We can't let Tarn get away." His voice was belligerent, as if he expected an argument.

"I don't intend to," Logen said, "but we need a plan. If he sees us coming, he might panic and kill Sara. We can't risk her, not even to capture him. If she dies, our hope dies with her."

Hope? thought Mena wearily. *What hope is there for us now, or for Sara either?* Tarn had her, and while she lived, she'd always be a threat to him. She could be dead already, and her murderer gone — vanished through a Gateway — completely out of their reach. Even if he'd kept her alive for some reason, they had no idea where he might take her. *Hope* was a foolish emotion under the circumstances. It was time they all faced reality. She stood and placed her hands on her hips. "And how do you think you're going to find them?"

She'd addressed the question to Logen, but it was Kelan who answered. "I can do it," he said, and there wasn't a trace of doubt in his voice.

He was so young, so sure of himself, even after everything they'd been through. It was admirable, in a way, but it was also dangerous. He needed to accept the truth, see how desperate their situation really was. He needed to grow up.

"Kelan," she said, injecting a mother's steel into her voice and expression, "Think for a moment. Tarn has a head start and you are on foot. You don't even know what direction he took once he was out of sight."

Unrepentant, her lanky son grinned down at her like the small boy he had once been, the stupidly long fringe obscuring his eyes yet again. He held out his right hand and slowly unfolded his fingers. On his palm lay half the promise charm. It was glowing, brighter than the daylight.

"Yes, I do," he said. "I dropped the other half in the wagon."

Tulley gave a great roar of delight and slapped him on the back. "Lad, you're a genius! Let's go!"

"Tulley, I think you should stay." Logen held up a hand as Tulley scowled ominously again. "Listen, my friend. Tarn came alone, but that doesn't mean he didn't give orders for his Guards to meet him here. They could be on their way right now. Thanks to Kelan, we have a good chance of catching up with him, but Fin can't come with us, and Mena has to stay to look after her." He smiled at her. "Mena is courageous, but she's not a trained fighter. At least one of us should be here with them."

Tulley gazed down at his sleeping wife. The ferocious scowl smoothed out. He nodded.

"I'll go with Kelan," Logen went on. "With his hunting skills, Tarn won't see or hear us coming."

"And when you catch up with him?" Tulley asked.

Logen shrugged. "We'll just have to take whatever opportunity Aal sends us."

Mena's hands dropped from her hips. *He's right,* she thought in surprise. *Aal is in control, not Tarn.* For a few minutes, she'd forgotten that.

Her eyes went to her son, standing proudly beside Logen. Their heads were almost the same height. Mena had been so used to thinking of Kelan as a boy, that he'd grown into a man without her noticing. He had surprised her so many times over the past two weeks. She'd known he loved to hunt, but she'd had no idea how skilled he was at tracking and finding his way through rough country. It was Kelan who had kept them out of sight of the Blueshirts before they'd met Garst. And it was Kelan who, time and again, had kept them fed.

And now, with his quick thinking, he might have made it possible for them to save Sara. Overcome with love, she jumped up and hugged him fiercely. When she let him go, he was blushing, but she thought he seemed pleased all the same.

They wasted no more time. As soon as Kelan had oriented himself to the charm, he and Logen raced away. Tulley remained on his feet, his eyes roaming in all directions, clearly on the alert for trouble.

Mena gathered up the long, purple-skinned carrots she'd spilled on the ground earlier. Thanks to Kelan's idea, they'd dug up two dozen or so. She handed one to Tulley, and then bit into another. The shrivelled root was tough and stringy, with a slightly bitter taste under the sweetness, but her energy began to rise as she worked her way through it.

When Fin woke again, Mena cut another root into small pieces and fed them to her one at a time. The older woman's colour began to improve. As Mena brushed damp wisps of hair back from her patient's forehead, something nudged her mind. She stopped, not sure just what she was sensing.

She closed her eyes and laid her hand on the crown of Fin's head. There it was again. As a Folk Healer, she transferred energy to her patients, but she received sensations back, too. They gave her guidance about where an injury or sickness was located, how severe it was, and how she should work on it. She'd already let this feedback guide her in treating Fin's head injury, but this was something different. Concentrating, she opened herself more fully to the perception.

Another trauma, but nothing to do with the wound on Fin's head. This was a much deeper hurt, and it wasn't localised. It was throughout Fin's body; it was everywhere. And there was nothing Mena could do about it. She was instantly and completely certain of that. This disease was beyond her power to cure.

She opened her eyes and stared into Fin's face, unable for once to hide her shock behind the reassuring mask of the healer. "Fin?" It came out as a whisper.

Fin sighed and gripped her hand tightly. "I knew I couldn't keep it from you, not with your skal, but I don't want Tulley to know. Not yet. I'll tell him myself at the right time."

Tears trickled down Mena's cheeks. "It's not fair."

"Fair?" Fin smiled wanly. "Maybe it's not, but many things happen in this life that are not fair. Why should it be any different for me?" Her hand tightened its grip, as if to drive her words into Mena's own body and soul. "It doesn't matter how long we live. What matters is what we do with the life we're given." She gazed intently into Mena's stricken eyes. "I have loved and been loved. I have done what Aal created me to do. I have used my skal with joy, and I have seen so much beauty. Oh, so much."

Mena squeezed her hand back, overcome that Fin was trying to comfort *her*. "I understand," she said, but she didn't, not really. She wouldn't be as accepting as this, if a fatal illness was ravaging her body. And yet, she'd also experienced love in her life and used her skal to the best of her ability. How could the other woman be so content to die?

She wanted to demand an answer, but Fin's face had grown pale and drawn again. It would be wrong to pester her with questions. Mena gave her hand one final clasp and released it. "I'll leave you to sleep." Fin's eyelids closed immediately, telling Mena she'd made the right decision.

She went a short distance away and lay down on the crisp carpet of Blighted leaves. Healing took energy, and she needed to rest while she could if she was to be of any use to Fin. Or to Kelan and Logen if, Aal forbid, they came back seriously hurt. She refused to entertain the thought that they might not return at all.

THIRTY-ONE

Sara

S ara lay on her side in the back of the wagon, aching all over. When Tarn had first grabbed her, it had been strangely satisfying to fight back. After weeks of hiding from unseen searchers, the direct physical confrontation had felt like a kind of release. But it hadn't done her much good. She was in Tarn's power, bruised and tied hand and foot. And every moment she spent here took her further away from Logen and the others.

Thanks to what she'd learned in the shed at Deep Lake, she could do something about one of those problems at least. She focused on the rope around her ankles, imagining the plant material it had been twisted from, willing the knots to slide apart. They loosened just like the others, the loops uncoiling and dropping away. She stretched her legs surreptitiously, craning her neck upwards to check that her captor hadn't noticed anything. He was facing away from her, his attention on the trail ahead. So far so good. Now for her wrists.

Seconds passed, with no change as far as she could tell. She concentrated harder, twisting her wrists until the cords dug into her flesh. Why wasn't it working? She felt the panic rise and shoved it down.

She tried again and again, with no result. Her stinging skin was being rubbed raw and still the rope wouldn't budge. Eventually the pain forced her to stop. For some reason, her skal wasn't operating any more.

Could she cut the bindings, then? Her blade, the beautiful one Tulley had given her, had been taken from her on the beach, and Tarn's knife and sword were back on his belt. There might be something sharp in the wagon, some tool the carter had left. She couldn't see properly, lying down like this.

Grunting from the effort, she wriggled into a sitting position with her back against the side, shooting a glance at Tarn to see if he'd noticed anything. He was leaning forward, flapping the reigns to urge the horse to go faster.

She shifted her legs under her and rose to her knees, but the horse had sped up, and the floor was jolting so erratically that she toppled sideways, wrenching her neck as she fought in vain to keep her balance. Back where she'd started, she swore under her breath and then pushed herself upright again, settling for a seated position this time. It would have to do: she wasn't risking another fall. She shuffled forward on her bottom, leaning down between her drawn-up legs to pore over every square centimetre of floor as she went.

A spark of light caught her eye, glinting from beneath some loose wisps of hay, just ahead of her. It looked like metal, but it was too small and round to be a blade. Even so, it might have a sharp edge. She scooted over and craned forward.

Up close, she recognised it immediately. What on earth was *that* doing here? She humped herself around until it lay within reach of her fingers, and then picked up the small flat disc, closing her hand tightly around it. It wouldn't free her wrists, but it might come in handy if she managed to get away.

She searched the entire floor of the wagon, finding nothing but hay and bits of rubbish. As she gazed down at yet another length of discarded rope, the question worried at her again: why hadn't she been able to untie her wrists? She stared at the short stretch of cord, then at the others lying around it. This piece was different. It was almost the same colour — a tawny yellow that matched the hay — but the braided strands were shiny and smooth, not bristling with tiny fibres like the others. Synthetic rope. It had to be.

This must be one of the "superior" products Tarn had boasted about bringing to Algarth. The hay merchant had bought it from him or his agent, and Tarn had found it in the wagon and used a piece of it on her wrists. No wonder her Greenhaelan powers had no effect on it — it wasn't made from plants. It was a huge relief to know she hadn't lost her skal, even if it couldn't help her right now. But maybe her other ability could.

If she'd recovered enough strength, she could shape a Gateway straight back to the others, and just disappear right out of the wagon. What a tempting thought that was, especially when she pictured Tarn's face when he discovered her absence. She had nothing to lose by trying.

She pictured her friends near the edge of the forest where she'd last seen them, and focused all her will on the image. She infused it with her deep longing to be with each of them, whispering their names under her breath: *Mena. Fin. Logen. Kelan. Tulley.*

Almost at once, energy began to seep out of her. It was a disturbing sensation: some vital part of her was trickling away like water down a drain, leaving her limp and gasping. That settled the question: she wasn't ready.

What if she jumped off the back of the wagon, with her hands still bound, and ran? If Tarn didn't turn around, he might not notice for quite a long time. Long enough for her to disappear from sight and start making her way back to the others.

But the horse had picked up the pace again, and the tree trunks were rushing past. She'd land hard. Even if she didn't break any bones, there was a chance of a twisted ankle. And if Tarn did see and come after her, he might be angry enough to kill her straight away this time. She couldn't hope to defend herself against him with her arms trapped like this. In any face-to-face encounter, he'd win, just like he had before.

Could she spring a surprise attack on him while his back was turned and shove *him* off the vehicle instead? She'd have to use her legs, kick him in the back. No, that was stupid, the kind of thing that only worked in movies. If she couldn't keep her balance on her knees, she had no chance on her feet. And she was probably too weak to do more than bruise him anyway, which would just make him angrier.

Think, she ordered herself. *You're a smart, educated woman. You even have magical powers, for heaven's sake! Work it out!*

Her thoughts went around and around, circling back to the same conclusion every time: if she couldn't free her hands, leap off the wagon or attack Tarn, her only other chance was to shape a Gateway. She couldn't manage it now, but if Tarn allowed her to live long enough, she'd eventually get her strength back, like she had at the castle.

But then what? She'd be back with the others and safe for now, but she'd also be exhausted all over again. What if shaping the Gateway affected her so much that she needed days to recover before she could try to cure the Blight? Tarn wouldn't wait for days. He'd have Guards out here to kill them all long before then.

Sara slumped against the side of the wagon and closed her eyes. Hot tears leaked out and spilled down her cheeks. She was bone-weary, scared, hurting, and most of all utterly fed up with her own constant overthinking. *This isn't a strategy game,* she berated herself, *this is life and death. Stop trying to see all the outcomes. It's impossible anyway. Just make a decision and act on it. Have the damned courage to take a leap of faith.*

Faith? Where had that come from? Fin and Mena were the experts on faith, not her. Although Fin had been right about one thing: the six of them had beaten some incredible odds, up until now. Maybe their luck would continue. No more second-guessing; a Gateway was her best chance. She'd stay here and conserve her energy until she was strong enough to shape one. She leaned against the vibrating wood and tried to get some rest.

Sara woke to find herself sliding across the floor of the violently rocking wagon; she jammed her legs under the driver's seat and braced herself, twisting her back but saving her head from smashing into the opposite side. Ignoring the jagged twinge in her lower spine, she struggled to rise high enough to see what was happening. The vehicle gave a mighty lurch and stopped dead, throwing her hard against the back of the seat. A hot spike of agony shot through her shoulder and down her arm. She cried out and collapsed again.

She lay gasping for a moment, and then pulled herself up one-handed and peered over the seat. Tarn was slumped sideways, motionless. Gingerly, Sara rotated her injured shoulder. It burned and throbbed, but it wasn't dislocated. She rubbed it while she looked around.

The steeply tilted wagon had come to rest on a muddy slope above a stream. The horse, still harnessed, stood in the shallow water slaking its thirst. Beneath its noisy sucking and blowing, another sound rumbled, rising and falling rhythmically. Sara couldn't place it for a moment. Then she knew: Tarn was snoring. She'd wondered if he was dead, but he was only asleep. Well, not exactly asleep, or the jolting would have woken him, too. He'd hit his head hard on the side of the wagon while they were fighting: maybe he'd passed out, leaving the horse to choose its own way.

Sara turned from him and worked her way up the sloping floor to the back of the wagon. Without giving herself time to think about what she was about to do, she closed her eyes tightly and rolled over the edge. An instant of weightlessness, before she landed with a soft thump, her shoulder protesting again. It could've been worse: the wet, deep mud of the river bank had broken her fall. The wheels of the wagon were bogged in the stuff. It sucked at Sara's hands and knees as she struggled to her feet. The rank stench filled her nostrils, and her soft shoes sank and squelched at every step as she slogged the rest of the way up the slope. The distance was short, but the slimy mud and her tied hands made it hard work, and she stopped at the top to catch her breath, glancing back the way she'd come. Neither the horse nor Tarn had moved.

From her vantage point, Sara tried to get some sense of where she was. She'd left the forest behind, but Blighted vegetation still covered the land like a nubbly brown blanket. A stout wooden fence stretched across her path, with small trees lined up in neat rows behind it. There were dozens of them, all the same height and shape, like rusty, open goblets on short trunks. An orchard, before the Blight had come.

Beyond the dead trees lay a large stone house and barn, surrounded by numerous outbuildings. It must have been a busy, productive place at one time, full of noise and movement. It was silent now, and somehow eerie. She wondered who had owned this farm, who had lived and worked here. She hoped they were still alive, wherever they were.

Her shoulders ached, especially the left — the one that had taken the blow in the wagon — and her legs felt like they belonged to someone else. But if she could reach the buildings, she might find a tool to cut the rope.

She rolled awkwardly under the fence, wincing as she regained her feet, and headed down one of the straight paths between the trees. The orchard grass had once been long and lush. The brown flattened remains made the going soft and slippery underfoot, but she moved as fast as she dared. She was more than halfway to the house when some instinct urged her to check back over her shoulder.

The hair rose on her scalp, sending a shiver through her body and down the backs of her legs. A figure was shambling unsteadily along a path that lay parallel to her own: Tarn. He'd shed his grey suit jacket and was in white shirtsleeves. He was only about ten metres behind her and the same to her right. His head was down and he was weaving from side to side, probably still dizzy from the concussion. He raised his head, and their eyes met. He roared and abandoned the path, veering around the intervening trees to get to her. His lumbering footsteps thudded dully in Sara's ears, a counterpoint to the rapid *thump, thump, thump* of her heart. She fled, her lungs fighting for air, her soft shoes sliding on the dry grass at every step. Any second now, his hands would be on her.

She spotted the ladder just in time. It lay across the path, almost completely shrouded by dead grass. She dodged around the end of it, barely saving herself from falling. An idea flared across her mind. She lurched back to the centre of the path, turned her head and shouted: "Leave me alone, you maniac! You *loser!*"

That got his attention. Arms and legs still pumping, he lifted his head to glare at her in outrage. His mouth opened in preparation to blast out a reply. She turned and ran again, praying she'd distracted him enough. If not, she'd just thrown away her lead for nothing.

Three steps, the impacts juddering up through her heels, then four, five, six. A deep grunt sounded, followed by a blood-curdling, high-pitched shriek. She faltered, shooting a glance back over her shoulder. Tarn writhed on the ground, clutching one knee. Energised by the success of her makeshift plan, Sara accelerated once more.

She reached the stable first, and ran straight through — in one doorway and out the other — into a cobbled yard. Turning sharply, she dodged a standing water pump and took a narrow passage between two wooden sheds. Emerging from the end, she spied what she'd been looking for, directly ahead.

Wide double doors stood open, displaying an interior space partitioned into open-fronted workrooms, each equipped with a bench and a stool. Soran's property had included a building like this, only less extensive. It was where all the craftsmen plied their trades: saddler, potter, woodworker, cooper. If any tools remained on the farm, this was where they'd be.

It took a moment for her searching eyes to adjust to the lower light inside, but then she saw it, sitting alone on a bench: a small knife with a bone handle. Turning her back so her bound hands could reach it, she picked it up, and then crouched down in a corner, out of sight from the doorway.

She twisted the knife upwards until she felt the blade pressing against the rope, then began sawing back and forth. Sharp pain shot up her arm and into her shoulder as her hand cramped, but she kept going, her breath whistling in and out as she forced her fingers to cooperate. All the time, she listened for the sound of Tarn's footsteps on the cobbles outside.

By the time the rope abruptly came apart, she'd almost lost the feeling in both hands. She brought her arms around in front of her body, gritting her teeth against the protests of her muscles and joints. Dropping the little knife into her pocket, she rotated her wrists, then rubbed her numb hands up and down her arms, gasping at the sensation of hot needles as the blood began to flow freely again. She rolled her shoulders, testing the range of motion. She was going to be very sore for a while, maybe a long while, but at least everything still worked. Now to find a better hiding place. If Tarn entered this building, he'd see her immediately. Staircases at both ends of the space led to a second storey. She chose the nearer one and climbed upwards like an old woman, one slow, heavy step at a time.

At the top, she knelt with a stifled groan and applied her eye to a gap in the floorboards. No movement below. He hadn't come in yet. But he would. She doubted the fall had broken his leg. The most she could hope for was a sprain, slowing him down. As long as he could move at all, he'd search every building until he found her. She surveyed the upper floor for something larger than the knife to defend herself with.

This area seemed to have been used mostly for storage. The floor was littered with broken remnants of crates and barrels, frayed pieces of rope and other refuse, but the former occupants had taken anything useful with them when they left.

A squeak from the staircase — shocking as a gunshot — froze her to the spot. A second one — he was coming.

She shook herself out of her stupor and sprinted on her toes across the floorboards, praying they wouldn't creak. Reaching the opposite staircase safely, she started down on shaking legs, gripping the rail tightly, trying to place her trembling feet on the outside edges of the steps. He mustn't hear her.

Footsteps stumped across the upstairs room as she reached the ground floor. Every nerve screamed at her to move. She darted out the door and into the yard, pulse throbbing, every sense on high alert. Adrenaline was keeping her on her feet for now, but it would wear off. She whisked around the corner of the building, and kept going.

As she wove her way through the maze of yards and structures, her thoughts narrowed to essentials: keep out of sight; step quietly; stay ahead. Only one of him; he couldn't surround her. Copper in her pocket; Logen would come. Survive till then. In one door, out another. Listen for footsteps, change direction. In. Out. Listen. Turn. Step quietly.

Another corner. Or the same one. A scrape to the right. Dart left.

Straight into him. He was quicker than her — so quick! — grabbing her upper arms before she could react. Eyes like glistening brown marbles bulged out from between red-rimmed lids. His mouth was set in a grimace of fury. He was going to kill her.

She struggled to twist out of his grasp, her shoulder singing with pain, but he only tightened his hold. She was helpless.

No, she raged, *not helpless! Don't you dare give up! Fight!*

Tarn took a step backward, keeping her at arm's length, his full, ruddy lips parting into a rictus smile. Sara's upper arms were trapped against her sides, but she could still move her hands. Fixing her eyes on his, she worked her right hand into her pocket. Still holding his attention on her face, she wrapped her fingers around the handle of the little knife and lifted it out.

One short step forward, then she struck upwards as fast and hard as she could. The sharp blade punched through his shirt and into his flesh, all the way up to the hilt.

He threw back his head and screamed, high and piercing. His hands fell away. He stumbled backwards, and the blade slid out. A spot of scarlet appeared on his white shirt, growing larger by the second.

The knife fell from Sara's nerveless fingers and clattered on the cobbles.

Tarn lowered his head and bellowed, pressing one hand to the wound, reaching out to her with the other.

She backed away, but he followed, his long fingers still clawing for her. Foamy pink blood bubbled from the corner of his mouth. What had she done?

"Turn around, Tarn, or I'll shoot you in the back!"

A look of confusion crossed Tarn's face. His arm dropped. He turned his head slowly towards the voice.

Sara's gaze slid past him, to light on one of the most beautiful sights she'd ever seen: Kelan, with bow drawn and eyes narrowed on his quarry, and Logen beside him.

Sara sagged against the wall. It was over. They'd found her.

She sat in silence between them on the driver's bench — with Tarn tied up in the back this time — and tried not to think about anything. Two or three times, Logen spoke a few words that sounded like a question, glancing sideways at her, but she refused to understand him. Finally, he seemed to accept that she didn't want to talk and returned his attention to the trail.

More than once, Sara felt her head begin to nod, but each time she roused herself awake again. She didn't want to sleep here, so close to *him*, even if he was tied up. The breeze wafted the carrion scent of his blood to her, making her gorge rise. She swallowed, and gazed off into the lifeless trees.

The light was dimming as they pulled up. Tulley helped her down. Mena ran over and hugged her tightly, exclaiming in excitement, but Sara couldn't seem to feel anything other than bone-deep weariness.

Mena sat her down and examined her. "Some bruises and abrasions, but you'll be fine. Food and a good night's sleep are what you need more than anything." She made Sara drink some water and eat some pieces of root that had been baked to tenderness in the fire.

Afterwards, Sara stretched out on the ground and stared up into the clear night sky. Sounds rose and fell around her. They resembled voices, or the songs of birds, or perhaps the stars humming to each other. Whoever or whatever they were, she wished they'd be quiet and let her sleep.

THIRTY-TWO

Sara

Everything came flooding back as soon as Sara awoke the next morning. She sat up, heart thumping, and looked for Tarn. He was seated several metres away, tied to the base of a tree. He wasn't facing her directly, but his head was up and his eyes were open. She discovered she was glad about that. She wasn't sure she could have lived with the knowledge that she'd killed him, even in self-defence. Seeing him alive, and still a prisoner, her spirits rose. In fact, she was feeling pretty good in general. Mena must have been working on her while she slept. Her aches and pains were gone, along with her exhaustion.

The day was cloudy but bright. The sun was merely a glow in the pearly sky, and the air held a fresh coolness that spoke of autumn. It would have been a beautiful morning, if not for the ugliness of the Blighted trees surrounding her.

Someone had unhitched and fed the horse. It was standing near the wagon with its head down, contentedly munching hay.

The others were gathered together a short distance away. Sara scrambled up and strode over to join them. "Here." She smiled at Kelan, holding out the half of the promise charm she'd found on the floor of the wagon. "I think this belongs to you."

The teenager took it and shrugged with would-be casualness. "It's a good thing you picked it up, otherwise it would've taken us much longer to find you."

His nonchalant act didn't fool her. Underneath, he was bursting with pride. And why not? "It did more than just lead you to me," she assured him. "As soon as I saw it, and knew someone would be coming, it felt like…a talisman, something to hold onto. It kept me from losing hope and giving up."

"And now," Logen said, "thanks to Kelan's brilliance and your bravery, Sara, we've turned the tables on Tarn. Mena says his wound should stop him from being able to shape a Gateway for at least a day."

Mena listened with her eyes lowered, stroking her hands repeatedly down her apron. "I'd never normally leave someone half-healed," she muttered. "But it was the only way to keep him here, other than knocking him out." She lifted her head. "And I won't be a party to that."

"We should kill him and be done with it." Tulley glared around the circle of shocked faces and flung up his big, calloused hands. "*What?* You think he deserves to live?"

Mena's lips tightened. "That's not up to us to decide."

Tulley's face grew redder. He snorted and gestured to his wife, lying asleep nearby. "After what he did to Fin? Tried to do to Sara? Who has a better right?"

"It's not about rights," Logen said, fixing Tulley with a level stare. "We're not killing anyone."

Tulley glowered back at him. "And what do we do after the wound heals? Stab him just a bit again?"

Sara felt herself pale at the memory of how it had felt to thrust the knife in. She shuddered. Mena noticed. She rounded on the stocky red-haired man, her hands on her hips and a fierce expression on her freckled face. "That's enough. Can't you see you're upsetting Sara?"

"It's an honest question," Tulley grumped. "What—"

Mena turned to their leader. "Logen, tell him to stop."

A strange half-smile was hovering around Logen's mouth. "We have at least a day until that happens, Tulley, and we're going to use it." He fixed sky-blue eyes on Sara. "How do you feel?"

"Good," Sara said hurriedly, thrusting away the memory of the wet sound the knife had made going in. Physically, it was true; Mena had done an amazing job on her. She felt better than she had in weeks.

Logen's smile broadened. "Then we're not waiting any longer. We're tackling the Blight right now."

Kelan peered out anxiously from behind his fringe. "You mean after breakfast?"

Breakfast sounded good to Sara. Despite her feeling of well-being, she was ravenous.

Logen chuckled. "Of course. We must get our priorities right. First breakfast, and then saving the world." It was a rare moment of humour from him, and Sara found she liked him all the better for it.

Kelan grinned in relief. "In that case, I'll have bacon and eggs."

"No, you won't." Mena sent a mock frown his way, her hands still resting on her hips. "You'll have roasted roots and be thankful for them."

Kelan rolled his eyes, so like a stereotypical teenager that Sara couldn't help laughing.

"That's a good sound," Fin called to them. She was sitting up now, looking much better than the last time Sara had seen her. Mena must have been busy on her, too. "Praise Aal, we'll hear more of it from now on."

After breakfast, which was filling if not exciting, they set about their preparations. They chose a tree well away from Tarn, who had been ignoring them all as studiously as they'd been avoiding him. Sara, Logen, and Fin gathered around the trunk, while the others stood watching from a distance, keeping their eyes out for any sign of Guards approaching.

"Now what?" Sara asked.

"We know the ancient Greenhaelen were able to combine their powers, but we don't know how they did it," Logen said. "If you're a Master Healer, then you're the key. You have to take the lead."

Sara was appalled. "But — I don't know what to do!"

"Neither do we, Sara," Fin said, "We just have to try. Aal will show us the way."

Sara still felt completely inadequate to the task, but what did she have to lose, after all? She stretched out a hand and laid it on the trunk, but immediately started back with a cry. Even in that split second of contact, the wrongness of the Blighted tree had assaulted her body, overwhelmed her senses. How could she heal it if she couldn't even touch it? All her doubts came flooding back, but she shook her thumping head and set them aside. She had a job to do. If her power was really as strong as Logen believed, maybe she didn't need to physically touch anything.

Keeping her hands well away, she pictured the tree in her mind and willed it to turn green and living again. Agony exploded, driving her to her knees. It was no good! She couldn't do this. Mena came up behind her and laid a hand on her shoulder. The pain receded. "Try now, Sara," she said. "I'll take care of you. You take care of the tree."

Biting her lip in determination, Sara regained her feet, closed her eyes and tried again, wincing despite Mena's assurance. But there was no assault this time. Instead, it was as though some invisible barrier resisted her will for a moment, and then gave way before her.

Sara's eyes flew open, her gaze already tilted upwards. High above, a myriad of fresh green leaves danced in the slight breeze, bright and joyful against the colourless sky.

A whoop of triumph rang out from Kelan. Fin and Logen were nodding and smiling. Mena's hand squeezed Sara's shoulder. She felt her own lips stretch into a grin. But this was only a first step.

She closed her eyes once more and imagined new growth spreading out far beyond the tree in every direction. This time, the resistance was stronger, and she struggled for a moment before it gave way like before. She opened her eyes. An area of about two metres in diameter around the tree was now covered with a velvety carpet of green. Ignoring the exclamations around her, Sara bent down. She brushed her fingers reverently over the friendly, round leaves of violets and clover, the delicate spears of new grass. She breathed in the wonderful scent of fresh growth and moist, living soil, and felt more alive herself. It was all so wonderful, but it was such a small area. An oasis of green in a desert of sterility and death. At this rate, it would take many lifetimes to heal all the Blight on the island. She needed more power.

She stood and spoke to Logen and Fin. "I'm going to try again. But this time, see if you can reach out to me with your skals."

They nodded and closed their eyes, but she kept hers open, focused on their faces. That seemed important. She dwelt on all the experiences she had shared with them, all the kindness she had seen in them. Their courage, their refusal to give up, their noble intentions, their good hearts. They were more than friends. They were family, and she loved them both. And with that, as naturally and easily as if she'd been doing it all her life, she reached out and gathered them in. They were like two small, warm, golden lights in her mind.

Amazed and grateful, still holding them in her thoughts, she turned her physical eyes to the green circle around the tree. *Grow,* she urged, and it began to expand. A tide of life rippled out. Gasps sounded around her.

A third golden light appeared in her mind, and then a fourth. Where had they come from? The green tide began to flow more quickly across the Blighted ground. Other lights winked into being. Soon there were over a dozen. The grass around the wagon was a deep emerald, ankle-high. The horse left its hay and began grazing.

Sara let her eyelids close. She didn't need her eyes anymore. She could sense the healing spreading, as the lights glowed in her mind, the lights of the Greenhaelen. She was gathering them in from all over Algarth. People she had never met, joining her, adding their skals to hers. Tears ran down her cheeks as she welcomed them. She'd never felt anything like this before. And still the healing spread.

"*No!*"

A new light appeared in her mind, hot and red. It spun in place, giving off sparks. The resistance Sara had felt earlier returned. As she pushed against it, she sensed the green tide slowing to a stop. She closed her eyes more tightly and concentrated harder.

But now the Blight was creeping forward again, brown consuming the green on every side. She pushed even more fiercely. The deadly advance slowed, and then halted. But no matter how hard Sara tried, she couldn't enlarge the circle of green any further. It was as much as she could do to hold the Blight where it was.

She knew what had happened: Tarn was a Greenhaelan, too, and, without meaning to, she'd gathered him into the link. Instead of working with her and the others, he was sabotaging them, breaking their concentration, willing the Blight to advance. Even though his skal wasn't as strong as hers, she wasn't sure she could do this with him fighting her every inch of the way.

She tried to call out, to tell her friends what was happening, but she couldn't make a sound, or even open her eyes. It was like being caught in a nightmare, unable to wake.

But she wasn't dreaming alone. And Tarn was a Mind Wender. She sent a thought towards the spinning red light, hoping he could hear it. "Tarn, stop! We have to heal the Blight!"

"No, not you! My destiny, not yours!" A blast of emotion accompanied his loud, echoing reply. The ghost of an image flicked past, too fast to see clearly. Before Sara could analyse what she'd seen and felt, the red light revolved to a stop. Its colour darkened to mahogany as it hovered in place, pulsing strongly. He was listening, waiting for her answer.

Just the thought of pleading with him, after everything he'd done, made her sick and angry. But success was more important right now than her feelings. She chose her words carefully, trying to reach any small bit of decency that might still exist in him. "Uncle, listen. The Blight is wrong. You're a Greenhaelan, too, you must feel how wrong it is. With your strength added to ours, I think we can beat it. Help us!"

"Help *you?* I don't think so." The words were confident, but his light had begun to pulse faster. It jittered in place. He wasn't as calm as he sounded. Maybe she was getting through to him.

"I know you planned to heal the Blight without help. But I've felt the extent of the damage now. Please believe me, Uncle: the sickness has gone so far, none of us is strong enough to cure it alone. Algarth needs all of us to work together, all the Greenhaelen. You can save your nation, and be a hero, just as you wanted to."

The light stopped its jittering. It hung there, still that deep red-brown, but now pulsing only faintly. Tarn was thinking, considering her words, perhaps feeling the strength of the Blight himself, as she had. At least, he hadn't rejected her plea out of hand. Some part of him, no matter how small, must want to respond. She only hoped that part would win out.

As she watched the brooding light, Sara found herself thinking about what she'd seen and felt from it as Tarn spat back his first refusal. There'd been anger, arrogance, and pride. No surprise there. But something else, too: pain and a sense of deep injustice. An image, gone in a flash, of a child, alone and crying in the dark. What right did this devil have to feel grief? What injustice had he suffered?

Unless — was that it? He'd made it clear in their conversation back in the castle that he resented being passed over by his father in favour of his sister, when he believed he was the rightful ruler, both by birth and talent. Even though Mendo seemed to have had good reasons for his decision, Tarn had been humiliated — found wanting — by his own father, the man whose footsteps he hoped to follow. It must have been devastating.

She was beginning to understand, now. He had carried that disappointment — that wound — all through his adult life, keeping it raw and open, never letting it heal. The pain of it was as strong today as it had been at the moment of his rejection. Maybe even stronger.

He'd been given so many gifts: wealth, position, and no less than three separate skals, one of them incredibly rare. But what good had any of that done him? Sara had seen the truth: underneath it all, he was nothing but a child crying in the darkness. Tears pricked her own eyes for the tragedy of a promising life wasted, a future twisted and ruined by bitterness.

Her thoughts convulsed. What was she doing? Pitying him? The monster who had murdered her parents, tried to kill her friends? *I don't care what he went through! People face worse suffering and disappointment every day. They don't all turn into murderers. He had a choice!*

Tarn was the one responsible for all the evil he'd done, not his father, and she'd never forgive him for it. But right now, she'd work with him, if that was what it took. She waited, willing him to rise above his own feelings and choose to do what was right, at least once in his life.

A subtle change was coming over Tarn's light. The difference was so slight at first that Sara wasn't even sure of what she'd seen, but after a moment or two there was no doubt. The colour was gradually lightening.

Soon it was a bright, cherry red. As she watched, it shifted to orange. Gold would be next. He'd made the right choice. He was going to help. Mentally, she sagged in relief.

But then the orange light gave one mighty pulse and flashed instantly to a red so dark it was almost black. His voice thundered in her mind. "I don't need you! I am Villembelt Tarn, the Saviour of Algarth! It is my destiny!"

She hadn't convinced him, and she didn't think she had the strength to heal the Blight with him fighting her, not even linked with all the other Greenhaelen. Her mind raced. If only she could contact Tulley or Kelan, they could deal with Tarn, knock him out or something, force him to break contact with her. She'd try again…

Blinding pain smashed into her. Instantly, every single light blinked out. She heard herself scream. Sudden daylight dazzled her tear-filled eyes. She staggered. Firm hands gripped her shoulders from behind, holding her upright. The pain began to recede. She blinked her eyes clear and twisted around to ask Mena what had happened. A broad, blue-clad chest met her eyes. Above it, a bearded face scowled down at her. And now her ears registered the sounds of fighting all around her.

"Hands behind your back." He was very big, and she no longer had a knife. She didn't think she could have brought herself to stab anyone else, anyway. Numbly, she waited as her hands were tied yet again, and she was ordered to sit under the newly-restored tree and not move.

Her worried eyes scanned the area, searching for the others. Fin was lying nearby, facing away from her, horribly still. Mena sat with her back to another tree, staring at Sara, her hands also tied. The Guards must have pulled the two of them apart, allowing the pain of the Blight to come crashing back in, breaking Sara's link to the other Greenhaelen.

Further away, Logen was still on his feet, holding off two Guards with his sword. Blood was running down the side of his face. The clash and scrape of metal chilled Sara to the bone.

Tulley was wrestling on the ground with another Guard, both of them grunting loudly. A second Blueshirt ran at them, sword raised high. Sara screamed out a warning, but Tulley gave no sign he'd heard her. A shriek burst from her raw throat when the Guard slammed the pommel of his sword down on Tulley's head. Tulley collapsed. The two men were on him in a flash. Even then, he didn't give up easily. A third Guard had joined in before they were finally able to overpower him. They threw him face-down and tied his hands and feet.

Logen was visibly tiring. Blood dripped from his sword hand as well as his head. He raised his arm again and again, but each time, the movement was fractionally slower, until finally one of the Guards knocked the blade away and put his own sword point to Logen's throat. *Please, no,* breathed Sara.

But the man merely waited while his companions tied Logen's hands, then withdrew the sword and looked around. Seeing no one left to fight, he sheathed the sword and swaggered over to talk to Sara's Guard.

Tarn was writhing in his bonds, demanding loudly that someone set him free, but he was being ignored for now.

Where was Kelan? Perhaps he'd already escaped. If so, Sara was glad.

A movement in the tree above her caught her eye. Kelan, of course. He was stretched out along a branch, poised directly above the two Blueshirts. His intention was horribly clear. With four other Guards nearby, it was insane. He was going to get himself hurt, maybe killed. Sara had to do something. "Wait!" she shouted, not looking at him, and hoping the Guards would think she was yelling at them. "Think about what you're doing!" She darted a glance upwards. He nodded to show he understood. Sara breathed a sigh of relief.

A split second later, the branch gave an almighty crack and broke off, taking Kelan down with it. He plummeted to the ground just behind the two Guards. Their swords were out again in an instant, but Kelan wasn't in any state to put up a fight. He was moaning and his leg was sticking out from the knee at a sickening angle.

It was over. Fin was unconscious, maybe even dead, and the others had all been captured. Logen was still losing blood, his skin ashen against his copper hair. One of the Guards was crouched beside Tarn, finally listening to him. He'd be free at any moment. And, as if things weren't already bad enough, a second group of blue-shirted riders was approaching through the trees. There was no escape this time, not for any of them.

All the sacrifice, all the hardship and danger, had been for nothing. Mena and Kelan, Logen, Tulley and Fin, would all die, and the Blight would keep spreading, destroying other lives, destroying Algarth itself. Why had Sara ever come here and given them reason to hope? What was the point of any of it? She hadn't been strong enough to defeat Tarn, and her weakness had doomed them all.

And yet, something, some stubborn core deep inside her, couldn't accept that, wouldn't accept it. *It's not over, I won't let it be. Not while I'm still breathing.*

She wouldn't shape a Gateway and leave them, not this time. She would battle with everything she had, against Tarn and for Algarth. Even if she failed again — or succeeded, and was killed anyway, never to see the future she was fighting for — that was no reason not to fight.

She reached out to the Blighted forest. The excruciating pain hit her, as she'd known it would, but this time, she was ready for it. She clenched her jaw and held on. It was every bit as bad as she'd expected, but that didn't matter. She wouldn't give in, not again. Almost before she finished the thought, the golden lights began to appear.

There was no sign of Tarn, and she tried not to think about him, in case that drew him in. She didn't know how long he'd stay out, or how long she could remain conscious with this agony coursing through every part of her, but maybe just long enough.

She closed her eyes and sent out the healing. Within seconds, she was blind and deaf to anything except the pain and the golden power, flowing through her and out over the damaged land. Linked together as one, the Greenhaelen of Algarth were obliterating the Blight.

Deepest red swamped her thoughts, momentarily blotting out the gold. Not just a single ball of light, but a wave, crashing into her. She struggled to push him away but felt the Blight's resistance increase once more. She tried to block him out, but she couldn't concentrate on him and resist the pain at the same time. The healing tide slowed. One of the golden lights winked out, then another.

No! She wouldn't stop. Even if they all left her, she would continue on her own. After all, she had been doing things on her own her whole life. She hadn't had the support of a family; she hadn't leaned on anyone. She had created her own life with no one's help. She just needed to try harder.

He was still winning. Her mind was on fire. How could he be so much stronger than her? She was a Master Healer!

But a Master Healer didn't do it alone, did they? They united the other Greenhaelen to work together. She'd felt that, sensed the joy and rightness of that. Tarn was only one, no matter how strong his hatred made him. By resisting him on her own, she was fighting on his territory. He was the one who'd chosen to stand alone, not her. Not anymore.

And with that realisation, came another. She'd only drawn in about twenty golden lights. Were there really only twenty Greenhaelen alive on Algarth? What about all the ones in prison? And the ones whose Green Healing was weak, only a second or third skal? There might be hundreds of them, mightn't there? Could she find them and bring them in, too?

She stopped fighting Tarn and sent her bruised mind questing out. She imagined the whole of Algarth, the way she'd seen it on Mena's map. She pictured herself flying over every inch of it, calling to anyone with even a trace of Greenhaelan skal.

Come, help us. Algarth needs you. Come to me. Please, come.

For long moments, nothing happened.

Then they began to appear, big and small, bright and barely glowing at all. Only a handful at first, but then dozens, scores, too many to count. She gathered them in and they danced with her.

"No!" Tarn bellowed. He spun violently into the midst of the other lights, careening from one to another, knocking them aside. But he couldn't stop them all, not now that there were so many. He screamed once, and then the red light abruptly vanished from Sara's mind. He was gone.

Bolstered by so many, the healing power raced over the land, but the further it reached, the more resistance Sara began to feel. It was like trying to push her way through thick, sucking mud. It couldn't be Tarn; he was no longer part of the link. It was the same resistance she'd felt right at the beginning, the resistance of the Blight itself, but immeasurably stronger now. How could a disease be resisting magic this way? She had no idea, but she was quickly becoming exhausted, and ready to pass out from the pain at any moment. She hung on. The healing slowed to a trickle.

Finally, Sara faced the truth. Her will was not going to be enough. Not even a hundred Greenhaelen working together was going to be enough. With the last of her strength, hardly knowing what she was doing, she cried out from the depth of her heart, in grief and desperation.

Can anyone else hear me? Algarth is dying! Please help us, we can't do this alone!

Instantly, a wash of white light flooded her mind, dazzling but somehow not blinding. The golden lights shone warmly against it. All of Sara's pain and exhaustion vanished, as if they'd never been, replaced by a cool sensation of pure energy and joy. The healing trickle grew and swelled until it was a torrent, streaming through her, over her, under her. It flowed through the forest, engulfing the Blight, and then spread in every direction, healing, renewing, refreshing.

It took eternity, and it took no time at all. And she was a part of it, carried along like a leaf in a stream, tossing and tumbling, rising and falling, until, finally, the current slowed, and subsided, leaving her rocking gently, like a child in a mother's arms.

When it was over, Sara knew, in a way that left no room for doubt, that the Blight was gone — all of it — washed away by the unstoppable tide.

The golden lights winked out, one by one, and the rocking sensation ceased. She was at rest, surrounded by a bright, profound stillness. But not alone.

Seconds passed, or years, and then the embracing whiteness began to break up and stream away. Glowing ribbons and banners swirled and slid from Sara's sight, faster and faster, stranding her in the growing darkness with no means of following. *No! Don't leave me!* The light was almost gone. *I don't understand! Who are you?* One last, brilliant wisp danced joyously as if in answer, and then vanished, leaving only blackness. She was bereft. Abandoned. Heartbroken. *Come back to me. Come back.*

"Sara! Come back!" Someone was shaking her shoulder.

Sara opened her eyes. Through her tears, she recognised Mena.

"Sara! You're awake! You've been unconscious for more than an hour. How do you feel?"

"I'm all right." It was a lie, but as she gazed into the other faces staring anxiously down at her, and at the green forest all around, it began to feel more like the truth. There they all were: Mena, Logen, Tulley, and even Kelan and Fin. And one other.

Sara blinked in astonishment. *"Niall?"*

It couldn't be, but it was: Niall Crawley, smiling his crooked smile and looking as much at his ease as if they were meeting at a party. "Hello, Sara Martin. Sage has been missing you. She's very glad to see you again, as am I."

Sara sat up. And there was Sage, standing a little distance away, her ears pricked and her big liquid eyes fixed on Sara's face. After that, Sara felt that nothing could surprise her ever again.

It seemed that they weren't even under arrest any more. Tulley introduced Sara to his brother, Bander, who had arrived with Niall and Sergeant Oren, of all people. They had brought the Guards from Fortune Creek with them, with questions for Tarn to answer. But that was proving to be a problem.

"Happened soon after we were captured," Tulley said. He was leaning against a tree with his brawny arm around Fin's waist, and he was grinning, despite the purple lump on his head. Whatever had happened to Tarn, Tulley was happy about it. "The Blueshirts had untied him, and he was blustering away, telling them to kill us all, when he stopped. Sat there for ages with his mouth gaping open like a fish, then gave a yell and fell over, out like a light. A bit later, he's up again and talking. Been talking ever since. The Blueshirts couldn't shut him up, so they carried him far enough away that they couldn't hear him."

"He's cracked," Kelan said cheerfully. His newly splinted leg didn't seem to have dampened his spirits at all. He twirled a finger in the air and rolled his eyes. "Completely mad." He pointed to where Tarn was sitting at the base of another tree. Even though he was completely alone, the Chairman's lips were moving, and he was alternately nodding and shaking his head.

"What's he saying?" Sara asked.

"He's telling the story of his life, would you believe?" Logen said, lowering himself down beside her. "He starts at his childhood, and tells it right up to today. And then he begins again."

"Including how he got rid of his sister and her family, started the Blight, and framed the Greenhaelen," Kelan added.

"And how he ordered Renn to hire men to attack the farmhouse and kill the Guards we left tied up in Fortune Creek," Niall said. "The first time he admitted that, I thought my dear friend Sergeant Oren here was going to do justice on him, right there and then." Oren was sitting to one side with Bander, listening placidly to the conversation.

"That reminds me," Tulley said to Niall. "Why'd you rush in to save the Blueshirts at that farmhouse, anyway? Would've thought you'd want to stay as far away from Warrant Guards as you could, considering the bounty on our heads."

"Ah, yes, I'm afraid that was the Councillor's idea. He rather insisted, said he was rushing to their rescue, with me or without me. Well, I could hardly leave him to be killed, I'd never have heard the end of it." He pursed his lips thoughtfully and ran a thumb and finger along both sides of his jaw, tracing the narrow band of black hair back to his chin. "It seems your brother has a distressingly noble streak in his character, Tulley. You should attempt to remedy it."

Tulley laughed, and Bander smiled tolerantly, but the look that Oren sent towards Niall was anything but amused. Somehow, Sara doubted that the stolid, dutiful Sergeant and the flippant man in black were going to become "dear friends" anytime soon, no matter what Niall had claimed.

"Anyway," Tulley said, "Tarn's finished now, for good and all. And so is Renn. Even with my noble brother reinstated, the Council's going to need two new members."

As they continued talking, Sara leaned back against the tree and sighed happily. Unbelievable as it seemed, they had done it. The Blight was gone, and Tarn was going to face justice. There was still a lot she didn't understand, but the rest of the explanations could wait.

THIRTY-THREE

Sara

After the trial ended, the six of them walked together in silence from the Council building to the tavern. Sara was busy with her own thoughts. She guessed the others were probably busy with theirs, too.

They were welcomed by the tavern owner herself, a surprisingly young woman whom Logen introduced as Bella. She was wearing a tightly laced red vest over a full-sleeved snowy white blouse, and the combination flattered her olive skin and the thick, glossy waves of her long black hair. The hem of her red skirt swept the floor as she led them to their table. Kelan couldn't seem to take his eyes off her. Well, she was very attractive, if about ten years too old for him. But when she left them, it turned out that Kelan's interest in her wasn't romantic.

"Isn't she the woman from that inn, the shady one you brought me to for the harvest festival?" he demanded of Logen. "Is she some kind of criminal?" He looked excited at the thought.

Logen leaned back. He was dressed more smartly than Sara had ever seen him, looking every inch a former Council member. His snowy shirt and olive-green tunic complemented the coppery tone of his newly-trimmed hair and beard. "Bella owns several businesses here in Eorna," he said placidly. "Some more respectable than others. She's an old friend. In fact, she's the one who arranged for Oren to be sent on a wild goose chase to Gadara after we escaped from the city. She has a lot of contacts."

Kelan smirked. "I'll bet."

Logen frowned him into silence.

No one seemed to know what to say next. It was strange, sitting together in full public view like this, and knowing they had nothing to fear. It would take a while to get used to. But the trial was over, and Tarn had been found guilty of treason and murder. He'd stopped his continuous telling of his life story, but was still eager to answer any questions put to him, alternately boasting about his brilliance and threatening what he would do if he wasn't reinstated as Chairman. He didn't seem to be aware that he'd lost his ability to Mind Wend and shape Gateways. After listening to him and to the testimony of Oren and the Guards, the reduced Council had been unanimous in their verdict. Tarn's property had been confiscated and he had been judged insane: whether temporarily or permanently, no one knew, but he would never be freed.

Asher Renn had been convicted, too, but in his absence. There was a rumour that he'd fled to Gadara and taken ship for Bregia.

Tulley scraped his chair back. "First round on me. Ale for everyone?" At least Tulley didn't look any different. His wild red hair and beard hadn't seen a blade since they'd all got back, and his shirt and tunic were as rumpled as ever. They all agreed to ale, and he stumped off.

Silence descended on the table again. Sara nervously smoothed the long green dress over her knees. She'd found it in storage at Edervale Castle. It wasn't her usual style of clothing, but one of the older servants had told her the garment had belonged to her mother, like the sage-coloured cloak. For some reason, it had seemed important to wear both to the trial, to stand and face Tarn in the clothing of the woman he'd murdered. Besides, Sara liked the garments, especially the cloak. She'd keep that, whatever she decided to do next. Her hands stroked the soft, thick fabric again. The gesture reminded her of Mena, always smoothing her apron.

Mena and Fin hadn't joined them tonight. Fin was very tired these days, and Mena had refused to leave her. It had been a terrible shock to Sara to learn that Fin was dying, just when things had all worked out so well for the rest of them, but Fin herself seemed to be at peace with it. Tulley would have stayed home with them, but Fin had insisted he come.

She said she didn't want him to spend all his time brooding over her, and ordered Sara and Kelan to bring him along.

They'd become a sort of family, in the last month: Fin and Tulley, Mena and Kelan. They were sharing a house in Eorna, with a forge out the back for Tulley, and a spare room for Mena, where she saw other patients in between caring for Fin. Sara had travelled up from Edervale to stay with them for the trial. Mena seemed to be thriving, despite her sorrow at Fin's condition, and Tulley said she was already getting a reputation in Eorna as an exceptional healer. There was no talk of Mena and Kelan returning to Soran's farm, and Sara was glad.

Tulley returned with a tray of brimming tankards. Distributing them around the table gave them all something to do. Before the awkwardness could descend again, Logen raised his drink. "To Bramley Gelt, a good and brave man, and one I was proud to call my friend. To Bram."

"To Bram," Sara echoed, along with the others. As she sipped without tasting, her gaze swivelled to Cahira, sitting directly across the table, between Niall and Kelan. The Skalsinger raised her own tankard slightly, but set it down again without drinking from it. She was in a beautifully tailored jacket of royal blue tonight, and her glossy dark hair was pulled back severely, emphasising her emerald, almond-shaped eyes. She looked polished and elegant, but her brow was furrowed and she was biting her lip.

Adric was the other one missing from this gathering. He was travelling and no one had known his exact location. Presumably he'd heard about the trial — the news of it had gone all over Algarth — but he hadn't turned up. Sara asked Cahira if she'd had any word from him.

Cahira shook her head. "Nothing. He was so restless after we reached my parents' house. He couldn't sit still. He kept going out on longer and longer hunting trips, and then, about a month ago, he didn't come home. I thought he just needed some time alone, but it's been too long."

"Don't worry," Niall said gently. He was in neat, unrelieved black, as usual. "I told you, I'm going to find him. I'll set out as soon as we get back." The habitual flippancy was completely absent from his face and voice.

Cahira's frown deepened. "You mean *we'll* set out," she said. "I'm coming with you."

"Cah," he began.

"No, Niall. Adric is family. I won't be left behind."

"But it might be dangerous. Don't you think—"

"I can look after myself." Her clipped tone brooked no nonsense.

"That's true enough, lass," Tulley said, ignoring the poisonous look Niall shot across the table. "You surprised me at Fortune Creek. I've never heard of a Skalsinger doing what you did. Those Blueshirts went crazy. How'd you learn to sing like that?"

Cahira spread her hands. "I don't know. I've never heard of it, either. But you were all being attacked, and I was...just desperate to do something, I suppose. I opened my mouth, and out it came." She chewed on her lip, this time in thought. "It was very effective, wasn't it? I really should try to find out more about it." A small smile appeared and hovered around the corners of her mouth. She turned to Niall with her eyebrows raised. "If our trip does turn out to be dangerous, I might be the one protecting you."

Niall opened his mouth to reply, but then seemed to think better of it. He took a long draw of his ale and addressed Logen instead. "So, my friend, have you decided, yet? Are you going to run for one of those vacant Council seats?"

"Yes, I am. Bander and Adara have agreed to support me, and I think I can do more good there than as a travelling Greenhaelan."

Niall flourished his tankard in a welcome return to his normally jaunty manner. "To Logen Rush, future Chairman of the Council of Six, and that rare creature, an honest politician."

Sara raised her own drink to Logen, seated beside her. This time, she was able to actually taste and appreciate the ale. It was slightly different to the brew in Fortune Creek, nuttier and with a hint of herbs, but just as delicious. She drank deeply and sat back with a happy sigh.

On Sara's other side, Tulley drained his tankard and slammed it down. "More drinks?"

"My turn, I think." Niall rose gracefully to his feet and slipped off through the thickening crowd.

Tulley gave a grunt of approval and leaned forward. "Logen, did you manage to pay that old carter properly? Mena was worried about it, made me promise to ask."

"Now, that's a very strange thing," Logen said. "Niall and I went looking for him down at the docks. We found some other men who were working for the merchants that owned Peddar's wagon, but no one had heard of him. The manager said they'd never employed a carter named Peddar. I don't know what to make of it."

"That's odd," Sara said slowly. "I wonder…" she trailed off, fiddling with the edge of the cloak.

"What is it, Sara?"

Sara raised her eyes to meet Logen's clear blue gaze. She felt a bit foolish, but it had been bothering her, so she pressed on. "It's just that someone else seems to have disappeared, too."

"Who?"

"I met her when I went to Edervale Castle, the first time. I was trying to escape from Tarn, and I went down into the lower levels. There was an archive there, thousands of scrolls and papers, and an old woman, Enge. She helped me. But when I went back, all the papers were gone, and so was she. I couldn't even find the room again. I asked about her, but the servants said they had never heard of her. In fact, the ones who go down to the lower level all the time swore there'd never been anything there but storage rooms. No archive, no domed chamber with a painted ceiling, no archivist."

"But what does it mean?" Kelan asked. "Peddar helped us and he's gone, and this Enge helped Sara, and now she's missing, too."

Niall had returned with more tankards. "Not just missing," he said, handing them around, "but apparently non-existent. I admit, it's intriguing."

"It has to mean something," Kelan insisted, his clear green eyes intent beneath his newly short fringe. Sara knew Mena's fingers had been itching to cut it for ages, and her son had finally agreed, saying it was a stupid fashion anyway, and a hunter needed to be able to see clearly. "One old man helped us…"

"Two," Sara said.

"What do you mean?"

"Two old men helped us. Peddar sold us the wagon, just when we needed it, and Garst led us through the foothills to Deep Lake. And then Enge gave me information about Gateways and slowed down the Guard so I could get away. Two little old men and one little old woman." She glanced around the table. "It can't just be a coincidence, can it?"

Back in his seat beside Cahira, Niall snapped his fingers. "Of course. It was Garst who warned the Blueshirts in the farmhouse that the mercenaries were going to attack them. I thought I recognised the description. A scrawny old man in filthy clothes, riding a mule, they said." His mouth quirked and one eyebrow lifted. "Sounds like Garst to me."

He was right, Sara thought. It had to be the same man. "And don't forget the wasps," she added. "That was pretty convenient, and then Garst came along right afterwards."

They were all silent for a moment, thinking it over. Sara took another long drink. It was getting warm in here. She untied her cloak and draped it over the back of her chair.

Kelan frowned. "But what about his 'diversion' at Deep Lake? All it did was wake the whole town up. It was really dark and quiet until then. We could've got away in that boat, without anyone knowing. I bet they noticed the missing boat and came after us much sooner because of Garst's fireworks. If he hadn't done anything, we might have stayed together all the way to the Blighted area, instead of losing Sara. How was that helpful?"

"I'm not so sure it wasn't," Sara said slowly, thinking it out. "If we hadn't been separated on the lake, I'd never have gone to Edervale Castle. I wouldn't have found out who I really was, and everything Tarn had done. I don't think I would have been so determined to defeat him, at any cost, and I'm not sure the Blight would have been cured at all. I might have just given up, the first time I failed."

She would still have gathered Tarn in, because he was a Green-haelan, and he would still have fought the healing, but she would have had no idea who he was or why he was doing it. And if the Guards from Talford hadn't arrived and attacked them, she wouldn't have been so desperate to heal the Blight right then and there, either. And what about Bander and Niall arriving with Oren and the other Guards, just in time to hear Tarn's confession and arrest him? Now it seemed Garst had had a hand in that, too.

"But has Garst disappeared too, then?" Kelan asked finally, after they'd spent several minutes talking it all out without coming to any definite conclusion.

No one seemed to know.

Sara emptied her second tankard and wiped the foam from her mouth. She wasn't sure she liked the idea that some sort of weird conspiracy of old people had been going on, even if it did seem to have been working in their favour.

Bella approached the table, trailed by two serving men carrying trays loaded down with plates of food. "Suckling pig, sweet apple gravy and roast potatoes. Compliments of the house for the heroes of Algarth." She smiled widely and gave a mock curtsy, her red skirt swirling.

Logen laughed up at her. "Thank you, gracious lady. And won't you join us?"

"Why not?" She crooked a finger and another chair appeared and was pushed in on Logen's other side. The lively tavern-owner seated herself and gestured to the serving men to set down the plates. Then she waved a graceful silver-ringed hand to indicate the steaming food. "Eat, eat," she urged in her rich contralto. "Before it goes cold."

The first mouthful almost had Sara swooning. The ale had been good, but this was heavenly. She filled her mouth with succulent pork and fragrant gravy and saw Kelan doing the same. The others were eating, too, except for Cahira, who was only toying with a potato, cutting it up and then pushing the pieces around her plate. Sara's heart went out to her. Niall had noticed now, and was quietly urging Cahira to try something. Cahira smiled sadly at him, but lifted a small forkful to her mouth. She chewed slowly and swallowed, then went back for more. She didn't look like she was enjoying it much, but at least she was eating.

"So, Sara, have you decided if you're going to stay at Edervale Castle?" Logen asked.

She shook her head and put down her knife and fork to fan her face. It really was getting hot in here. And noisy. She leaned towards Logen and raised her voice. "I'm not sure. It still seems incredible that I actually own a castle, but I suppose it's true."

"'Of course it is," Logen smiled. Tarn isn't allowed to benefit from his crimes, and he admitted that his father had been intending to leave Edervale to your mother. The Council ruled that it's yours."

"I know, it's just a lot to take in. It's a beautiful place, and it's where my mother grew up. I spent the first five years of my life there, and I've been getting some flashes of memory back. But I left a whole life back home in Wattleford, the only life I knew for twenty years. I know I was born here, but I feel like I'm from there."

She was glad she'd finally told them all the true story of how she'd appeared in the forest near the Erdal farm. She'd done it as soon as she could after the Blight had been cured, not knowing how they would react. To her relief, they'd taken it in their stride. Everyone had said they understood why she'd lied, and Fin had hugged her. They were all better friends than she deserved.

But now, she had to decide her future. She didn't want to be like Tarn, living some kind of double life between both worlds, but she'd been thinking about it for weeks now and was no closer to a decision. Where did she belong? She really didn't know.

Kelan leaned forward, a solemn look on his face. "Don't go back there, Sara. Like Bella said, you're a hero in Algarth now."

"Fin and Mena would miss you if you went," Tulley said gruffly. His plate already lay empty in front of him, and his brawny arms were crossed above his prominent stomach.

"I'd miss them, too," Sara said. "I'd miss all of you." Tears pricked her eyes. She was getting maudlin. That ale must have been stronger than she'd realised. She'd better eat some more to soak it up. She picked up the cutlery again, and then paused. They were still looking at her. "Oh, let's talk about something else. Kelan, what's been happening with you?"

He answered proudly around a mouthful of food. "I'm going to enlist as a Blueshirt, at least until my skal comes in, and maybe even after that, if it's Strength or Swiftness. Commander Oren says they'd be glad to have me." Oren had been promoted by the Council a few days ago.

"And how is the good Commander these days?" Niall asked. "You know, I believe we really bonded, after that fight at the farmhouse." The crooked smile appeared. "Brothers in arms, and all that. Does he ever ask after me?"

Kelan snorted in amusement, another loaded fork halfway to his mouth. Then he froze, staring at something over Sara's shoulder. The fork clattered onto his plate.

Sara swivelled her head. A young girl in a pink evening dress was entering the tavern on the arm of a richly dressed, older man. Sara couldn't quite believe her eyes. "Isn't that..."

"Rassil," Kelan said flatly.

Mena's former maid was almost unrecognisable. Her pale blonde hair was braided in an elaborate crown, pierced with jewelled pins. Her blush-pink dress was fitted in the bodice, then fell in generous, graceful folds to the floor. The thick, glossy fabric was embroidered all over with a design of seashells, outlined in tiny seed pearls. Sara couldn't stop staring.

For a split second, Rassil's round, blue eyes fixed on the group in the corner, and then her gaze passed straight over their heads. She gave no sign that she'd recognised any of them.

Apparently unaware of the sudden tension around her, Bella chuckled. "So, that's Merchant Boroden's new diversion. The gossip has been all over town, of course, but I haven't seen her before. Hmm, pretty enough, but surely she is little more than a child."

"She's eighteen," Kelan said, still in that dead voice. "Her birthday was two weeks ago."

"Gossip?" Logen asked under his breath. "What's the story, Bella?"

The tavern keeper lowered her voice. Sara leaned forward, straining to hear. "They say Master Boroden's wife found her working in a dress shop and took a fancy to her. But when she brought the girl into their home as a personal maid, her husband took an even greater fancy. Now

Mistress Boroden is on an extended visit to their country home, and her former maid is…well, as you see," she finished delicately.

Sara turned anxiously back to Kelan. How was he taking this news? The teenager was staring fixedly at his palm.

"Are you all right, Kelan?" Sara asked.

He tilted his hand towards her. The two halves of the promise charm lay side by side. "I should get rid of this. I don't need it now." He absently rubbed a fingertip over the bright copper. The two pieces of the charm slid smoothly together with a click, making a complete oval. The fine, interlocking lines engraved into the surface began to glow silver.

"Kelan!" Logen said, reaching across to grip his arm. "Congratulations!"

The others echoed this, Tulley even going around the table to slap the teenager on the back. Kelan just sat there, staring down at his hand.

Sara had no idea what had just happened. Logen must have noticed the puzzlement on her face. "Once a promise charm is activated, anyone can break it apart and use it. But putting it back together again isn't so simple. Kelan's skal has come in."

Finally, Kelan looked up with wide eyes. "I'm a *Charm Shaper?*" His horrified expression of disbelief was almost comical.

"Never mind, Kelan," Niall said, wickedly. "I'm sure you'll be the very best hunter at the Academy."

Kelan groaned.

The party broke up soon after that.

It had been good to see the others, but Sara was no closer to making a decision about her future. What was she going to do?

THIRTY-FOUR

Rhin

Astari Rhin, Disciple of the Third Echelon — known in Algarth as Commander Asher Renn — stood alone at the bow of the merchant ship, peering with unseeing eyes over the grey, choppy waves of Windras Strait.

Four years, wasted. The bitter reflection tightened his grip on the chill metal railing, but he refused to permit his emotion to rule him. A lesser man might have been apprehensive about what awaited him, but fear was not something he allowed himself, either. Decades of the pure, harsh discipline of the Temple of Kolos had burned out all such weakness. He did indulge a small feeling of satisfaction that he would never again need to associate with the idiot, Tarn.

The fool had seemed an ideal choice: a man of weak mind, strong ambition, and no scruples. Under Rhin's influence, he had willingly appointed "Asher Renn" as Deputy Chairman and Commander of the Warrant Guards. At that time, the Guards had been nothing more than a few score of amateurs, unworthy of the name. Rhin had set to work immediately, transforming them into a properly trained, equipped and disciplined force of almost five hundred men.

Tarn's pathetic delusion that he was a powerful Mind Wender had also served a purpose. He had never once suspected the superior mental talents of his Deputy, always standing faithfully nearby whenever a mind was compelled to Tarn's will. Rhin's mouth twisted in contempt. It had

268

not been easy to endure the man's endless preening, his patronising manner, but he would be the perfect scapegoat if one were ever needed. Careful preparation always included a contingency plan.

Rhin braced his legs against the rise and fall of the deck as he went over the main points he needed to include in his report. The mission had begun well. Under Tarn's leadership, the Council had strengthened Algarth's economic ties to the Bregian government, signing binding trade contracts and encouraging business owners to do likewise. Many of the agreements included large loans, secured against properties and future harvests. Merchants and farmers lined up to take advantage of this rich new opportunity for expansion.

Rhin's original orders had been to secure Algarth as a subject province within six years. But when Tarn had told him about the Blight and his idea to blame the Greenhaelen, he had seen his chance to accelerate the time frame. He had set the Guards to hunting the Green-haelen to extinction and informed his Master of the new situation. Rhin pursed his cold lips and nodded. Yes, he had behaved correctly, followed procedure. His actions thus far could not be faulted.

And the spell-charged powder the Master had sent in return to his message had worked perfectly, transforming a natural disease into something more virulent and contagious. The crops of Algarth would wither, season after season, until all those merchants and farmers, even the government itself, would have no choice but to default on their contracts, activating huge financial penalties. Loans would be called in, lands and property seized by Bregian creditors.

With the Blight progressing nicely towards this inevitable conclusion, Rhin had been poised to enact the second half of his plan. Under his influence, Tarn would declare publicly that he was a Greenhaelan and could cure the Blight. After he failed, a shocked Commander Renn would produce "newly discovered evidence" that proved Tarn had created the Blight himself. He would order Sergeant Oren to arrest Tarn and charge him with treason. If it became necessary, the former Chairman would confess, at the same time swearing that his Deputy had not been involved in any way.

According to Council law, Deputy Renn would then be offered the Chairmanship. Rhin would become, in effect, the ruler of Algarth, with sole command of the Warrant Guards, the only trained military force on the island. He had calculated that within another year the small nation would be completely under Bregian control.

It would then be a simple thing for the Master of Disciples to use his own talent — strengthened by power channelled directly from the great god Kolos himself — to reverse the effect of his powder and make the land productive again.

The icy wind gusted into Rhin's face and over his naked scalp, sending a shudder down his spine. He raised white-knuckled hands and pulled his hood over his head, but the shivering didn't abate. With a snarl, he spun from the rail. Victory had been within his grasp — he'd almost been able to taste it — and then everything had fallen apart. That damned Greenhaelan girl! How had she accessed so much power?

Rhin's boot heels rang on the wooden deck as he enumerated his grievances. First, the obliteration of the Blight. Second, the moron Tarn's breakdown and confession. Third, and worst, Oren's discovery that his supposedly dead Guards were very much alive, and his capture of one of the mercenaries.

The first two setbacks could have resulted in no more than a delay to Rhin's plans. Even with the Blight gone, there would be other ways for the new Council Chairman to undermine the country, once Tarn was declared unfit for office. And as for Tarn's accusation of his Deputy's involvement in everything — well, a madman's word was hardly trustworthy.

Rhin reached the stern, and drew his cloak tighter. He pivoted, staggering a little on the pitching deck, and resumed his pacing. Yes, he might have salvaged his position, given time, if it hadn't been for that cursed Oren. Promoting him to Sergeant had been a mistake — Rhin admitted it to himself — his only mistake as far as he could tell, but a catastrophic one. Oren was ambitious; Rhin had seen that appetite for recognition and advancement glinting brightly across the surface of the man's mind, and thought to use it. But in neglecting to look deeper he had somehow missed what lay below — the true bedrock of Harl Oren's character — a juvenile devotion to honesty, loyalty and justice.

The Sergeant had been so outraged by the discovery that his superiors did not share these values, that he had encouraged his rescued Guards to spread the story far and wide before he had returned to Eorna to confront his Commander. Not even Rhin, with all his talent and training, could Mind Wend the entire population. He had been left with no choice but to flee.

The waves were growing larger, and the ship was beginning to buck. Rhin lurched the last few steps to the forward rail and clutched onto it again. The coast of Bregia was visible now, a narrow line of white cliffs rising from the tossing grey ocean. They would arrive soon, and the Master would demand a full analysis of exactly how Rhin's plans had gone so awry on the very brink of success.

If Rhin was a fool, he might try to blame his failure on nothing more than bad luck, unfortunate co-incidence. But he knew, as well as the Master, that neither luck nor coincidence moved the levers of the world. Rather, every outcome was determined by will clashing against will, power opposing power, strategy countering strategy.

He lifted his head, baring his teeth in defiance of the freezing gale. Someone had been working against him. Someone with power. They had supplied the Greenhaelan girl with the ability to overcome the strengthened Blight; they had broken Tarn's mind beyond Rhin's ability to control; and they had led Oren to the farmhouse at the very moment the mercenaries were attacking. It might have been this Aal, the local god they all talked about, or another player unknown to Rhin as yet, but an unseen force had been manipulating events.

Not that Rhin would plead that as an excuse, either. Excuses were signs of weakness. He had failed; he would be harshly punished for that, and rightly so. It was even possible that the punishment would end in his death, but it was unlikely. He had many talents, and his Master seldom threw away a tool that might still be of use.

The coast of his homeland was approaching. Fighting the buffeting wind and the heaving deck, he worked his way along the rail until he was close enough to grab the frame of the cabin doorway and haul himself inside. The wind cut off, leaving his ears ringing in the sudden silence. He paused for a moment at the top of the steps to secure his balance, and then headed below to gather his few belongings. He would have other opportunities to prove his worth. As the youngest Disciple ever to have risen to the Third Echelon, he had no intention of resting on his achievements. One day, he would sit in the Master's Chair, answering to no one except Kolos himself.

Back on deck, as the helmsman guided the now docile boat deeper into the sheltered harbour, Rhin turned an admiring gaze on the tiers of splendid white buildings rising from the waterside to the clifftop. Even this small coastal city reflected the majesty of the Bregian Empire, its superiority to the nations around it.

Rhin's current defeat would achieve nothing in the end except to delay the inevitable. The taste of personal failure might be sour in his mouth, but he had not been the only Disciple dispatched across the Strait. One of the others would succeed. Whoever the unnamed enemy was, they could be no match for Bregia, or Kolos. And the tiny, backward island of Algarth was only one front, after all, in a war no nation but Bregia even knew had been declared. They would learn.

Rhin pushed back the hood and twitched the cloak into its proper position on his shoulders, ready to disembark and face the future.

Sooner or later, the entire world — including the foolish little land of Algarth — would bow before the might of Kolos the Great. And Astari Rhin would be at the front and centre of that glorious victory, basking in his triumph and securing his rightful portion of the spoils.

THIRTY-FIVE

Sara

Rain dripped dismally from a steel-grey sky the day Sara returned to her garden in Wattleford.

It was autumn again, but more importantly, it was her birthday. Her real birthday, not the one they'd randomly allocated to her in the Martindale Children's Home. She'd found the record in Edervale Castle: Ilsara Loren, born to parents Elana and Serd Loren on the second day of the final month of autumn, twenty-seven years ago.

She'd already learned from Tarn that her last name was Loren, but *Ilsara* had been a shock. She'd told the people who found her wandering on the road after the car accident that her name was Sara, and that was what Tarn had called her, too. It must have been her pet name in the family. *Martin* had been added later, because she'd grown up in the Martindale Home and hadn't seemed to know her last name.

Surveying the sadly neglected garden, she was moved to try a small experiment in spite of the weather. She chose a sad, shrivelled violet growing in a crack in the paving, and willed it to heal. It greened up straight away, its round leaves unfolding and spreading, its stems straightening proudly. She was still a Greenhaelan, even here. After what Tarn had told her about Mind Wending in this world, she'd thought that might be the case, but it was interesting to have it confirmed.

Raindrops plopped and splashed around her as she crossed the patio and lifted the pot under which she'd hidden her spare key. Still there. She let herself in the back door and sat down at the kitchen bench.

She shivered, drawing her green cloak more tightly around her. The room was cold and smelled damp and musty. It was dark, too. She automatically reached out and flipped the light switch. Nothing happened. The electricity was off, of course: the bills hadn't been paid. There wouldn't be any hot water, either. Were the same sheets still on her bed? The clothes still in the wardrobe upstairs? What happened to a person's property if she went missing for almost a year and had no living relatives? Would she still have access to her bank account?

She recognised that these questions were just a way of procrastinating, but it was very disorienting to be sitting in a kitchen equipped with a refrigerator and an electric stove, in the house she'd lived in before she had any idea of her real identity.

Disorienting or not, she needed to make a start. She'd already decided what to do first. She was just sitting here putting it off because, despite running the scene over and over in her head, she still had no idea what she was going to say.

She slapped her hands on the counter. Enough stalling. Time to face Jackie. She rose and trudged back outside into the rain.

A week later, the two of them were sitting out on Sara's patio, enjoying the late afternoon sun, drinking from large glasses of red wine. The bottle had cost more than Sara usually earned in a week, but this was a special occasion and she'd felt like marking it with a little extravagance for once.

She gazed across the garden, where healthy chrysanthemums, dahlias, salvias and hundreds of other flowers bloomed, their colours bright and lovely in the low golden light. She'd cheated a little to make the show so abundant, she admitted that, but she wasn't sorry at all.

The electricity was still off, so she'd been staying with Jackie, but she wanted to have this particular conversation on her own property. She'd never been any good at lying, and her sharp neighbour hadn't believed her amnesia story for a moment. But Sara had simply kept insisting that the last eleven months were a total blank, until Jackie stopped pushing, saying only that she hoped Sara would be ready to talk about it one day.

Sara took a slow sip of the delicious wine and gazed fondly at her friend, who was tugging at her ginger curls and talking animatedly about the local Conservation Action Group's planned trip to the Brogan Mountains next month. Jackie had already caught her up on all the important news. As soon as it had become clear that Sara was really missing, the police had questioned everyone who knew her. They concentrated heavily on Stephen Cooper, as the last person to have seen Sara on the day she vanished, but the investigation was dropped for lack of evidence. That didn't stop some people from continuing to suspect him, and his practice had suffered.

As soon as Sara had heard this, she'd visited the police station to assure them she was alive and well. Then she'd called on Stephen at his surgery. There were several chatty patients in the waiting room, and they spread the story of her reappearance to the whole village. She'd allowed the local newspaper to interview her, but refused to talk to any other media. She had no intention of becoming some kind of celebrity. She was a gardener, and that was all she wanted to be.

Jackie, her eyes alight with glee, had also related the story of Melville Barnett's mysterious disappearance six weeks ago, followed by the collapse of his commercial empire as the police investigation uncovered numerous illegal activities and financial irregularities. Deprived of her chief antagonist, Jackie had already thrown herself into several new causes, including something to do with halting the smuggling of rare Australian orchids.

Sara sat back and stretched, being careful not to spill even one precious drop of the wine. She was stiff from spending so much time hunched over a desk the past few days. There'd been a ton of paperwork to get through before she could reclaim her real life, but now it was all completed. She and Jackie talked late into the night, and then Jackie hugged her tightly, something she'd never done before. Sara hugged her back.

Lying in bed in Jackie's spare room the next morning, the memory of that hug warmed her. A year ago, she had considered Jackie to be her friend, her best friend. But she hadn't known anything about real friendship, not until she met Mena and the others. She'd always been scared to show too much, *feel* too much. If you didn't care about anyone, you wouldn't be destroyed when they abandoned you. And if you locked up those other, dangerous emotions — anger, grief, fear, loneliness — they'd be powerless to wreak devastation on you or anyone else. Life would be smooth, predictable, safe. She had thought that was maturity, self-control, but it had simply been cowardice.

Feeling deeply was a risk, but it was a risk worth taking. Meeting Fin and Tulley had taught her that. Fin was dying, and Tulley was going to lose her, but it was certain that he wouldn't have swapped the time he had spent with her for anything. Neither would Sara. A tear trickled down her cheek. She brushed it away.

And then there was the white light that had answered when she had called for help. It had been more than a light, more than love and joy and power, although it had been all that. She knew, without any doubt at all, that it had been a person. A person she would have given anything to know better. But even though that person had left her, she would never regret the experience. And perhaps, just perhaps, they would meet again. She hoped so.

She showered and dressed, then went downstairs. Outside, it was still dark.

There was no need to wake Jackie. They'd both said all they needed to say last night. Although Jackie didn't know it yet, the money from the sale of Sara's house was going to her. No doubt she'd use it to further one of her causes. Sara approved of that. Passion was important, and so was fighting with all you had for what was right. Algarth had taught her that, too.

She'd told Jackie, and everyone else, that she was emigrating to England, where there were exciting career opportunities for a gardener, the kind that couldn't be found in Australia.

Well, it was close to the truth, except for the part about England.

The sun was just rising as Sara Loren, wearing her mother's sage green cloak, strode into the wild, passionate, glorious mess of her very first garden. She sank to the damp earth and allowed the deep longing to well up from within her. She was going back to her real life, the one she'd been born to live, the one she yearned for.

"Home," she whispered joyfully, and let the dizziness take her.

END

ABOUT THE AUTHOR

Lyn Webster is a retired teacher who has spent a considerable portion of her life exploring imaginary places from the comfort of her favourite reading chair.

In the classroom, her greatest joy was taking her students on similar journeys and equipping them to launch out on their own.

Newly retired, she experienced a deep yearning to explore a brand-new destination and share its stories. After a few false starts and wrong turns, she found herself, along with her protagonist Sara Martin, on the magical island of Algarth, where she's been spending most of her fictional time ever since.

Lyn lives, writes and gardens in regional Australia, another strange and wondrous land, with her husband and a small enthusiastic dog.

Catch up with Lyn via her website, **www.lynwebster.com**

Lyn also blogs about books and reading at **www.twobooks.blog** Or come and say hello on Twitter @TwoBooksBlog